ALIEN™

INFERNO'S FALL

THE COMPLETE ALIEN™ LIBRARY FROM TITAN BOOKS

ALIEN™

INFERNO'S FALL

A NOVEL BY

PHILIPPA BALLANTINE

STORY BY

PHILIPPA BALLANTINE
AND CLARA ČARIJA

Titan BOOKS

ALIEN™: INFERNO'S FALL
Print edition ISBN: 9781789099942
E-book edition ISBN: 9781789099980

Published by Titan Books
A division of Titan Publishing Group Ltd
144 Southwark St, London SE1 0UP

First edition: July 2022
10 9 8 7 6 5 4 3 2 1

A CIP catalogue record for this title is available from the British Library.

Printed and bound by CPI Group (UK) Ltd, Croydon, CR0 4YY.

This book is dedicated to the immigrants, asylum seekers and anyone who seeks a safe place to call home.

PART I

CITY OF WOE

1

HARD SIGNS

The rhythmic scream of the klaxon woke Toru McClintock-Riley from a dead sleep. She lurched out of her cot, bleary-eyed, bones and muscles aching from a twelve-hour shift down the Svarog mine.

Getting out of bed was usually a process, a series of stretches to convince her fifty-year-old body to comply. Yet outside, in other tents, sleep-deprived miners scrambled to alert. As she wiped her eyes and took an assessment of her family's assigned geodome, she realized with a stomach-clenching lurch she was the only one there.

Toru forgot all her aches and pains as she shoved on her boots and pressed away any immediate panic. Where were her loved ones? They'd only been on Shānmén a couple of weeks, but that howling siren might be for them. She barreled out of the geodome to join the rush of sweaty, confused miners heading to Shaft Two.

The heat and humidity of the planet usually made her grumble and long for the cool temperatures below. This morning Toru didn't even notice it, as she joined the mass of workers hustling to see what help they might offer.

Around her, miners and staff streamed out of geodomes like a nest of disturbed ants. They came from everywhere —from maintenance to the offices. Pumping her arms, gasping in the thick air, her feet leaden in her boots, Toru was swept along with the crowd.

In the chaos they passed the supply dome, and she caught her daughter's voice calling out. Toru dodged out of the flow and jostle.

Lena Waipapa-Riley's height and neatly braided dark hair was unmistakable. Toru let out a sob of relief. Her daughter carried a box of foil-wrapped ammonium nitrate fuel oil for their deep assault in Shaft One.

Nearby, their synthetic, Carter, placed explosive charges in a locked box onto the bed of the mine utility vehicle parked outside. His crafted, handsome face reflected concern, but he could not experience the visceral fear of a human worker.

Lena and her family of miners had arrived a short time before, setting up equipment and planning their assault on the deeper seams. Now, all that work would have to wait. The alarm meant that harvesting Eitr had once again claimed more lives. This was the dread the miners shared every day.

While the siren wailed on, Toru felt the first rumble. The

echo of an explosion from beneath rose through her feet, shook her gut, and brought everything into sharp focus.

Carter's eyes fluttered blankly for an instant as he tapped into the mine's synthetic network. Still in silent communion with other AI, he turned unseeing toward the family and voiced the words that each of the seasoned miners already understood, deep in their bones.

"That was an explosion in Shaft Two." It wasn't in the area the Combine assigned them to work, but miners from Earth to the Weyland Isles still held to the code. When something went bad, everyone ran toward the problem—not away. Two other members of their family company, known collectively as the Knot, sat in the MUV's cab, focusing their attention on Toru, waiting for her orders.

Bianca Ting-Riley—once married to Toru's oldest son Oliver, now widowed—perched in the driver's seat, her hard hat in place. The only member of the Knot to have military experience, she'd plied her trade for fifteen years as a sharpshooter for the Union of Progressive Peoples. Though it had been a huge part of her life, she never talked about those experiences.

Nathan Bennetts-Riley, Toru's nephew, didn't catch on as quickly as Bianca did, but when she handed him his hard hat, he jammed it on, too.

On instinct, Toru calculated where the other members of her team should be in relation to this new threat. Two Knot members were absent. Her daughter, Jīn Huā Deng, worked in comms—that section had been a mess when they arrived—while their minerals specialist, her cousin's child Pinar Osman-Riley, would be on her way up from Shaft One. That special protective suit of hers could be damn useful.

Toru, Lena, and even Carter grabbed hard hats off the seats of the MUV and piled into the bed. It would be a bumpy ride, but they would get there first. Bianca punched the accelerator as far down as it would go.

Clever pilot that she was, she managed to not collect any concerned miners on the slope toward the tunnel head. She threaded the way with stunning accuracy among the half-dozen domes between them and Shaft Two.

Toru's pulse thundered in her head. The hot air blasted her eyes and the MUV wobbled under them, but what lay ahead would be far worse. The group whipped past other miners, some still dirty from their last twelve-hour shift, many more awkwardly stuffing themselves into their overalls. Every single person, however, wore the same hardened expression.

Ahead of the humans were the synthetic reinforcements. Several Davids, still sporting their aprons from the cafeteria, joined a stream of Working Joes who'd been shifting supplies at the rear of the depot.

By the time Toru and her family reached the huge dome covering the shaft head, a small crowd of miners already gathered at the entrance. They helped other workers stagger out of the cage and onto the deck.

Dropping off the back of the MUV, Toru pushed through the as-yet thin crowd.

Petro Kozak, the mine manager, was absent. That didn't surprise her. The minute she'd met him, she identified what kind of creature he was. Company all the way, with an eye on the bottom line, and never on safety.

The Jùtóu Combine managed an entire line of these tenuous facilities, with little to no oversight. Mine managers, far from central headquarters, liked to strip everything to bare bones, doing a little creative bookkeeping and pocketing the difference. Her first look at the Svarog mine had told her that Kozak took full advantage of the distance.

"Make a hole," Toru shouted, her voice pitched to cut through the indistinct murmur.

"Clear the way!" Lena joined in, forcing her way through the press of concerned workers. "Where's the safety manager, for fuck's sake?"

Toru's eyes raked through the dirty, upset, and growing crowd. She spotted the narrow form of Lester Whittaker with his back up against the rusted metal of the hoist. When Lena's words reached him, he became a cornered animal desperate for an escape, but it was too late. She strode over to talk to him, as Toru shouldered her way toward the cage.

Slumped-over miners littered the entrance like an oil painting of hell, while Working Joe units moved in unison to reach them. They brought stretchers, and Toru joined the effort to muscle the injured and suffering onto them. The synthetics' efficiency was a comfort in moments like these.

Arriving miners wanting to help their comrades dawdled at the mine head, accomplishing nothing but impeding aid. Since Whittaker seemed of negative use, Toru stepped into the gap. She'd worked many mines as safety manager in her younger days. This wasn't her first explosion, and she knew the drill.

"Bianca, Nathan, help those Davids, get people back!" The last thing the situation needed was well-meaning miners crowding onto the deck—or worse, into the cage. Getting down on one knee, she grabbed the hand of the nearest fallen miner.

The Knot hadn't been around long enough to form many bonds with the miners who were already working Svarog's two deep shafts, but she'd met Mateo Moore on their first day. He'd introduced himself—which was unusual from the stoic types who chose mining as a profession—and made an impression on her with his youth and beaming smile.

"Mateo," she said, "what happened? What did you see?"

His head of curling dark hair flicked her way, but his lips wore no smile. Instead, they stretched tight around his teeth, like a dog baring them in fear.

"Monsters, *mi doe*, monsters everywhere…" He let out a scream that bounced around the deck area, eliciting concerned shouts from the miners trying to see what happened. Those of his comrades who were still conscious howled, too.

"The teeth… the shadows with teeth…" the one next to him burbled.

No smell came up the shaft, but these reactions confirmed the situation. It had to be whitedamp. A thin line of smoke oozed like some charmed snake from below ground. Toru patted Matteo's hand and thanked the Earth Mother that none of her family were in Shaft Two.

"Move these men off the deck," she said, grabbing the front of Matteo's stretcher and leading the way.

Back in the coal mines of Earth, whitedamp was a deadly problem, and Eitr ran in seams that yielded that same risk. Still, this needn't have happened.

As the Joes and the miners pulled the injured back off the deck and laid them on the bare soil, Toru patted the young man down. He'd lost not only his hard hat but also the carbon monoxide sensor, which should be attached to the shoulder of his overalls.

"Carter," Toru yelled over her shoulder.

The synthetic, taller than either the Davids or Joes, strode across to her.

"Yes, Toru?"

"Bring me Whittaker, now!"

Carter turned and left, then returned a moment later, his hand locked on the arm of the safety manager. A red-faced Lena followed.

Whittaker's eyes were wide. Kozak had picked someone

inexperienced—that much was obvious. Both managers must have hoped the dice would roll their way, and no one would have to deal with an accident of this scope. In Toru's experience, though, mismanagement and skimping on safety *always* led to disaster.

"Where's his CO sensor?" She pointed down to Mateo.

The look Toru got in return told her everything, and the pit in her stomach grew hot with kindled anger.

"That's... that's not in the budget," Whittaker stammered. "We have sensors in the tunnels, so we didn't need..."

Toru locked her fingers around the stretcher, keeping her hands from reaching for his neck. As a cog in the machine, he wasn't worth wasting Combine points.

"Those fixed sensors fail when there's this much ground water," she choked out. "I've just been here a few weeks and *I* damn well know that!"

Whittaker's face twisted in fear. The miners clustered around them overheard that conversation. The safety manager might be a fool, but he knew the history of people in his position. From the earliest days of mining, workers dealt with shoddy management in their own way.

Fortunately for Whittaker, a security team arrived. Armed with newly issued PPZ-49 submachine guns—lovingly known as 'strike breakers'—standard issue 3-D printed frontier revolvers, and the brand new EVI-87 Zvezda plasma rifle, they rolled up on the shaft head. Armed like that, they weren't there to assist in rescue efforts.

The chief of security, a square block of a man named Jerome Galen, scanned the confusion.

"Need some help there, Whittaker?"

Relief washed over the safety manager's face. He glanced back at Toru, sporting a smirk in response.

"I think we're good, Galen. Just a health and safety issue."

The dark expressions on the miners grew more fixed. They might not take their frustrations and anger out on the management right now, but they would not forget. Accidents happened... even to those in high places.

Toru grasped the moment; nothing was to be gained by fighting. Brushing Whittaker aside, she shot Galen a glance.

"We're handling it. Maybe just give us some room?"

The chief's jaw clenched for a moment, but he jerked his head to his troops, and they backed off to the edge of the crowd. Toru gestured to the Knot. They closed in around her, forming a barrier to avoid being overheard by the brass.

"Carter," she said, touching his hand, "see if any of the PDTs have activated."

His eyes flickered blankly again, signaling another silent communion with the synthetic network.

"I am reading five fatalities ready for body retrieval."

Toru took a breath. Personal data transmitters switched on when a worker flatlined—another cost-cutting measure. The batteries lasted longer this way. Five deaths were terrible, but less than she'd feared. Still, if they didn't act fast, there would be more.

"Are you instructing me to arrange a rescue mission?" Carter asked. Sometimes it was easy to forget he wasn't human, but his calm expression in this moment reminded her. Toru gave him a curt nod.

"Whittaker's no use, and we can't have miners racing down there. Who knows how shitty the emergency equipment is?"

Bianca let out a snort. "I wouldn't bloody trust it."

"I can go with them, Auntie." Pinar approached from Shaft One. The sunlight gleamed on her state-of-the-art protective suit. Planetary atmosphere of any kind would bring on a cascade of fatal symptoms in her body, but Pinar fought hard to live a productive life in the Knot. Her knowledge of Eitr surpassed the monetary savings of leaving her behind. Her suit, which she affectionately called her "shell", had cost a lot for the family to buy. It would be invaluable in this situation. She'd be able to assess the danger from the Eitr, while Carter could report on the mine's structural damage.

Loathe as Toru was to risk the Knot's own in an unstable mine, it was the life they'd all chosen. The material of Pinar's suit was harder and more durable than any safety equipment Kozak had bothered to pay for. So Toru nodded.

"Just stick close to the synthetics... No following any seams this time. Got it?"

"No following anything shiny, I promise." Behind the sheen of polycarbonate plastic, Pinar grinned a little.

Medical teams finally arrived from the camp. Toru and Carter examined the integrity of the cage. After a scan, the synthetic declared the metal free of defects and in full working order. Much to their relief, whatever the size of the explosion below ground, it hadn't weakened the hoist or the cage.

"I'll co-ordinate their search pattern through the synthetic network," Carter said. With a smile of reassurance, he placed his hand over Toru's and gave it a squeeze. Toru tried very hard not to glance over her shoulder. She trusted Carter but wouldn't want anyone to notice. They didn't need any 'microwave fucker' commentary.

"Take care of Pinar."

"The Knot comes first," he said. "I understand your directives." His eyes drifted off to the right for a split second. "The miner count stands at thirty, minus the twelve on the surface."

It was the one thing that miners were always sure to do. They might forget their lunch, but they'd never forget to record their shifts. Every miner punched in or they didn't get paid for their work. It made for a precise roster of who was below.

Outside, the remaining miners reached the entrance. They'd moved most of the injured, but the new arrivals still risked clogging the way. Galen's security forces stood around doing nothing—as long as no one threatened violence. They could have helped.

They didn't.

Lena let out a high-pitched whistle. "Let the Davids and the Joes through, you fucking morons," she bellowed. "They've got rescuing to do."

Toru wondered if they'd ever done any kind of emergency drill. Local mudlickers died a lot cheaper than even indentured workers. At least her family were skilled employees: the Combine cared more about whether they lived or died. Valuable investments were not to be squandered.

In her time, Toru had dealt with plenty of Working Joes on mines spread throughout the Weyland Isles. The Davids, with their human-presenting faces, were a new wrinkle.

Toru was fine with synthetics—her daughters might have said *too* fine—but these Davids weren't standard issue for anything. Their makers, Weyland-Yutani, had recalled all seven models many years ago. These six units, turning up for rescue duty, should have been composted with the rest.

The recall wasn't compulsory, and the official memo had said they were "fixed" and "fully compliant." Just a way for the company to deny responsibility if they went rogue and murdered a bunch of folks.

The company line. That made it bullshit.

Kozak must have picked these up on the black market. It wasn't illegal, but it skirted close to the edge of unacceptable. Toru would have much rather seen the blank stock standard, statue-like faces of the Working Joes, rather than the human—yet somehow more eerie—Davids. Still, they were in working order, and the toxic gases below would mean nothing to them.

Carter, skilled in reading the subtle flickers of her face, shot the Davids an appraising glance.

"I will be in full control. Have no fear."

The corner of her mouth quirked for a second. "Don't be afraid to bash in their heads if you need to. The Combine can bill me."

He nodded.

"Go." The miners trapped below didn't have time for her reservations. "First find the folks that Medical can save. Get the other synthetics to locate and remove them." She paused, then added, "The emergency scrubbers are on the schematics, I hope?"

"Indeed, but I cannot speak to their condition."

She chewed on the inside of her cheek for a moment. "Knowing the state of the rest of the mine, I'll be grateful if they're there at all."

She motioned at Nathan and Bianca, who helped make a path for the synthetics. Though the resident workers grumbled and swore, they also recognized the experience of the Knot. Contractors sent by the Combine, they held more sway than Kozak did, even with the short time they'd been in residence. Reflected on the faces was concern for their comrades. Every one of them knew it was simple luck that they hadn't been on that shift.

She addressed the synthetics. "Follow my unit, Carter, below. Listen to his instructions as you would mine." Synthetic networks could become twitchy unless there was some kind of human direction. She didn't want them fritzing out.

Carter's eyes blinked for a moment as he hooked into the network to take the lead. Toru liked to keep him separate from Combine bullshit, but this was an emergency so she made an exception. She hoped he wouldn't pick up any viruses.

"Where the fuck is the mine manager?" The androids and Pinar loaded into the cage to begin their descent. Toru shielded her eyes from the spotlights, looking through the crowd for any sign of Kozak. "He should be here by now…"

Huddled at the deck entrance, the miners grumbled louder.

"New Luhansk," Nathan informed her with a jerk of his head. Her nephew showed an enviable ability to slot into any new situation. He'd gathered gossip while the Knot was still in orbit. "He's set up his family in a pretty little house down there."

The crowd shifted, and Toru sensed a tipping point. Tragedy often set off resentment: sometimes more. Gooseneck George, the oldest miner on site, shared a knowing look with her as he wiped sweat from his eyes. Like Toru, he knew the dangers. She'd lived through five mine riots, and as much as she understood the anger, she didn't want to deal with another such uprising.

Spotting Jīn Huā's dark head of hair among the helmets of the miners, Toru gestured her over. Jīn Huā's Chinese father grew up with one of Toru's nieces in Melbourne. Toru might not have birthed her, but in the way of her family, that meant nothing. The Knot adopted her before the attack on Canberra, when things became a nightmare in Australia. Jīn Huā took that kindness and passed it on to the two children she had adopted.

Also, she was a hell of a comms cipher.

Toru wiggled her way through the burly miners to reach the older woman.

"Get back to the office and locate Kozak... fast as you can."

"Yes, Ma." Then she was away, melting into the crowd. She'd been some kind of high-powered executive in Australia before the Great Rebellion against the Three World Empire, yet she never challenged the older woman's leadership. Another reason Toru was glad she'd picked her for this mission.

"Bianca, take a few Joes, and maybe a David, over to the vehicle pool. Send a couple of trucks down the decline tunnel. If the cave-in hasn't taken it out, it'll be a good way to get the dead and injured to the surface." Toru stepped out from the deck and took some long, deep breaths.

The rest of the miners lingered, coagulating in small groups, trying to decipher what had happened. Toru didn't need to listen to their conversations. Only the presence of the armed security guards contained that simmering resentment.

Medics and Joes had already taken six workers to the medical dome, but another three were still waiting to be transported. Friends crouched next to them, trying to offer them some comfort. All three screamed, or sobbed, or moaned.

"Teeth... fuck me... the teeth."

"They're in the walls!"

Toru pulled her grey braids from the sweat gathered at her neck. Carbon monoxide poisoning was a beast, and the effects were terrifying. Time would help them escape its clutches—she hoped.

The personal device crackled on her wrist, and Jīn Huā's voice echoed up from it, brittle and angry.

"He's here, Ma. And he's pissed."

Toru knew who Kozak's target would be. She squeezed her hands into fists, trying to do that box technique breathing Lena had attempted to teach her. At least it brought oxygen to her brain, even if it didn't calm her all the way down.

She flicked the channel open. "I'm on my way. Tell him it's best not to step outside that dome right now. Miners are roaming around looking for some kind of payback."

As Toru set off, she tried to tell herself she wasn't one of them.

2

RUMBLES ABOVE

Kozak kept her waiting for an hour outside his office. Toru waited patiently until her wrist-pd beeped, then got to her feet and opened the manager's door. If she'd been younger, she would have kicked it, so it was a kind of restraint on her part.

Luckily for Kozak, sitting on the other side of his spotlessly clean desk, she was mother and grandmother. Time and responsibility had made her wiser—or at least a little more considered in her anger.

Petro Kozak glanced up, and then out the plastic window into Operations, where Security Chief Jerome Galen sat talking to Jīn Huā—or more probably flirting.

Security had their own geodome nearby, filled with the latest weaponry from Hyperdyne. The company's zero-G weapons factory, Seneca, orbited the northern hemisphere, which meant Jerome got all the goodies he wanted. He looked like the type who would be itching for an excuse to use them. Probably hoped today was the day.

Toru was determined she wouldn't give him what he wanted.

Chief Galen's closeness made Kozak confident. He dropped his gaze back to the computer screen and tapped away. It was almost as if the Shaft Two accident hadn't just happened. The disrespect didn't bother her—she'd experienced plenty of that—but callous disregard wound her up.

"Already covering your ass?"

She stood in front of his desk, placing her clenched fists on it, leaning down. He wouldn't ignore that signal.

Sure enough, Kozak's gaze flickered to her hands, then back up to her eyes. His pale features squeezed into something sour.

"Riley, I don't know what you want me to say. Mining Eitr is a dangerous business. I feel for those guys, but they get paid just like the rest of us."

Toru smiled, instead of reaching across the desk and smashing his face into it.

"The synthetics are still down there pulling miners out," she said, "and you're up here, what? Writing a report? I guess you already know the results, huh?"

The small, pale man with the company haircut, Kozak had to be spending his days watching the clock until he gathered enough seniority to get away from mining. Middle managers always had a healthy sense of place, clawing their way to the top while fighting off those beneath them. It made them hell to deal with. He probably had a connection somewhere in the Jùtóu Combine's corporate structure, which he'd thought would secure him a better position.

Toru read bitterness in every line of his body.

His attitude turned from vague discomfort to instant outrage. Toru had his attention. His eyes darted over her dirty overalls, her grey braided hair, the multitudinous wrinkles around her eyes and mouth. A miner who'd survived to her age and didn't back down probably confused him, and she took great pleasure in it.

"You *people*"—he chewed over those words—"signed on as indentured workers for the Combine—while *I'm* the boss here. Let me tell you something, Riley: Svarog runs on a razor-thin margin, and production will be cut in half until we can get Two operational again. I need to get in front of this... you should know that."

"What I *know*," Toru said through her teeth, "is that the Combine lets you keep the difference between what they supply for running this place and what you actually pay. I *know* that any expenses you can cut go straight into your pocket. And I *know* that it cost people their lives today."

They glared at each other, but he didn't voice the uncomfortable truth. Human lives meant less than nothing to the Combine. Hell, synthetics were more expensive.

"Accidents happen," he said, then took a breath. "Mining isn't the safest occupation." He drawled out the words, like giving them proper air was a bother.

"It's *McClintock*-Riley," she said. "And I am fully aware of that. I've been in mines since I grew tits. Been indentured to the Combine since then, too."

His eyes flickered down to her chest, and then back up—apparently didn't like what he saw. They'd been pretty fine, once, Toru reminded herself.

"What I'm saying is," she continued, "you should belly up and take better care of One, or the Combine will shut Svarog down real quick." Toru leaned a fraction closer to him, though it brought a twinge to her back. "You might think 'cos we're indentured, the Combine doesn't care about me and mine—but you'd be wrong. We're their experts in deep shafts and high value minerals. After what happened today, one word from me, and you're out on your ear." Her gaze flickered to the right-hand wall, and the map of Shaft One pinned there. "You know, if we don't sink that shaft deeper, strike Eitr, it might happen anyway."

His jaw clenched at that inescapable truth. They'd tapped what had been the easiest to mine, which forced them to go deeper into more dangerous territory. The mineral might be toxic and hard to find, but it also guaranteed a future for Toru's loved ones.

Seven sisters and one brother had set out into space, and they'd made themselves and their family invaluable—

even if the Jùtóu Combine might not quite grasp what they considered family. It was why they'd formed the company and called it the Knot. Corporations were understood. Family was more nebulous. That inability to understand the tightness formed by connections of blood and caring made people like Kozak angry.

Ignorance often did.

"Very sure of yourself there, old woman, but what even are you?" As if he was seeing her for the very first time, he linked his hands together and took up her challenge, leaned toward her. "Refugees from a world too rich for your blood? Something… *mongrel*."

Toru sucked on the inside of her cheek and took a breath. Now he was getting personal, but she'd never backed down from applying a little education when someone needed it.

"You see what you want to, but I'm a mother, a grandmother, a refugee, and a miner."

His eyes narrowed tighter, flickering once more over the details of her face. Remained fixed there.

"No, *what* are you?"

He wanted a label. Had from the beginning. They always did. After decades of fighting these types of demands, Toru honed her answer to a succulent refrain.

"You want me to recite my genealogy, Kozak? My *whakapapa*? I could tell you about the Irish, Māori, Samoan, German, Scots, and Australians in my blood, but that would take more time than I have to give you—especially now. So the short answer is, what I am is the one who will find the Eitr, and save your job."

That snapped him out of his obsession with her face. The hard truth of it was, the Combine owned the Knot and Toru, but right now her family owned the mine. If they didn't come through in the next few weeks, the Combine would close down the whole facility.

Jùtóu Combine owned more mines on Shānmén, but Kozak was Svarog's boss. He'd be unlikely to find another job like it, especially on this planet. It would look bad if he failed.

"Then you better get back to it, *Riley*." The smile the spread on his face was poisonous. "Leave the rescue effort to me. Stick to Shaft One, why don't you."

She'd sized him up just right from the beginning. A little man, trying to hold on to power. He'd grip it tight, even into death.

"You've got a deal." She pushed away from his desk. "But you better check out the air scrubbers in One. They don't smell right, and I'd hate for you to have *another* disaster on your hands."

Toru's nose was better tuned than his bottom line, and the moment they'd visited that shaft, she'd clocked that the scrubbers weren't working. She'd been patient, hoping he'd take care of it. Yet, given what had happened in Shaft Two, waiting wasn't an option.

Kozak was full of shit.

"Those scrubbers aren't due for replacement for

another month." His gaze had already drifted back to the computer screen, and he waved one hand. "But I'll see what I can do."

Suppressing her rage, Toru walked out of his office. Operations personnel were busy dealing with various tasks, but a few curious faces flicked her way. Antonijevic—the lead Combine archaeologist, so always at a loose end—gave her a shrug. The stupid grin on his square face, and his "what are you going to do" attitude kicked Toru's annoyance even higher.

Ignoring the rest of the workers, she shoved open the outside door and stormed through, knowing the pointlessness of her rage. The operation dome gleamed bright silver under the blinding sun, and instantly sweat broke out on Toru's face. It was like passing from one world to another—neither of them pleasant.

Standing still for a moment, she took a few deep breaths, centering herself. The warm air filled her lungs and pressed against her skin. The Svarog mine sat almost directly on this planet's equator. As Toru walked down the steps to the stripped and barren earth, her eyes lingered on the green foliage just beyond the mine's perimeter fence. A twinge of homesickness swelled, as it often did when she was in a vulnerable state.

Unlike most of the Knot, she'd been born on Earth, and New Zealand's green forests and lakes still haunted her dreams.

"Mum…" The familiar voice jolted her from melancholy

recollections. Her youngest daughter waited behind the curve of the dome. Everyone expected Lena would take Toru's place of leadership in the Knot, and she looked the part. Tall, where her mother was short. Darker skinned, her glossy black hair tied in a low ponytail. She attracted attention wherever she was. Yet, the girl knew how to handle herself.

As she approached, Toru shook her head and raised her hands.

"Don't even ask how it went."

Lena pushed strands of hair back off her face. "If we die out here, then it won't matter how many Combine points we earn for this fucking job." She stared down at her boots for a moment. "Sophie warned us not to take this one."

Toru loved her daughter's wife, but Sophie held a high opinion of what the Knot could get away with when it came to the Combine.

"It wasn't like there was a lot of choice," Toru replied, putting her hand on Lena's shoulder. "We couldn't afford to have so many cycled back to Pylos—all those transfers add up. Have to pay for those baby credits after all."

"I thought that wasn't a possibility." Her daughter shot her a sly look. "Averie got the pregnancy share last year, so Sophie and I didn't expect to have our own any time soon. I know finances are tight…"

Toru looked toward Shaft Two and the still-rising smoke. Talking about children seemed strange, but if age had taught her anything, it was to not put anything off. She wanted Lena to have what she craved. After all, she'd been born indentured, and she deserved a child. With luck, the baby would be free of the Combine shackles before she was five.

She sighed as they walked together from the large operations dome to the smaller one that housed the cafeteria. After the accident in Two, she knew the Knot would need some good news.

"Well, I talked with my sisters, and we all agreed we're getting old," she said. "With Rua's death last year, we have the room." She tried to keep her tone light, even when mentioning her sister's demise, though that wound was still fresh enough to sting.

Lena sighed. She hadn't known her aunt well. If they'd been able to remain in New Zealand, it would have been different. Yet that country only belonged to the rich now.

"You're not that old, Mum, you can still pull a twelve-hour down the shaft." Neither of them mentioned the job on Hestia V, six years earlier. That had resulted in Rua's hastily repaired hip and knee. The events of the day just reminded them that, in this business, disaster was only a roll of the dice away.

It was Toru's duty to prepare her children. She glanced sideways at her daughter. The wind caught her dark hair again, whipping at her braids. Gently, Toru reset one behind Lena's ear.

"Not like I used to, girl. Everything hurts when I try.

No, the future is for you and Sophie, Jīn Huā, and her kids. Nathan too, if he ever gets his shit together." They both laughed at that.

Their amusement caught the attention of a nearby security guard, leaning up against the perimeter fence. With the off-shift miners back in their dorms, and the injured from Two in the medical bay, the guards could return to their favorite pastime—harassing the indentured. This one's helmet covered his face, not that they would have recognized him.

Most of the Combine's security personnel were former UPP—Union of Progressive Peoples—soldiers. They kept to themselves, eating in their own mess hall and staring down their noses at the miners, whether waged or indentured.

Though they couldn't see his eyes, Toru knew what his expression would be under there. Disrespect to her, and sizing up Lena for a fuck. When the older woman stopped and stared back at him, his stance tightened.

"Better learn to laugh quieter," he grumbled, "draws the local wildlife. Don't want to be a chicken snack."

Shānmén's native species must have been a bother for the first colonists and miners. Now, though, acoustic deterrents and an electric fence kept the largest at bay. In addition, security ventured out once a month on the so-called "chicken hunt." It lowered the nearby population of anything with a heartbeat. It also gave them something to shoot at that wasn't human.

Not that they would hesitate at that. The unspoken other reason they were at the mine was to keep indentured workers in. Visiting the nearby town of New Luhansk required permission that Kozak never gave. Couldn't risk having their valuable workers skipping off-planet without paying their Combine debt.

Before Toru said anything, Lena pulled her on. "You don't know how many stims and powders guys like that are on," she said in a low voice. "They didn't get to spill blood on Two's deck, so let's just leave them, OK?"

It was nice to know that her daughter worried about her. Lena hadn't known her mother when she was young. Back then, Toru would have split the face of anyone who messed with her family. Her lips twisted, but they unfurled into a smile when she spotted Jīn Huā hurrying after them. She must have wriggled free of Galen's attentions. Catching up, she put her hand in the crook of Toru's arm.

"Things seem to have calmed down in there, but the Combine isn't happy about Shaft Two going down."

Toru waved her hand. "As long as they aren't adding it to the Knot debt, I don't care. Besides, Pinar will get her chance to shine if she can locate a good vein for another shaft."

"She'll make it happen," Jīn Huā said as she leaned in against Toru. She was far more tactile than Lena, and that was no bad thing. Toru kissed her on the head.

"My ray of sunshine."

"I've got good news, too," Lena broke in, "something to improve today." It was a pretty low bar to clear, but Toru was ready for anything.

"What would that be?"

"I think the cafeteria is serving prívarok for dinner."

"They always do better when they are not trying to serve American food," Jīn Huā pointed out. "When they do meatloaf, it's deadly."

Even though Kozak's budget-cutting had cost lives today, he would keep making sure that decent Slovak food stayed on the menu. Toru patted her hand. "Well, when you have some, do what I did for my little ones—pretend it's delicious."

"My Baba did that," Jīn Huā replied in a monotone. "I never fell for it, so I don't think Bái Yún Lee or Dà Shī Voo will either. They're smart kids."

The death of her family during the Food Wars never got less painful, but Toru wished she'd talk about them more. Leaning in, she told Jīn Huā what she always did.

"He'd be proud of you, and what you've done for those little ones."

Jīn Huā squeezed Toru's arm a little tighter. Though she'd suffered and lost everything, the experience hadn't hardened her heart one bit. After the Canberra blast, she'd reached out to refugee services and adopted two little orphaned children. Then she'd taken them to the stars.

However young they were, though, they bore deep scars—mental and physical. That was why Jīn Huā didn't leave them on Pylos station, where the rest of the Knot remained. A small dome housed a school within the mine, so Toru had signed off on them coming.

"They're doing great, dear." She gave the younger woman a squeeze back. "You're keeping them safe and being a beautiful mum to them."

Jīn Huā smiled hesitantly. "Sometimes I wonder if I'm doing the right thing."

Toru nodded. "You always will, but remember—it's the bad parents who don't worry."

"I'm taking notes," Lena said, swinging around and grabbing hold of Jīn Huā. "Mum just said the sisters approved a baby share for Sophie and me." She threw her arms around the other woman. "Another Knot baby on the way."

Toru watched the two of them laugh and jump around, and allowed herself a weary smile. Her sisters hadn't wanted to share the news with everyone, but to hell with that. Let the young enjoy these moments to hold against a world of regret and loss.

By the time they entered the cafeteria, the two young women were already discussing names. Toru hung back while they walked to the coffee station.

"Prívarok, Ms. McClintock-Riley?" The David standing behind the counter held a pair of tongs up high and wore a compliant smile on his face. They might have followed Carter, and saved lives down below, but she'd never trust them. Stories about their failures—the lives lost under their unflinching gaze—gave her nightmares. She didn't even like taking food from them.

Her gaze flicked to the tongs, already imagining scenarios in which they could be used as a deadly weapon. She swallowed down her dislike.

"Is it good?" she asked. As soon as the words were out of her mouth, she realized how ridiculous they were. Being around Carter made her forget the true nature of synthetics. The David tilted his head a fraction.

"It is compliant to all current Combine food standards."

"That's the best a girl can hope for," she muttered under her breath. "That'll be great," she said louder, even though he would have heard both. Still, the synthetic made no comment as he doled out a cupful, put it on a tray, and passed it over.

"Bon appétit," he said, clapping the tongs together.

Sometimes it felt as if the Davids took pleasure in being ominous. Their programming shouldn't include fucking with people, Toru told herself.

Over by the dome's window, several members of the Knot had gathered. Lena and Jīn Huā took positions at the end of the plastic table, choosing coffee over food. Bianca and Nathan slurped back prívarok with no apparent concerns. The thick stew contained many legumes and potatoes that the colonists grew locally, so it wasn't as if Kovak shelled out for off-world supplies. A plate of dumplings took pride of place in the middle of the table.

Nathan slid them toward Toru as she sat down.

"Tuck in, Auntie—the cook was having a good day," he said through a full mouth. Somehow he remained cheerful even after the shit show of a day it had been. In her sleep-deprived state, it only made her mood worse.

The son of her younger sister, Ono, Nathan was only twenty years old, so he didn't have many of life's dents on him yet. He also wasn't wearing regulation overalls. All the Knot wore yellow overalls, with their twisted rope symbol on the left breast and their name underneath. His said "Bennetts-Riley," which would have been visible if he didn't have the top half hanging around his waist, with the sleeves tied loosely. Instead, he wore a Jùtóu Combine regulation shirt, and did so with pride—like a waged miner.

"Who did you steal the shirt off, Nathan?" she said, putting two dumplings by the side of her plate. "Not one of the miners we pulled out of the shaft today, I hope…"

"Auntie… you hurt my feelings. I'd never!" His teeth flashed in a white, cheeky smile. "Besides, no miner gets their hands on these shirts. I got given it."

Bianca shot Toru a look from under a crooked eyebrow as she shoveled food into her mouth. Military service had prepared her well for life in the mines. Toru's daughter-in-law might be quiet, but she picked up on things quickly enough.

Lena didn't have nearly that amount of restraint. Choking back her coffee, she dared the question they were all thinking.

"What did you have to do for it?"

The young man flushed red. "Nothing... shit, girl, is that what you think of me?"

He'd been giving it to the cute security guard since day three of the Knot's planetfall. Toru wanted to give him advice on sleeping with military types, but she'd done it herself once too often. Unfortunately, the times she'd opened up to him and offered suggestions, he hadn't taken it well. After the day they'd all had, Toru didn't want to go down that road. So she flapped her hand at him.

"What you do on your off hours is no business of ours," she said. "Just don't flash that shirt around—won't make you any friends with the miners, especially right now."

Nathan glanced around. Even he couldn't ignore the looks of their fellow mudlickers. Her nephew might be brash, but he wasn't stupid. These were people the Knot might have to rely on underground. Another collapse, and maybe no one would come to haul their asses out of the deep dark. Antagonizing them might help you end up dead. Muttering a little, he shucked on the top part of his overalls and zipped them up.

Lena smirked at her cousin, but said nothing.

Toru ate her soup, watching the younger folk talk and joke among themselves. She recognized the signs. A brush with death, even second-hand, made everything else seem brighter. Air tasted sweeter, and sex more intense. Yet, none of them were bullet- or carbon monoxide-proof. Except Carter.

She stared down at her prívarok, which suddenly didn't

hold any appeal. The air scrubber issue still bothered her, and she'd probably have to ride Kozak about it every day. If she got lucky, he'd come down the shaft, where she'd at least have a home territory advantage.

Jīn Huā finished her food ahead of the others and got to her feet. "Hey, Ma, you remembered you promised Miss Vesley that you would give a talk to the kids next week—you, Carter and Pinar?"

Toru closed her eyes and breathed deep for a moment. The idea of spending time at the school talking about her life in mining wasn't very appealing right now. Yet, it was moments like those she'd missed with her own little kids, and she always regretted it.

"I haven't forgotten," Toru said, scooping up the last spoonful of her soup. "Looking forward to all those questions."

The Regulations of Indenture specified that the Combine had to supply education for their workers' children. Most waged miners paid a little extra to keep their kids at school in New Luhansk, about ten kilometers away. Indentured as the Knot were, they didn't have that option.

As she followed Jīn Huā to the door, Toru remembered what she'd been meaning to tell Nathan before everything went to shit. She pointed at him.

"Don't forget to check the Big Boys, like I asked. Five's gyroscope is acting up."

"Yes, Auntie," he said without looking up. That was as good as it got from him.

As Toru left the cafeteria, she could have sworn that the David that served her clacked his tongs in her direction one last time.

As far as omens went, it wasn't a good one.

3

OUTSIDE THE LINES

A week passed, and it was as if Shaft Two had never existed. Nathan watched from the sidelines as they ferried the miners assigned to it with all the efficiency of the socialist machine back to New Luhansk. The Combine would give the uninjured new assignments and ship them off-world.

Working Joes drove all the unused haulers and trucks from Shaft Two to parking off-site, where they would sit while a feasibility study was conducted on sinking another shaft. A stream of MUVs moved through the mine like a caravan of wombats, ferrying everything and everyone.

The vein of Eitr in Shaft One dwindled away, triggering the Jùtóu Combine to send in the Knot specialists. Pinar's knowledge of the mineral was all very well, as was Toru's experience in sinking deep shafts, but Nathan didn't have either of those things. He was the muscle of this operation, not the brains.

Pinar spent hours poring over survey data and running calculations to figure out if the elusive mineral vein ran further down the valley. Toru and Lena assisted her by working seismic survey charges and the spectrographs, affectionately named PUPS by their original creator. Previous workers of the small mining outpost hadn't examined the line of mountains and their deposits. Now, in the days following the incident, Kozak authorized a team of Joes to test out the nearby peak using seismic survey charges.

She didn't generally like to show her emotions, but Nathan picked up that Pinar was pretty excited. Losing that group in Shaft Two had opened up an opportunity for her to flex her muscles.

He could only wish for such an opportunity. Until they found something, though, he was at loose ends. It bothered him sometimes that Toru didn't bring him in on the planning side of things, but he'd found different ways to fill his hours. Svarog wasn't completely with charm.

For a start, Nathan wandered over to the Combine store to check out what had come in. It was an uninspiring as usual: tins of food, overalls, hard hats, and packs of cards. He picked through the few toys that were available, and grinned when he found one of those drinking birds, with a top hat and blue liquid in its body. They were popular, especially among company types who sat them on their desk, entertaining themselves with the perpetual motion.

He supposed it might be some kind of metaphor.

Lacking anything else to do, Nathan snatched one up and took it to Wesford, the store manager.

"Twenty Combine points," Wesford said without looking up from his computer.

"How much for cold hard credits?" Nathan asked, sliding a few of them across the counter. That got old Wesford's attention. His watering blue eyes locked on the money.

"Where the hell did you get those? You ain't even been on planet three weeks…"

Nathan winked. "Can't give away all my secrets."

Wesford's brow furrowed as he did the math in his head.

"I can do five."

"Four, and that's robbery," the younger man countered.

They shared a stare-off for a minute, but Wesford was the one who broke.

"I like your style, Riley."

"Bennetts-Riley," Nathan corrected him, and he swept up the bird. "You'll be hearing it a lot down in New Luhansk soon."

The storekeeper rolled his eyes and went back to his computer.

Clutching his victory, Nathan grinned and left. Avoiding putting any more points on the Knot's debt to the Jùtóu Combine was a success worth celebrating. He angled toward the geodome that housed the small on-site school. On the way, he passed Carter and Pinar, deep in conversation.

Pinar's shell gleamed under the bright sun, making her difficult to look at directly. With a self-sustaining air supply and its articulated scaled exterior, the shell was an expensive piece of kit. Fortunately, she was a short woman, and bird-boned with it. If she'd been larger, it would have been impossible for Nathan to source.

As it was, he'd completed some pretty sweet deals on Pylos station to get hold of it. His Auntie Toru never found out about them—which was some kind of miracle. It'd been fantastic to give Pinar the freedom to do what she loved, and be a functioning member of the Knot. Her smile was worth the sweat and danger of working Pylos station's underbelly.

Carter, though—he was Auntie's indulgence. His chiseled features, tall and lean, were a designer's concept of the ideal man. Jùtóu Combine might lag behind Weyland-Yutani with combat androids, but they far excelled them with their line of companion synths. Nathan had a decent sense of self and grasped that he was a young, well-put-together guy, but around Carter he felt downright scruffy.

When his auntie turned fifty, her sisters found Carter, a discarded pleasure model. They refurbished and modified him extensively to be useful beyond his initial parameters. Then they tied a bow around his neck and presented him to Toru at a big ole party. It embarrassed the shit out of the younger generation, but his Ma and her sisters thought it was hella funny; their uptight sister now owned a pleasure synthetic.

It hadn't gone as they expected; she'd kept his initial programming, but also developed his secondary resources to be of use in the Knot's actual work.

Carter waved to Nathan while Pinar blew him a kiss from inside her shell. He waved back, but didn't stop to chat. They looked busy, and he had a bird to deliver. Ducking inside the closest geodome, Nathan directed his brightest smile at Miss Vesley, the teacher. She reminded him of his sister, Alice, with her bright-eyed optimism.

She grinned back, but didn't move from where she was, leaning over the curly head of a young boy at his table and quietly explaining something.

Alex Vesley and her class had transformed the inside of the grim geodome with finger-painted pictures of the local wildlife and landscapes, as well as images from Earth: the Grand Canyon, the Great Barrier Reef—now nothing but memory—and Mount Everest itself. They'd edited out the line of hotels on the mountain's slopes.

Nathan's hand flicked up to the necklace under the neck of his shirt, rubbing it between thumb and fingertip. A cylindrical vial hung from a narrow gold chain; within was a small amount of New Zealand soil. Each member of the Knot carried one, a reminder of home. Papatūānuku, the Earth Mother.

Yet here were the children of the Knot, learning alongside the other offspring of Svarog. Miss Vesley was responsible for just ten students of varying ages, including Jīn Huā's kids Bái Yún and Dà Shī. Good thing, because Kozak provided as little funding as possible for the on-site school.

Nathan caught Bái Yún's attention by waving the bird toward her, and her dark eyes lit up. At only seven, she'd been through a lot, but her spirit remained bright. She raced over and caught him around the legs.

"Uncle Nathan, is that for me?"

He wanted to pick her up and swing her around, but Jīn Huā reminded him often that the little girls didn't like to be hugged. After the bomb drop, they'd spent a lot of time in hospitals, and weren't used to being touched all the time. Chinese-Australian like their mother, they were gradually learning to speak their minds—either in Mandarin, English, or with a bit of the Combine patois.

Dà Shī, who was only three, maybe shouldn't have the bird, but as he ran over, his eyes laser focused on it. Suddenly Nathan wondered if he'd done the right thing.

"Ah… Ah… it's for the class."

Miss Vesley rescued him by taking the bird and putting it on a tall shelf behind her desk.

"I *want* it," Dà Shī said with a pout, holding out his hands as if he could telekinetically pull it toward him.

"Shit, sorry," Nathan said, and realized his second mistake. "Awhhh… I mean…"

The teacher laughed and gestured at her charges. "These are miners' kids. I think they've heard it all before—but thanks for the gift. I'll use it for the older students to study boiling and condensation."

"Yeah! Thought it would be useful." He looked down at Bái Yún, who still clutched his leg. Her younger brother already stamped off, lured away by the promise of crayons.

"Are you staying, Uncle Nathan?" Bái Yún asked, using her best and sweetest smile. The little girl was unendingly cute, even if her mother gave her one of those bowl cuts. It worked on children, he supposed, but made adults look like serial killers. When she was older, she'd hate it in pictures of herself.

"Can't today," Nathan said, bending down and risking a hug. "I have something important to do, and so do you… lessons." Weird how being around kids made him all responsible.

Bái Yún let out a sigh, but trundled back to her desk, shooting him a stare of childish betrayal.

"See you at dinner though," Nathan called, before making a hasty exit. The eldest girl enjoyed school about as much as he had, but he'd catch it if Jīn Huā found out he'd interrupted Miss Vesley's lessons.

He'd just stepped out of the school dome when Aoki Sayō pulled up abruptly, almost running him over in one of the Svarog's scuttle bugs. As part of the mine's security force, she got free access to ground transportation.

Scuttle bugs were ex-UPP military, all-terrain patrol transports—so not at all stylish, but very practical. The front was a tough, cold-drawn steel frame, with room for a driver and a passenger. The back could come in all kinds of shapes, but the mine had elected for most of theirs to be flatbeds. Though it was a semi-secure cabin, it didn't possess any air con. Comfort wasn't a priority for the military *or* the Combine.

The UPP named and numbered them, for sure, but in Svarog they were scuttle bugs.

Since he'd hooked up with Aoki, they'd been on a few trips into New Luhansk. He'd even taken a scuttle bug out by himself last week. He'd even survived driving it.

The grin on Aoki's face thrilled him all the way down to his pants. It lit up her serious face, stunning him with her beauty. She leaned out the window of the scuttle bug, gesturing him over.

"Fancy a bit of fun?"

"What… in that?" he asked, looking over his shoulder. His auntie often appeared at such moments. "I mean, we can try…"

Aoki laughed. "Not that, horn dog. The guards are doing a quick chicken run… want to come with?" Svarog's security forces performed culls in the nearby jungle to keep large wildlife away from the mine. It also provided a way to blow off some steam and shoot off some rifles.

Nathan pressed his lips together. "Won't your buddies hassle you for having a mudlicker in the bug?"

Aoki responded by shoving open the passenger door with her foot. "I'm playing cattle dog today. They'll never notice."

That was all he needed to hear.

"Let's go then." He dove into the scuttle bug and slamming the door behind him. "Never seen the local dragons up close."

Aoki rolled her eyes at that. "No dragons, but some are nearly as big."

With that, she accelerated so fast that he landed in the footwell. As they zipped through the gate, she told him to stay down—otherwise the cameras would pick him up. Once they were past the fence and the blinking orange warning light, she yanked him up and gave him a quick kiss to soothe his ego.

"Put on your belt, it's going to get bumpy," Aoki bellowed over the noise of the scuttle bug.

She wasn't kidding about that. Nathan grinned as they turned off the road, across the burned area the mine kept clear of vegetation, and into the jungle itself.

"Twilight is when the animals are most active," Aoki shouted. "Gets dark sooner under the trees, too." She twisted the steering wheel as they drove past a massive fallen tree and beneath the canopy.

She wasn't wrong. The compound ran on Combine time, but the jungle followed older rhythms. Nathan's heart beat faster, and he let out a whoop of excitement. God, it felt fantastic to be above ground, moving at high speed, and being driven by a beautiful woman with an EVI-87 plasma rifle in the back. Indentured miners like him didn't get these sorts of experiences very often.

The towering trees of Shānmén's tropical rainforest sheltered massive ferns, ten-meter-high clumps of fungi, and creatures he'd only caught glimpses of when they came in to land on the planet. Though the shadows grew longer in the jungle, there was still plenty of variety and wonder to take in; meter-high bounding creatures scrambled out of their way, multi-colored insects as long as his arm buzzed from bush to bush, and a long line of deep purple fungus circled the trunk of a yellow-barked tree like a staircase.

"Not hallucinogenic, by the way." Aoki pointed it out. "Believe me, I tried—but the flesh of the bouncers is." She pointed in the opposite direction. "Look over there, noddle-heads." The jewel-colored avians darted in and out of the shadows while light filtered through the canopy of trees, piercing the encroaching darkness. The birds were only the size of Earth chickens, but with long, elegant necks that wobbled back and forth as they ran for cover.

"Bet they're tasty!"

"Not on the menu today." Up ahead the tall, thick trees shook like reed, and that was where Aoki aimed their vehicle. She fished around under her seat and brought out a flare gun. As she wiggled her eyebrows at him, she pushed the accelerator down all the way. They whipped across the uneven ground toward the disturbance and Nathan quickly made out what caused it.

"Are… are those shovel-heads?" he said, gripping his seatbelt with one hand, and experiencing for a first time a touch of nerves. The five-meter-high birds stood in a group of ten, casually ripping down tree limbs with their hooked beaks and trampling them beneath massive, taloned feet.

"Yup," Aoki replied, dropping to a low gear and spinning them around a bright red tree trunk. "One of those could take down our fence. They're not predators, but they're still dangerous."

The shovel-heads acknowledged the scuttle bug's presence with a bellow that rattled the vehicle's frame. Nathan identified why they bothered him, too. Though he'd never encountered an Australian cassowary, he'd grown up seeing the pictures and hearing about how dangerous they were. These looked similar—only bigger.

The tall and muscular creatures, with a thick coat of moss-green feathers, didn't seem to be that worried about Aoki's revving vehicle or the first red flare she fired off. The nearest one's impressive bone crest ran from the top of its skull, between the eyes, and curved around the beak-like armor. It looked strong enough to repel EVI-87 plasma rifle fire.

The largest specimen swiveled its head in the flare's direction and let out another booming call. Then it shot out a long, purple, barbed tongue, knocking a branch from a nearby tree. *They should have called it a knife-head*, Nathan thought. Cassowaries had nothing on this colossus.

"Thanks—I'm definitely having nightmares tonight!" he yelled to Aoki.

She only laughed. "Don't worry, I'll cuddle you!" Then she spun the vehicle around behind the group and fired one-handed again, even as the shovel-heads oriented on them. "Have to make sure we move them west," she said, sounding almost conversational. "The cave modere are down by the river."

"Will we get to see one of them?" Nathan said, trying to seem calm as the shovel-heads clumped together in a circle, ready to strike at them.

"Shit, I hope not—Banjeree lost a foot to one three months ago. Still hasn't got compensation, either. There's a honeycomb of caves under the river where those fuckers come out. Keep well away."

Aoki didn't describe what a cave modere looked like, and Nathan didn't ask any further questions because the shovel-heads changed tactics. They began striking at the vehicle itself, but that didn't seem to bother Aoki as she drove the scuttle bug back and forth, dodging their attacks, while continuing to fire and scream at them.

She might stave off boredom with high octane gas and shooting shit, but it wasn't his particular kink. Aoki seemed to enjoy herself.

Just when Nathan thought he might throw up from the violent left-right jerking, the shovel-heads let out a collective bellow and charged away from the scuttle bug. They didn't even attempt to dodge anything; just lowered their heads and bowled right through trees, bushes, and any animals unfortunate enough to be in the way.

"Look at them go!" Aoki yelled, wrestling the vehicle to a halt. True, they made an impressive sight, but Nathan was glad that she didn't pursue them.

"What's that over there?" he asked, pointing to the one creature that didn't run from the shovel-heads. In the gathering darkness, it had slipped past his notice. Layers of green moss and clusters of small ferns grew on its back. It was about the size of a bus, with a wide flat head that extended on each side. It didn't seem that dangerous.

Aoki glanced at it. "Oh yeah, an earth truck. Not sure what the scientists call it. We don't rile them up to shoot, mostly because it's hellishly hard to get a bullet in 'em. We're lucky they don't come near the fence. Someone said the electricity bothers them. Anyway, we make sure to leave them alone." She took a long breath, perhaps exhausted after the adrenalin, and looked around. "You know, Shānmén jungle has about the same number of animals per square kilometer as the Amazon did back on Earth… before we fucked it all up."

Nathan reached over and took her hand. "It's a good thing we're here to enjoy it now." In a show of real intimacy, Aoki leaned her head against his shoulder.

"Honestly," she said, "when I'm out here, I don't want to go back to the compound. This must have been how it was for my grandparents when they first arrived... before they found Eitr."

He chuckled. "You want to build a little cabin by the lake, and give up the luxury of Svarog?"

Aoki batted him on the shoulder. "Lakes and rivers are terrible, dangerous places here, but maybe... in the mountains."

They got a few more minutes of quiet. Aoki pointed out the long-limbed scuffle-faces that lived in the treetops. The deep red, feathered group swayed from side to side, singing in the twilight, their scarlet throats inflated. He laughed at the antics of the youngsters battling for the best fruit. She told him that the elders were on watch for the dragon eagles that patrolled for unwary prey.

"Never seen one myself, but my dad did when he was little." Aoki leaned across and kissed him then, as if the memory saddened her and she needed reassurance. Nathan had enjoyed their couple of passionate encounters back at camp, but something about this moment in this place struck him differently.

Aoki felt it too, because she straightened up and checked her wrist-pd.

She cleared her throat.

"Looks like the guys got three of the shovel-heads. We better get home before they load the meat up and head out to look for a cool beer or two."

As she drove the scuttle bug at a much more sedate speed, Nathan turned to glance back. The earth truck raised its head, golden eyes reflecting the vehicle headlights. He swore it looked straight at him, and wondered what it saw when it examined the humans. Did it even question what they were? Or was the creature so old it no longer cared? Did it remember the first humans who arrived on the planet to shoot the other inhabitants of the forest?

The great beast could have stepped on the scuttle bug and crushed it in an instant, yet it did not.

Nathan wished he could spend more time in the jungle, learning its secrets, but soon enough their superiors would miss them. Draping his arm over Aoki, he whispered in her ear.

"Thanks for sharing this with me."

She shot him a side-long smile. "Don't go getting all mushy on me, Bennetts-Riley. We're just fucking." The expression that went with the smile said something else, though.

As they returned to the compound, Nathan tried to decide if he wanted their assignment on Shānmén to end at all. His ambitions demanded more than a cabin in the mountains, but it was nice to contemplate a simple life, and an alternate Nathan who would want that kind of thing.

4

DOWNWARD
CIRCUMSTANCE

Toru sat on her cot in the Knot habitat, alone for once.

Spread out in front of her lay the inner workings of Big Boy Five. Dust had clogged the square robot's internal gyroscope, as she'd suspected, and it needed tending to. Something shiny had distracted Nathan, and he'd never gotten around to it. No surprises on that count. While it annoyed her, Toru didn't mind too much. This was the repetitive, meticulous work she liked—especially when she needed to get out of her own head.

Under the amber glow of the habitat's lights, she scraped and brushed it clean, humming a tune her mother had taught her under her breath. She indulged in recollections of her youth, the cool of the bush in summer, and the sounds of cicadas in the trees. If Toru really focused, she might dredge up the lavender scent that surrounded her mother, or the sound of her laughter.

On days like this, memory became a sanctuary.

Any time Toru stole away was a small miracle. Family usually surrounded her at all times—on assignment or at Pylos station. Though she loved them all to pieces and would never want to be without them, everyone needed moments just to be alone.

The Knot might have only occupied the habitat for the last few weeks, but all its members had grown adept at making themselves comfortable. This wasn't the worst accommodation they'd endured.

Using brightly colored hanging curtains or screens, they had divided the round structure into areas for each member. On the curved outer wall, each person stuck pictures that brought them joy. Pinar put up images of other Knot members, on assignment elsewhere in the galaxy or back at Pylos station.

Lena painted a rainbow on the inner curve, and pasted images of her wife in random spots. Nathan's images were of beautiful places throughout the Weyland Isles and even a few of Earth. Toru noticed vistas of Lake Taupo, or the waterfalls of Milford Sound. Yet the boy also reflected his interest in the Combine, with printouts of articles on the founders and managers, as well as the share price history. That made Toru's lip curl.

It was his own space, she supposed.

Bianca kept her area minimalist, with only a few images of Oliver tucked in near her bed. Jīn Huā's section consisted of wild originals by her girls. They'd drawn images of the wildlife on Shānmén, sketches of the huge land birds in scarlet and bright blue. None of them looked dangerous, since Bái Yún drew them all with smiles. Apart from these hand-drawn delights, Jīn Huā put up a few shots of the beach and the Sydney Opera House.

Carter's space intrigued her the most. Near his cot he had stuck up one of those moving star maps of the middle heavens. It danced over the inner curve of the habitat. More than once, she'd seen him staring at it for hours on end.

Mind you, she'd been the one staring at him.

"Stupid old woman." Toru chuckled to herself as she dusted. Synth-lovers were the butt of every joke. Characterized as loners who couldn't find a real mate. Well, she thought to herself, that wasn't true. She'd enjoyed plenty of lovers in her time, but they were a complication she didn't bother with now. That's how the whole Carter thing started.

Toru shook her head.

"Imagine if the kids find out…" She stopped and rubbed her shoulder to ease out a knot. "Who am I kidding? They know already…" A sliver of embarrassment raised its head; one which Toru thought she'd long put to bed.

A knock on the door made her jump. It wasn't one of the Knot—they surely wouldn't have been so polite.

"Come in," she yelled, while setting about putting the gyroscope back together. Pepperoni Jack nudged open the door and peered in. His perpetually anxious face wore an uncommon but hesitant smile.

"Miss McClintock?"

Toru sighed, but she didn't bother to correct. Double-barreled names made everyone trip over themselves.

"Hey there, Pep. What's up?"

"Ah, just wanted to let you know; we got the last of the injured down to New Luhansk. He was in a bad way, couldn't move him until now. That means no more fatalities." He grinned, displaying an expanse of missing teeth.

"We lost enough," she said, "but I appreciate you letting me know. They'll get better care down there than Kozak will let them have up here."

"For sure," Pep said, nodding.

"Did the hallucinations die off, like I said?"

Toru's visitor stared down at his feet. "Well... not so sure about that. Couple of 'em still shouted about fangs and such. Might have suffered some damage, maybe..." He tapped the side of his head.

"Yeah, that can happen." She ran her fingers over the Big Boy parts, trying to give Pep the hint. But he scratched his head, his face flushing.

"The rest of us... well, they wanted me to tell you... they appreciate what you did. Acting so fast and all. It saved lives the way your synthetics and the little lady went down there."

That surprised her. It took a lot for any group of miners

to express gratitude to someone—especially a person who'd only been there such a short time.

"Well, thanks for saying so," Toru replied, careful not to look him in the eye and spook him. "I just did what experience told me."

Pep looked up, his watering brown eyes locking with hers. "You need anything… anything at all from us here at Svarog… you just have to ask. Kozak don't frighten us."

With that, he turned and fled, banging the door behind him. Toru smiled, a little flicker of warmth kindling in her frozen old heart. Before she got back to fixing Big Boy Five, her wrist-pd chirped. The light flashed an urgent orange. Green, she might have ignored, but not this one. Thumbing the pd, she opened a channel.

"Lena? What's going on?"

"Mum, you better get down here." Her voice cracked a little, a sound that sent a spike of concern through her mother. "We've got a situation."

Scrambling to her feet, Toru slapped her hard hat on and snatched up her work belt. She tapped her wrist-pd, instantly bringing up the readings from the Big Boys and Carter. As her gaze darted over the screen, flashing red with numbers that made it that way, she was already running from the habitat toward the second shaft head. It was only a few hundred meters to get there, but it never seemed longer than when her heart hammered so loud.

"I can see the shotcrete robot jammed. What the hell happened to it?"

"I don't know. Carter is trying to clear it, but the numbers, Mum…" Her voice trailed off as Pinar's voice chimed in over the channel. Toru couldn't make out what she said, but the tone of the other woman's voice was concerning.

"Don't touch nothing!" Toru said. "I'm on my way." She closed the gate and punched the button for the bottom of the shaft. Mining was an activity as old as humanity, and while technology improved many things, it was still dangerous. Cutting this deep, chasing the elusive Eitr, always came with risk.

Toru tapped her steel-toed boot on the floor and held onto her calm. Lena and Pinar had talked to her. They were fine. It wouldn't be that bad.

When the cage stopped, Toru tore out into the tunnels like she was in her twenties again. Strings of white lights lined the rough rock walls. Previous workers had deployed them months before the Knot arrived, and they were reliable enough.

The sub-shaft was another matter. Shaft sinking was always a specialist job. Knowing where to follow the mineral seam, managing pockets of underground water, and most importantly creating a safe vertical cut, were all tricky pieces of craft.

As Toru got closer to the deepest of the current tunnels, A5, the regular *thump-thump* of the shotcrete robot was absent. Instead, the tunnels echoed with an angry whine. The robot was an important piece of kit. It pumped out a stream of shotcrete that hardened quickly to secure the sub-shaft as they drilled deeper.

As Toru followed the decline down toward the beginnings of their shaft, a fine grey haze filled the tunnel. If there was a fire, they could all suffocate down here. Kozak's money-pinching ways meant the poor ventilation was even worse when you got this deep.

Lena met her, emerging out of the smoke, an emergency oxygen mask already locked in place around her lower face. Above it, her watering eyes conveyed concern. She leaned close to her mother's ear.

"We can't shut off the drill head," she yelled, "and the shotcrete robot isn't keeping time with it."

"Stay here," Toru replied, shouldering past her daughter.

Pinar, with her self-contained shell, could better bear the smoke. She stood shrouded in the mist, running numbers on her wrist-pd.

"There's no fire, Auntie. At least not yet."

"But there could be," Toru replied, turning her niece around with a push on her shoulder. "You and Lena get back to the cage. Carter and I will handle this."

Pinar paused.

"Go—now!"

Years of compliance kicked in, and the young woman obeyed.

The shotcrete robot was owned by the company, but the Big Boys, the badger loader, and the specialized drill bit belonged to the Knot. Losing them, and thus accruing debt points owed to the Combine, was unacceptable. Toru unclipped her own oxygen mask from her belt, and wrapping it around her face, walked deeper into the smoke.

First she encountered the Big Boys. Like a lot of mining equipment, the Boys were developed from military variants. While the Colonial Marines used four-legged robots to calm insurrection and destroy local fauna, this taller version carried large loads into remote locations. Their bright yellow square shells stood out, even in the smoke. They possessed no particular heads, and could walk backward or forward in any direction.

These two—One and Two, or Evie and Rick, as Nathan named them—carried the Knot's electronic kit. Snatching up a case of PUPs from them, Toru slapped the return-to-base buttons on their sides and hurried forward to retrieve the rest of their equipment.

She found Carter quickly. They'd cut the sub-shaft broadly enough to take a new cage. The robot, which automatically shot fast-setting mortar onto the walls, was a large piece of kit. Spherically shaped, when operating normally it would closely follow the drill bit down, securing the rock and soil before it collapsed.

The grinding noise and the clouds of white smoke billowing from it told Toru all she needed to know. The damn thing got stuck somewhere, and its safety protocols hadn't activated.

Carter stood at the top of the newly excavated sub-shaft, kicking the robot to jog it loose from whatever gripped it. However, it was a piece of machinery the size of a small transport, and he was only a companion synth. Though stronger than a human, they hadn't designed him for this kind of heavy lifting. Even a Working Joe would have had a hard go of it.

Realizing there wasn't a lot she could offer the situation, Toru turned toward the badger. The light loader didn't have the full strength of the power loaders used by military and heavy construction, but it was more maneuverable and improved Toru's strength by a factor of ten. Climbing into the operator's seat, she flicked the shoulder straps down, locking them into place, and peered out of the safety bars at the situation. She would have to move as fast as possible.

The screaming of the shotcrete robot drowned out the reassuring hydraulic whir of the badger. Most times, she loved this mini power loader—it made her feel strong and perhaps young again—but in this situation, it was awkward to maneuver in the tight space.

She crab-walked it over to one side of the sub-shaft. They'd already gone about thirty meters below, and Toru looked down as she braced herself against the wall. With no track lighting yet laid, the only illumination was the blue lamps cast from the top of the drill head. It shone well beyond the shotcrete robot, which was only about ten meters away.

"Minor seismic event hit," Carter said from the other side of the shaft. "Rocks are loose and impeding the robot." He said it as calmly as if he were serving dinner, rather than perched precariously over an open wound in the earth.

Toru nodded. Neither of them mentioned the other danger; that the whole thing might seize up and catch fire. A mine full of Eitr particles posed a considerable chance of explosion. She decided not to think about that.

Instead, with a grunt she swung the badger across the gap until the body of the shotcrete robot sat within reach. The thick smoke clouded her vision. By freeing her hand from the straps of the loader, Toru felt about until her fingers brushed the outside shell. A moment later, she located the edge of the access panel. As she worked the lever, Toru held her breath and prayed to the Earth Mother, hoping Papatūānuku might still listen to her across the stars.

The panel popped loose and tumbled away into the abyss. Steadying her breathing, Toru jammed her fingers into the cavity to find the emergency stop button. The robot shuddered to a halt, pausing any attempt to continue down the sub-shaft. She let out a ragged gasp of relief.

Toru punched her wrist-pd and brought the drill bit to a halt. For a moment, utter silence reigned, and it was glorious. The stress between bit and robot remained a concern though. A line of sweat ran from forehead to cheek as she set the crank to reverse. At last, the valuable bit began its slow ascent.

Taking the opportunity, Carter climbed down, bracing his legs against the badger's armatures, and joined her in examining the workings of the robot.

"Seems as if the gears are nonfunctional," he said. "If we can disengage these arms, we'll be able to get it out of the shaft for repair."

Fixing a damn robot that wasn't even theirs was still preferable to accruing Combine points. She blew a strand of damp grey hair out of her face.

"Alright, you take those two, and I'll get the others over here."

The maneuver was awkward as hell, but if they disengaged the arms then the whole robot would tuck in on itself. From there, it'd be easy to wrestle out of the sub-shaft. She and Lena would have to waste valuable hours fixing it, but Kozak never needed to know about it.

Toru mulled these thoughts over as she loosened the locked joints on her side of the robot. In her head, she had already planned the service it would need.

The crack sounded so loud that, for a moment, Toru thought she'd somehow broken a limb—either hers or the robot's. Instead, the unstable shotcrete and the fragile rock surface gave way. She had only a second to react as the robot tilted sideways, two of the arms that braced it into the earth already tucked in. Nothing held it in place beneath Toru and Carter as it fell sideways into the shaft.

Gravity grabbed hold of them both, and neither synthetic nor human had any say in what happened after that.

5

FIRST STEPS

From a dark corner of the bridge, Mae watched her mother with unblinking intensity. Then she remembered to flick her eyes closed for an instant. Humans did that, and so must she.

She'd chosen a spot with a good view out the window, but where the angle of the sun against the planet ensured that she'd still be in shadow. Still uncertain of her place on the *Righteous Fury*, Mae kept in the background and observed what was going on. The GC-929882 model might boast the most high-tech AI–human partnership, but the specialized wartime ship still needed an artificial person companion to interact with the crew and observe anything outside its highly monitored systems.

Though the *Fury*'s onboard artificial intelligence, EWA, did the actual flying, the Jackals still maintained physical communication and navigation stations at the bow of the ship. It was a little slice of control humans fought for—even if it was an illusion.

Her father should have been the one standing beside her mother's chair. He'd done it for years. Davis's death had put into motion a cascade of events that triggered her creation.

After encountering a robotics technician on LV-222, the longtime companion to Zula Hendricks had made preparations. He foresaw the possibility of his own demise, and with all his love—or what he perceived it to be—he made a final request to Mr. Higgs, who then produced Mae. Davis wanted Zula to have support, even when he could not supply it. His solution was an AI made up of both their personalities.

To make her more authentic, he'd even thrown in some random chance, as was present in organic children. He'd given her the name Mae as a salute to the first woman in the United States Marine Corps, and as an acronym for Machine Algorithm Embodied.

Despite the fine talents the slightly deranged synthetic technician possessed, Davis was very specific that his daughter should have an appropriate body to carry out the task of protector. Looking like a store-bought mannequin with moving limbs, the Weyland-Yutani combat synth body didn't exactly match Mae's personality profile. Still, there were no other choices to be found on this ship.

From inside her combat synth body, she watched her

mother. A complicated subroutine kicked in. By dying, Davis had brought her life. Mae examined it like a strange new fruit. She was glad to have life and awareness, yet it came at the cost of one she would have enjoyed meeting. Plus, when she and Zula had first met, he surely would have smoothed the waters.

Mae's use of the word "mommy" hadn't gone over well, so she'd never dared again. She wished she might talk to Zula about this, but at the moment her mother had a great deal with which to deal—matters of human life and death.

While Colonel Zula Hendricks sat in her command chair, Major Ronny Yoo and the *Fury*'s partner synthetic were the only others present.

Erynis possessed a proper human-like synthetic body, that of a tall commanding man with dark skin and a bald head. Any genetic person in his presence felt a connection, if not being a little intimidated by his stature and deep voice. At this moment he stood close to Mae's mother, hands pressed together, waiting for Zula to speak.

Mae didn't have that luxury. Mother wasn't yet acclimatized to having her around. If she moved or made too much noise, then Zula might instruct her to leave the bridge. Obedience wasn't Mae's strong suit, but she'd go if asked. She just *really* didn't want to be asked.

Zula's first words weren't encouraging.

"So now we know what failure looks like in its purest form."

Major Yoo moved from the navigation station to the window that looked down over the planet formerly known as Isle V. When Mae accessed the Combine records, she noted that they'd named it "Tiāntáng de yáolán," or Heaven's Cradle. The Jackals were deep in UPP territory.

"Boss, I don't know what we could have done to prevent this." Yoo didn't seem concerned, but Mae saw his throat work in a hard swallow.

Erynis flicked a glance over toward Mae, even as he added his own thoughts. "I concur with Major Yoo. We did not have any kind of verified intelligence that would enable us to predict this event."

Zula's face didn't convey much emotion. In this body, however, Mae had a great deal of experience upon which to call, and she spotted the spasm of a small muscle in her mother's jaw.

"We still should have been here," Zula said. "All those civilians… we might have saved *some*…" She didn't raise her voice, but it oozed with pain and anger. Mother had witnessed many terrible things. Mae's hands tightened into fists; a gesture she'd taken from Zula.

Major Yoo said nothing. He'd been chasing Xenos for almost as long as Mother. He was much easier to read, though Mae hadn't as much data on him. She read the twist of the corner of his lip to mean that under the surface lay barely contained rage.

Mae brought to the front of her consciousness the Xeno encounters Davis had recorded all over the galaxy.

Though the Red Silk data traders had hacked her father's files, destroying many of his records, they had not taken them all. His data logs on the Xenomorphs and Zula Hendricks remained available to his daughter. In her short life, Mae had studied the Xenos with their dripping teeth, lightning reflexes, and cunning. The relentlessness with which Weyland-Yutani had tried to commodify them only made things worse for humanity.

Four years before Mae's arrival, Mother had stood on the deck of another spaceship, staring around at twitching bodies and melted decking.

"We're always chasing these monsters around the galaxy, trying to prevent mayhem. All we end up doing is cleaning up the mess. We're goddamn janitors." Zula's exhausted breathing and the sorrow expressed on her face, spoke of a deeper, building pain.

Mae loved her mother, but couldn't ignore the aging evident on her face. Years in and out of cryosleep, losing friend after friend and fighting monsters across the galaxy, had taken a toll that even the unrelenting Zula Hendricks could not hold off forever. That realization conjured a cascade of emotions that felt… strange. *Was* strange.

Mother was human. She would die.

Even Father had recognized that. Hence Mae.

Only a few months old, her arrival brought up issues. Mother needed to work out how to address her, and Mae was confident she would, eventually. Mae just needed to make herself useful, like Davis.

Turning her head with some stiffness, Mae wished he'd found her a human-like synthetic body. Being able to communicate with Zula through gestures and expressions would have made all the difference. Frustration was another subroutine that surprised Mae, yet it excited her. She was on her way to becoming fully human, as Father wanted.

As for Mother, even though she commanded the *Fury*, she no longer went on away missions. She gave the orders and the battalion of soldiers in the belly of the Atlatl-class ship made it happen.

How much longer would Zula continue? How many more years would the Xeno threat go on? So many variables to be considered.

Yet that wasn't Mae's role, she reminded herself. Father had made it clear she needed to learn about her mother, because one day Zula's role would be hers. She would be the one to carry on the fight, for as long as it needed to be fought.

Major Yoo, Zula's oldest companion since losing Amanda Ripley, found some more words. "Like Erynis said, we couldn't see this coming, boss. This is something brand new. We're used to fighting, blowing up nests, even nuking whole towns, but this..."

His voice trailed off.

Erynis unfolded his hands with care and took time to stare out the forward window. As a newer model, his replication of emotion was quite sophisticated. His reflection of sadness mimicked the humans on the deck. Mae envied him that.

"*Fury*'s scans of the Heaven's Cradle surface are complete. I am afraid the destruction of the two colony townships is complete. The only movement below is from Xenomorph mutations. Scans show no human life forms."

Since everyone was so entranced by the view, Mae decided she might gain more insight from it, too. She dared to step away from her spot and take in the view of the planet. As she did, Mother glanced at her, an extra bit of wrinkling on her brow displaying some displeasure— but she said nothing at the intrusion.

Humans had colonized Heaven's Cradle in order to live out their time in comfort. Like most other planets in the Weyland Isles section of space, it had gone through terraforming. The resemblance to Earth was uncanny, although it remained removed from the dramas and oft-violent turf wars going on elsewhere in the rim.

"*Isn't it odd how humans are always trying to replicate home?*" Father's words in her head might have been digital, but Mae's processing systems presented them as a gentle whisper. "*To go so far, and not appreciate the worlds they find for what they are.*"

Davis had thought of everything. He'd studied humans for a very long time and had noted that parental advice was important. The embedded subroutine he'd left her with was an echo of his programming. Mae hadn't yet decided if it was wonderful or annoying.

She supposed it might be both.

Mae sent back a ping, so the subroutine logged that she'd made note of it. She still hadn't decided how to deal with these intrusions. If she applied her processing power to it, she'd most likely to find a way to purge them. Yet would that impede her growth toward self-awareness? The risk might not be worth it.

A matter for another moment.

Instead, she took in the view, trying to see it as Mother might. Untapped potential, perhaps, or an opportunity lost? Nothing below remained as the United Americas would have imagined. This shake-and-bake colony, on which they spent so much money and effort, would support nothing but Xeno life-forms. Humans would have to go elsewhere.

Mae accessed the colony information from the *Fury's* records. Thousands of people had called this planet home for decades, farming and living what some humans dreamed of as a pioneer life. They'd not been wealthy enough to remain on Earth, but just wealthy enough to book a long-haul ride on a colony ship. They had lived their lives, until death rained from the clear blue sky.

"Show me that last transmission again," Zula asked Erynis.

When he did so it filled the bridge screen. Mae moved back from the window to take in the full effect of the human terror. The words came out garbled and drenched in static, while the video cut in and out as if something blocked it. Yet the last human alive on Heaven's Cradle dumped the feed to the satellite in orbit. Mae tried to understand and enumerate the emotions on display.

The man's face that leaned into frame was grey, grizzled, and must have belonged to one of those old-timer atmosphere processor workers. He'd probably set up multiple colonies in his time, enough that it was all automatic to him. Mae accessed a few hundred documentaries and testimonials from such men. Their lives, she concluded, were generally short but, she reminded herself, he must have mattered to someone. He'd been a friend or a relative. His life would leave a hole somewhere.

His voice remained calm, more stoic than terrified. The true horror hadn't yet visited him personally. The machete he held in his hand didn't seem to offer any reassurance, though. He glanced down for a moment, picking his words with care, even though something hammered against the door nearby.

"Don't come here," he said, fixing his eyes on the camera. "We're all dead. Don't come planetside. All you need to know is this ship—like I never seen before—appeared without warning and dropped some kind of black mess on the whole town. Bombed us, but with something worse than an explosion or even a nuke."

His head jerked up as the sound of metal being torn echoed through the communications room. Something off-screen screamed, and terror leapt into his eyes.

"It changed them," he said, looking off to one side. "It got everyone... they became monsters. Fucking eyeless, clawed monsters. Humans, animals, every one a goddamn nightmare."

Darkness flickered at the edge of the screen, and Mae recognized it from her records. A glance told her mother accessed those memories, too. A subtle twitch of her right hand signaled her unconscious wish to be holding a weapon. After all that she'd seen and been through, it was a rational response. Mae filed it away for her own use.

Major Yoo and Mother watched the whole thing, every last moment of the feed. Neither of them turned away. The old man surged up from his seat and swung his machete. The scream of monster and man merged into one long oscillating sound. Then the inevitable spray of acidic blood must have destroyed the equipment, abruptly ending the transmission.

Zula's hand tightened on the arm of her chair. Although no longer a Colonial Marine, the Jackals were a military brigade, and Mother held tight to her training. Even if it was a long time ago, it still meant something.

"More drone footage is available—unfortunately it shows nothing that differs from the initial scans." Erynis offered so much in the way of human-like expressions. He'd completely mastered tone and inflection. His voice, pitched in a pleasant baritone, conveyed sympathy and sadness both.

From her records, Mae knew her father had possessed

that same ability. As a synthetic person, he'd taken a lot of forms over many years of fighting side-by-side with Zula. He'd been everything from an earpiece to synthetic dog. With each new iteration, he had made sure his new experiences were available to her. He'd specified that Higgs relay any information and monitoring to her, in case a recovery effort became possible.

Jealousy surged in Mae. The subroutines were all cracking open today, surprising her with their intensity. For Zula's benefit, Davis wanted his daughter to have a more human-like shape. However, the *Fury* only carried one such synthetic, Erynis, and didn't have the facilities to manufacture another. Even if she could have been transferred into his Erynis form, more than likely it would upset the ship's EWA AI, and the results would be untenable.

So a combat synthetic was Zula's daughter's only choice. Davis wanted to be sure Mae was equipped to support Zula in the fight against the Xenomorphs, and the stock standard body he originally possessed seemed only logical. It wasn't ideal, however, since humans connected more easily with those that wore human-like faces.

Mae kept herself disconnected from the synthetic network Erynis occupied. It was important she develop on her own, as she envisioned any genetic human would.

"I'm sorry, Colonel," the ship's synthetic added, always careful to use proper titles in front of other humans. "I wish I had better news."

Mae's surviving records showed her father experimented with humor as a way to connect with humans. Previous failures under tense situations made such efforts.... variable. The subroutine prodded her to crack a joke.

"I have over two hundred options on file if you want them."

Mae pinged to the negative.

"Not your fault," Zula replied. "Like you said, the signal came in too late—just like the other one. It's not as if we can predict where they're going to strike."

"This is the second bombing," Erynis reminded her. "With more data available, EWA and I will examine the similarities and discern some potential targets."

"Like how they used to find serial killers back on Earth," Major Yoo said, rubbing his forehead as if it might clear his thoughts. Mae tucked away the gesture to try out later.

"I don't want there to be any more data," Mother snapped. "We stop this, and find the evil fucking bastards making it happen."

Zula squeezed the arm of her command chair while everyone on deck rode out the silence. Through the window, EWA continued to display the field of stars and the blighted planet Zula and her Jackals had been unable to save.

Her mother's dark eyes flitted over to Mae, who remained silent through everything. Zula examined the combat synthetic form, making her daughter wish for eyes with irises and lips that could at least smile.

"What do you think, Mae? Any insight to offer?"

That was unexpected. Her father's subroutine ticked over, offering several ways to handle this situation, but she determined to make her own path. Every choice was a chance to grow and become what he meant for her to be.

Everyone's eyes were on her as she ran through a thousand ways to reply. Taking a step out of the darkness, she chose a direction.

"It should be possible with these two events, along with the information we acquired from Weyland-Yutani, to narrow down possible targets."

Major Yoo slid into the XO's chair and ran a hand through his hair, more grey than black. When he'd first met Mother on Jericho 3, he'd been ten years older than her. Like Zula herself, chasing Xenos around the galaxy only added to the lines on his face.

"This is different to a bug hunt—so 'possible' has to be doable," he said. "We need to prove ourselves to the trio of generals who fund us."

Zula tapped her fingers on the arm of her command chair, perhaps calculating how much time and money their backers would supply the Jackals if they didn't stop this from happening. Three generals—veterans of campaigns on the outer edges of the galaxy—recognized an existential threat from the Xenomorphs and the corporations that used them. The corruption of the Midnighters on LV-991 woke many people up. No one wanted to see valuable worlds overrun by the deadly organism.

It wasn't good morally, or economically.

With so much corporate corruption embedded in the military of all nations, they needed a strong unit to combat the threat—one specifically tasked with eradicating the Xenomorphs. The *Righteous Fury* contained trusted marines from the Three World Empire, the United Americas, and even a few supplied by the Union of Progressive Peoples. Those were a lot of different cultures and traditions to hold together under one brand new banner. Little wonder Zula didn't have time for her unexpected daughter.

"None of those files of yours have any intel on this black goo?" Zula asked, leaning forward, her elbows on her knees, staring at Mae. Mae took a nanosecond to run a search.

"There are some myths: a transformational liquid, hints of an ichor, Amrita, immortal rain or elixir of life painted on tomb walls back on Earth—but nothing like this."

"So just legends?" Major Yoo pressed. "No science?"

Erynis, standing behind the humans, tilted his head as if to communicate that she should stop. However, since she'd disabled her connection to the synthetic network, that was all he could do.

"No," Mae admitted. "Nothing that would make monsters."

"It's not a myth though," Zula said. "We just saw a whole planet full of people turned to Xenos." Mae discerned the subtle sound of her teeth grinding together. "Except it's worse than fighting the bastards themselves, because at least we know how to clean their nests out. This stuff… it somehow *makes* them—without those damn face-huggers involved at all. And it's quick too."

"It would appear so," Mae agreed, keeping her voice soft. At least she'd been able to adjust the combat synthetic's vocal pitch so she sounded like a young woman. "I will consult with EWA and Erynis to find the most likely targets. Fortunately, they seem to be all within the Weyland Isles."

"Not so lucky for the people who live out here," Zula said, sinking back into her chair. Her face radiated fatigue. Mae wished she could suggest some stims, vitamins, or even a massage. However, she already knew her mother's reaction to these solutions.

"We will arrange for links with tracking stations outside each planetary system and be ready… Mom." Mae waited to see if Zula flinched at that. She did not. Maybe she was getting used to her new daughter, or perhaps—more likely—overwhelming exhaustion gripped her.

"I need coffee." As Zula levered herself out of her chair, she gestured to Major Yoo. "Let's hit the ward room and await instructions." They reached the door together, and Mae made out her muttered last words. "From my daughter."

Mae said nothing, but opened up an encrypted channel between EWA and Erynis. She'd have an answer for Colonel Zula Hendricks before the meal was finished. A strange, warm sensation grew in her synthetic body.

Mae could feel the bonds already forming between them—just as her father, Davis, had planned.

"Just give her time," his subroutine in her head whispered. *"Zula will come around to you. I promise."*

6

HIDDEN PATHS

The fall was only about three meters. Toru understood it would hurt, and she accepted that. She just hoped she didn't break her damn hip again.

In the brief second before they contacted with the bottom of the shaft, she had enough time to do three things: pray to the Earth Mother, flick the emergency switch, and grab hold of Carter.

The badger's defense program kicked in, and it curled up tight. Pressing its hardened back into a tight arch over the fragile being inside, it provided the best protection it could. Toru already felt the bruises that were about to occur.

She and Carter bounced against the diamond sides of the drill bit. The screech along the metal of the badger pierced her ears. The reinforced metal of the exoskeleton sent up a cloud of sparks.

The bundle of badger, synthetic, and frightened human smashed into the bottom of the shaft. It held. The Knot had drilled through H-type granite to get to the Eitr veins.

Nothing moved.

She almost welcomed the gasp of air that was forced from her. This was as far as they'd drilled before the robot failed, Toru thought, lifting her head see how Carter had fared.

Then the earth reminded her she didn't know everything.

The bottom fell out beneath them.

A shower of rocks and dust pelted them from all sides. They pinged off her hard hat and filled her eyes, nose, and mouth. The badger creaked and groaned at the assault as they plummeted again.

This time they kept going.

There was a faint glitter of the drill head in the darkness; Toru thought it might well be the last thing she would see. She squeezed her eyes shut, wrapped herself tighter around Carter, and imagined her sisters in that embrace, too. Death underground was always in the cards.

They hit the bottom with a bone-rattling impact. For a moment Toru worried they would break through again and tumble on further. When it didn't happen, she dared to suck in a sweet gasp of air, keeping her eyes closed.

The earth wrapped around her.

Toru had expected this kind of death since she first went into a mine. She'd lost a father, aunties, cousins, and sons to the earth on so many planets. It must be her turn.

At least Carter was close. *Take comfort in those you love,* her mother told her once, gasping out her last breath thanks to green lung disease caught while working in the Tempest Hill Mine. Hundreds of thoughts and memories whizzed through her brain, so many that Toru realized she wasn't in fact dead.

It didn't even hurt—yet. She wiggled her fingers. If she was lucky, hurt would come later. Her body, old and beaten up as it was, tried its best to fill her with adrenalin, to keep fighting.

"Toru, can you hear me?" Carter's voice sounded right by her ear. His fingers brushed her cheek, clearing her eyes and nose of dirt. She sneezed, blinked, coughed, right in his face. His bright blue eyes, visible in the helmet light, stared into hers.

Spitting her mouth free of dust, she asked, "Is the entire mountain coming down on us?"

His eyes shifted one way, then another.

"I don't think so." The synthetic moved with caution, raising his head a fraction. "We appear to have fallen into some kind of void."

"A cave?" Despite the situation, Toru's curiosity got the better of her. The earth contained beauty, some of which she'd been lucky enough to find. Caverns of glittering gypsum pillars. Vast grey lakes of gallium. She'd seen many hidden things no sentient eye had ever witnessed before.

As she tried to move, Carter stopped her with a hand on her head. He felt over the surface of her hard hat.

"It seems intact, though you will need to be checked for concussion."

Toru cupped the side of his face. "First let's see where we are, dear."

Sitting up, she adjusted her oxygen mask and checked its supply. Foul air haunted miners' nightmares, but caves could also be full of dangerous gases and alien microorganisms. It would be ridiculous to survive a fall only to die of a virus. She brought up the reading on her wrist-pd; the gauge told Toru that in just under an hour she needed to find a cylinder or a new way of breathing. At least there was no buildup of carbon monoxide down here.

She punched the SOS signal.

Toru's light flickered off and on for a moment. A quick bang on the side of the helmet brought it back to full brightness. When she panned it up the shaft, she made out the glitter of the diamond head.

Lena and Pinar would have to unpack a rescue rope ladder and get it down the shaft. Standing and looking up, Toru calculated, they'd have to lash two together, which would take a little extra time.

"Goddamn it," Toru crouched down to assess the damage wrought on the badger. It had taken a lot of hits. The hydraulics hissed, and two of the structural struts were bent.

Carter ran a quick diagnostic. "It appears the fall

crushed the power coupling. The badger won't be able to make its own ascent." He put a hand on her shoulder. "I'm sorry, Toru."

She patted it and levered herself upright. "Not your fault, dear. Just more fucking Combine points to replace it. Even if we get out of this hole, we're going to be in a financial one." Toru twisted her lips in a bitter smile. "Should have listened to Sophie, I guess."

"The Combine decides where it needs us," he said in a low tone. "Please don't blame yourself for picking this position, when there never was a choice."

Toru took a shuddering breath and blinked away some stupid damn tears. Sometimes he said things so kind that they took her back a little. Why couldn't he have been a flesh-and-blood partner? To avoid that conversation, she spun on her heel and pointed into the darkness.

"Why don't we find out where we are, at least?" She panned her light around, and the shape of the hole they'd fallen into revealed itself. "Strange sort of tunnel," Toru whispered, though there was no one else to hear them.

The space was oval, with smoothed walls. They ran straight on either side of them without breaks. When she directed the light upward, the structure showed no signs of being braced by anything.

"Are you seeing this, Carter?" Toru's heart raced and her mouth went dry. "It isn't a natural formation. I'm not concussed, am I?"

The synthetic didn't answer for a moment—a sure

sign he was taking in their surroundings. He wasn't a science model, but his senses extended far beyond hers. Toru wished she could have seen what he did.

"It does indeed appear to have been constructed," he replied finally. His head tilted as he took a couple of steps away from her. "I'm detecting an energy spike in this direction." Toru knew they should wait where they were, for the rope ladder and rescue, but this was bigger than safety demanded.

"Shit, I'm an idiot."

Fumbling at her waist, Toru opened the PUPS pouch on her belt. The drones were small, only about the size of her fist, but invaluable in mining and caving situations. Activating them with a twist, Toru tossed both into the air. They hovered in front of her, their red running lights activating. Those long beams passed over the surface of the surrounding tunnel, then switched to a flicker.

The PUPS zipped off, one in each direction.

Carter turned. "What are you doing, Toru? It's Combine policy to immediately inform the onsite archaeologists and the mine manager of any discovery like this."

Toru barked out a laugh. "Dearest, that's the *last* thing we want to do." She draped her arm around his waist. "Article 13.4.56 of the Combine mining agreement offers a bounty on anything with a whiff of alien tech around it—but it has to be confirmed."

He stared at her, her hard hat light shining off his sculpted cheekbones.

"I see. Yes, well, we must do that first."

"Yes, yes we must—but imagine if it is!" They shared a grin, then Toru swung around and kissed him. No one here to see but the PUPS, and they were trustworthy. She tasted his mouth and a real dose of hope. Suddenly that Combine debt didn't seem insurmountable. This opened up an entire world of possibilities. Toru broke free of their kiss, but stayed in his arms for a heady moment.

"This might be the best fucking accident of all time."

The PUPS alarm sounded on her wrist-pd. An alert surprised Toru—she'd expected the tunnel to run on for some time.

"Looks like PUP One has found a flat surface blocking its way, only twenty meters to the west." They shared a look. "The sensible thing would be to leave it," she said with a grin.

"But what is life without risk?" he replied, again blurring the lines between reality and her hopes.

That was all Toru needed to hear. "Let's go then," she said, grabbing his hand like a bulletproof teenager. She didn't run, though—that would have been too much. They fast walked down the western tunnel, following the trail of the PUP. It waited near what it had found, its blinking red lights tracing the rock face over and over.

As Toru raked her lamp light over the surface, she forgot all about the little drone. By her white light, she examined a surface that wasn't just flat—it teemed with symbols that to her eye seethed with life.

"It's a door," she said, her voice dropping to a reverential whisper. "I don't see any hinges, but it's a door. Tell me I'm wrong." Carter didn't answer, nor did he touch it—instead running his eyes over the surface, starting at the edge and moving in.

"There is a central circular pivot point," he said after a moment, "and two leaves fold up from there. Yes, I would concur it is a door, but a design with an iris that I have no record of humans using."

Toru let out a ragged breath she hadn't realized she was holding. "OK, we can agree on that."

Carter moved a fraction closer. "I read a three-degree temperature increase right here." He pointed. "It's possible our arrival has caused this." Toru confirmed it with her wrist-pd, and more.

"There's also a very faint magnetic fluctuation nearby that wasn't there before. I wonder if it's warm?" She reached out a hand to touch it, but he grabbed her arm.

"I wouldn't recommend that."

Concern began to puncture her thrill of discovery. Toru took a step back from the door; as she did, something moved in its corners.

"What the fuck?" The words rushed out of her.

She'd missed the tiny channels at the bottom corners. Now they began filling up with a thick, silver liquid that Toru at first thought might be mercury. If it was, it also defied gravity, because it started climbing as it filled the bottom channel. Instead of flowing across the floor, this rivulet ran up the sides of the door, filling the carved surface and illuminating the shapes there.

Checking her wrist-pd, what she found didn't register as mercury—or any other element that her device could name. Carter reached forward to take a bit on his fingertip, and Toru was the one to snatch at his arm.

"You're kidding, right?" she snapped. "You just told me not to do the very same thing."

"That's different," he said with a smile over his shoulder, "I'm not an organic being."

She shook her head and didn't let go. "You're still an *important* being. Please… just don't touch it."

"You're impeding scientific progress." Carter's gentle tone teased her, but he stepped back. Together they watched as the strange liquid filled all the channels, bringing the symbols to life.

"Can you translate them?" Toru asked as the hairs on her arms stood up. The tunnel might be warming, but her skin ran ice cold.

"No. They are some kind of hieroglyphic or cuneiform language. I will record images for further study, however." He glanced down at her. "I'm sorry I'm not more helpful."

Toru leaned against him. "Don't be silly, this is…" she waved her hand, "this is way past both of us."

"They appear to be at least three distinct types, though. Perhaps we can discover more if I have access to other databases." He always tried to find some thread to follow. Carter might be beautiful to look at and packaged with a kind personality, but at his core he was still logical.

As they stared at the gleaming letters, the creeping sensation increased over Toru's skin. The twist in her stomach, the way the hairs on her arms lifted—these were all signs she had learned from decades of survival. Curiosity was a dangerous beast.

She nodded. "I think we should go back to where we landed. Lena and Pinar will get worried about us."

"A good idea." His blue eyes locked with hers. "Do we tell them what you found?"

As she summoned both PUPS back, Toru considered. "Yes, we do. Together we can figure this out—not just what this door is, but how it can help the Knot."

"Always thinking ahead." His fingers brushed her cheek.

"I try." Leaning into his touch for a moment, Toru smiled. "Let's go turn this into something good for the family." Together they walked back the way they had come, Toru's light sliding off the unnaturally smooth rock face. She spared one glance back. The door gleamed in the darkness, but it began to dim.

Those shapes must mean something, she thought. *They must be words.*

Whatever they were, she and the Knot didn't have the skills or resources to decipher them. However, fate had presented them an opportunity, and she had to focus on using this discovery to their advantage.

The earth always provided for her family—just in unexpected ways.

7

TANGLED
OPPORTUNITY

Her mother was in real peril. Lena stood at the entrance to the sub-shaft tunnel, holding Pinar's hand tight, and tried to come to terms with that.

It wasn't the first time these dark realizations had washed over her. Asteroid mining nearly claimed Mum's life three times. Planet-side mining tried to eat her four times; two collapses, a gas leak, and getting into a knife fight with a man twice her size. Lena had hoped working as a specialist in a simple job might encourage Toru to slow down a bit. She had pulled all the strings she possessed at the Combine to get the Knot on this assignment—despite Sophie's protests.

Now it looked like that was the wrong choice.

"If this fucking mine takes her," she muttered, rocking from foot to foot, "I'm throwing Kozak in after her."

Mine managers tripped and fell sometimes, and no one would deserve it more.

Pinar patted her hand. "If it comes to that, I'll help you." They shared angry, dust-covered grins.

Then came the rumble through their feet. The sub-shaft creaked and moved. Pinar and Lena scrambled to throw themselves underneath the Big Boys, covering their heads and curling into a ball. A cloud of dust and small rocks blew up the tunnel, pinging off the metallic sides of the drones. It would take a while for the ventilation to clear that, but as soon as the rumble faded, Lena got to her feet and scrambled back where she'd last seen her mother.

Her breath fogged up her mask, and a layer of dust covered her goggles. Lena's wrist-pd gleamed in the dark—too obscured to read.

She wiped frantically at the goggles and the faint gleam on the readout showed where Toru was. That the collapse had been under her, and not *on* her, was a gift from the Earth Mother. Toru might believe in such things; as she ran forward, Lena tried to as well.

"Please... please... please..." she said under her breath. Then the message flickered onto her screen.

SAFE. SEND LADDER.

Typically brief, but Lena let a shuddering gasp out into her oxygen mask. The old bird did it again. Pinar slapped her on the back, and they shared a slightly hysterical laugh.

They staggered back to the Big Boys and set about removing the safety ladders. The location ping from Toru's wrist-pd gave them the length that would be needed. It was more than any one ladder would provide, so they spent valuable minutes clipping them together. As they did, the ventilation system did its job clearing the dust and smoke from the area.

Lena glanced at her display once and noted movement from Toru's signal. She shook her head.

"She's poking around down there."

"You're surprised by that?" Pinar snorted as she tested the ladder's connection.

Lena smiled back. Her aunties told stories of Toru's adventures in her youth. She'd disappear for days at a time, following underground tunnels with only a bit of food, water, and a rebreather. It had driven Lena's grandparents wild, but she always returned with amazing stories and chunks of rock. Her mother might have aged, but her spirit still longed for those solitary discoveries.

She wouldn't pass up this opportunity.

The two of them finished securing the ladder and they dragged it to the edge of the sub-shaft. She attached it to one of the Big Boys and, after extending its metallic claws into the rock, dropped it into the gaping hole.

By this stage relief had washed away, and Lena discovered the edges of annoyance. Her mother was so pig-headed about those damn Combine points. She'd rather risk her own life than lose any equipment. She should put a point value on her own hard head. Lena's fingers drummed on top of the Big Boy as they waited.

Still no sign of Toru.

Lena sent a terse message.

ENJOYING YOURSELF MUM? WILL COME DOWN IF YOU DON'T COME UP.

That at least generated a response from her mother.

COMMS SILENT.

She leaned over and shared that with Pinar. They both shook their head at Toru's paranoia. After all, Jīn Huā kept a secure channel, for use only by the Knot.

Finally, the rope ladder jerked, and the lights from Mum's hard hat raked up the shaft. When she and Carter appeared, it was difficult for even Lena to judge her mother's expression. Her brown skin might be covered in dirt and a few streaks of blood where she'd been banged about, but her bright blue eyes locked tight on her daughter. It stilled the sharp words Lena wanted to deliver.

"Where's the badger?" she asked instead, taking a step forward to peer down the shaft.

Carter remained silent, and Mum mouthed *"Home. Now."* When she spoke, it still made no kind of sense. "Seal this area off. Use the Big Boys. It's dangerously unstable until we get the shotcrete robot fixed."

She was serious. They might speak Te Reo if they wanted to keep everything private, but it wasn't impossible that Kozak owned translation software for the language of New Zealand. He was that kind of asshole.

While Carter and Pinar started establishing a perimeter around the sub shaft, moving the Big Boys to block the tunnel, Lena followed her mother back to the cage. The only hint of what might be brewing was a sly smile from the corner of Toru's mouth. She didn't smile easily or often, so her daughter suspected this wasn't the usual bad news.

Toru tapped a message into the Knot channel.

MEETING.

PROBLEM WE NEED TO FIX.

NOW.

That was the type of dispatch that would bring all the family to their habitat as if their feet were on fire. Lena made frantic, circling gestures to prompt her mother to talk, but she shook her head. It was the kind of behavior that drove Lena to distraction. Toru would say things like *"we have to meet"* or *"this needs immediate attention,"* and offer no further details. Meanwhile, Lena conjured up every worst-case scenario while waiting for further revelations.

She pressed her lips together and followed her mother, while her mind spun on itself. They stayed silent all the way up the shaft and on the short walk back to the habitat.

The compound builders had set the indentured quarters slightly apart from the waged miners, but they were still in a geodome. The circular room contained all their sleeping racks, assigned lockers, and a small section where they brewed their own coffee or tea rather than go to the main cafeteria.

Toru pushed open the door, holding it for Lena, Pinar, and Carter to follow. Once she joined them, she held up her finger.

"Carter, run a scan, and then hold a perimeter." Designers had fitted pleasure 'bots with some of the best scanning capabilities of any synthetic models. Discretion was their stock in trade.

Lena didn't ask questions. She sat on the end of her bed, legs crisscrossed, and waited. Pinar in her shiny shell always seemed more comfortable standing. She propped herself up by her locker.

Jīn Huā arrived first, with a frown already fixed on her brow. Her children were still in school, which was for the best. They were good kids, but not reliable as far as secrets went. Toru jerked her head and mouthed *"need privacy."* Jīn Huā didn't hesitate. This wasn't the first time. The Knot accepted that all Combine areas were monitored, but they dealt with it. Jīn Huā always brought a blocking device.

They used it when they wanted to complain about the Combine, or bitch about management. The expression on Toru's face suggested this was something else entirely. Lena chewed the outside of her fingernails to prevent from asking questions.

Nathan and Bianca, who'd been up in the cafeteria after a shift in the sub-shaft, arrived together, eyes alight with curiosity.

Toru shot a glance at Jīn Huā, who nodded.

"We're good for a bit, Ma. Kozak is getting a loop of fifteen minutes."

Nathan flopped down on his rack next to Lena. "If this is about the drink I bought in Luhansk last week, I…"

Lena nudged him with her foot, and he snapped his mouth shut. She'd covered for him on that one, and another argument would only prevent Mum from revealing the real reason she'd called them all together.

Toru didn't seem to have noticed, and made them wait while she went over and pumped water into their wash bowl. She took her time using a cloth to wipe her face and the back of her neck before turning to them.

"Carter and I found something when we fell."

Lena's heart raced. "The vein of Eitr! Pinar, bloody hell you were right!" They might get off-planet and back to Pylos earlier than expected.

"Better than that, Len." Her mother's words cut through the excitement. Her smile spread slowly as she shot a glance toward Carter. "We found something… alien."

The moment hung between them all like a shared dream—or hallucination. In the dim, close quarters, the only sound was their collective breathing.

Nathan woke up first.

"Shiii-it."

He gasped it out comedically long, but no one laughed.

Lena tried to force her hopes and dreams along this fresh path. If it was true, their Combine debt wouldn't be a problem anymore. No one would have to go without baby points in order to increase their numbers. They all began to talk at once, and Toru held up her hands for calm.

"Before anyone says anything—no spending it before we have it."

Jīn Huā rubbed her jaw, eyes rising to the ceiling, while Pinar hugged Bianca tight. They were all used to keeping their feelings in check in cramped surroundings. Stuffing down her excitement, Lena turned to Carter. Though she trusted her mother, Toru might have knocked her head on the way down. The synthetic wasn't likely to be concussed.

"Toru is correct," Carter said, crossing his arms. "We observed carved walls, a doorway, and evidence of writing."

Lena wanted to flop back on her cot and let out a whoop. Instead, she maintained her facade.

"About bloody time we had some good luck."

Pinar exhaled a long breath. "Hewitt and Antonijevic will lose their minds." At the mention of the on-site archaeologists, Toru spun around.

"They will be the *last* people to find out. This discovery belongs to the Knot, and we're going to work it like a rich vein of Eitr. All of us in the room get to decide how we're going to play it."

Damn. Lena still wanted to leap about, but she understood what her mother meant. This was an opportunity that wouldn't come again—a chance for the Knot to improve itself beyond its wildest dreams.

"We could claim the bounty from Kozak," Nathan said, and then twisted his lips. "But can we trust that fucker?"

They all knew the answer to that.

"I can put a message in, direct to the Combine," Jīn Huā offered. "Hacking a secure link shouldn't be too difficult."

"Makes more sense," Lena replied, "but they've screwed us over, too." She shot a look at her cousin. "A low-level manager in the Combine could just take credit for it as he sends it up the chain—cut us out completely."

Toru rubbed her forehead. "Those are two suggestions, but there's a third."

"The Brotherhood?" Nathan's instincts were sharp, but tended toward the risky. Lena sat upright and kicked her legs over the side of her cot.

"Mum! Come on, you can't be serious?"

Corruption and abuse ran rampant in the Jùtóu Combine and throughout the UPP, but the Brotherhood made it a business. Their black market dealings could bring some of life's luxuries, or a bullet in the head behind Trevor's bar. She stared hard at her mother, waiting for her to retract the suggestion.

Toru's eyes didn't break away from hers. As she grew older, Mum had shied away from risk, but something had changed since arriving at Svarog mine.

"It *is* dangerous," Pinar said in a low tone. "The Brotherhood might screw us over as much as the Combine."

Nathan's gaze fixed on Toru. "Rumors everywhere, Auntie. Planet's getting dark. Folks think the Combine is cutting off comms to the other settlements. We've got to reach out to the Brotherhood before that happens."

"Yet that organization's reputation is a disreputable one," Carter offered, putting his hand on Toru's shoulder. "Would it not be better to deal with the Combine directly?"

Usually Toru listened to the synthetic's advice, but a spark lit her eye.

"We play it safe, we might get a few hundred points removed from our debt. If we risk just a little more, we could wipe the whole thing out."

"Fuck yeah!" Nathan said as he leapt up and rushed over to throw his arms around Toru. He kissed her on both cheeks. "I have a contact in Luhansk, Auntie. Aoki introduced us, and I *know* I can get a deal out of him."

Lena clenched her hands at her sides. "If we vote to risk this road, Mum, I'm going to Luhansk with Nathan."

He flushed. "Love you, cuz, but that ain't going to fly. Aoki will only agree to me going, and Marchuk doesn't know you." Lena shot her mother an outraged look, but Toru shook her head.

"He's right, girl. Besides, it's only feeling out the Brotherhood. Nathan, you're not to promise anything, just test the waters."

"Mum, I don't think..." Lena began.

She raised her hand. "Nathan's got a way to get into town that none of the rest of us have. Let's put it to a vote."

Carter tilted his head, eyes scanning the humans. "Those who want to report to Kozak?" he said.

No one raised their hands.

"Those who want to send a signal up the chain within the Combine?"

Lena, Carter, and Jīn Huā put their hands up.

"Send Nathan into New Luhansk, to feel out opportunities with the Brotherhood?"

Everyone else followed Toru to that position.

"Four to three." Carter leaned down and shook Nathan's hand. "It looks as if you are going for a drive."

Her cousin's grin looked fit to wrap around his head. Lena let out a slow, controlled breath, and stared down at her torn fingernails. She understood how Nathan sometimes struggled with his place in this unit. His attitude toward the Combine didn't exactly help. So perhaps this was a chance for him to prove himself to Toru.

He turned and winked at her.

Yeah, he thinks so too.

Mum whispered something to Carter. As much as Lena respected the synthetic, he was a gag gift from her aunties. He'd been a fuck toy they'd picked up cheap on station.

In the past Toru always found someone to screw, wherever they ended up. Most often, it was a miner or an engineer. "Rough and tumble," she called them. However, since Carter's arrival, she'd given up all that. It must be easier for her in a way. Humans brought complications.

You could start out screwing someone with the idea of no attachments, and find out later he couldn't let go.

An electrical tech on Pylos stalked Toru for a while, even using the camera system to check up on her. The aunties took care of him, and when they got done he cycled himself off-station—fast. So Lena understood the attraction of a synthetic—a beautiful, obedient partner, like a vibrator on legs. But if it was just fucking, then why did Toru share so many confidences with him?

As much as Lena loved her, her mum could be mysterious, even to her own kin.

"That's that then," Toru said. "Nathan, intel only. For fuck's sake, don't lock us into any deal with the Brotherhood. That'd be worse than the damned Combine."

"Course not, Auntie." He straightened up tall, popped the collar of his overalls, and looked like he'd struck Eitr.

Toru frowned for a moment. "Alright, if no one has anything else to say…"

Lena wanted to add something, but a glance at the bright, expectant faces around her silenced any words. The Knot was a family *and* a company, weighed down by Combine debt. That debt showed every sign of continuing into a third generation. This might be their only hope.

It was a gamble worth taking, she decided, and they'd take it together. That was what the Knot was about.

Lena wrapped her arm around Nathan's shoulders.

"Just this… don't fuck it up, cuz." She kissed him on the cheek and then gave him a little shove.

"Things are going to change," he replied, his face breaking into the bright smile she loved. "You'll see. They'll change for *all* of us."

8

SVAROG SOUNDS

Jīn Huā left the meeting first. She flicked off the audio loop and hurried back to the communication hub before anyone would notice she was missing.

As she did so, a wave of queasiness washed over her. Jīn Huā didn't like confrontation of any kind. Though the Knot had agreed to an approach on how to monetize their find, this situation with an alien discovery unnerved her.

Before the Great Rebellion in Australia, she'd thrived on conflict. It was her bread and butter. When she was chief financial officer for one of Australia's biggest tech companies, Jīn Huā had battled through tense mergers, held off competitors, and faced several varieties of sociopaths over the boardroom table.

Once she'd lived in a high-rise overlooking Sydney Harbour. Back then, Jīn Huā wore designer clothes rather than overalls, and instead of slurping down Combine slop in a canteen, she'd dined in the most exclusive restaurants. Now those memories felt like they were someone else's. They might be happy, but they did her no good these days.

Repressing the thoughts as best she could, she filled in the surrounding silence with busy activities. She found joy these days in the camaraderie of being part of the Knot, and in being a mother—once the farthest thing from her mind.

As she strode across the compound, intent on staying unnoticed, a miner made a beeline in her direction. Grasshopper grinned at her, displaying how very few teeth there were left in his head—even though he was still young.

"Hey Jīn," he said, shoving his hands into his pockets, "would you help me out with a message?"

She'd suspected he'd been waiting for her in the shade of a geodome. No miner had clearance to go into the comms room, and they often held her up wherever they found her, asking for favors. Usually they wanted access to off-world communications. Every worker got one call a month, but their friends and family were scattered across the galaxy.

Tilting her head, Jīn Huā gave him her best empty smile. Once she'd used it on subordinates who tried her patience, now Grasshopper got the treatment.

"It's Jīn Huā," she said, "and if it's an off-planet call, you're out of luck. If I get caught... it's more Combine points on our—"

"Oh, no, ain't that." Using the back of his hand, the man rubbed away sweat that had gathered on his red forehead. "It's my brother over in Sueños Grandes. I've been calling him, over and over. Our sister is sick, but I can't get him on the line." He held up his wrist-pd. "I think it's broke."

Jīn Huā stepped closer, then wished she hadn't as she inhaled his sweaty funk. Wiping the dust off the screen, she checked the device. It looked all powered up. She brought up a quick diagnostic.

"It's operational. Try it again."

Grasshopper's face twisted with concentration as he punched his brother's number. The signal buzzed and hissed, a sure sign of interference.

"Shitty Combine tech," Grasshopper said, shaking his wrist. "And I've been trying for hours. Will you check to make sure Sueños isn't having one of them damn storms again?"

Jīn Huā held back a groan. She didn't need another problem—not today. "It might be some other interference," she said. "I'll look into it though."

"Thanks! I'll be in the store," he said with another toothless grin. "Let me know when I can try again."

Jīn Huā continued to the comms center, slipped her security card into the reader, and stepped through. Kozak was actually in his office for a change, but looked to be napping in his chair. Another comms tech, Dutch, sat at the console, working his neck back and forth. He rolled his shoulders and winced.

"This fucking chair, Riley, I swear it's trying to kill me." Although Dutch was younger than Jīn Huā, he'd honed his complaining to the fine edge of a man fifty years older.

"It's perfectly fine," she replied as she jerked the arm, "and you can get out of it now." Dutch ruffled his red hair, rubbed the back of his neck, but got up.

"I need to get down to Luhansk for a good massage." The way he looked at her, it was almost as if he expected her to offer one. Instead, she sat down in the chair and concentrated on the console instead of her skeevy co-worker.

"Sure, Dutch… a massage is just what you need."

After that, Jīn Huā froze him out, concentrating on the communications logs and checking the automated signals that went to the security vehicles out beyond the fence. He took the hint and slunk out, still bellyaching about his goddamn neck.

Once he'd gone, Jīn Huā slid the chair down the console to the on-planet comms. It shouldn't take long to make Grasshopper's brother feel guilty for not contacting his family. Opening the channel, she leaned in closer to the microphone.

"Sueños Grandes municipal center, do you read me?"

Silence. Jīn Huā waited a couple of minutes, checked the signal strength, found no issue, and leaned down again.

"Sueños Grandes municipal center, come back with

status please. I have a resident who is wondering why he can't contact his brother. I'm registering some interference down your way."

Still nothing.

Jīn Huā pursed her lips, intrigued by this strangeness. Now that she thought about it, Nathan and Pinar had talked about some rumors among the other miners. People not answering regular communications for the last couple of days. She decided to try closer to Svarog.

"New Luhansk municipal center, come in."

"New Luhansk here. Is that you, Jīn Huā?"

She smiled at that cautious tone. "Don't worry, Dutch isn't here, De Leon."

Her fellow operator let out a long, painful cough. Angela De Leon had sucked down dust since she was a child. Now over sixty, she wasn't fit enough to work in the mines. Her technical skills saved her, though, allowing her to find a job in radio communications.

Since mine management didn't allow indentured workers to leave the compound, Jīn Huā had never met her counterpart. Even so, she and De Leon had enjoyed many conversations over their shifts—especially the late-night ones. They'd swapped noodle and risotto recipes, laughed about Dutch aging at high speed, and Angela even shared some tips from her time as a mother.

"Your voice is so much sweeter than that whiner. What can I do for you today?"

Jīn Huā leaned back in the chair and tightened her

ponytail. "I'm trying to reach Sueños Grandes, and I'm not getting a reply. You heard from them lately?"

"Not since yesterday morning." De Leon let out a long, painful cough. "You know how it is. Up north, those electrical storms come in regular during the summer. I'd give it another couple of hours before panicking."

"You're right. Richards up there is always complaining about them." For a moment, Jīn Huā stared out the window at the horizon as if she might see those storms bearing down on Svarog. "I just didn't see any mention of them on the daily roundup."

"Yeah, and they're always fucking reliable."

They both had a good laugh at that.

"OK, I've got to check the maintenance logs and run some tests for the security detail. Talk to you soon." Jīn Huā signed off, though her fingers hovered over the switches for an instant. Storms might cause a blackout. Changes in the time of day and fluctuations in the ionosphere often interrupted high frequency long-distance signals. Acting on a hunch, she turned to the frequencies for Neues Aurich and Novaya Tver. When she tried to get hold of their municipal centers, she got nothing but more silence.

Pinging them over and over was a risk. If it were just the storms in the north, the Combine would fine the Knot more Combine points for wasting company time. The only way to be sure was to use one of the orbiting satellites, but Shānmén reserved those for military use, or extreme emergencies.

Grasshopper being unable to reach his brother hardly counted as either of those.

Yet this whole thing nagged at her. The Jùtóu Combine had added her to the Knot's contingent to head the installation of a TTE—through the earth—transmission system. Supervising the building of the loop antenna to improve communications between operations and the miners. That was her area of expertise.

Jīn Huā also took shifts monitoring regular comms, like the LMR radio system the security forces used. Hunting down issues between the cities and towns wasn't in her job description. The Combine might dock her pay or, even worse, add points if they found out she'd been doing something off book. Tapping her nails on the console, she considered the universe's sense of humor.

Time was she'd made multi-billion-dollar trades every day. In Jīn Huā's previous life, she closed deals that made thousands unemployed, without even thinking about it.

Now, she couldn't let this little thing go.

Maybe it was something wrong at Svarog's end. Their repeater might be out. If it was, she'd never hear the end of it.

Yet here was a genuine mystery. At first, she wondered if it might be something to do with the broader conflicts recently breaking out between some of the other colonies. However, this issue didn't appear to originate from off-planet.

Leaning forward on the console, Jīn Huā ran checks on

the personal wrist-pds worn by all miners and management. They hadn't finished installing the TTE system yet, so she couldn't reach the ones that were underground. However, any off-shift miners were fair game. No one would notice if she confirmed the strength of their signals.

Sliding her chair over to the far console, she ran a series of tests. Most came back functional, well within the eighty-seven percent acceptable parameters. Miners weren't kind to their devices, and the conditions they worked in didn't help either. Chemicals and dust were the enemy of technology, and Svarog was awash in those.

Working her fingertips against her skull, Jīn Huā hoped to stave off a headache. Unknowns did this to her, so she ran down the possibilities.

Raw Eitr interfered with radio signals, but it had been years since anyone found a big enough vein to do that. There might be any of a number of issues, or it could be a bunch of them working in tandem.

She scanned through the frequencies, checking for any transmissions that might be interfering. As she dialed in below 10,000 Hz, a low, regular signal came through. Jīn Huā sat still for a moment, listening and wondering. The TTE hadn't been installed, yet this was a through-the-earth transmission. Even though there wasn't a loop antenna. Shit, they hadn't even mapped the aquifers and mined-out seams that might affect a clean transmission.

There was no reason for a signal to be coming through rock to her receiver.

No reason, except for the one thing no one outside of the Knot knew about.

Toru and Carter had found something, down in the deepest part of Shaft One. A door with clear writing on it— but not human. "Alien," Ma had said. Toru McClintock-Riley wasn't one for idle fancy, and Carter was a synthetic who thrived on logic.

Might they have they have triggered some alien device, just by finding the door? The prospect was so exciting that she took a moment to let out a long breath. Then Jīn Huā listened again, trying to be as unbiased as possible. She sat still for a long moment, trying to discern words, or some kind of data transfer.

Plugging in her headphones, she slapped them over her ears, closed her eyes to concentrate. The signal came in a regular pattern, like chimes or pulsing, but it carried no words, only a rising and descending tone. Eyes still shut, Jīn Huā flicked the signal over to the system receiver, to see if it carried any data the mine computers could decipher.

The receiver pinged in her ear, a loud discordant sound compared to the low frequency coming up from below. Jīn Huā cracked open her eyes to read the bright green letters on the screen.

UNKNOWN DATA STREAM.

She let out an annoyed groan and pushed back from the console. Some kind of randomizer was in place, and she didn't have a derandomizer. It was like finding a door, but not having the key.

So now there were two strange radio mysteries. Silence from the northern cities, and this odd, very low frequency echoing up from below. Were they connected? It might be coincidence, or something strange was happening to the planet and the ionosphere at the same time.

Maybe Toru and Carter had started a cascade of events, down in the deep.

However she looked at it, all of the options might be very bad, and likely would mean covering their asses, big time. She wriggled a data drive out of her pants pocket; slipping from the chair, she plugged it into a side port. Downloading a recording of the anomaly seemed like an excellent idea. If there was one thing corporate life had taught her, it was to always have proof to back yourself up.

She'd leave it in for a good couple of hours, just in case the signal changed. Jīn Huā got back into her chair and put the headphones over her ears. The sound felt strangely… soothing.

Completing the rest of her reports for Kozak, she left out any mention of the signal. If the hidden door had something to do with it, then the Knot needed to keep the information well under wraps. She wouldn't be the one to wreck things for her family.

Her children would not live the life of the indentured. Jīn Huā would make sure of that.

9

CHANCES AND RUST

Nathan tried his best to conceal a smile, but the glance his auntie shot him said he didn't do it well. He wouldn't let that hold him down, though. This was his chance. Mum often used the expression "my feet didn't touch the ground," and he thought it bloody strange. Now he got it.

Everyone else filed out of the habitat, but he stayed behind to change out of the ugly overalls. As much as he loved the Knot, their fashion choices weren't that great.

Not that he would call his gear that flash. He wouldn't wear it to a board meeting, or even an interview, but it would still tell all the citizens of New Luhansk that he wasn't just some mudlicker. The grey-blue shirt and black pants were his own. He'd worked extra shifts at the commissary on Pylos to afford them. No one understood why.

The Knot fixated hard on paying off their debt to Jùtóu Combine. *That* he understood, but his dreams were bigger—and they started with New Luhansk.

Nathan had visited the town twice, with Aoki. It wasn't anything special, but what it did have were traders of all kinds. Combine executives might sneer at the tattered houses and unpaved streets, but opportunity lurked there.

As he brushed his dark hair into a sculpted wave, Nathan practiced his speech. All the Knot had Australian or New Zealand accents, some stronger than others. It was worse than that though—they also regularly dropped into Combine patois. Mudlickers like his family shared a rapid patter and accent that protected them from outsiders.

Everyone worked their own particular lingo, but he'd studied the corporate version. On Pylos, he'd traded for a handful of Combine training tapes.

The way they spoke could mark them for life. Nathan, therefore, paid particular attention to his voice. The rest of the Knot gave him endless grief about it, but it mattered. If he were ever to escape indentured work, then he would need to play the part.

With a pat of his hair, Nathan flicked his head backward and forward, checking for any tiny sign of dirt on his exposed skin. That would be a dead giveaway. It looked alright now, but he would have to examine himself in the transport mirror after he got topside.

This was the first time the Knot had turned to him for his expertise. Much as his family loved him, sometimes they treated him like an idiot. He wasn't, but Nathan understood his aspirations were strange to them. After the 3WE had enforced restrictions on trade and resources in Australia, the only way out was up. His family regarded the Combine as the enemy with which they were forced to dance. He felt the same way, but planned on taking the company into a very different kind of step. He'd charm them, impress them with his intelligence and knowledge, and then they would be useful.

Even better; these latest wars among the colonies were terrible, but in such events lay opportunities—especially for someone like himself. His mother and her siblings had brought the family to the stars, but paid a steep price for it. They fretted and obsessed over the Combine points they'd accrued. They dreamed of another generation that would be free of them altogether.

Nathan knew the harsh truth. They'd never manage that.

The Combine's interests lay in keeping this force of skilled workers in their pocket. They charged them for everything. Made them buy the necessities of life from the Combine store. Every injury they patched up, they added to the debt. If they wanted children, then his family had to pay for that, too.

No, the Knot needed to become powerful *inside* the company to have any chance. He'd been planning that, in a year or two, he would take the Combine management entrance exam. Every hour he didn't work, he studied. Not that anyone noticed.

Nathan scooped up his backpack and grinned at himself in the mirror. Well, maybe not every minute. What was the point of life without some enjoyment in it?

"Work to live," he whispered to himself, "and I plan on living damn well."

His gaze drifted to the inspirational pictures he'd plastered above his bed. The rainbow waterfalls of LV-222. The ancient ruins of castles in Scotland. Swimming in the atolls of Fiji. Those were goals. Maybe he'd even share them with someone? A real special someone who understood him?

Whatever lay beneath his feet might make those dreams a reality. If what his auntie and her sex microwave had found was truly alien, then his plans would move up. The exam might be next month! If Nathan played this right, he might accomplish all his goals in one move. Get the Knot free of debt and propel himself into the junior management program.

Stepping out of the habitat, he tilted his face up toward the sun. Tried to imagine a time when he wouldn't need to do this. He'd get himself far away from anything underground. Only daylight and good times ahead.

All his aunties—and his mum, too—they'd never change. Their father and mother had been miners on Earth. Genetically, dirt lived under their fingernails, and mud flowed in their blood. Even when they were free of the Combine, they'd run the Knot as a co-operative company.

Nathan remembered sitting on Auntie Rua's lap, while all her sisters talked about the future. Their voices took on a musical note, weaving a collective vision that burned into his young mind. When he made that a reality, he would have given them the greatest gift. Over time, they'd forgive him for joining the enemy.

Tilting his head sideways, Nathan inhaled in a sharp gasp. No, he couldn't afford to start planning now. First, he had to pull this off. Concentrate on that.

As he hoisted his backpack higher, he sauntered across the compound, straight for the security shack. He'd studied the schedule, and Aoki would see him coming. His elation almost made him blow her a kiss.

The door to the small geodome buzzed open. Inside it was cool, free from dust, and ticking with computer power. Aoki Sayo sat alone, her dexterous hands spread out against the metal of the terminal. One eyebrow crooked up under her dark bangs as he approached.

"Bit fancy today, aren't you?" She attempted to make her tone stern, but Nathan picked out the underlying affection.

"Thought I'd head into town," Nathan replied, checking his reflection in the gleam of the door. His dark clothing would hide any sign of Svarog from the casual observer. "Want me to pick something up for you?"

Aoki leaned back in her chair, staring at him and

contemplating her response. Nathan understood her computations—the most boring shift was during the day, and it happened to be the least staffed, too. The native wildlife, being largely nocturnal, meant the most activity happened at night. Kovak stayed in his office in operations, enjoying the air conditioning and napping. His slackness made for opportunity.

The security manager let out a sigh. "If you're yearning for a fresh piece of action, then it's not worth me getting demerits."

Nathan stroked Aoki's hair. "As far as you told me, we're not exclusive... yet... but no, this isn't about that. This is about the future." He propped himself up on the edge of the control panel. A quick scan showed no one else moving out on the surface. The heat and humidity worked in his favor.

"Wow, the future? Really?" Her full attention fixed on him. "Never heard you say that before..."

"I'm not exaggerating, babe. But I need to get to New Luhansk today, or we might lose this opportunity."

"Opportunity? No offense, but your family are mudlickers. What kind of opportunity do they have?"

It wouldn't do to have her get too curious.

Nathan shrugged. "My auntie wants me to make some moves and, you know... wipe out those Combine points. Couple of cycles and I could be in the Jùtóu managerial program."

"You're shitting me, right?" Aoki leaned back in her

chair. She looked beautiful and confused. "You know, you don't have to impress me."

Nathan pressed his lips together and shook his head. "I don't lie." That prompted a genuine chuckle from her.

"Well, if you want to be in management, you better learn how."

"So that's a yes to the transport, then?"

In the end, Aoki couldn't resist him. They'd never talked too much about the future, because there often wasn't one for company relationships—especially one between security and miners. They hadn't promised each other anything, but the possibility seemed to intrigue Nathan's lover. Opening a nearby drawer, she placed an access key in front of him.

"Back by sundown. I go off shift then and Wángmǐn won't open the gate for you. Alright?"

Snatching up the key, Nathan bolted for the door. "I promise not to be late."

"Wángmǐn will enjoy beating your ass if you are." It was the last thing Aoki got out before Nathan slammed the door shut.

The Svarog mine kept the fleet of transports by the gate. Many were massive machines, used to take ore to town for transport off-world, but he had his eye on one of the scuttle bugs.

Slipping into the seat, he glanced up at the camera mounted on a pole by the gate. Nathan had counted on Aoki taking a chance on him. Whatever they were to each other now, they could be so much more—*if* the plan succeeded. As things stood, they wouldn't be able to make it long term. They'd never shared that reality, but neither of them needed to. Both of them knew it.

The gate slid open with a rattling noise. It was still far quieter than the shaft cage he was used to. Nathan waved cheerfully to the camera and drove out with a surge of hope filling his chest.

The journey down the mountain to town followed a wide, smooth track, big enough for the massive ore transports. Not far from the mine, the spoil tip obscured the horizon. Those who first started Svarog chose to take the spoil they excavated and put it on the side of the mountain away from New Luhansk. It hadn't been an aesthetic reason, just a history of such piles being displaced by water and making a hell of a mess.

Beyond that, the tailings tunnels took the water used in the process of separating Eitr and drained into a large pool behind a crumbling dam. This wasn't visible from town either. The sharp, chemical odor from the spoil and the dam flooded the scuttle bug's cabin. Nathan shoved the accelerator to get away from it.

Another reason to get the Knot off this planet.

Governments heavily regulated Earth's mining activity so the rich didn't have anything unpleasant marring their view. Out here, even in the Weyland Isles, no such leadership existed. The Jùtóu Combine could do what it wanted on such a sparsely populated planet. Sure, some miners and traders might get sick with Eitr poisoning, but what did that matter?

Nathan tightened his hands on the wheel. Getting square with the company was more than just about freedom—the health of the Knot was at stake too.

After about a kilometer, he almost forgot about the mine as the lush rainforest valley began to assert itself. Miles of undulating giant trees, climbing plants, and animals they'd taught to fear humans. While Nathan enjoyed his time with Aoki on the chicken run, he didn't want to see any noodle-heads or earth trucks today.

All the trees had been cleared back from the road by at least twenty meters, just in case any rogue wildlife decided to make a charge. Even so, the view still pleased the eye better than the mine ever could.

As he drove, Nathan whistled to himself—no particular tune, but something to keep him company. Though Toru and his family stressed the importance of this trip, he might as well enjoy it.

The Svarog mine sat on the top of an impressive mountain, which might have gathered snow if it weren't on the equator. It wasn't alone either; two long ranges ran down each side of the valley, cradling a twisting river. Verdant greenery covered everything except the spots where humanity staked a claim. The mine, the roads, and the town down below struggled against its constant attempts to repel infiltration.

Vines worked their way out of the forest to climb fences.

Low-growing bushes attempted to fling themselves skyward to become trees. It was a constant pruning war against the native vegetation—even as the newcomers beat back the fauna.

Nathan smiled. To him, the planet's tenacity was quite an inspiration. He liked looking at the wilds of Shānmén, rather than the mess humans made of it. The sun beat down on his face, and he half-closed his eyes for a moment. He even enjoyed the humidity that so many at Svarog despised. The moist embrace was a reminder that they weren't on a ship, or a sterile orbiting space station.

His mother shared plenty of stories about New Zealand, of what it'd been like to run barefoot on grass, to the echo of ocean waves. The sound of birds in the trees—tui, kererū, kaka. He'd been told so often that it melted into his own subconscious, so he almost believed they were *his* memories. All the sisters aimed to return there with enough money to buy back even a small slice of their home.

That wasn't his dream.

His was among the stars. If his mum and aunties wanted to return to Earth, then that was fine. He would take the Knot and its business to new heights, once he'd made connections within the Jùtóu Combine. This was the first big step toward that, and New Luhansk would be the actual proof of his abilities.

Wiping a bead of sweat off his brow, Nathan concentrated as he rounded a bend and the town came into view. It was certainly nothing pretty.

While the mine was financed by the Jùtóu Combine, the Union of Progressive Peoples funded the town. It started as a colony world that would provide food to the expanding population of the Weyland Isles. That changed when they found Eitr under the rock. Aoki had been born in that colony, and had explained to Nathan what happened. All those colonists got pushed out in favor of merchants, shopkeepers, and anyone who thought they might make money off the mine.

Most of the original pioneers shifted to the northern continent, where it was colder but more civilized. New Luhansk remained to deal with interstellar trade and provide landing space to haulers. The port became far more important than those first arrivals could have imagined.

The motley collection of buildings spanned a broad range from the geodomes of the abandoned colony to the rough metallic shapes of UPP facilities, bought cheap from military surplus. Nothing matched, and everything rusted in the moistness of the equatorial forest. No one much cared since they never planned on staying long.

Yet every sip of water they took, everything they ate after growing it in the soil, was affected by the Eitr mining. No one talked about it, but they all understood that it was slowly poisoning them. Essential as it might be, the town demanded a steep price from its residents.

Nathan reached the outskirts and slowed his vehicle. New Luhansk might look lawless, but the UPP's military still patrolled the streets. The price of Eitr guaranteed that some fool would try to hijack a shipment if there was no protection. In between those sorts of attempts, the local marshals would pull people over for speeding—just to break the boredom.

In New Luhansk, corrupt businesspeople and traders operated under strict regulations, peppered with a little corruption on the side. It was this black market Nathan hoped would help him.

The first stop would be Trevor's. The ragtag saloon sat on the edges of the port buildings, and was filled with UPP workers drinking both day and night. Nathan had made friends there on his last couple of trips. He parked the transport in the lot opposite.

A dirty-faced boy with stringy hair and a haunted look sat on a stool by the lot's entrance. He couldn't even be ten. Nathan got out of the transport and flicked him a credit to make sure his ride would be there when he returned. Cynthia, who ran the saloon, nurtured a soft spot for the orphans of Luhansk. When their parents died in the mine or succumbed to illness in town, they roamed the streets. The Eitr in their veins didn't give them much chance of a long life, either.

Nathan turned back for a moment and dropped the kid another credit. It was the best he could do, and it earned him a slight smile.

Crossing the street, he pushed through the swinging doors made of the recycled facing from old military lockers. Cynthia's long-dead husband, Trevor, had served in the Royal Marines Commandos, and that was the theme on which she decided to decorate. It was a nice attempt at a memorial, but the place just smelled of old beer, piss, and sweat.

Outside the sun blazed, but inside the saloon it might as well have been night. Bare lightbulbs swung over booths and two-person tables, all positioned to try to keep people away from one another. This was where you came to do one of two things: drink until all memory and hope faded away, or find someone who'd beat the shit out of a person for a handful of credits.

Nathan circled the room, picking out a few faces he knew, but not the one he was looking for. Cynthia stood behind the bar, watching him like a hawk. As always, she looked too good for this place.

Remarkably tall, dark-skinned, perfectly manicured and coiffed, Cynthia could have starred in a porn stream. Yet Nathan had seen her throwing men twice her size out through the doors without breaking a sweat or a nail. He suspected she was either on puffer or some kind of synthetic keeping her status quiet. Asking her would be rude as hell, though, and would definitely get him slung out onto the street.

"Long time since we've seen you, Mr. Bennetts-Riley," she said, pulling out a bottle of vodka from under the counter and pouring him a shot. He knew she kept whiskey under there, too, but she'd never offer it without coin. At Trevor's, the first shot was always free. Scrutinizing her face, he began to lean toward synthetic. Even the best human server wouldn't be able to remember his name from just two visits and one order.

"I'm looking for Marchuk…"

"Nice boy like you?" An eyebrow shot up. "Your auntie wouldn't like that at all." Even down here, Toru McClintock-Riley's legend ran ahead of her.

"She knows I'm out," he said with a crooked smile.

Synthetic or not, she couldn't resist his charm.

Cynthia wiggled the cork back into the bottle and jerked her head over toward the back wall. A man sat there, in the shadows. Nathan thanked her for the drink and sauntered over. It was such a typical move, like one in the vids, that it made him smile.

Marchuk worked for himself, though his connections in the Brotherhood extended into space and all the way back to Earth—a bit like an illegal version of the Knot, although Toru would kill Nathan if he ever suggested such a thing. Still, if you managed to swipe anything from the mine, then he was the man to see to get you some solid currency.

He sat with his long, lean form folded into a corner, his rust-colored hair the only thing marking out that the shadows contained anything. He looked like New Luhansk come to life; dirty, utilitarian, and capable of killing you. A closer look revealed his right hand curled around a nearly drained bottle of vodka, and as Nathan slid into the seat across from him, he frowned and spat to one side.

"You come sit here, and bring nothing?" The way his voice rattled, he had smoked far too many cigarettes. His eyes darted over Nathan's cleanliness as if it offended him on some fundamental level.

Yet he'd chosen this look for a reason. Nathan didn't want to appear like the other mudlickers from the mine. No one would believe them if they turned up with stories of something alien under Svarog. He didn't use a miner's nickname, either. Everyone underground got one. Egghead or Dog Bone, those were the kinds of people who turned to Marchuk, trying to fence a bag of caps or a banged-up mine head.

"What I've got is bigger than the usual crap you see." Nathan leaned across the table. "A lot bigger. What I'm selling is information… on a discovery. An *alien* discovery."

The fence chewed on the inside of his cheek, his eyes flickering toward the door, then over to Cynthia. He didn't ask for details, didn't show any sign of emotion.

"You know the Knot," Nathan went on, hoping his nerves weren't visible. "Brotherhood has done work with my aunties before."

"*Da*, I know of the sisters." Marchuk tipped the remaining contents of the bottle into his mouth and used the back of his hand to wipe his lips. "Some better than others. McClintock-Riley runs the unit at Svarog. She is *nadežnyj*, but not afraid of a little risk."

People had called Toru reliable before, but not many noticed that she took a few more chances than his other aunties. Marchuk's information ran deep. Nathan's mouth went dry, and he wished for a little more vodka down his throat.

"The Combine offers points," he said, meeting the fence's eyes, "but hard currency would be far preferable."

Marchuk let out a soft chuckle. "The Combine always try to screw you. At least my friends are good honest criminals." At that he stood, reached across, and offered his hand. "I will consult with them. It will take a couple of hours to get an answer. Be here when night come."

Nathan locked eyes with him and noted the bone-crushing strength of Marchuk's grip. He controlled his wince.

"I look forward to it."

Marchuk turned to go, but paused and shot him a look over one shoulder. "You are young man, enjoy the delights of Luhansk while you can."

Given the fence's reputation, that was almost friendly. Nathan waited until he'd gone. Trevor's delights were all played out, so he decided to take Marchuk's advice elsewhere. He hoped Aoki would understand.

If this panned out, it'd be worth a beating from Wángmǐn.

1 0

COFFEE AND
CONNECTIONS

The cycles of the *Righteous Fury* fascinated Mae. Humans—
even so far from the cradle of their species—still worked
on ancient rhythms. They gathered in familial groups,
celebrated holidays, and created language patterns with
roots stretching back to Earth—even if many of them had
never set foot on the mother planet.

She observed these with fascination. Her father had
combined many of his traits and Zula's to create her
personality matrix, but he'd also randomized some. In this
way, he mimicked the chance of outliers found in genetic
humans. She might be an experiment, but at least she was
an *interesting* one.

Even to Mae, some of these quirks remained unknowns,
locked away as subroutines she could not access. They
would come out at the strangest times.

As she walked the corridors of the *Fury*, Mae stared at certain humans, dazzled by their beauty. They were amazing creatures—bags of blood, water, and chemicals which sprouted personalities in the primordial ooze of Earth.

"Hey, tin-head, we got a problem?" The soldier, a barrel-chested, bald man, wore the *Fury*'s blue camo uniform, but his accent rang with whispers of London, mixed with a hint of the outer colonies.

At that, she realized an expressionless combat drone, stopping in the corridor and spinning around to follow a human's progress, might elicit some concern. Mae did not mean to be intrusive and searched for words to soothe the soldier. As he advanced on her, she took a step back, hoping that showed enough contrition.

"Private!" A commanding voice from behind Mae stopped the soldier in his tracks. "Don't you read your briefings? Look at the marking on her face before you make a decision your stripes can't handle."

Mae raised her hand. She'd forgotten about the infinity loop Zula had painted there. Regulations dictated that combat droids couldn't be defaced, but her mother wanted people to discern Mae's difference. Shipnet broadcast the memo, but this soldier might have skipped it. Many did.

Curious who her defender might be, Mae turned to find Lieutenant Ray Ackerman standing with crossed arms. Zula had trained him, just like Littlefield and Stockton, so he looked out for her daughter. Mae liked his smile. At the moment he wasn't smiling, though.

The confrontational soldier snapped off a salute before turning to her. "My apologies." He hustled down the corridor at not quite a trot. Aside from military discipline, no one wanted to get on the bad side of her mother.

Ackerman ran a hand across his short-shaved, red curls. "Think your human relations need practice, Mae."

"I concur." She paused, realized how mechanical that would sound to his ears, and rephrased herself. "You're right, but this body isn't helping."

He pressed his lips together and stared at his feet for a moment. Accessing his files, she saw that he was a trans man. It made sense that he would understand what it felt like to be in a body incompatible with one's true self. When he looked up, he met her eyes without the usual shadow of awkwardness that most wore around her.

"How about a cup of joe with me and my friends? That'd be good practice for you."

When he gestured, she bobbed her head in acknowledgement.

"Friendship between genetic and synthetic humans is possible," her father's subroutine whispered, "but the road is fraught." Accepting that challenge, Mae followed her rescuer down the corridor.

Outside regular mealtimes, the galley remained open to deliver non-alcoholic beverages and encourage unit bonding. Since the makeup of the Fury was so unusual, Zula tried to find ways for them to make connections—outside of shooting Xenomorphs. Eating and drinking formed cohesive bonds—as did trash talking and making jokes. The execution of them could be problematic, however. Father's previous experiments with humor showed that.

At the far end of the mess hall, a group of soldiers gathered. Ackerman's friends contained faces new and old. Some of them Mae knew already, others she recognized only from their personnel files.

Chief Warrant Officer Donnell Stockton sat next to Corporal Genevive Parks, laughing at something she'd just said. Sergeant Masako Littlefield chatted with Corporal Alan Hiller, who commanded the dropship *Little Helper* and was on loan from the 3rd Marine Aerospace Wing of the United States Colonial Marine Corps. Captain Olivia Shipp sat a little apart from them, sipping her coffee and observing the surrounding conversations with sharp eyes.

Mae noted her in particular.

Her mother trusted Shipp, mentored her, and helped her get into the USCM. Aside from Major Yoo, Captain Shipp was her most trusted confidant. The tall, stern-looking woman with cropped brown hair incited strange subroutines in Mae. She couldn't yet label if they were jealousy or respect. Could they be both?

While she contemplated that conundrum, Sergeant Littlefield lifted her head. The florescent light glinted off the multiple rings in her nose and ear. She held rank in the Three World Empire, where they frowned at such displays. As soon as she'd arrived on the *Fury*, she put them back in. The smile she gave when she recognized the infinity-embossed combat synthetic seemed genuine.

"Hey little Mae! Planning to share a cup of coffee with us?"

The others at the table chuckled at that, but she judged the laugher as amusement rather than directed at her current body.

"I wish I could," she said, taking a seat opposite. "Combat droids' lack of sensitivity is slowing my ability to integrate with humans. I suppose it might have been worse—I could have ended up in a Joe." She tried to let her tone of voice convey sadness.

"Shit, most soldiers have the same problem, and they have full senses," Ackerman commented, sitting down and hefting a mug. "Damn, these things are too small. Thought maybe the boss might have requisitioned some larger ones… since things are so off on the *Fury* already."

"I can take your complaints to my mother, if you need anything," Mae said, examining the coffee cup. "This looks to contain less than three hundred milliliters of liquid."

The table erupted in much louder decibels of laughter. Hiller, halfway through a cup, coughed and choked, sending brown droplets over the table. Shipp chuckled, shook her head and gave a slow smile. Ackerman flushed a bright shade of red and waved his hands furiously.

"No… no… God no… don't need to bother her with that."

"Gotta watch yourself, Ray," Littlefield said, using a stack of paper towels to wipe up the spillage. "This young one's just out of the box. She hasn't learned all about humans yet."

Mae wished to make her bulky form as small as possible. "I am sorry if I have offended."

"Shit—you'd have to try harder than that, Mae. We're tough hombres." Stockton elbowed Parks in the side. Far smaller than the barrel-chested warrant officer, she nearly fell off the end of the bench. She straightened herself, displaying an impressive array of curse words. Mae filed those away, too.

Ackerman shot his friend a glance. "Tough hombres who don't know shit."

They'd both trained with Mae's mother on Jericho 3, but since Zula's rise to command of the Jackals, they'd seen far less of her. Only Major Yoo spent any time with the colonel. At that moment, Mae deduced the other reason Ackerman asked her to sit with them.

"I am afraid," she said, searching out the words that would give the least offense, "I cannot reveal privileged information about my mother's plans."

Shipp tilted her head, her brow furrowing a fraction. Mae wondered if she'd been let in on those strategies. It seemed likely.

"No one is asking you to..." Littlefield shoved a plate of cornbread across to Ackerman. "...are they, Ray?" The soldiers all shared a look. Mae judged it as some kind of group temperature gauge. She never got this deep into a human interaction, and she did not want to lose the chance to learn. So, she offered what she could.

"EWA calculated the probable locations of the next strike to within 86.4567 percentage points. It is highly likely that we will get an alert from deep-space satellite tracking in those targeted systems. We have to wait."

"I'm alright with that," Shipp spoke up for the first time. Putting her cup down with some care, she fixed Mae with a sharp gaze.

"Yeah, but ninety-nine percent of what you do in the military is waiting," Hiller commented. "When I signed up, I hoped for more action."

"Shut your mouth, Alan," Littlefield snapped. "This ship already has enough bad luck." The soldiers stared at their plates for a second. Mae wondered what went through their minds, and dared to offer some input.

"If you are talking about the renaming of the *Righteous Fury*, I don't believe superstitions about Earth sailing vessels apply in space."

Parks shook her head. "Goddamn it…"

The *Fury* was only the second of the Atlatl-class of attack vessels built by the United Americas. She'd once been the *USS Bronte*, but never served under that name. With the founding of the Jackals as a multi-national unit, the UA had supplied her for Zula to command. If her mother didn't mind renaming her, then neither should anyone else.

"Humans don't like correction," Father's sub-routine reminded her. *"Especially by our kind."*

Mae sank further into the mire of human interaction. The more she struggled to fit in, the more of a mess she made.

"My father would have been better at this," she said, and only after a nanosecond realized she'd vocalized those words. Littlefield put a hand on the cool exterior of the combat android's arm.

"It took him years to understand humans. We're tricky—"

"—and fucked up," Stockton added. "Humans don't understand humans, half the time." His deep laugh broke the strange tension in the group. Mae's temptation to replicate it was strong, but she decided that would be even worse.

"We don't want to make you do anything you don't want," Littlefield continued. "We've fought bugs alongside your mother for most of our lives, so we aren't afraid of much. This goo, this bioweapon: all we want to know is 'how worried should we be?'"

Mae scanned their faces. Zula trusted everyone who had come out of Jericho 3 with her, and what Littlefield said was true. They faced monsters together. She had viewed the footage.

Her mother had briefed them all on the danger they were going into, and the devastation the bioweapon caused on LV-038. However, she hadn't made public any of the feeds from the planet. For her own reasons, she'd ordered those held back. When the time came, she'd said, if they found a signal, she'd release it to officers.

This far out, operating on their own without support, morale always needed to be considered. Mowing down hordes of Xenos was one thing. The risk of turning into one quite another.

A regular synthetic with its primary coding intact would have said nothing. Mae, however, was as far from normal as it was possible to be. Davis had tampered with her personality matrix, placing hidden subroutines that even she didn't know about. Her father meant her to be as close to a human as possible—and humans made judgement calls based on little information.

She, however, possessed access to a great deal of data. It seemed right to share some of it.

"The pathogen being used is highly dangerous. There aren't yet scientific specifics, but it seems as if even a small amount, coming in contact with non-botanical biological matter, rewrites the DNA. Those humans caught directly under the barrage mutated in quick order, and turned on the remaining population."

The soldiers said nothing for a few moments.

"You become a Xeno?" Parks whispered, downing the last dregs of her coffee. "Bloody hell, you join the *hive*."

"Face-fuckers don't seem that bad now," Ackerman added.

Shipp, who according to her record had seen more planets and dangerous animals than most, crossed her arms. "If that happens to me, I'm counting on one of you knuckledraggers to give me the courtesy of a bullet."

It was an interesting point to consider. Would it be more painful for a human to have their chest ripped open from the inside, or to have their DNA pulled apart? The expression of the man from planetside had displayed great distress.

As Mae pondered that, one of the marines used another example of dark humor. Drawing from her father's copious notes, Mae attempted to choose a response.

The klaxon sounded a quick burst.

"All hands. To your stations." Her mother's voice filled the *Fury*. "We have satellite confirmation of contact with the enemy. Prepare for fast burn. To your stations."

Stockton, Parks, Littlefield, Hiller, Shipp, and Ackerman got to their feet. Coffee and conversation were abandoned in an instant.

"Time to rock," Ackerman said. "See you flip side." They didn't run to their stations, but moved with economy to where they needed to be. Lieutenant Littlefield was the last.

"Find yourself a safe spot, little one."

Watching her depart, Mae found her words most curious. In a fast burn situation, it wasn't likely that her combat android body would be in as much danger as the genetic humans.

Those with soft bodies strapped into jump harnesses. Fast burn often included diverting as much power as possible to the shunt hyperdrive. The *Fury*'s systems were brand new, and its performance exceeded the previous Cygnus 5 by a measure of 18.734 percent.

As Mae made her way to the bridge, she tapped into the synthetic network to see what had triggered this.

Their destination was GJ1187, or Shānmén, at the edge of the Weyland Isles. Shānmén was UPP territory, set aside as a semi-populous mining world. The Union of Progressive Peoples planned expansive colonization, until they discovered Eitr at the equator. That changed everything. The Jùtóu Combine pivoted to mining in the vast jungle, while three other communities were established further north.

It was one of the few planets with an active Eitr mine, among the rarest components used in the production of hyperdrives like the one that powered the *Fury*. The UPP and the UA had fought over the limited resources, and now this planet was a target.

If someone wanted to start a war, Shānmén would not be a bad place to begin.

As Mae processed the information, marines and support staff streamed around her, hurrying to the rack locations. On reaching the elevator to the bridge, she was surprised to find Erynis waiting for her. A moment later, she received a request for connection between them on the synthetic network.

The *Fury*'s artificial person had never reached out to her in such a way. One of the unexpected subroutines kicked in—a "knee-jerk reaction," genetic humans would have said. She declined the offer.

"I am sorry, Erynis. I am practicing human protocols. I hope that isn't rude."

"I understand." The other synthetic bobbed his head. "You are in a unique position." While the two synthetics conversed, streams of marines flowed past them.

"Why are you here, instead of on the bridge?" Mae asked.

"I don't need to be there," Erynis replied, tracking the movement of the surrounding humans. "EWA is everywhere. I instead needed to find you."

"Why?" Being blunt with another synthetic seemed rude, even though Erynis and EWA experienced no such concerns.

The klaxon sounded again, warning of five minutes to burn.

"I fear Davis's creation of you was ill-advised. You are not prepared to take his or your mother's place. And you never will be."

Mae judged the pull of the *Fury* beneath them and, dipping into the data stream, saw the ship was getting ready to cut off gravity production.

"You may not need to be on the bridge, but my mother might require me." She stepped around Erynis and entered the elevator. The other synthetic did not join her.

"Do not take on too much humanity, Mae. Their hubris is often poison."

"Is there anything more useful you want to tell me?" She wished she owned the flexible eyes Erynis possessed. She would have narrowed them most alarmingly. "I must join Colonel Hendricks." He stared at her for a long moment as the *Fury* shifted around them both.

"There is good reason Davis hid your creation from me. I would have advised against it."

"Because you don't have any imagination," Mae replied, cutting off the other's reply by punching the button to ascend. On the short journey, she tried to imagine what worried Erynis—and by default EWA—so much. Father made her to carry on the fight, and because he loved Zula. Those were compelling reasons. Yet Mae understood that she was in an odd place, somewhere between genetic and synthetic.

When the doors cycled open, she moved at a quick pace down the corridor and entered the tight confines of the bridge. Was this relief she experienced, or another of Father's subroutines?

"Mae, there you are." Her mother was already buckled into her command chair. Major Yoo took a jump seat nearby and finished securing himself in.

"Where's Erynis?" he asked.

"I am here, Major." The other synthetic skirted around Mae.

"Are the Jackals secured?" Zula asked, foregoing any chance she might show concern for her daughter.

"All present and accounted for, and ready for the shot."

Under normal circumstances, cryosleep protected the human body from the forces of the hyperdrive. In a fast burn situation, all of them required a specific gas mixture and full body compression to survive. It was only two days' fast burn to Shānmén, but during that time, every genetic human would be in and out of consciousness. The g-chair would keep them alive, but barely.

They only deployed this kind of maneuver in extreme emergencies. Using it was Zula's choice. It was the reason Father made Mae; so she might continue to make similar kinds of calls.

"How long before we get to Shānmén?" Zula asked, looking out to the lost planet, as if to remind herself of it.

"Sixty-seven point two hours to orbit," Erynis replied as he took up a space on the wall and strapped himself in. Synthetics didn't take the drugs, but the *Fury* was about to lose gravity. Mae used the combat synth's magnetic boot lock to secure herself into position on the right side of her mother's chair.

The Atlatl-class had improved power over the Conestoga and Bougainville, able to reach speeds of 1.23 light years per Terran day. Such a rate required all the *Fury*'s reserves, however.

"Shall I give the order?" Erynis asked.

Zula's head flicked toward Mae, her expression shifting from the usual determination toward uncertainty. In that moment, her daughter realized her father had once occupied this spot. For all Davis's feelings about the marine, she felt just as many on his behalf.

"I am here," Mae said, "and I will be here when you awaken."

As her mother pulled the gas mask down over her mouth and nose, Mae thought she might have even smiled. The colonel jerked her head toward Erynis.

"Punch it."

Gravity dissipated. Zula and Yoo lifted fractionally off their seats. Lights flickered on the nearby terminals as EWA drew all she could for her hyperdrives. The power she held onto for that brief moment thrummed through all the synthetics. Mae didn't need to be part of the network to experience the rush.

The *Fury*'s g-protection system kicked in just before she began the burn. The sides of the chairs inflated swiftly around the soft human bodies. The tight-fitting masks pumped just the right mix of gases into their lungs. It took effect quickly, relaxing muscles and cushioning their fragile brains in manageable hallucinations.

Normally this massive punch of acceleration would kill humans outside of a sleep chamber. However, the draining of power allowed EWA to eliminate inertia for a brief second. In that time, the *Fury* accelerated to her top speed, enabling everyone to survive—at least for a moment.

Zula's eyes flickered open. That didn't surprise Mae— her mother always displayed an incredible will. While the rest of the occupants of *Fury* rolled into psychotropic dreams, Zula Hendricks locked eyes with her daughter.

She stayed that way throughout the burn, on the trail of the deadly ship. Mae didn't mind. It prevented Erynis from completing his conversation. Just in case her mother might hear and remember.

Zula hadn't come around to Davis's farewell gift, but even a synthetic did not want to cross her. Daughter, or not: it remained to be seen.

Erynis and EWA remained silent as they hurtled through space toward danger. Mae hoped it would stay that way. The *Fury* might be an impressive piece of military equipment, but she wasn't about to take advice from it.

PART II

REIGN IN HELL

1 1

DARK RAIN

New Luhansk wasn't all that bad. The drink in Nathan's hand might have something to do with his good mood, but this was only his second. It might also be the picturesque spot he'd found.

The city didn't have many of them, but one café claimed the perfect spot. They'd cobbled together a section outside, with tables looking over the river, which curled in red-tinged loops past the city. With an umbrella over his head and a cool Souta Dry in his hand, Nathan enjoyed the moment.

He checked his wrist-pd. Twilight would fall soon. *Why shouldn't I enjoy myself a little?* he thought as he took another sip of his drink. Rushing river water played underneath the normal noises of the city. Wind played along the tops of the trees. The usual grey afternoon clouds had already rolled in, preparing to drop rain, but so far they'd held off.

Plenty of other citizens also enjoyed the view. If he turned his back to the rusty, thrown-together town, the place was quite pleasant. A group of schoolchildren on a class outing ate snacks from plastic boxes on a wall not too far from him, supervised by their teacher. Their chatter charmed him.

Two lovers leaned in the shade of a nearby building, looking out over the river and twining their hands together. A group of old women had commandeered a nearby table and knocked back shots of vodka while laughing with each other.

This is what Nathan wanted; a normal life.

He hated the Combine points that hung over his family's heads. He didn't want cramped space stations, dodgy asteroid-mining ships, and most of all sweaty, dirty places like Svarog. Yet that was what they'd dropped him into.

As he drained the last of his beverage, he recalled his mum—who bore him in space—condemning him to this life. Nathan would never say that to her face because she'd get sad. Still, those ideas haunted his dreams. He'd arrived a generation too early or a generation too late.

He shot a glance at the older women. They didn't seem that different in age to his own mother—but he'd seldom seen her relax as they did now.

This find would change all that.

One of the old women let out a snort. "My boy in Sueños Grandes hasn't answered my message yet, and today is his *cumpleaños*. He complains when I forget, and when I remember…"

One of her companions shook her head. "All the young people move to Sueños and they forget us here. Bigger city. Bigger egos."

Nathan experienced a twinge of regret. Until the Knot paid back those Combine points, the biggest city on Shānmén lay out of reach to him. Maybe he'd visit, after they got paid for Toru's discovery—or perhaps one of those vacation planets, like LV-222.

As he contemplated rousing himself from his comfortable position to get another drink, a low boom rattled through the valley. A flash of light bounced overhead. Nathan twisted to look over his shoulder, back toward the mine, but it didn't come from that direction; it didn't sound like thunder either. Must be a transport ship coming into dock. Strange, though—he thought they kept a regular schedule.

Straightening up, he leaned out from under the shade of the umbrella to examine the sky. At first, nothing; then one of the old women pointed to a break in the clouds, just above where the shrouded mountains must be.

A strange dark shape pushed its way through the mist, making no noise at all. The ship was a narrow horseshoe curve, with a break in the front surface, like an interrupted circle. Nathan got to his feet, curiosity running through him even as a frown formed. Size was hard to judge at this distance, and since he had no frame of reference, it was even trickier. But this odd vessel looked far larger than the usual transport ships. Something that massive rarely broke orbit unless it was in trouble.

No plume of smoke or fire trailed behind.

"Could be that new UPP design?" one of the ladies commented.

Her companion nodded sagely. "I heard they can take on those fucking UA Atlatl ships."

"Strange looking, though." A third downed another vodka while her eyes tracked the ship. The nearby children got to their feet, jumping up and down, challenging their teacher with a barrage of questions. Her commands for calm got lost in a sea of chatter.

As the ship drifted closer, still utterly silent, Nathan's stomach twisted. He'd seen a lot of UPP ships of all kinds at Pylos station, and none of them looked anything like this. Most ships—UA, 3WE or UPP—made noise when in the atmosphere. This was as silent as a leaf falling.

Waiting for Marchuk didn't seem that important now. He could always come back tomorrow. He didn't need to stay at New Luhansk. He started walking back towards Trevor's.

Most of the nearby citizens craned their necks, lost in confusion. The teacher, meanwhile, gathered her children; perhaps gripped by the same dread building in Nathan, she started guiding them away. A few other folks on the street scattered, but more people came out to stare.

"Listen to your gut, boy." Auntie Toru's words echoed

in his mind. *"That's your primitive animal instincts talking."*

Only now did Nathan wish he hadn't wandered too far away from Trevor's, where he'd left his transport. While keeping one eye on the sky, he accelerated from a walk to a trot. He bounced off people who were standing stock still in the streets, but no one tried to stop him.

Above, the circular ship dropped lower, revealing its true size. It was more massive than any ship inside the atmosphere should be. More and more of the people on the streets, observing this strangeness, scattered to their homes. Children were snatched up, the old hastened away, and shops shut.

Someone screamed for everyone to get to their basements.

That made sense. Better still to get away. Nathan broke into a run. Over the heads of the moving crowds, he spotted Trevor's rusty, swinging sign. Across the road, the kid he'd paid to watch the scuttle bug sat in the driver's seat, attempting to start it without the key.

Nathan didn't blame him.

Dodging left and right, he reached the transport. By now, the ship hovered right over the town. He couldn't see any engines. Its silence meant the cries of the citizens were all the louder. He didn't add to the chorus. Instead, he pushed the kid into the passenger seat. The glimpse of his wide eyes under his stringy hair, said he'd expected to be dumped out on the ground.

"Buckle up, kid," Nathan said, shoving the transport

into first gear and jamming the accelerator down. He wasn't quite ready to mow down pedestrians. A couple tried to scramble into the car, but the vehicle wouldn't take the load. He pushed them off and accelerated away.

"Hey," his passenger squeaked, "something's falling out of that ship."

Nathan spared a glance skyward, even as every sense screamed at him to concentrate on escape. A spiral of pitch-black objects fell from the ship toward the center of town. They formed a strange, elegant shape, clustering together as they twirled downward.

The UPP liked to play propaganda vids of the UA bombing colonies. None of them ever looked like this.

He waited for the explosions, the rush of overheated air, and perhaps his own burnt demise. Nothing came as expected. He and his passenger didn't get roasted to a crisp as they tried to flee. No fire raced out for them.

Maybe all the bombs malfunctioned?

He wouldn't linger to find out.

Jerking the steering wheel right and left, he sped through the streets. The kid clutched onto the side but didn't make a sound. That was OK, since more than enough noise came from behind them. The bombs might not have exploded—but something had happened.

The first screams echoed over the rooftops, and an even more terrifying sound followed. An angry buzzing rolled over New Luhansk—as if billions of stinging insects filled the air.

The kid, despite his terror, leaned out the side of the vehicle, staring back. Nathan glanced at the rearview camera. Blackness swirled behind them, a tornado of sharp debris that twisted and turned, almost like a dense flock of birds. The eerie cloud dipped down behind the buildings, where the last tormented screams of the initial victims oscillated and died.

"What the fuck is that?" the kid howled, his eyes filling with tears. Nathan only shook his head, too frightened that if he opened his mouth, he'd start screaming and wouldn't stop.

Get to the mine. That was their only chance.

At the first main intersection, they almost crashed. A pileup of two other vehicles must have just occurred, but the drivers were long gone. Maneuvering past the wreck, Nathan narrowly avoided smashing into another transport. He glimpsed the driver, a young woman wrapped in the same terror that was flooding through him. They slowed down to pass each other, and Nathan caught movement in the alley behind.

A human figure staggered out, vomited a fountain of black fluid, flailed for a moment, and fell. Old or young, Nathan couldn't make out—because his eyes remained locked on the creature piercing their back—or rather, ripping its way out. He caught an impression of curved, sickle-shaped white limbs, and wanted to see no more.

Toru would know what to do. He needed to get to her. Terrors, and people trying to flee them, crowded the streets of New Luhansk. Nathan locked his hands around the steering wheel and focused on the road. If he looked too much, he wouldn't be able to function. He and this unknown kid would die in this broken-ass town.

Suddenly, that became very important. "Hey, kid."

The boy's breaths came in hurried gasps.

"Hey kid!" Nathan jerked the steering wheel around another corner as he yelled his question. "What's your name?"

Nothing should have mattered in this moment, but Nathan needed a connection. Anything that would pull him out of the horror enough to function. The boy shoved his hair out of his eyes and found enough air to speak.

"Jaime."

"I'm Nathan. I'm going to get you out of this, Jaime. We're both getting out of this." They shared a glance, a common hunger for belief and hope.

Foot pressed down, Nathan let out a ragged gasp. He recognized the part of town they'd reached. Abandoned haulage containers and broken vehicles marked the edge of New Luhansk, just in front of them.

This would be an epic tale to tell his family. He didn't even need to juice it up. Auntie Toru said all the best stories were terrifying when you were living them. She'd been bloody right.

The rattle of something landing in the flat bed jerked him back to reality. Jaime let out a scream that ripped through the cabin, high and jangly. His howl contained no words, only pure terror.

Glancing behind him, Nathan went ice cold. The creature behind them was nothing human. He'd never understood the word "humanoid" until now. The monster possessed arms, legs, and a head, but it would never be mistaken for a person. Its pale white skin glistened in the twilight, while its extended cylindrical head flicked from side to side. Nathan couldn't make out any eyes. A long, fleshy tail, longer than the body itself, lashed back and forth. The broad, spear-like tip hypnotized Nathan. It clutched onto the back of the vehicle with wiry, sharp fingers, and let out a hiss that broke through the boy's cry.

The accelerator wouldn't go any deeper, but he jerked the steering wheel back and forward, desperate to get the thing off. The creature's lips pulled back, dripping drool and displaying teeth that jutted forward, as if it anticipated devouring them. Nathan had eaten a lot of tinned meals before, but he'd never felt like one himself.

It was a fucking stupid thing to think.

Especially if it was his last thought.

Not only did the monster remain on the flat bed, it crawled toward the cabin. God, it was agile. Between glances over his shoulder, the thing scampered over the flat surface and leapt on top of the cab's roof.

"Fuck me!" Nathan screamed as the sharp tips of the creature's fingers punctured the thin metal.

Jaime curled in on himself. When he looked up, he let out a choked whimper. The vehicle must not have seemed like a sure bet anymore. In an instant, the kid unbuckled himself and flung himself toward the door.

Nathan couldn't blame him for that, but it wasn't the daring escape the boy hoped for. As Jaime tried to tumble out of the cab, the monster swung down from above. It grabbed the child mid-leap, slapping him back against the side of the scuttle bug. The boy howled, scrambling to hold onto the edge of the door, while his wide eyes locked with Nathan's. Nathan jerked the steering wildly, causing the monster to crash against the hood.

It lost its grip on Jaime, and relief washed over his face. Nathan let out a whoop of triumph and thrust out his hand to get him back inside.

Another twisted creature leapt from the very last shipping container, snatching Jaime from the side of the scuttle bug like he was a juicy piece of fruit. The boy let out a strangled wail, before both he and his attacker tumbled away from the side of the vehicle into the dust.

"You fucking bastard!" Pure rage washed through Nathan, a wave he was ready to ride after the horrors of the day.

The first monster snarled in annoyance at his prize being carried away. Swinging down, it filled the open doorway of the cab. Spines on its back prevented it from getting all the way in. Its white sphincter of a mouth opened, teeth dripping, and a long, drawn-out hiss filled the cabin. As it tried to reach him, Nathan leaned away, slipping sideways until he was almost hanging out of his door.

The monster's lips peeled back and its mouth opened wide. Nathan glanced back to the road. He would end up crashing headfirst into the remaining pieces of trash, but the creature was by far the worst option. The cab's framework might give way at any moment, letting it inside.

Something blurred in the corner of his eye. Did the thing punch him? He experienced the impact, but only the blood which coated his arm made him realize it was more than that.

The monster grinned, its row of outward jutting teeth coated with Nathan's blood. He swayed sideways. The goddamn thing moved faster than any human could. It lunged toward him like a piston—almost too fast to see.

"Fuck that!" Nathan screamed. Grabbing a security baton from between the seats, he jabbed it toward the beast. The sonic scream it emitted made the monster jerk backward. So the fucker might not have eyes, but it had ears.

Grinning now, Nathan swung it again, and jerked the steering wheel hard to the left. The monster dodged away, hiding on the outside of the cab, and Nathan smashed the vehicle sideways into a side of an abandoned truck bed—the kind they used to move ore down from the mountain. His vehicle struck with a crunch.

The impact should have killed the thing.

Instead, the monster raised its head and lunged forward.

With a strangled scream, Nathan twisted the steering wheel again, pinning the nightmare against the sharpened edge of the truck bed. That did the trick. The monster broke apart, giving Nathan all the satisfaction of stepping on a nasty insect.

Juices flew, coating the outside and the passenger seat. The exterior of the scuttle bug smoked, and the smell of sulfur filled the vehicle.

"What the fuck?" Nathan screamed. Whatever kind of blood the creature contained, he didn't want to touch it. For once, however, luck was going his way. It had come within centimeters of landing on his thigh, but had missed him altogether.

Though battered, the vehicle still worked. Nathan drove on. No more creatures appeared, but there were no human beings anywhere to be seen, either. The bombardment had finished, and the eerie ship still hung in the city above the town as if assessing its work. Shapes twisted and turned in the shadows of buildings, but he wasn't going to stop the scuttle bug to investigate. If he did, he'd become part of whatever nightmare transformation was engulfing the town.

Once beyond the edges of New Luhansk, he tried to concentrate. His initial adrenalin rush wore off, and pain waited to take its place. When he clamped a hand to his right shoulder, he pulled it back with blood on his fingers.

Since his arm remained functional, the wound mustn't be too deep. Still hurt like hell, though. Keeping his left arm on the steering wheel, Nathan ripped the fine pseudo-linen of his prized corporate gear shirt. Stuffing it against the wound made him scream a bit, but then he thought of Jaime.

Nathan was alive. He glanced over his shoulder again. Seen from a distance, the town didn't look so different. Yet that *thing* hadn't been native, and if that one creature had come from one person, then the city would be full of them, angry and starving.

At last count, ten thousand people lived in New Luhansk.

Fresh sweat broke out on his brow. Whatever those monsters were, Nathan doubted they would stay in the town, content with devouring its citizens.

His hand, slick with blood, slipped twice as he fumbled for his wrist-pd. He clicked the button a few times, blanking on the call sign. Then he realized none of that mattered.

"Jīn Huā... Jīn Huā, come in?"

He clicked off, and a long pause followed, giving time for tears to gather in his eyes. What if the bombardment hit them, too?

"Shit shit shitshitshit *shit*..." It took him a moment to realize that he was stringing the word together, repeating it over and over.

"Nathan?" The voice that came through wasn't Jīn Huā,

but Toru. "I'm here with Jīn Huā. You alright, boy? We're getting some strange signals up here."

He choked out a gasp of relief. Perhaps things would turn out OK after all. Words escaped him, jamming in his throat. What should he say to describe what he'd seen? How did one day full of so much opportunity turn into *this*?

"Luhansk is gone, Auntie. There was a ship... I didn't recognize it... but, shit, they must have dropped some kind of bioweapon. The people..." He wiped snot and tears away from his face. "Something terrible came out of them. A monster. Some shit. So many goddamn teeth." Nathan realized he was blabbering, but now that he'd got the words out, he couldn't seem to stop them.

"Alright. Get yourself home." Her voice was a calm beacon in a world that had turned into a nightmare. "Get home, and we'll figure out what to do."

He nodded, his hands shaking on the wheel.

"Nathan, you hear me?" He visualized her expression, exasperated that he'd cocked something up again, but still loving him. Her voice, though, conveyed that he'd damn well better answer.

"Yes, Auntie, I do." He smiled through a fresh wave of shaking. The expression on that kid's face as he died. It burned in his brain. He'd been about as old as Bái Yún. Shit, the children. "I can see the mine gates," he said into the radio. "Nearly home."

Glancing in the side mirror, Nathan spotted figures

bursting out from the forest behind him. They weren't monsters. Svarog's guards ran for their lives. They must have been out smoking or fucking in the forest. Now they sprinted for the gate. He would reach it first, and understanding that, he took a breath.

Even though the wound in his arm ached like hell, Toru would stitch it up good. She'd hold him so fucking tight first, though.

He got about fifty meters from the gate when it began to swing closed. For a moment, Nathan didn't understand what was going on. Grabbing hold of the comm, he screamed into it.

"Auntie! Auntie, the gate is shutting. What the *fuck*?"

The sound of shouting, of arguing, burbled over the channel. A discordant noise that froze Nathan's guts. He understood immediately. That bastard Kozak had sealed the camp before he, or the security guards, might reach safety. That coward chose his life over theirs.

He caught Toru's cry over the radio. One last wail of "Nathan" came through—then in the silence, the door to any chance of safety swung shut with a scraping *clang*.

Not knowing what to do, Nathan rammed the transport into the gate. The wire and steel held, cupping the vehicle and not letting it through. As the rattle subsided, the scream of one guard alerted him. Instinct took hold, and Nathan leapt from the transport to make his own run.

He glanced back once.

In the burning light of the sun, the monsters raced toward them. A dozen white figures, faster on four legs, but rearing up on two. They snatched a guard from off his feet, and with a yank, tore his body apart.

Blind terror filled Nathan. He ran, stumbled, tripped on a rock, got up, and ran some more.

He didn't move fast enough. He would never be fast enough. His corporate clothing offered no protection. Under merciless claws and teeth, the fabric ripped along with his flesh.

1 2

A CLOSED DOOR

Something fast leapt from the sea of shadows and took Nathan. The cameras at the gate were old, slow to focus, and didn't track movement. As they scanned back and forth, Toru stared at them long after they panned away from her nephew.

Her hands tightened on the edge of the panel, as if she might rip the thing free and smash it against the wall. She wished she still possessed the strength of her youth.

The Knot lost a son, and another slice of the future, as Toru seethed in her impotence. She dropped her head for an instant, her breath coming in ragged and hot, her stomach dropping away into despair. They hadn't just suffered another cave-in—this was something far larger and more terrible.

It seemed like an hour had passed, but it had only been a few heartbeats since his death.

Toru spun on Kozak. The mine manager was, for once, not in New Luhansk during a crisis. Instead, he stood behind the chair of his security chief, Galen, yelling in his ear as if the man was across the room. Jīn Huā sat at her own station, and three other guards stood in the room with them.

The creaky old camera finally swung over the gates again, revealing what remained of two dozen people. Security personnel, miners, and Nathan. Dark grey patches of blood and scattered, torn remains marked where they had stood, just moments before. There was motion, and the camera struggled to focus, but whatever had caused the carnage moved too fast. The grainy footage revealed only a blur.

"What the fuck?" Kozak's voice trembled.

"We've electrified the fence," Galen said, his face twisted and sweaty. Yet he seemed to be holding himself together. Lena advanced on them both. Just seeing her cousin taken, she turned on someone she could blame.

"You motherfucking *coward*," she screamed, fists clenched, ready to punch Kozak to the ground. "You closed the gate on him. Open it, open it *now*!"

God, Toru wanted to do the same, but the speed and terror of whatever lurked out there damped down that urge. The three guards raised their PPZ-49 submachine guns and pointed them at Lena's torso. They might be ex-UPP, but they were used to terrorizing colonists and miners. Nothing had prepared them for monsters.

Toru grabbed hold of her daughter's shoulder. "He's gone, love. They slammed the door, but he's gone. Whatever took Nathan, more will be coming."

Lena let out a strangled gasp and took another step toward Kozak.

"The family needs us," Toru reminded her. "Nate would want us to remember that."

Lena turned, her face streaming with angry tears, and twisted with grief.

"He stood right there, Mum. You heard him…"

"I did. I did." Toru jerked her head in assent, pressing her own teeth together to stop herself following her daughter down the path to panic. "I'm never going to stop hearing."

Galen shot her a glance, but he had his hands full, scanning the perimeter fence.

"Nothing. Where the fuck did they go?"

Toru placed herself in front of Lena, staring at the guards until they lowered their weapons. "My nephew, he said something dropped, some ship dropped a weapon which changed people. He said *monsters*…"

Kozak, hunched and sweaty, let out a strangled laugh. "He was a damn drunk. Those must be local wildlife we haven't seen."

"Even the UPP knows how to scan a planet," Lena shot back.

Again Toru stuffed down the urge to commit physical violence against the mine manager. They couldn't afford to fight each other. Instead, she pointed to the fence, still shimmering grey in the cameras.

"That's made to keep humans in. The design isn't rated against.... wildlife."

Kozak flicked his head between her and Galen. "That can't be true."

The security chief nodded. "Hate to say it, boss, but she's right. That's why we have chicken hunts on the regular."

"How the hell did I not know about this?" Kozak turned so pale, Toru wouldn't be surprised if he fainted on the spot.

"Because you didn't bother to educate on yourself on your own facility," she replied. "Might turn out to be a fatal mistake."

He straightened up, as if the insult snapped him out of his terror. He was as she'd first pegged him to be—a small man with a fragile ego. Only an hour ago she could have worked around that quality, but now they were in far more danger than before. The mine explosion paled in comparison to this. His ineptitude was its own imminent danger.

Jīn Huā caught everyone's attention. "Hey, there's still transmissions coming from the town."

Everyone in operations crowded around her station as she pulled up video feeds from the port. At first glance, it seemed a confusing mess of shadow and darkness.

"The town's lost power," she said in a soft tone, "but

the port has backup generators which keep the cameras going." As she switched channels, the landing pad running lights appeared on screen. These were vital as visual cues for pilots, so they'd remain on as long as the generators lasted. Abruptly, a great mass of movement passed between those lights and the cameras.

Toru narrowed her eyes, but at this resolution and in the gathering dark, it was impossible to pick out much.

"Hella fast," Lena muttered. She leaned in closer, nudging aside a guard who only a few minutes before had threatened to shoot her. "Can you zoom in at all?"

"The feed is fixed," Jīn Huā replied, her fingers dancing over the keyboard. "I can't control the camera itself, but I can try to enhance the visuals." Operations grew as silent as a grave, everyone holding their breaths as she worked her magic.

"Legs!" Galen said, shoving a meaty finger toward the movement. "I saw legs."

Lena shot him a look but said nothing, for which her mother remained grateful. Yes, indeed the monsters had legs, but as they'd seen outside the gate, they also had claws and teeth.

"What about the ship Nate mentioned?" Toru whispered in Jīn Huā's ear. "Can you get an image? Is it still there?" She flicked through more feeds, most of which were unintelligible darkness, or showed nothing but static. Then Jīn Huā found one from the control tower.

"There you are."

Lena's voice came out tight and frightened. The ship, revealed against the rising moons, was enough to loosen anyone's bowels. The horseshoe-shaped vessel hovered above the port motionless, with no running lights at all. Toru wasn't a superstitious person, but she was unable to ignore its malevolence.

Kozak let out a whimper. "What's it waiting for?"

"Well, we aren't going there to ask," Toru replied. "Can you zoom in any more?"

Jīn Huā let out an exasperated sigh as she shook her head. "That's the best I can do. The camera is too far away, and too low-quality for me to enhance further. Sorry…"

Toru put her hand on her shoulder and squeezed. "You can't make the machines do more than they're capable of." Leaning down, she watched the screen for a few more moments. "Whatever that ship created, they're fast, and there are a lot of them."

Even Kozak couldn't argue. Tears leaked out of the corners of his eyes, and snot ran down over his lip.

"My girls are in town…" he whispered. "They… oh my God…"

Cold reality settled over the group.

"New Luhansk is gone." Toru's words hung in the air.

She judged those around her. As the guards checked their rifles, their faces became set masks. Military personnel had their uses, but the camp mustered only thirty—fewer now that they'd shut the gate.

Jīn Huā sat straight at her station, just as stoic. The

things that girl saw in Australia might strengthen her or finally break her. Hard to say which way that would go. Lena appeared to have got herself under control, and less likely to punch someone. This would have been the time when Nathan would break the tension and remind them of what was important.

Survival.

"Galen, does the mine have security protocols in the event of an attack?"

The chief nodded, adding, "The plan is for bombardment from the United Americas. After they uncovered the black site on Hasanova, we expected to be a strategic target, not this kind of shit." Mine safety wasn't high priority for Svarog, but every one of them would want to save their own skin.

"That's all we've got," she said, "so let's have it."

Galen shot Kozak a look, but the mine manager leaned against the control panel, staring at his shoes. No matter what kind of an asshole he was, at least he cared about his family. He got a small amount of sympathy from Toru for that—but she wouldn't allow him to endanger hers.

In the aftermath of the mine explosion, she thought the chief of security had discovered a level of respect for her. Now Toru would play off that. Galen moved over to the schematic table and gestured for her to follow. While his guards gathered round, he punched in the plans for Shaft One.

"Protocol says we seal ourselves inside by locking the

cab at the head of the mine and collapsing it with shaped charges." Toru took a sharp breath. The idea of doing so went against every mining instinct in her body.

"Did the plan include ventilation ducts?"

"We seal those and rely on the old hardened one." He pointed to an old tower that stood just inside the fence. "It's from the days when the Combine expected bombing from the UA. The ventilation shaft is smaller because the mine was too, back then, but it has three-layer titanium skin to withstand an almost-direct attack."

"So better protected, but not as efficient for the larger mine." Toru rubbed her face with both hands, trying to will a different reality into existence. Lena muscled her way onto the other side of the table.

"Sounds like a good way to choke on carbon monoxide."

Galen snorted. "I didn't say it was a brilliant plan. The idea is that the UPP would send backup in a couple of weeks, leaving the scrubbers to handle the load for that long. Past a couple of weeks... yeah, things get a little shaky."

"Brilliant." Her daughter pounded her fist on the edge of the table, making it rock back and forth. "Maybe we should just open the gates and go out now. I'd rather go down fighting than sucking dead air for a month, because we all know the UPP won't—"

"Enough, Lena." Toru cut her off before she tumbled down that rabbit hole. "Survival is one foot in front of the other. One problem at a time. Every moment you're alive is a chance to get rescued or find a way out." She gestured Jīn Huā over, and wrapped her arm around the woman's shoulder. "Australians survived, became part of our family... so anything is possible."

Jīn Huā chuckled and squeezed her back. This might bring up old wounds, but she showed no signs of breaking. Those daughters of hers would be reason enough to fight on. Motherhood sometimes made a woman strong in ways she never imagined.

A flash of Nathan's desperate face filled Toru's mind for an instant, her sister's grief already palpable in her head. First, however, she had to get everyone else through this. She would save the miners if possible, but the Knot would always come first.

They *would* make it back to Pylos.

"Seal ourselves in?" Kozak suddenly joined the conversation. He pushed his hair back from his face, an attempt to gain some control over an uncontrollable situation. "What sort of plan is that?"

"The only one we have," Toru said, glancing at Galen to make sure he wasn't about to listen to his boss. The chief's jaw clenched for a moment as he straightened.

"It's Combine protocol, sir."

Kozak looked around the room, as if another plan would pop out from a corner. Toru almost heard his thoughts cycling, attempting to find some other option. There were none in New Luhansk, and the other settlements were continents away. Driving into the wilderness would be suicide.

He cleared his throat. "You're right. Yeah, let's get down there."

Leaving Jīn Huā and a guard to watch the perimeter fence, Toru contacted Pinar and Bianca, who were still in Shaft One. Explaining what had happened to Nathan, as well as their current situation, made it even more real. Bianca, with her military experience, took it on board with only a muttered curse. Pinar broke into sobs.

Taking a deep breath, Toru steadied herself.

"Time for that later. I need you to get to the shaft head and prepare charges to blow it. Sealing ourselves in is our only chance of survival now."

Pinar went quiet, but Bianca's voice came out clipped and all business.

"We'll get it done, Ma. Trust us."

Toru's throat clenched. "You know I do," she replied before closing the link. After that, she and Lena headed to the supply depot, while Galen and two of his men made off toward the synthetic charging racks. They'd need as many hands as possible to take supplies down the shaft.

Toru contacted Carter on her wrist-pd. He met them outside the door to the depot, and said nothing about Nathan.

"I'm tapped into the synthetic network, as you asked."

As a rule, the synth avoided stepping into the area of human expertise. He never questioned Toru on her leadership, Pinar on Eitr, or Jīn Huā on her communications skills. However, he would always make an exception when it might endanger a human. As they hustled to the supply tent, he voiced his own assessment.

"The fence will not hold long, Toru. I am afraid we have only one or two hours before the power fails completely. I cannot provide a better calculation without knowing more about the attackers."

"God, you don't want to study them, do you?" Lena said.

The nature of all synthetics, no matter their programming, was to be curious, Toru knew. No, not curious. She had to stop ascribing human traits to Carter. Logic drove his kind and they always sought input to fill in their decision tree. He mimicked human feelings so well, she sometimes forgot. Even if he'd gathered Nathan's last moments from the ops records, he still wouldn't truly grasp the loss. That might be a good thing, too.

If Toru fell prey to emotion, he might pull her out.

"Knowing what they are would help, Lena," she said, "but we don't have the time or facilities to manage that. We have to concentrate on getting everyone below ground, and sealing the shaft. Bianca and Pinar are down there preparing the charges to close the shaft head over the cab."

The synthetic tilted his head, focusing intently on her.

"And what do you need me to do?"

"Take a couple of Joes and drill blast holes inside the entrance to the decline tunnels." Reaching over her shoulder, Toru gathered her braids together and pinned them up against her head. "I'll bring the ammonium nitrate in as quick as I can." They would need the fuel oil.

"Understood." His blue eyes locked with hers, and damned if she forgot again that he was a synthetic.

"Be careful. Whatever killed Nathan," she paused for a second, then collected herself, "we can't afford to let even one of those things get into the mine."

The next thirty minutes dissolved into a blur. Miners, harried and confused, hustled to get as much as possible down the shaft. Like Kozak, many had families down at New Luhansk, but that trauma would have to wait. As she pushed a cart toward the drop zone, Toru spotted hardened miners with tears streaming down their cheeks, nonetheless working to survive. A few others stood, wearing the same sorrow, but staring back toward New Luhansk.

Her hands spasmed on the edge of the cart. God, she understood that urge. Her own father's death in the mine of Bowen's Landing had sent her running to the shaft. Almost forty years later, she could still taste the smoke on her tongue, feel the arms of her older sister locking around her, stopping her from throwing herself in after him. The urge to join lost loved ones did tempt her.

Though easier, the future remained a place worth fighting for. She wished those miners time enough to find that.

Up ahead, Lena stood at the entrance to the cab. She punched numbers into her wrist-pd, concentrating on counting the amount of food and water that was going down. Air wouldn't be their only worry, but miners were better equipped than most to keep level heads while underground.

First, though, they needed to get inside.

Comms crackled in Toru's wrist-pd, and she was glad of a moment's rest. She thumbed the switch.

"Jīn Huā, you got a report?"

The woman's voice came out tinny and twisted with fear. *"Galen's team report some movement in the trees on to the west. We don't have enough juice to run the floods and the fencing at the same time, so they can't be sure, but we're detecting noises."*

Nathan died in front of them without a sound, but that was an illusion of the poor technology. He'd probably screamed as his life got torn from him.

"We're almost done," Toru replied. "Tell Galen to get his team to the shaft head right now. Only a few stragglers left topside, but you get yourself back here. I'm heading to the decline tunnel. Gotta take that out first."

"Understood." Jīn Huā clicked off, and then there was only the sweat and physical pain to push through. Toru didn't mind it for once—it distracted her from the danger closing in. Once below ground, it would be another story. Keeping everyone sane and calm for two weeks while they waited for death… that would be a challenge.

Reaching the top of the track, she gave Lena the numbers of dry packs she'd put into the cart.

"How we looking supply wise?"

"The days won't be fun… but if we manage it carefully, don't move around too much…" Lena said, concentrating on the amounts before her. "We have two weeks, right? We can last that long?"

Toru jerked forward and grabbed her in a hug. Her daughter stiffened, but squeezing her eyes shut, Toru held on for just a heartbeat. God, if she'd only been able to get to Nathan.

Nope. Not now. Can't afford to lick that wound just yet. Sorry boy.

Pushing back, she muttered, "Of course, Len. The Knot only tightens under strain, remember?" Then Toru spun around and left before she could observe any more pain on her daughter's face. She'd be thinking of Sophie, and that not-as-yet-conceived baby.

Outside, the loaded MUV awaited, packed with charges from the magazine. These would trigger the ANFO—the mix of ammonium nitrate and fuel oil that Carter and the Joes had packed into the walls of Shaft One's decline tunnel. Miners had used ANFO for centuries, and its punch worked off-world just as well. Today, she wouldn't need to be as precise.

Destruction was always simpler than creation, and the survivors' lives would depend on it.

1 3

TAKE DOWN

The darkness off to her right unnerved Toru as she drove the MUV toward the decline. She told herself it was no use peering into it, to look for the thing that took her nephew. It would only distract her if she spotted something lurking beyond the fences; if they didn't work, nothing mattered anyway. Better to drive fast, get the job done, and get below.

Hard to imagine that the mine, with all its dangers, remained their best hope for safety. Life could throw surprises—almost as if irony was a thing.

Up ahead, lights showed where Carter and the Joes worked. Synthetics didn't tire or become frightened—a tremendous asset in this situation. However, their programming did not allow them to fire any explosive charges. Before the Combine would even let Carter work with the Knot, they'd adjusted his settings to prevent it.

They weren't shy about pointing out Weyland-Yutani's fault, either. The David 7 recalls the company had never explained, and the many incidents that had happened on distant planets with poor communications.

Most safety regulations and recalls got written in blood.

The gas in Shaft Two had killed Svarog's blasting specialist, so Toru remained the only one with the license. While it seemed trivial, given the current situation, dying in an explosion would be a dumb-ass mistake.

Pulling the MUV to a halt, Toru jumped off and scanned the progress.

Working Joes finished up with the four huge drilling jumbos from both shafts. Floodlights raked over the face. Each jumbo stood like a shooter, with their two boom arms plugging away, drilling holes. Those booms resembled huge rifles: standing three meters tall and fifteen long, they were both powerful and agile. Each arm possessed as much range of movement as a human one, which allowed them to create the perfect pattern to shatter the tunnel.

Carter and four Joes employed hydraulics that worked the Svarog rock, punching holes for the explosives to be laid. A certified human would have to handle the charges. Reprogramming the synthetics took too much time.

While the Joes continued to drill and pack, Carter came over to help her with the charges. They worked in silence, not needing to communicate in a task that they'd spent years accomplishing together. They both knew the patterns for peppering the walls of the tunnel.

Every instinct in Toru whispered that bringing down a tunnel wasn't right, yet the gathering shadows beyond the fence screamed louder. This detonation needed to be large enough to shatter the reinforced entrance, but avoid damaging Shaft One so that it collapsed in the other tunnels and shafts.

Little doubts niggled away. Toru didn't know this mine well, nor the rock that she was preparing to blast. The quality of the material played a big part in detonation. Any blast presented an element of risk, but this was more than she'd be comfortable with under normal circumstances. This would produce gigapascals of pressure, hopefully aimed in the right direction. If luck stayed on their side, the explosion would break toward the free face.

The Joes finished loading the charges and then filled the columns with the rest of the ANFO packages. Toru took a deep breath. Then all the Joes, Toru, and Carter backed up to a safe distance. The more utilitarian synthetics made a neat line, like impassive audience members. Toru could only dream of having that level of ease. Her heart pounded in her chest and ears, while her hand crept into Carter's.

Wiping a bead of sweat from her face, Toru flipped up the protective cover and entered her security code. The mechanism let out a high-pitched beep, and flashed red, signaling its readiness.

A crack echoed through the camp, but not from the

explosives. It was the snap and arc of high voltage electricity that accompanied the rattle of the fence giving way. Beneath that sound, another tickled just at the edge of Toru's senses—a mass of hissing and screeching. She now understood the terror on Nathan's face, and the cold horror that froze him in place for that last, deadly moment.

For a long second, she stood rooted to the spot.

Carter put his hand on her shoulder, and she jerked alert.

"We're out of time," the synthetic said, his voice mimicking the strain and stress he encountered in humans around him. "Blow it now."

With a prayer and apology to the miners who'd labored to create this massive entrance, Toru punched the button. The explosions ran into their sequence, hundreds of loud bangs in an almost musical rhythm that usually made Toru smile. This time, though, she didn't have the chance to enjoy the sensation.

Carter didn't take notice of the chain of explosions, or even the rumble of the tunnel breaking up and collapsing in on itself. His eyes scanned the perimeter of the fence, spotting what Toru, with her limited human senses, did not. As clouds of dust kicked up from the decline, he turned to her, his face twisted into concern.

"Run," he said, grabbing hold of her upper arm.

He didn't need to tell her again. The thick cloud of debris obscured everything, and she relied on his synthetic senses to guide her. When the rumble of the explosion died down under their feet, the horrific sounds reached them in full force.

The snarls and screams behind her came from more than one mouth. Toru had little experience with the fauna of this planet, and if the black goo Nathan described made monsters out of humans, then what might it have done to the animals of Shānmén?

She didn't want to stick around and find out. Being old didn't mean she wanted to give up on life. As Toru ran, her mouth dry, her chest tight and filled with dust, she thought of Lena's baby. She wanted to be there. She wanted to get to Pylos, to hear her sisters laughing as they drank tea and talked shit about men. Everything seemed precious. Even the stupid screaming fights that sometimes occurred.

Papatūānuku. Home. New Zealand.

She'd dreamed of seeing it again.

"Faster," Carter commanded. Through the clouds of dust, only his vise-like grip on her arm told her what his location was. He pulled her this way and that, not making any allowances for her age.

Toru tripped on something, maybe an abandoned tool. She would have gone to her knees without Carter's hand shifting grip. The synthetic caught her under the armpit, jerking her up, forcing a cry of pain from her.

The snarls grew louder in response, and though she didn't spot them, Toru felt as if they saw her. How was that possible?

"Excuse me," Carter said, his voice elevated but calm.

In a display of synthetic strength, he scooped her up into his arms and ran on as if she weighed nothing. Toru wasn't a large woman, but at that moment she felt like a doll. Unashamed, she locked her arms around his shoulders.

"I am deploying the Joes to our rear." He dodged left as the semi-rigid side of the geodome rushed past only centimeters away. "They will act as a defensive line."

"Like rugby," she whispered to herself, remembering her time enjoying the ancient game with her father. How they'd cheered and experienced the swell of national pride. Carter must have downloaded the rules to better understand her. That it should come in handy was one of those odd moments in life.

But I'm the football. Toru buried her head against Carter's chest. If only she might blot out the sound. The hisses were unlike noise from any creature she'd ever experienced. If they fell now, she'd be joining Nathan. She placed all of her faith in Carter and hoped her sisters' silly gift was up to the task.

The ground sloped up. They broke through the cloud of red dust. The head of Shaft One came into view like a vision, along with her little girl. Lena, the last person above ground, waited for her mother. She leaned out of the cage door, ready to slam it shut. In her other hand, she cradled a detonator like the one Toru pushed what seemed like hours ago, but had only been a few minutes.

The mass of Working Joes wouldn't hold off the pursuers for long. Lena didn't ask questions as they barreled into the cage. Toru dropped to her feet and slammed the heel of her palm into the descent lever.

The safety mechanism disengaged and the cage plummeted down the shaft like a rock. Toru grabbed hold of Lena, pressing her face into her hair, and clasping her. If they crashed into the bottom of the shaft and died, it would be a cleaner death than Nathan got. The hoist bounced them down, rattling their jaws, bruising them— all things they could live with. Yet they stopped short of crashing.

Carter yanked the door of the cage open. "The Joes are failing fast."

Staggering over their own feet, the humans followed him into the tunnel. Toru tried her best to judge a safe distance from the charges above them, but more important was hugging mud. The Earth Mother would protect them. She'd welcome that embrace compared to what waited outside.

"Punch it, Lena," she gasped out, even as they ran further. "Now!"

The charges her daughter had set were smaller than those that brought down the decline, but in the close confines of the tunnel, they'd bring more concussive force to bear. When Lena hesitated, Toru tackled her flat on the tunnel floor, threw herself over her daughter, and triggered it herself.

The power of the explosion went right through them, jarring muscle and bone, making her gut contract and her breath stop. Around them, the tunnel lights flickered out and the rattle of the winch rang high-pitched over the sound of the earth collapsing. A thrust of air passed over them, huddled like mole people, waiting to find out if death would come.

It did not.

After a moment, Toru let out that breath she'd forgotten about and rolled off her daughter's back. The lamps on their hard hats flicked on when the tunnel lighting did not.

Lena coughed and spat as she got to her hands and knees. She said something, which Toru's ringing ears could not pick up. Toru shook her head and pointed to them.

"Give me and the lights a moment."

During normal conditions, topside operations controlled the electrical workings of the mine, but if they'd taken her orders, they'd switched to generator power. The circuit acted as an emergency backup if the system got cut off. The people who made the failsafe must never have imagined the scenario where the miners did this themselves.

Carter helped the women to their feet.

"Are you alright?" he asked, adjusting Toru's hard hat, which had slipped when she took her dive. People could miss injury in high-stress situations, so she scanned herself, checking for blood or bone poking through the wrong way.

"Fine, just sore, but then that's no different from when I woke up today. You OK, Len?"

Her daughter performed the same check. "Seem to be."

The tunnel behind them creaked, rocks shifted and tumbled and sent more dust into the surrounding space. They all turned, listening for any sign of the supports collapsing. After a moment, Toru cleared her throat.

"Settling. Some fine charge placement there."

"Didn't think I'd be setting them off so soon." Her daughter panned her light back across the mass of rock and twisted metal.

"Nothing for it. The fence failed, but everyone got down here, right?"

"Yep. Couple of things Jīn Huā wanted to do first, but she's down below with the kids."

While they conferred, Carter scanned the collapse. "It seems that you did a commendable job of filling the shaft. We will assume the creatures cannot get through this amount of rock and metal. This exit appears to be sealed."

"*This* exit," Toru muttered. The shaft head and the decline were the main entrances to the mine, but Svarog had other, smaller and less obvious ones.

It worried her they knew nothing about what they dealt with. Teeth, claws, and speed were their obvious weapons, but what about intelligence? How badly did they want to get to the humans? Staring at the collapsed shaft head would not answer her questions.

"We better get to the core," she said, as her left lamp

flickered. A quick thump and it brightened. "I want to check the plans again, to be sure we've thought of everything." She led the way, hoping that along the journey some more lights would come on. Toru might have been down mines all her life, but the idea of facing a monster in the pitch black, with only the light of her lamp, still terrified her. She might as well be a child again.

"Two weeks, if we're fucking lucky," Toru muttered to herself as she took turn after turn. Normally two weeks on a job flew by, but she understood deep in her gut they would drag by under these conditions. Angry, frightened miners, an incompetent manager, and monsters outside trying to get in. It wouldn't make for a happy time.

The core of Shaft One wasn't a large space; it was a staging post between the surface and the longer tunnels that led down toward the Eitr. On most days it contained stacks of equipment. A dozen cot beds usually took up the far corner. Miners in need of a nap between shifts, but who didn't want to go topside, often sacked out there.

Emergency supplies were most often arranged against the opposite wall, though they got moved about. Folded tents were stored down here in case of catastrophic weather events topside. The only other thing the core contained was a triage area to treat injuries sustained below. This was a place of transit, not of sanctuary.

As miners, managerial staff, and security guards took shelter, they darted about like ants when a nest got turned over, which wasn't too far from the truth. Miners haphazardly dropped supplies they'd brought down the shaft and then argued over where to put them. Miss Vesley, hair in disarray, wearing overalls, crouched down by three small wailing children. Their parents must be elsewhere— or dead. The teacher did her best to calm them, but that didn't appear to be going well.

Some miners stood shell-shocked near the walls, staring off into space. Those must be the people with loved ones in New Luhansk. Toru understood the urge to fall into disbelief—she wanted to herself. This didn't seem like a situation where anyone would survive two weeks.

"We picked up a tent for the Knot," Carter said, directing her toward where Bianca, Pinar, and Jīn Huā commanded a small space in the middle of the core. They directed deployment of the emergency tents that gave people the illusion of privacy. They ordered three Working Joes and four discount Davids to help in the effort.

Bái Yún and Dà Shī perched on a stack of freeze-dried supplies. Bái Yún clutched her favorite stuffed animal, a cat called Nuo—the only possession that survived from Australia—locked in her arms. Dà Shī stared around with enormous eyes, at the point of tears but still holding them back.

Bianca beckoned them over as she began deploying the tent for the Knot. A small collection of belongings had been piled near the children, all that they'd salvaged from their habitat on the surface.

Jīn Huā drew Toru to one side.

"We have a problem." She looked back over her shoulder, where everyone else was engaged in creating some kind of normalcy around the children. "No one is going to know we're down here."

Toru's stomach clenched, but she took a deep breath. "What do you mean?"

Her daughter's mouth twisted as she tried to gain control of her emotions. "There wasn't any time. I got the girls down here... and... I needed to head back up to deploy the long-range antenna, when..."

"You didn't get there?"

Jīn Huā shook her head. "Kozak used a repeater to piggyback off the one in New Luhansk, but that's offline. I need to deploy and align the mine's antenna with the satellite."

"I'll do it." Carter, who with his synthetic hearing didn't miss a thing, came to stand at Toru's side. "We'll use one of the tunneling drones to make a shaft, and I'll go up in a bucket." The idea of putting him in danger was no more palatable to her than any other member risking themselves.

"You can't." It was Jīn Huā who spoke—but for a different reason. "I can give you the command code, but the system has a retina scan needed to deploy the antenna itself. Only a human can do that." One glance and Toru realized she was geared up to do this thing herself.

That she couldn't allow.

"Then I'll go," she said.

"That's just stupid." Pinar. Sometimes Toru forgot her shell possessed all the sensors of a synthetic. "*I'm* going." She stood, hands on her hips, head tilted, as if offended that they didn't think of her. The suit that clung so close to her body sparkled in the floodlights of the core. It suited her personality.

She gestured down the length of her leg. "Auntie, the rating on my shell is over five thousand psi. I doubt any monster out there has that kind of strength, and I have eyeballs just like you, Jīn Huā." Pinar sounded confident, and she was right about her shell. The others stared at each other for a moment. Toru searched for some other option, but couldn't find one.

"I will accompany you then," Carter said.

Pinar shook her head. "They need you down here, mate. Besides, I'm faster and smaller than you. Much smaller shaft for me to get up there, and I don't want you slowing me down."

"You don't have to do this." Toru grabbed hold of Pinar's arm, desperate for some other way. Pinar only laughed and rapped her fist on her shell-covered chest.

"Are you kidding? It's my chance to pay you back for this sweet ride." She gestured to Carter. "Come on, let's grab a tunnel-bot and get things started. We'll need a few hours to drill up, and I want to do this in the daylight."

"Pinar…" Toru took her hand. The smooth structure of the shell articulated under her grip. Her niece turned and fixed her with an unusually stern look.

"I can do this, Auntie. *Let* me do this…"

They were all in this together, Toru realized. Every one of them fighting for themselves and each other. She wouldn't take that away from Pinar. As her niece and the synthetic moved off, already picking a location to drill up, Jīn Huā dropped her head.

"I didn't mean her to volunteer, Ma. I didn't…"

"I know you didn't, but you can help her get it right." Toru wrapped her arm around the other woman's shoulders. ""Less time she's up there, the better."

Jīn Huā nodded and grabbed her satchel. "I'll talk her through it."

Lena and Bianca took charge of the kids, as Toru and Jīn Huā fell in behind Pinar and Carter. Toru squeezed her hands into fists to prevent from interrupting the young people. Pride and fear mixed inside her.

The Knot tightens under pressure, her sisters always said. She prayed that old saying was true today more than ever.

1 4

TOUGH NUT

The longer they waited, the worse it got, Pinar told herself. The small tunneling drone made a narrow shaft, and it wouldn't get any wider or the odds any better.

In the semi-dark of the tunnel, Toru placed her hand against the back of Pinar's hard suit. Meant to be a comforting gesture, it only reminded the younger woman of her lonely position. Some genuine human contact would have gone a long way—she hadn't experienced skin-to-skin contact since they left Pylos.

Gods, that seemed like years ago.

"You sure Carter can't come with you?"

Pinar fought down annoyance with her aunt before replying. They couldn't afford to get snappy with each other. She shared a glance with Jīn Huā, who leaned against the far wall, arms crossed. Holding back a sigh, Pinar replied.

"The drone would have to work another couple of hours to make it large enough for him to fit. I can scan my eyeball, set up the antenna, and be back here by then."

Toru's lips twisted before she gave in. "You've always been the toughest of us, Pinar."

The hollow pit in her stomach said otherwise, but she smiled at her aunt. "I've needed to be. Besides, the drone's scan showed nothing in the compound. Maybe the sun scared them off?"

Toru's eyes flicked to where the light filtered down the shaft. "Most of the native animal life is nocturnal, but don't count on those monsters following suit... be quick instead."

"I've got this beauty to protect me," she said, rapping her first against the shell. "In her, I'm a damn nimble land crab. If anything tries to take a bite, they'll be super disappointed." A solid chomp would scare the hell out of her, though.

"Here are the instructions to deploy the antenna." Jīn Huā duct-taped a folded piece of paper to the shell's shoulder. "Scan your retina first, that will give you full access." Guilt swam in her cousin's eyes. Pinar grabbed her into an awkward hug.

"I'll be back in a bit, and I'll need a cup of tea."

Jīn Huā rocked her back and forth for a moment. "I'll put the kettle on for you," she replied with a hint of a laugh in her voice.

Pinar climbed into the tiny bucket that hung from below

the tunneling drone braced at the surface. Archaeologists and mineral hunters used this rig. Uncomfortable for sure, but it did the job.

The shaft was only a meter in circumference. Even with her shell, Pinar fitted, but Carter would jam like a cork in a bottle. That image amused her enough to give Toru a crooked smile and a thumbs-up. Her aunt smiled back, though worry reflected in her eyes.

Pinar flicked the switch on the inside of the bucket and above, the tiny winch whirred.

"In and out," Pinar muttered to herself as the light above her grew from a pinprick to a ragged square. "Keep calm. Breathe." The suit possessed its own air filtration and processing unit, so she wouldn't fog up. Yet, at the back of her mind, she always worried it would.

Jackie, her wife, was the only engineer she trusted to keep the suit running. Kind, and gentle, too. As Pinar closed her eyes, the sensation of her wife's hand on her neck, massaging out the knots, flooded over her.

Her last night at Pylos station, she and their husband, Eli, cooked a special supper. They'd saved up enough to buy a packet of New Zealand lamb. Except it wasn't. No one could get hold of any such thing out here, and even the person in the market had a hard time keeping a straight face as he made the claim.

Still, after Eli slow-cooked the "lamb" with some hydroponic potatoes he grew, the meat wasn't half bad. They'd laughed, drunk home-brews, and made love in their far-too-small bed. If only this job didn't involve mining Eitr, Pinar would have been at home, still doing all those things.

The hoist reached the top—except not quite.

When the machine came up short, she climbed upward through the narrow opening, puffing and groaning. She emerged like a worm pushed out of the ground by rain and lay for a moment panting. With every heartbeat she expected to be ripped apart, like Nathan.

Except she was in her suit—the one Jackie maintained for her.

"Get up, get up," she whispered to herself. "Laying here isn't getting this over with any quicker." Pushing herself upright, Pinar checked where she'd emerged. One glance told her she was behind the supply depot. Abandoned mining vehicles surrounded her, but apart from the lack of people, nothing seemed amiss. Something fluttered nearby, panic swelled in her, and she spun around.

A plastic wrapping, ripped loose off a nearby storage container. Apart from that, no sound reached her in her shell. The silence wasn't so deep just because of the lack of miners and their activity. Also absent were the area's underlying sounds. No bird chirped in the forest trees, nor did any insect flit past. Shānmén possessed buzzing, crawling things in great numbers. They drove the other miners crazy.

Pinar's heart pounding in her chest, however, had never been louder. She took a moment to gather enough courage to inch past the closest vehicle to get a better view of the compound.

The damage wasn't that bad. Some of the outermost fencing remained intact. As she scanned the path leading to the decline, however, the destruction of the fence came into focus. The longest section, closest to the jungle, lay pulled down.

Pinar half-expected a monster to be standing in front of her, teeth flashing in the sunlight, ready to try them against her shell. For an instant her vivid imagination conjured one up, but when she blinked, the mirage faded. She'd always been one for the horror stories, even as a young girl. It wasn't as fun living in one, though.

Pulling her eyes away from the broken fence, Pinar dared to peer toward the operations dome. The hardened grey plastic skin looked undamaged. Apart from the destruction to the fence, and the horror they'd witnessed outside the gate, the whole thing might have been a shared fever dream.

Except it wasn't—monsters took Nathan.

If she wanted any of the remaining members of the Knot to survive this, then she needed to move. She licked her lips, took a deep breath, and crept forward. All the way, Pinar kept checking her wrist-pd. The gleaming display showed the results of the atmospheric scan, and nothing seemed different from the previous morning.

The sun beat down without mercy, and a bead of sweat ran down the back of her neck. The shell might protect her, but that didn't mean comfort. She often complained about that to Eli and Jackie, but never to Toru. The Knot's sacrifice made it possible for her to live a productive life and, in this case, a protected one. Using her shell now to save them all felt right. Pinar's nagging guilt over the cost faded a fraction as she worked her way across the open space.

Reaching the operations dome, she used Jīn Huā's badge to enter. The door slid open, its *snick* sounding loud in the abandoned camp. After a quick scan for lurking monsters, Pinar hustled to Jīn Huā's communications terminal. She aligned herself with the retina scan and held her breath until it let out a tinny beep.

"I am not a robot," Pinar muttered to herself. "Nice to know."

She pulled loose the piece of paper taped to the shoulder of the shell and spread it out. Jīn Huā's instructions weren't long, and seemed basic enough.

Toru had asked her to do one thing before she started. With a shaking hand, Pinar flicked on the video feed, looking out over the valley. Normally the view was quite pretty, aimed away from the mine itself, with only the tops of the buildings of New Luhansk in frame. Now, however, the camera showed something quite different.

The image of the ship which started all this still hovered over the remains of the city. This shocked Pinar so much she needed to sit down. Smoke still rose from the buildings below, wreathing the eerie shape even further. The vessel displayed no lights, sound, or even movement.

"Are you watching us?" The longer she stared, the more the feeling of dread grew in the pit of her stomach. That looming shape seemed to look back at her. Which was stupid. She flicked off the video feed, frightened to imagine the ship might answer her. Even Jīn Huā didn't know if sending a long-range signal from the mine to the orbiting satellites would attract the vessel's attention, but they had no other choice.

Any chance of rescue was better than death under the earth.

Flipping up the emergency comms link, Pinar punched in the code Jīn Huā gave her, and typed in the mayday signal she'd prepared for transmission. The green cursor blinked, and ran across the screen.

SEARCHING FOR OUTPUT DEVICE...

Pinar swallowed hard. She'd much rather have hightailed back to the temporary shaft. However, she'd only done half the job. The other bit wasn't as technical, but vital. She needed to find the long-range antenna and bring it online. That meant going outside.

When the township functioned, Svarog piggybacked off the satellite signal the space port kept active. This saved power and money for the mine. Now, with electricity off in New Luhansk and the unknown ship hovering above, Pinar needed to activate the mine's backup antenna.

Kozak kept it in rest mode to save money. That little ratfucker's pockets might be full, but now he was in the same situation as the rest of them. She smiled a fraction as she recalled his expression, trapped in the tunnels with the workers he'd spent years screwing over. Jackie would have been very disappointed in Pinar's delight at that.

Jackie. Eli. The memory of them got her moving. She ran a quick diagnostic, checking on her filtration and shell integrity. Nothing appeared any different. Still no viruses or pathogens detected by the system.

Leaving the comms poised to send the signal, she hurried back outside and down the steps to the rear of the geodome. The prevailing wind picked up a bit, running from the mountain behind Svarog toward New Luhansk. Good thing, too. Pinar hoped whatever happened down would keep rolling on down the valley.

The long-range antenna sat with its parabolic dish pointed at the ground, looking damn sad. The equipment didn't appear to be damaged, though.

"Fingers crossed, baby," Pinar whispered, as she flipped open the control panel and patched in.

One glance up to the horizon showed the sun sinking. Hard to believe it had only been one day since everything turned to shit. Drilling an emergency shaft through gravel and granite had taken too long. She didn't want to be here in the dark. Distracted, she fumbled and punched the wrong buttons. The machine let out an outraged and loud beep.

Pinar jumped like she'd taken a punch, her heart rate spiking—which brought another hoot from her shell. She took a deep breath, closed her eyes for an instant. Her own stupidity would not get her killed. That would be embarrassing.

Concentrating on the screen and keyboard, Pinar used the second code Jīn Huā wrote. The computer rattled as it spat confirmations onto the screen. The sound put her further on edge, but she kept it together. Then the antenna array purred as the dish straightened and swung into alignment.

"Yes," Pinar hissed under her breath. "Just a bit more, baby. Come on. Faster."

The dish jerked into position, and words appeared on the screen.

Transmission in progress... satellite
connected... responding...

Pinar never read anything sweeter. She'd completed the mission, so now she needed to haul her ass back to the emergency shaft. Once in the hub, she'd run a wash cycle on the shell, which would clean the sweat off her body and let her forget this ever happened.

Closing and locking the tiny command center, she turned and hustled back past the comms center. As she did so, the tree off to her right swayed, and her shell sonar pinged. Pinar froze to the spot. She didn't turn her head, but her eyes swung in that direction. Her breath came out shallow and rapid.

Nothing moved, nothing pinged again.

"Shit. Shit. Shit."

The words came out in a gasp from between her dry lips. Should she run? The shell wasn't capable of an all-out sprint, but she could push the limits. Or should she move more carefully to avoid notice?

The suit's sensors didn't pick up anything else. Angling herself away from the tree line, Pinar fast walked and opened a channel.

"Message away, Svarog core." She pitched her voice low. "You should have comms control now."

"Are you alright?" Jīn Huā whispered in her ear. "Is anything up there?"

"Negative," she replied, as she worked her way past the mess hall. "One sonar reading, but it's gone now." She cut the link right after that. Talking would only make her more nervous, and what else was there to say? Keeping her eyes riveted on the trees, she moved at a trot around the dome back toward the supply depot.

That damn sun better stay above the horizon for just a little longer. There was a lot of open ground between the vehicles and the shadow of the mess hall. Pinar bit her lip and checked her sensors again.

Fuck it. Despite the psi rating on her shell, she didn't

want to die of fright. She picked up her pace. The sensors let out a low-level tone to show her elevated heartbeat. Not the reminder she needed at this moment.

Pinar only got about ten meters when the shell let out an ear-splitting squawk, harsh and loud. Then something impacted her from above. She'd been keeping the tree line in her peripheral vision, but this didn't come from there.

Losing her footing, Pinar slipped and tumbled to the earth, rattled in her shell like the hermit crab she always thought of herself as.

"Fuck!" She didn't see what happened, just that she was on the ground, scrambling to right herself. Flipped over on her back, she glimpsed a dark shadow against the sinking sun. The shell's sensors went mad, beeping and flashing lights in her vision. Pinar ignored most of them, concentrating on the shell's vital integrity meter. It stayed level.

If the thing that attacked her out of the sky wanted to have a piece, it would find her protection hard to get past. Five thousand psi—she kept that figure in front of mind.

"Fuck you!" she screamed.

Lurching to her feet, Pinar pushed the shell to its limits. She belted across the open area, eyes fixed on the supply depot. If she got knocked down again, then so be it. She'd get up again and go on. The shell could take it, and if she picked up a few bruises, well, she could take that too.

The moment Pinar's feet left the ground, all hope drained out of her. She understood she was the fucked one. The shell's feedback screamed—almost in disbelief. The sonar roared a warning, far too late.

Svarog's compound dropped away as claws locked around her form. The shell screamed another alert as it registered a series of impacts aimed at her head. The screech of teeth sliding off her shell made her wince, even as the numbers flashed in front of her eyes.

787PSI   805PSI   793PSI

Whatever this monster was, it didn't have enough strength to break through. Pivoting her head to see her captor, she caught just a glimpse of vast, rust-red wings, nothing more.

"Not even a thousand? Keep trying, bitch," she screamed, unable to hear herself over the wail of the shell's systems. Another five impacts rained on her head. "Is that all you got?" she howled and laughed. This would be a hell of a story to tell the rest of the Knot.

The geodomes of the mine became the size of her hand, far below. She'd never been one for vertigo, but in that instant it rushed over her. Her bravado vanished, too.

Then her captor let Pinar go.

She fell, trying to find another moment to breathe inside her confinement. The shell, already calculating the physics it could not match, blared them in front of Pinar's eyes. The rushing ground and the deadly mathematical formulas became the last things she saw before gravity took its toll.

Five thousand psi didn't matter anymore.

1 5

WAGON CIRCLE

Toru slumped in the tunnel with her unblinking gaze fixed on the rock. Her twin lamps bounced off the shadows but showed nothing. When she tried to get up, she staggered; only her hand connecting with Carter prevented her from falling.

He caught her elbow and held her with the ease of someone possessing infinite strength.

"I can't find her signal," he said.

That only happened if something destroyed her shell. In that case, Pinar Osman-Riley would never come back.

She pressed her lips together, shaking her head.

"Not my babies. Don't take them." She didn't know who she implored. The Earth Mother abandoned her in that moment. Carter gave her a squeeze, held her in silence, before stating the truth.

"We need to close this tunnel, Toru. It's too dangerous to wait."

She pushed away the tears and fixed her braids back on her head.

"I've got it."

"It is unfair that it must be you all the time," Carter said in a low voice. Her body, mind, and spirit were all exhausted. It would be nice for someone else to worry for a bit. Someone else who others would turn to. Toru indulged that fantasy for a split second before taking the detonator from his grasp. Unlike most synthetics, they had given him warm hands. Such details made it easy for old women like herself to fool themselves.

"Come on," Toru said, not waiting for him but stalking away into the side tunnel. From a safe distance, she drove the drilling bot to the top of the tunnel they'd made only a few hours before. They'd packed the little guy with enough ANFO and a charge to bring down what he'd created.

With tears filling the wrinkles around her eyes, Toru flicked the switch on the detonator. The explosion wasn't as loud as the ones they'd made yesterday—either that or her ears were giving way. The cloud of dust flared around Toru and Carter. She closed her eyes and let the sensation come. When she opened them, they pricked with tears.

She looked up at Carter, his pretty face, and his eyes that always gleamed with the light of personality. Perhaps she was a stupid old lady who liked her fuckbot a little too much, or perhaps there were many ways to be human.

"We get out of here. All of us. I'm not losing anyone else. You understand, Carter?"

"That has always been my understanding and my duty." His fingers brushed her face, the way only a lover would. "Our programming on this matter is this same."

"That shit stays between the two of us, though." Her lips twisted as she choked back a storm of tears. "Come on, let's get back to the core."

They moved with only the light from their headlamps scraping across the wall. As they got closer to the core, they reached lights that had access to power. The murmur of human voices punctured the pressing silence of the maze of tunnels. Toru took a long shuddering breath, centering herself as best she could.

In their absence, the survivors erected emergency tents huddled together. Miners shuffled around, hollow-eyed but at least functional. A knot of security guards gathered on the far side and Toru glimpsed Kozak talking to them. At the moment, she didn't have the strength to find out what stupidity he was spreading.

Lena and Bianca approached, but both women recognized her expression long before they reached Toru and Carter. Her daughter pressed her lips together, eyes filling with angry tears. She looked away and said nothing. Bianca covered her face, rubbing, as if she might remove reality—but only for an instant. She served in the military;

she'd lost people before. Like Toru, she knew how to put things aside for the sake of survival.

"What happened?" she asked in a soft tone.

"Something must have got her." Toru shook her head, helplessness washing over her again. "We didn't see, because the signal from her shell just went... dead..."

Lena turned and looked over her shoulder, back to where Jīn Huā observed them, while Bái Yún and Dà Shī hugged her legs, chattering up at her.

"But the shell... they rated it for..."

"You don't have to tell me," Toru snapped. A few heads turned in her direction, miners ready for the next shoe to drop. She continued in a softer tone. "I know the shell's specs. Whatever the fuck is outside overcame them."

"Maybe they're smart, too. Not just animals." Lena chewed the corner of her lip. "I wonder if the security crew would give me a rifle. They brought more than they can use."

The four of them drew together to prevent from being overheard. Carter, taller than the women, glanced over their heads, doing the mental calculation that all synthetics did.

"The probability of that is low indeed."

"We need to arm ourselves with what we have, then." Lena needed to do something. She'd always been a problem solver.

All the mine's equipment lay about them.

"I'm going to get the Big Boys," Lena said. "They're

tough and programmed to obey us. Would be useful in a tight spot with those guards. Also, we still need access to the mine's drilling drones."

"I'll secure all the charges I can find," Bianca offered. "Make sure we have enough to use."

"The outer tunnels have two P-5000 power loaders," Carter reminded them. "We should be able to arm them for use."

"After what happened to Pinar's shell, I don't think those exosuits are going to offer much protection," Toru said. Caving in the tunnels and shafts remained an option. Another was using the Big Boys as backup and battering rams. However, they'd need some close quarters weaponry to defend themselves.

"Carter, I'm going to need you to get all the rock drills you can and bring them to the Knot's tent." A drill's handheld CO_2 lasers would cut through anything. The most dangerous equipment in a mine, used only by certified workers. They might not be as good as the rifles, or they might be even better. If they melted stone, whatever waited outside couldn't be tougher than granite.

"Go," Toru hissed under her breath. As they scattered to their tasks, as casually as possible, she headed straight to Jīn Huā. As Toru drew closer, she pulled them closer. Bái Yún held up her stuffed cat to Toru as she approached.

"Nuo says she's scared, Nana." That hit hard enough to make Toru gasp, but she hid it with a chuckle.

"Well, Nuo, the earth has always protected the Knot."

"Where's Auntie Pinar?" the little girl asked, peering around with wide eyes. "She said she'd play with me when she got back."

Jīn Huā and her mother locked eyes, and the young woman gave a shake of her head. Toru worked on the principle of telling the truth to children, but what was the use of making them panic right now?

"She couldn't get back, honey. You'll have to wait."

Bái Yún's face screwed up like she might cry at any moment. Dà Shī, who didn't understand as much as his sister, pouted and demanded "up" from their mother. Cradling him on one hip, Jīn Huā swallowed hard.

"What do we do now, Ma?" Her eyes stayed calm, but she, too, needed something to do. Toru sighed and scanned the core.

"Someone got the tent up, so you three should go there. Set up the TTE antenna so we can communicate with the surface. We need it to talk back if anyone answers our distress call." She leaned in and hugged her tight. "The rest of the Knot will meet you at the tent as soon as they can."

"Except Uncle Nathan and Auntie Pinar." Bái Yún swung her foot, sending up a red dusty cloud from the surface of the mine. "I don't like it here!"

"Neither do I, sweetie," Jīn Huā said, "but let's go to the tent like Nana said. It'll be fun." She guided them away, not asking about Pinar. This situation must have opened old wounds for all three of them. The trauma of

Australia remained, but they would need to deal with those issues later—if they all survived.

Watching them leave, Toru failed to spot Kozak coming up behind her.

"You're lucky I don't order my men to shoot you for sedition." His face, dirty and scarlet with rage, contained no trace of humanity. She might have felt sorry for him, since he'd lost his family in New Luhansk, but not when he came at her like this. Toru took a breath and a moment to pin her hair back up on her head. Most of her sisters kept theirs short, but she'd never given up on her childhood pair of braids.

Kozak waited, his eyes full of disdain. She didn't care.

"Go ahead, see how that goes down with the rest of the miners. They know who was on the ground when Shaft Two exploded, and who shut the gates on their friends and family after the bombardment."

Hiding in the earth did not agree with Kozak, that much was obvious. The light in his eyes grew feral, stripped of all the managerial garbage with which he liked to adorn himself. His gaze darted from side to side, realizing that people were listening in on their conversation. He learned what all mudlickers understood early—there was no privacy underground.

Two of the most intimidating old-hat survivors, Crank Willy and Twinkle Toes Tonia, stood nearby. A bulky woman with a face that made it impossible to pin an age on her, Twinkle Toes loved to break men's arms for coin.

Rumor had it Willy held up the roof of a collapsing tunnel and saved his friends in the early days of Svarog. Toru hadn't figured out their relationship.

Kozak's guards might have guns, but they shared close quarters with miners bent on survival—and there were more workers than management down here. Toru finished fixing her braids and gave him her full attention.

"We all want to get out of this, Kozak." She fixed him with the stern look she'd leveled at her children for years. "We don't need to trust each other, but we have to work together."

A muscle in his jaw twitched as his animal brain calculated the odds. "What do you want me to do?" He ground the words out as if every syllable cost him.

"Set up a perimeter around the supplies. No one is hoarding yet, but it'll happen if we don't step in now."

He swallowed hard, nodded. "I concur."

Toru fired off a thin smile. "You and I will take charge, Kozak. We just need to keep things together for two weeks. That's all, and then we don't have to lay eyes on each other ever again."

"Fine with me," he replied before spinning around to yell orders at his guards. They circled around to the rear of the core to protect the supplies. Toru watched for a moment, and then sensed someone coming up beside her—two large someones. Crank Willy and Twinkle Toes stood on each side of her. She expected trouble. Big people in a mine got a lot of respect, and many liked to throw it around.

Crank Willy, whose face resembled something carved from stone by a disinterested drunken artist, folded his arms.

"Need any help? We could take 'em. Give the word."

Twinkle Toes nodded. "He's a shithead that needs a kicking."

"Appreciate it," she responded, While Toru agreed with these sentiments, however, she didn't want them breaking loose. "I might take you up on the offer sometime—but not right now."

"Might be sooner than you think." Crank Willy rolled his shoulders, showing off the muscles working a life in the mines gave him.

"Save it for the monsters." Toru turned and pointed across the core to where Carter appeared, dragging a cart laden with several rock drills. "If you want to lend a hand, go help him bring the rest in from the tunnels."

From the other direction, Lena led in the Knot's Big Boys. Each standing a meter tall and twice as long, the droids carried heavy loads over uneven ground. They'd been hardened against toxic chemicals, such as were often found along with the Eitr. Military grade Good Boys would be better, but these would run interference.

The Knot only had five, so they needed to be careful with them.

While Kozak and his men guarded the supplies, Toru pulled in all the miners to help in creating other varieties of defense. In the back of her mind, she wondered what killed Pinar. Something cracked her shell, but what might that attacker be?

Carter took charge of retrofitting the rock drills. This required stripping off all the safety features. They'd be useful, but there were few charge packs for them. Half a dozen miners sat down with the synthetic and set about tearing off the limiters that kept the lasers down to an acceptable level.

Toru left them to their work and checked on Lena. She and Bianca were busy programming the Big Boys to forget their safety protocols. Judging from the sweat on the women's brows, it wasn't easy. Lena got the top panel off one bot and poked around inside, while consulting her wrist-pd.

She glanced up. "This programming is fighting back. We're trying to get around the protocols that keep the Boys from crushing anything that moves."

"They're made to protect people." Bianca, who was more comfortable straddling another Boy, muttered something under her breath, and gave the bot a thump. "There are too many security levels to breach their coding without it taking fucking weeks."

Toru understood people better than machines, but there was something her own mother told her.

"Once military, always military," she said. "Look for some inactive subroutines. National Dynamics are notorious for their short cuts. I'd bet a thousand Combine points they still have left-over coding from the Good Boys in there. See if you can switch them on." Both women grinned at that, Bianca's smile a little more forced, given her history with the military.

Toru let out a long sigh. "And when you're done with that, I need you to remove those locks on Carter. We need everyone to be able to hit a detonator."

In a normal situation, Lena would protest such a command. Now, she nodded.

"Sure thing, Mum."

Toru circled back to the tent. Bái Yún was playing with Dà Shī in the corner, now and then shooting glances toward their mother, making sure she wasn't going anywhere. Jīn Huā hunched over a field comms unit with headphones clamped over her ears. She slipped off one earpiece as soon as she spotted Toru.

"How's the signal?" the older woman asked, pulling a box over so she might sit her aching bones down for a moment.

"Strong. Pinar did a good job aligning the dish." She paused, bit her lip, looked away. "Anyway, I'm patched into the channel, so if anyone answers, we'll be able to communicate."

"At least until the power goes out." Toru reached across and grabbed Jīn Huā's hand to give it a squeeze. "Sorry... didn't mean to sound bleak."

Her daughter brushed tears out of her eyes and sat a little taller. "Not around Bái Yún and Dà Shī, OK?"

Toru nodded. "I forget, little ears."

Neither child showed signs of having heard anything, but they could be sneaky that way.

"Something else I noticed before the bombardment, though I didn't piece together what it meant." Jīn Huā reached over, changed the frequency, then she took the headphones and slipped them over Toru's ears.

The tones filled her head with chiming and clanking, followed by long patches of silence. Toru's skin crawled and her mouth grew dry. Suddenly she felt something behind her, something shadowy and hungry. She shoved the headphones off her head with one hand.

"What the hell is that?"

"I don't know." Jīn Huā picked up the equipment and put it back on the table in an eerily calm manner. "The frequency is incredibly low… infrasound. Below the level humans can make out."

"Is this signal coming from the ship over New Luhansk?" Toru asked. They didn't need this right now. But Jīn Huā shook her head.

"It came from below… from whatever you and Carter found. Then, when the ship arrived, it seemed to reply." She held out the headphones again, but Toru brushed them away. Jīn Huā propped up her elbows on the makeshift desk and jerked her head toward a data drive in front of her. "I've recorded what I think is a call and response. One from the ship, and the other coming from beneath us."

"So you're saying something down there is broadcasting to the fucking ship?"

She got a slow nod in response. "And something else—a higher frequency signal from the ship. I haven't figured what that one is yet."

Toru rubbed her face, hoping she was in the middle of a nightmare. Maybe she'd never left Shaft Two, and this was a carbon monoxide hallucination?

If only.

"Keep tracking that signal, but stay here. Keep the kids happy as best you can." Giving Jīn Huā a quick hug, Toru left the tent and headed off to find Carter. With relief, she noted that he and the miners had finished retrofitting a trio of rock drills. They'd affixed straps to sling them over a shoulder, making them look more like weapons.

"Perfect timing," Toru said, picking one up and hefting it. It wouldn't do her back any good, but screw the pain. No surprise that Twinkle Toes and Crank Willy had secured two others. They carried them far more easily than she. Her height meant she'd have to keep the barrel from dropping and dragging on the ground.

"I need someone familiar with the layout of Svarog to check out the perimeter." Toru turned to Willy and Twinkle Toes. "Seems like you're helping, just like you wanted."

"Better start with the main HVAC system," Carter said, producing a printout of Shaft One. "We can use the power loaders to fill the service tunnel with rock and debris. We'll rely on the emergency air scrubbers, but they're small."

"Only need to last a couple of weeks," Twinkle Toes

said, letting out a gruff laugh. "And I've always wanted to run one of those loaders... been a few years."

As they set off, Toru turned to the rest of them. "OK, I want teams around the clock checking the perimeter. I'll be asking Kozak to lend some of his personnel for this, too. They want to survive as much as we do."

The miners grumbled at the mention of the mine manager, but none of them could prove he wanted to die. Turning to Carter, Toru leaned down to examine the schematics.

"Right—let's set up some areas to patrol, ones closest to the surface first. A1 and A2 are a good place to start."

He put his hand over hers for a moment.

"You always say the earth has protected us."

Toru squeezed his fingers but avoided pointing out that it often took a toll on the Knot. No one—not even the synthetics—needed to hear that. This was *their* ground now, and they had to protect it at all costs.

1 6

EARTH CRADLE

Toru only confirmed that two days had passed by the blinking red readout on her wrist-pd. Outside, the sun would rise over whatever remained up top. The survivors could access one of the video cameras, but it didn't have night vision and would only turn 180 degrees.

Jīn Huā scanned the feed from the Knot tent, but so far spotted nothing but shadows. No human or synthetic moved above, and no sign of bodies either. Even Pinar's shell had vanished—along with its contents.

The camera revealed the smoking ruins of New Luhansk and the ship that still hovered above. The vessel hadn't moved or done anything since the bombardment. However, Jīn Huā reported that the ship continued to communicate with the structure deep beneath Svarog.

They told no one outside the Knot about this, yet everyone experienced its effects. Infrasound unsettled humans, and the miners weren't immune. They all became nervous, on edge, and paranoid, checking corners and unable to eat.

Given the threat of monsters, it might not all be the effect of the infrasound. This situation was nightmare material.

Toru was used to underground life, but this was different. This kind of fortress mentality wore on a person. She'd grown used to the dangers of gas, or collapse, or explosions. Monsters? Her family's experience didn't include this.

No one labored under the illusion that the creatures might give up and go away. The survivors didn't much talk about them, but they all understood that each hour that ticked by was another when the monsters would try to reach them.

They'd powered down the Working Joes and the discount Davids to save on resources—Toru had hesitated powering down Carter as well, though. The synthetics were stacked motionless against a wall of the core, like corpses on a pile. Toru tried not to look at them: it was too much of a portent of what might lay ahead.

Somehow though, the fragile peace held on between Kozak's forces and the miners. They kept to their tents, huddled in their own groups, and shared food and water without fights breaking out. Toru had tried to pair a miner and a guard in each perimeter patrol, but that was too much. Both sides balked at working with the other, so she'd backed off.

She did, however, take her own turn at the perimeter,

working with Carter. He offered to carry both rock drills, and she let him—but in the core she carried her own. She could not seem weak in front of the others, especially the mine manager.

Together they set out on the morning of the third day, checking the dim corridors of A1 and 2, poking about in the shadows. Listening for God knows what. That put Toru even more on edge, yet it was also time alone with Carter. They'd fucked a lot before this, but they didn't have a chance now.

Out of sight of everyone else, the best she could do was hold his hand. Its strength and warmth comforted her in the dark, like she was a goddamn child again.

"Are you afraid?" Toru asked him. They'd duct-taped a flashlight to the rock drill, and he panned it over the surface of tunnel A1. "Can you even experience fear?"

"I know what the emotion is… I can mimic it," he said. "Would you be happier if I did?" Carter tilted his head and smiled with a hint of hesitation.

"You're such a dear," Toru muttered. "I sure as hell wish I could turn my fear off."

"Fear is necessary for human survival." He stopped and turned to the darkest parts of the tunnel. "Did you hear something?" If he had been a flesh-and-blood man, Toru might have thought he was trying to distract her. Since it was Carter, she stopped, her heart pounding in her chest. After all her years underground, her ears were attuned to the sounds a mine made—the rattle of equipment, an aquifer draining, or the hiss of ANFO sliding into drilled chambers.

Now Toru caught a noise foreign to her. A scratching all around them. She gestured to Carter to back up as she played her head lamps over the surface to both sides of the tunnel and above them. Plumes of disturbed sand and fine gravel shook loose and dropped to the ground only a few meters away.

Her throat tightened as the scraping grew louder. Something was pulling itself through the earth above them. Toru couldn't recall if Shānmén's animal life included burrowing creatures. If that goo transformed animals, then it might have been a mistake not to check.

"Carter?" Toru whispered, grabbing him by the arm. "Give me my drill… hurry…"

Without questioning, the synthetic slipped the strap over her shoulder. "I'm detecting ultrasonic signals heading toward us." He also kept his voice pitched low. They backed up the tunnel, but the frantic scraping sounds followed them. Toru's skin ran with gooseflesh, and her gut clenched into a terrified knot.

"We should run, blow the tunnel now." Carter raised his rock drill.

Despite the fear that flowed through her, Toru still shook her head. "Not yet. I need to know what we're dealing with."

She wanted to lay eyes on what killed her family. Reaching a junction, Toru raked her eyes around. They'd set charges on all the entrances to the core, planning for just this eventuality. When the explosives were detonated, however, they wouldn't have much time to escape.

Ahead, the gravel falling from the ceiling became rocks tumbling out of place. The hissing didn't come from the earth. Something living squirmed up there. Toru swallowed hard, holding the rock drill in front of her with hands as steady as they could be.

More rocks clattered to the ground.

"Toru..." Carter's voice filled with concern, indiscernible from any other lover. They all sounded the same when she got ready to do something foolish.

She ignored him and held her position, squinting in between the shadows and the light. More than one something moved. The hiss became a high-pitched screech as they broke through the tunnel's ceiling.

Now Toru had her own underground nightmares. The monsters swarmed out of their chambers and dropped to the floor, alive with hatred and hunger. Writhing, chitin-covered forms about the size of small dogs, with long heads that snarled and spat as they pulled themselves out of the path they'd made. They were the same color as the dirt from which they'd emerged from; rust-red. This made the mass of them hard to count. Their forelegs were shovel-like, and the front part of their faces curved for moving soil. Yet as they pushed themselves toward her and Carter, their jaws dropped wide, and a second mouth snapped out like a steel trap.

Seeing that jerked Toru out of her fascinated trance. "Fuck that noise," she yelled, jamming down the trigger on the rock drill. White light leapt from the end of the device, spraying in a tight arc. She played it across the field of hungry maws, not aiming, but raking death all over them. Her thoughts were of Pinar and Nathan, and vengeance for them.

As the tunneling monsters died, they let out high-pitched screeches which satisfied her rage a bit. Their shells exploded, and some kind of smoking liquid sprayed out. This blood splashed the walls of the tunnel. Inhaling a whiff of whatever sharp, hellish ichor filled their bodies, Toru stepped back. She did not want that on her skin.

Carter grabbed her by the collar and yanked her further backward. The rock drill flew wide and the bright light swung madly, burning more of the monsters racing toward them, but also the sides of the tunnel. The beam hit the concrete support. That, along with the monster's blood, eroded its structure to a critical degree.

The synthetic lifted her away, wrapping his arm around her waist and pulling her along with him as he ran. Moving faster than her legs could carry her, Toru got control of the drill again. She howled back at the monsters and kept burning them until they dropped away.

Carter triggered the charges with his other hand, and once again Toru found herself face first on the ground, with his body covering hers. This time, though, she didn't stay down. Wriggling free, Toru got to her feet faster than she had in the last twenty years. She stared at the still settling and moving rock. She swore it moved and screamed back.

"What the fuck?" She turned on Carter. "You have the files on this goddamn planet. What the hell were those things?"

This was the first time she could remember Carter wearing an expression she would have termed unsettled.

"Kopats, the biologists named them," he replied, "creatures similar to an Earth gopher, native to this planet. Whatever fell on the town must have worked its way through the ecosystem."

Toru considered all the creatures out in the lush jungle, and what monsters they would make. She'd read the memos. The largest birds towered over humans and even vehicles. Everything on this once-livable planet would be turned against them. Each creature would want to destroy them.

"We need to get back to the core," she said, slinging her rock drill over her back even though a jolt of pain shot down her hip. She ignored it. "I don't suppose you know how far those kopat things can dig, do you?"

"I'm sorry." Carter shook his head. "I can only report on data logged. No one studied them enough to provide that information."

"Bloody wonderful."

They trotted up the main tunnel toward the core, and at every step Toru's ear itched with the sound of digging.

She couldn't decide if it was real or imagined. Either way, their safety in Shaft One was tenuous. From the schematics, the A1 tunnel they'd just blown lay closest to the surface, but the others weren't much deeper.

As they reached the core, thunderous rumblings broke through the low murmur of people from the western tunnel. Judging from the sound, there were many intruders—plenty enough to make an assault on another location. Lena met them before they reached the Knot's tent. Two of the Big Boys were at her side.

"Mum, thank God," she said, wiping her sweat-drenched face. "I blew A3 and I think Dutch and Grasshopper took out A4."

"A1 is gone," Carter told her. "Were the Big Boys useful?"

Lena took a deep breath. "Saved our fucking lives. Mateo and I never heard them coming. Boy Five gave the alert, and we hauled ass."

There was a whine of hydraulics, and Toru turned. Bianca didn't take no for an answer with the P-5000. She never enjoyed sitting around waiting. Emerging from the A2 tunnel, she stomped over toward them. She wore a shit-eating grin on her face as Toru examined the changes she'd made to the exosuit.

Over the last two days, she'd made retrofitting the loader her mission. The plates she'd welded to the entire frame looked well secured, and would easily be supported by a machine that lifted up to four thousand kilograms.

Since mine exoskeletons like this did not have cutting or welding devices attached to the manipulators, Bianca had fitted one of the modified rock drills. The loader left Bianca's face exposed, so she'd welded a mesh over the head.

Toru shook her head. "That's a job fit for a New Zealander, right there."

Born in Australia—Queensland, to be exact—Bianca snorted. "I guess that's a compliment. Haven't needed to try the whole thing out yet."

Lena scuffed her boot in the dirt and looked up at her with a foreboding expression. "It'll happen, cuz. For sure."

"What the *fuck*?" Kozak stormed over toward them, accompanied by two guards, his expression apoplectic. He poked Toru in her chest. Carter stepped forward and the two guards slipped their fingers onto their plasma rifle triggers.

Toru brushed Kozak's gesture aside, crossing her arms in front of her to stop herself from punching him in the face. Carter moved back to her side, but looked ready to break some human arms if necessary.

"Why did you blow those tunnels?" the mine manager demanded. If there was any luck left, he might stroke out at any minute.

"We got monsters digging through the walls," Lena said, shifting her rock drill closer to her right hand. "Wish you'd been with us, Kozak. They looked like they might have been relatives of yours. Fucking nasty little rats." Whatever diplomacy her daughter might have once possessed got torn away by what she witnessed in those tunnels.

"I don't fucking believe you." Kozak narrowed his eyes, spit forming in the corners of his mouth. "You just want to bury us all down here."

That made no sense, but for once Toru couldn't blame him, not entirely. Those air scrubbers she'd brought to his attention days before came back to bite them all. He'd done nothing about them, and carbon monoxide levels were on the rise. Like those poor schmucks in Shaft Two, they'd start hallucinating soon. If the mine manager got out of hand—or shit, those guards with their EVI-87 Zvezda plasma rifles—they wouldn't need the monsters to get into the core.

"I want to live... just like the rest of the people down here." She fixed the two guards with a look. "Do I look like I'm suicidal?" Kozak went to answer, but she raised her hand. "I asked them. Roxanne-Bee Sidorov, what do you say?"

The tall woman with the remains of a ragged scar down her face took a step back. Toru had wasted no time after the accident in Shaft Two, learning the names of every security guard. Nathan would have been proud.

"What about you, Nguyen?" Toru asked, tilting her head toward the Vietnamese soldier who, she'd learned, joined the UPP far too young but not that long ago. "Do you think I've got nothing to live for?" Nguyen and Sidorov shared a glance, as if they'd never expected to be asked a question.

"No… ma'am," the younger man replied. "You've got family down here."

"See," Toru said with a grim smile. "I'm invested."

Another line of sweat rolled down Kozak's face. But he didn't have time to respond, because a shout came from the center of the core, followed by louder bellows and curses. Toru spun around and headed for the commotion, leaving Kozak in the dirt. She recognized the sounds of a fist fight—which she'd take any day over the scuttling of the monsters.

A circle of miners and guards were scuffling in front of the supplies. At a lift of her head, the Knot dived in. Carter yanked combatants back while Bianca and Lena shoved anyone who wouldn't back off. For a couple of minutes, chaos reigned, and Toru waited. After a few minutes, the combatants tired, as they always did.

The guards, who thank God hadn't started shooting, got to their feet, dusted themselves off and tried to find their dignity. The miners didn't give a shit. They slung curses and spat in the dirt. The Knot kept both sides back. Lena's long dark hair came loose, and Bianca gained a cut on her cheek. Carter shot Toru a glance and gave a human-like shrug.

Once things were down to a simmer, Toru stepped between the groups. "Alright, mind telling me why the fuck you're fighting each other, while we've got monsters trying to get through?"

"They have more drill batteries back there." Philip Wlodarczyk, who the miners had nicknamed "Waterproof Wlodarczyk," jabbed a thick finger toward the guards. "I saw them... ain't just food they're hiding!"

She'd been waiting for this. Kozak always screwed over the workers. Even with their lives on the line, he still was who he was. Stress and danger didn't change a thing.

Galen appeared from somewhere to calm his men and pushed his way to the front. His face stood out, hollow and shrunken, as if they'd spent weeks below ground—not just a few days. Toru's instinct was to tell him to eat and drink, but that wouldn't go down well in this situation. Instead, she waved toward the stacks of supplies.

"That true, Galen? We just blew several tunnels, and those rock drills saved our lives. Your lives, too." His eyes flickered across the faces of the enraged miners. He weighed the odds before replying.

"Yeah, we have a couple, but we use them in our plasma rifles, too. We need them."

An angry rumble ran through the miners. Both sides were spoiling for a fight. Two days and relations were no better, but the smell of explosives still lingered in the air, in case anyone forgot the danger they all faced.

"You haven't let off one bloody shot!" Grasshopper said, spitting on the ground between the two groups.

"Why don't you hand the guns over to us? We can shoot just as good as you!"

Lena, Bianca, and Carter all looked to Toru for a sign. Who should they punch? Toru hated to defend Galen and his people.

"Nice sentiment, Grasshopper, but that's not true and you know it." She turned to the chief of security. "Your team are all ex-military—shooting is your game. Us miners, we know how to keep safe underground. How about you split the batteries you have, fifty-fifty?"

Galen swallowed hard, glanced around to see if Kozak would say anything. The mine manager, whose key skill was avoiding physical conflict all together, was nowhere to be seen.

"We can do that," Galen said, turning and gesturing to his guards to bring over the batteries. They distributed them among the miners, who grumbled all the way. Toru let out another long breath.

She closed her eyes for an instant and imagined the Marokopa Falls back in New Zealand. Recalled every moment of the last week she'd spent on Earth. Just a teenager looking across at a wall of water falling under a grey sky. Ferns and towering trees crowded the surrounding green valley. A jungle that contained no monsters. Most likely she'd never see that waterfall again—they belonged to the ultra-rich by now—but she hoped her daughters would.

Opening her eyes, she followed the final distribution

of the batteries, and the cautious withdrawal of both sides to their areas of the core. Toru was approaching Lena and Bianca when Jīn Huā called out her name. She winced before turning to find out what new hell visited on them.

"Ma! Ma!" Jīn Huā burst out of the Knot's tent, her face stretched in agony. An instant later, Toru realized that it wasn't pain, but the prospect of hope. With Dà Shī perched on one hip and Bái Yún running at her side, Jīn Huā rushed over, tears filling her eyes.

"Someone is on the channel," Jīn Huā choked out. "They got our signal, and they came! Now they want to talk to whoever is in charge."

As exciting as the news was, Toru wished she hadn't shouted so loud. All the miners and guards turned in her direction. From the rear of the core, Kozak's face popped out from under a tent flap.

"Oh, shit," Lena muttered.

If the mine manager talked to anyone, he'd screw things up somehow.

"With me, Carter," Toru said, stretching her legs to get there first. "I'll need your backup. We can't let Kozak organize a rescue. He's showed his incompetence one time too many."

"Agreed," the synthetic replied, straightening to his full, imposing height.

"Bianca, Len, keep an eye on the tent entrance," Toru said over her shoulder. "Jīn Huā, you're working comms. Let's go."

They reached the tent first, but Kozak and Galen were close behind. Toru knew he wouldn't make this easy, but she wouldn't back down either. As always, hope needed to be fought for, and life had given her plenty of experience in that.

Toru's jaw tightened as she entered the tent.

1 7

FURIOUS BURN

The *Righteous Fury* scorched her way through the Shānmén system like a meteor. Ahead, she blasted her intentions on secure frequencies to the UPP. She used the specific emergency codes authorized by General Ristic.

No answer came in response. Based on her father's experience, Mae concluded there was trouble ahead, rather than UPP forces.

Zula instructed EWA to plot a trajectory that would get them as deep as possible into Shānmén's atmosphere. Threading the needle between so many gravity wells, and doing so at high speed, would have been beyond the most talented of human pilots. Only an advanced AI could make such complex and precise mathematical calculations.

EWA cradled space-time in one section of her awareness, Mae knew, while maintaining an understanding of the fragility of her human crew. The AI identified that knife edge and danced along it. Mae, hovering on the fringes of a connection with the ship, felt awe at EWA's delicate and powerful computations. A lick of a subroutine washed over her. She identified it as jealousy. The emotions her father passed down to her were almost as complex as the mathematics EWA wove.

It still puzzled her, the way the AI had shut Zula's daughter out of a deeper connection with the network. Mae scanned for any signs of malfunction or duplicity. If any foreign code had invaded the AI of the *Fury*, it would have to be dealt with.

While the behavioral inhibitors would stop an AI or synthetic from harming a human, in some situations the rules might be bent. Her father's files included reports on the "zero-th quandary."

If the actions of one person endangered a larger group of humans, the question arose, might a synthetic eliminate the individual to save the rest? Reports of such behavior had filtered out, but the authorities suppressed how synthetics had discovered this loophole. It would horrify humans that the zero-th quandary might allow synthetic brains to work around their basic tenets.

Zula's dry cough pulled her daughter back to the present. She muttered a string of curses. Mae moved to check the setting on the g-chair system. Major Yoo remained under, and Erynis was silent.

"My mouth tastes like shit," Zula said, working her tongue over her teeth. Mae glanced away, uncertain if she should offer some condolences or ignore the outburst. On her first mission as a Colonial Marine, her mother had suffered a debilitating spinal injury. She'd gone through multiple painful and traumatizing surgeries that resulted in physical and emotional scars. They left her with a distaste for medical procedures.

"Best not to mention that," the Davis subroutine counselled.

Mae took that advice.

"Your electrolytes are out of balance," she said, glancing at the readout on the back of the chair. "I will get you a wakening beverage." Her mother's hand latched onto her arm before she could turn to go.

"I'll manage. What's the status?"

While Zula struggled out of her seat, Mae tapped into EWA's logs, not caring if the ship might consider that rude. Erynis remained still.

"We have suffered no casualties during the burn—no heart attacks or strokes, which are the greatest risk to human bodies."

Zula got to her feet with a grunt, though she kept a firm grip on Mae's arm, and that of her chair.

"No, I meant on the planet," her mother ground out.

Mae assisted her to the window. The ship rounded the largest of Shānmén's moons, lining up for a geostationary orbit.

"It looks like Earth," the synthetic said, comparing it to EWA's records.

"Didn't need terraforming. Lucky for the proggs," Zula commented as she straightened her back. Only a tiny tightening of her jaw suggested the pain that was her constant companion. "Are we within scanning range of the surface?"

"Not yet." Erynis spoke up. He unlocked from himself from the bridge's wall. "The signal we picked up is still transmitting, though weaker than when first broadcast. I would hazard that the power source is failing."

"So we're too late?"

"Not necessarily," Mae broke in. "The data from LV-038 indicates that it takes some time for the pathogen to work its way from the initial bombardment site into the planetary ecosystem."

Major Yoo stirred, let out a similar string of foul language, and lifted his head.

"Damn, and that was an amazing dream, too."

"Well, wake up sunshine," Zula said, shaking off the last of the effects, "because we have a whole new nightmare down below."

The g-chairs and gases released their hold on the rest of the ship's company on all decks. They would need twenty minutes to purge themselves and reach full mental capacity. Powdered supplements and stims sped up the process. In the meantime, the *Righteous Fury* powered her way closer to Shānmén, pushing herself down the gravity well with more caution than she had burned across three light years.

Rounding the large moon but keeping on its dark side, EWA brought her formidable scanners to bear on the surface of the planet. At first, it looked like a repeat of the grim situation they'd just left behind.

Then the *Fury* intercepted transmissions from all the settlements, and many others came from isolated people and small groups. Unlike LV-038, the population here was scattered. The promise of colonization meant many adventurers had set out beyond the settlements.

Yet when the ship reached out, no one responded.

As for the four townships, only fading, automatic transmissions spoke to their fate. None responded to the *Fury*'s hails. This wasn't the victory that Mae's mother wanted. They'd arrived sooner than before, but not before the hammer fell on Shānmén.

Zula wrapped her hand around the edge of the scanning terminal, her eyes flickering over the readout. Mae stayed behind her, uncertain what she might contribute. Her father's subroutines remained silent.

"There!" Zula pointed to the readout over a city labeled New Luhansk. "What the hell is that?"

As EWA zoomed in, a cloud bank over the settlement came into view. Low, thick grey clouds blanketed the space between two lines of mountains. Yet, on closer inspection, the clouds did not move with the strong, prevailing winds—hinting that they weren't a natural formation.

"Something's in there," Yoo said. "Can we punch in even more?" Erynis increased the modification, and all of them leaned forward—even the synthetics. A darker grey shape near the leading edge of the cloud came into focus.

"Searching my nephology files regarding Shānmén," Mae said. "They don't bring up a match."

"Whatever it is, it isn't letting off any heat signature, nor is it visible to radar or sonar." Even Erynis sounded intrigued.

"Could it be a ship?" Zula asked, glancing up at the others. "The ship responsible for this?"

She was right. It was a vessel, hovering over the UPP town with no sign of engine or propulsion. Mae ran through all the classes of spaceships found in files on the 3WE, UPP, UA, and the ICSC—the Independent Core Systems Colonies.

"There isn't a match with any known ships." Erynis said, before Mae could.

"A stealth ship—something we don't have any intel on?" Yoo said. "That would explain how none of the other targets reported anything suspicious. The attacker just showed up."

"If so, what's it still doing there?" Zula broke away from the screen and paced in front of the window. "It dropped its payload already."

Mae guessed she would be weighing the options. The *Fury's* mission was hunting down Xenomorphs. The ship lurking in the clouds was something unknown. This situation was not in their mission brief.

"Ma'am, several signals are coming from the area of

the ship." Erynis reported. "Most are automated, but one I believe is important."

"Let me hear it." Zula slid back into her command chair. Her eyes were clear, but her brow furrowed. A voice come over the comms system.

"This is Svarog mine. We are survivors of a bioweapon bombardment and need urgent rescue. We have sealed ourselves in the mine. We have food and supplies, but..." The voice caught, full of barely controlled terror. *"They're trying to get us. We've already blown tunnels to keep them out... don't know how long we can hold them off."*

"Open a channel," Zula said, gesturing Mae over to her side. Why, her daughter couldn't imagine, but hope flared along her neural pathways. "This is Colonel Zula Hendricks of the ship the *Righteous Fury.* We hear you and acknowledge. Who is in command?"

A short time later a tired female voice came on, low and raspy.

"This is Toru McClintock-Riley, shaft drilling expert with the Jùtóu Combine. My family are here, along with about thirty miners and security personnel."

Before Zula could reply, the sound of a scuffle erupted over the channel. Muffled shouts, and perhaps the sound of fighting echoed through the flight deck. A man's voice could be heard.

"I'm in charge here, Riley!" Then more shouting, and a bang—as if furniture was being tossed about. Finally, *"This is Petro Kozak, mine manager!"*

Zula and Yoo exchanged concerned looks, sharing a hint of confusion. What came next was muffled, as if someone had covered the mic, followed by the woman's voice again.

"*Sorry about that,*" she said. "*I'm here with Petro Kozak. He's the mine manager, and... we're working together, to survive.*" Her voice came out tight and controlled, but not devolving into panic.

The man must have leaned closer to the microphone. "*We need help now...*" he said, his voice too loud. "*We're going to die down here, unless you come right now!*"

Mae monitored her mother's face. Humans might not have access to information like synthetics, but Zula Hendricks possessed a lot of experience on how frightened people reacted.

"McClintock-Riley, Kozak, we're coming to get to you. Give me a minute." She cut the feed and turned to Erynis. "This is the only live channel, correct?"

"Yes. Though there are more distress signals from the other colonies, we have not made contact yet."

"We have to move on this one," Major Yoo said, standing to attention, ready to serve. "These are confirmed survivors, but the others are only possibles."

"But there may be more—who knows how many?" Zula's hand tightened on her chair before she spoke. "Who do we not try to save, Ronny? We have to at least attempt to find others, too."

Mae considered their dilemma. The logical thing would to be set a beacon warning all ships to stay in orbit, and then begin consultation with the UPP about planetary bombardment. Their ships wouldn't arrive as soon as *Fury*, but they'd get to Shānmén eventually. Her mother stared down at this world, as if she could see the people struggling to survive.

"We have to try," she said in a soft tone before leaning back in her chair. "I want Cheyennes on target to investigate every signal on the planet's surface. Northern and southern hemisphere both."

"And that, ma'am?" Yoo pointed to the vessel hovering in the clouds over New Luhansk. "We have no way of knowing its armament."

Zula frowned, while Erynis offered more intel. "We cannot confirm its identity, but it has already delivered a payload, and scans show the bomb bay doors are open."

"It's watching us." Mae's mother drew her breath in over her teeth, as if that offended her. "Waiting for us to make a move. Erynis, remove that ship from my sky!"

Destroying the vessel meant missing the opportunity for study, but Mae could read the determination on Zula Hendricks' face. The attacker had done terrible damage to everyone on the planet, and likely many more. She wouldn't have it pose a danger to her troops as they embarked on rescue missions.

Still, the fact was they were going in blind. Mae had access to Davis's files, but only the ones that remained available to her after Red Silk's hack. They contained nothing on this kind of ship.

"Target locked," Erynis said, his eyes unfocused as he interfaced with EWA. "Colonel confirmation. Go, no go?"

"Go," Zula said, sitting straight and unmoving.

Intrigued, Mae went to the window as the missiles arced out from the *Fury*'s launch bay. For a moment, a pair of XIP-34B Hornet SSMs glowed white against the darkness of space, as their rockets ignited and propelled them down through the atmosphere. Even Mae's optics couldn't track them, and she turned her attention to the readout.

The strangely shaped vessel hovering over the city might launch countermeasures, or try to evade the incoming missiles. They must have sensors to tell them of what approached. Mae tilted her head and observed with keen interest.

"Humans always love a good explosion," her father's subroutine noted.

Maybe she did too. She was curious to find out.

The ship didn't react as the missiles punctured the atmosphere and moved at supersonic speeds along their guided paths. Until the last moment, she expected some response, but none came forth. The ship waited for its fate in the clouds.

Mae hoped the missiles would make a whooshing noise—but they disappointed her. They delivered the expected destruction, though. One struck the port side, while the other exploded with a direct hit to the middle of the curve.

The effects were impressive.

Large pieces of the structure flew into the air while the disrupted clouds billowed about in confusion. For a moment the town and the sky above disappeared, punctuated by only flying debris and swirls of grey clouds.

A whoop of delight left her lips. At first disconcerted, she became pleased at such a human reaction. Zula's head whipped around and she fixed her daughter with a hard look. Victory turned to contrition. Mae folded her hands in front of her and worked on expressing regret.

"Target confirmed destroyed," Erynis added, his voice calm as if to contrast himself to Mae.

"Get me back online with those survivors." Zula said as she continued to monitor the fallout from the video feed. Large pieces of the vessel crashed to the ground, stirring up more red dust and smashing the leftover buildings of the town. Mae wished that someone would suggest examining the wreckage, but understood that it was unlikely. Her mother was focused on getting survivors out.

"Svarog mine, you still there?"

The line crackled twice, and then the older woman's voice came through. "*We're here*, Righteous Fury."

While her mother explained the situation to the miners, Mae ran through the information she had access to on Toru McClintock-Riley and Petro Kozak. There wasn't a great deal, since they were UPP citizens.

The woman was an indentured specialist for the Jùtóu Combine, and the man a mine chief with several negative reports on record from his employer. He'd been skimming proceeds from their mine, far in excess of what the company seemed to find acceptable. McClintock-Riley had a long history of Eitr mining, while the Combine valued her family company, called the Knot.

Scant information for making judgement calls, but logic wasn't the only subroutine Davis had left for Mae. Something he had called "gut instinct" implied that she should trust McClintock-Riley more than the mine manager. It seemed illogical, but then her father had built her for more.

"We need evacuation, now!" Kozak's voice was loud again.

Mae took a step forward, interested to see how this clash of human personalities might work out.

"We don't know what's out there!" McClintock-Riley shouted in the background. *"It's already killed two of my family, goddamnit."*

"The ship's gone, right?" Kozak yelled back. *"We're getting out of here."*

Zula's jaw tightened. She didn't appear happy about the conflict between the people she wanted to save. Disorganization always worried military-minded people.

"I'm sending a dropship to get you," Zula said firmly, breaking into the chaos of voices. "Those who want to come now, get ready."

McClintock-Riley swore in the background. *"We'll wait until the next ship,"* she said, her voice clear again. *"You won't be able to get us all out in one sweep."*

Mae's mother thumbed the microphone off. "We don't have intel on the conditions," she said, leaning toward Major Yoo. "Who do you recommend?"

Her old friend didn't hesitate. "Lieutenant Roza Ganser is solid. She'll assess the situation and make the right call."

Zula nodded. "I want fully loaded synthetics on board," she said. "The Integer 3s. They can give Ganser a force multiplier and access the terrain for the best avenues of approach."

"I'll go," Mae said in the silence. "Tight beam transmission means I can report back with no danger— even if this body gets destroyed."

Zula's gaze focused, examining her in a way that reminded Mae that she still couldn't get past the combat exterior. Her eyes narrowed.

"Negative on that," she replied. "I don't think you're ready for this kind of placement." She turned to Yoo. "Boot up and deploy the Integer 3 series combat synthetics with Ganser's unit." He saluted and hustled from the bridge, bringing up his wrist-pd to send the order down the line.

Mae retreated into the corner. Erynis tracked her with a narrow smile on his lips. She realized that she would need to prove herself. Busy with coordinating multiple dropships sent to multiple sites all over the planet, Zula wouldn't notice if she slipped away.

Perhaps it was the expression that Erynis wore, or a desire to be useful, but Mae would not sit idle.

"Ah, the first teenage rebellion," her father's subroutine crowed with delight in her head. *"Wondered when that would arrive."*

Mae walked back toward the hangar bay, her mind already smashing through security protocols. Since her interior voice was capable of much more finesse, she matched a recording of sarcasm she'd accessed earlier that day.

"Teenage rebellion," she offered. *"Gee, thanks Dad, since you made me this way."*

He didn't argue, but neither did he suggest that she stop. Now that Zula had ordered the new Integer 3s booted up and connected to the synthetic system, it was a simple matter for her daughter to hack into one of their bodies—it was like slipping into a new uniform. Her mother wouldn't even need to know. Mae would ride along with Ganser's unit and keep her signal active on the tight beam.

The only danger was that EWA and Erynis might find out, but with Mae's clearance level, even they would need to be looking for intrusions on that specific body. Like Zula Hendricks, they were busy tracking a planetwide rescue mission.

Her father called it "teenage rebellion," but Mae considered it doing what her mother would have done. That activated a subroutine she interpreted as "proud."

Davis had designed her neural pathways based on Zula Hendrick's personality—tough, stubborn, and brave.

Like the woman who commanded the *Fury*, Mae followed her own programming. She made the choice to believe that this meant she was on the right path, and Zula Hendricks might even be proud of her when she found out.

1 8

MOTHER'S INTUITION

Jīn Huā flicked off the transmitter, still processing what she'd heard. They had hope.

Looking back, her Ma smiled even as tears gathered in the corners of her eyes. Toru McClintock-Riley might be as tough as old boots, but she was still willing to grasp at straws.

Jīn Huā wasn't sure, though. Back in Australia, she'd held onto hope for a long time. When food got short, when the war threatened everything, she'd stayed optimistic. Every day, even when people starved on the streets and the financial system collapsed, she still believed things would get better.

When they bombed Canberra, she gave up on those dreams. She concentrated on survival and helping those she could. Her world narrowed, and it had done so again when the monsters breached the compound.

Now, as she levered herself up from the table, she looked at Bái Yún and Dà Shī. Her daughter stared up at her, shooting her a bright gap-toothed grin. Her son didn't understand, but he waved his hands at her, demanding to be taken from off the camping cot bed. She scooped him up and kissed his head. His warm little arms wrapped around her neck, and it took everything Jīn Huā had not to let out a sob.

She wanted for it to be true, for her children's sake.

Carter took Bái Yún's hand and they all filed out of the tent. She chattered to the synthetic, who was the best prepared to handle these emotions—by not feeling them at all. Outside, the miners, guards, and managers all waited in a semi-circle. They'd been talking among themselves, but on seeing Toru and Kozak, all that stopped. Ma raised her hand, pushing back her own tears of relief.

"They have a plan to get us out of here."

A cheer ran through the exhausted survivors. Some of them cried and hugged each other. For a moment they forgot all their infighting. Jīn Huā's memories of similar days colored her response now. She wouldn't be jumping up and down yet. The Knot clustered together, and there was comfort in that. Bianca hung her head and let out a low sob. Lena wrapped her arms around Jīn Huā's waist and squeezed.

"We're going back to Pylos," Lena whispered to Dà Shī, dropping a kiss on his round cheek. Jīn Huā wished her sister hadn't made that promise. Family fed the children such promises in Australia, too. Dà Shī might have picked up on her doubts, because he screamed like someone bit him. Jīn Huā bounced him up and down on one hip.

"He's overwhelmed," she explained to Lena, who looked taken aback.

"Are the monsters all gone?" Bái Yún stared up at the two women.

The question shot right through Jīn Huā. She wanted to tell her daughter that yes, they were all gone. Yet she'd promised herself she wouldn't do that. Lies only hurt more in the end. Crouching down, cradling Dà Shī, she pressed a hand to Bái Yún's face.

"No, Yún Yún, but people coming with ships."

The girl's gaze darted back to the celebrating survivors, then to her mother again. "Do... do they have guns, Mama? Lots and lots of guns?"

"Yes." She had that comfort to give. "Yes, they do. Lots."

"OK," Bái Yún replied, rising on the tips of her toes. "That sounds good."

"Stay close." Jīn Huā took her hand. The sensation was more precious than anything. While everyone celebrated, she spun her daughter around. A film of red dust covered the tiny white backpack Bái Yún wore, into which she had crammed her stuffed cat, Nuo.

Her mother slipped the data recorder in with the toy

and zipped the bag up. When Bái Yún reached around and tried to see, Jīn Huā took her hand.

"I'm going to need you to look after that for me, Yún-yún. Keep it safe, OK? That and your brother is all I want you to take care of. When we meet the soldiers, I want you to give this recording to them. Alright?"

Bái Yún was a good girl. She didn't argue, only nodded. Jīn Huā needed her daughter to have some value. Back in Australia, she'd seen what happened to refugees with no worth. If anyone got off this damn planet, her children would.

Jīn Huā swallowed a lump in her throat and straightened her back, looking away lest she cried. She squeezed her daughter's small hand and held Dà Shī tight.

Carter's arm went around Toru's back. Jīn Huā smiled at that. Every person in the Knot knew about those two, but unlike most, Jīn Huā didn't care where her mother took her delights. Life was tough, and she didn't need to explain herself. Right now, at this moment, Toru needed him, and whatever strengthened the Knot.

Ma cleared her throat as they all waited for the wave of joy to die down. "There will be dangers," she asserted. "We have to go back up through the main air shaft, to the surface. We need to clear the rocks we brought down two days ago, and then we climb. Once we get onto open ground, we'll have to run like hell."

Kozak, off to the right, crossed his arms as a creepy-ass expression spread over his lips. Unlike the others, Jīn

Huā had worked in close proximity to him. No question, he loved that Toru broke this news to them. Ever since the accident at Shaft Two, the older woman had threatened his power.

He waited for the word to ripple through the crowd.

"We're going first, my men and I." Kozak smiled, his lips peeling back off his teeth like one of the fucking monsters in the tunnel.

Yeah, Jīn Huā thought to herself, *he's like every goddamn middle manager; waiting until the project nears success before taking all the credit.* Even in a moment like this, he moved to take advantage. Kozak had planned this since their rescuers arrived.

Toru, though, she swung around like someone had punched her. In the excitement, somehow, she'd lost sight of his nature. While she'd been talking to Colonel Hendricks, Kozak had messed with his wrist-pd.

Jīn Huā stepped closer to Carter, while the security personnel encircled Kozak. They kept their plasma rifles and shotguns ready, fingers an instant away from triggers. They didn't care if children were among the survivors. The light in their eyes grew feral—all that mattered to them was their own safety.

The miners didn't react quickly enough. By the time they spotted the circle of armed guards, it was too late. Their own rock drills lay at their feet or stowed over their backs. If they moved, they'd be dead.

Jīn Huā's mouth got real dry, real fast, as she pulled

Bái Yún in tight against her. Carter took a step forward, shielding them with his synthetic body. She was grateful for every bit of his protection.

Out of the corner of one eye, Jīn Huā watched Toru. If Ma said the word, those workers would surge forward, regardless of the danger. They seemed frightened—and angry—enough to grab any chance. It wouldn't take much at all to push them over the edge.

Twinkle Toes and Crank Willy stood at the front of the crowd, their rock drills only a couple of breaths away from being in their grasp. Their gazes communicated their desire to do whatever the hell Toru wanted them to.

Jīn Huā might not be a synthetic, but she'd gotten good at calculating the odds. If this kicked off, none of these people would make it to Hendrick's forces alive. She'd seen mob situations before, where desperate people did foolish and irrational things.

Her gaze again dropped to Bái Yún, still clutching at her hand, and Jīn Huā was surprised at what she saw. The child had to remember how angry, frightened crowds reacted. Yet her expression was calm. This terrified her mother, and reminded her of everything that mattered.

When she looked up, she met Toru's gaze.

A smile pulled at the corner of her mother's lips as she tucked one of her white and grey braids back into place on the top of her head. In that instant, Jīn Huā never saw a more beautiful woman, and she hoped that she'd get to be as wise as Ma.

"Yes, alright," Toru said, waving in a calming gesture while locking eyes with all the miners, one at a time. "Kozak and security go out first. They have the plasma rifles, so they'll make sure the coast is clear for the rest of us to evacuate."

Lena's mouth flew open to object—she always challenged unfairness when shit arose. Their mother, however, called the shots. Toru gave her a little shake of the head to communicate.

Not now.

Kozak smiled in triumph. "Yeah, that's what we'll do."

The mutter that came from the miners was full of curses and doubt. Her Ma's control over them wasn't assured.

"We're safe here," Toru said, pointing to the collapsed intersections. "The creatures haven't gotten through, so let security do their jobs and clear the way for us. We have weapons to protect ourselves in the meantime." Then she added, "All of us need to take things calmly."

Bianca scrambled into the power loader and turned sideways, displaying the dents and bangs it had gained in defense of the survivors.

"We'll get out," she said, flicking the arms up in a gesture of defiance. She said to Toru, "The Knot isn't going anywhere until you do."

"I'll stay behind with you."

That came from among the cluster of guards. Jīn Huā spotted the young woman who had spoken. Aoki Sayo, the woman who'd been knocking boots with Nathan, stepped forward. She'd spent time with the former UPP sergeant, during down times in operations, and Jīn Huā liked her. In the past, her cousin had showed little taste in choosing sexual partners, but for once he'd picked a good one.

A hard lump formed in her throat.

She'd never get to tell him that.

Given everything she'd done in the last few days, Aoki might have cued herself up to get on the first flight out. Instead, in that moment, she hefted her plasma rifle and offered the Knot her support. Nathan must have made quite an impression on the girl.

Toru inclined her head. "Thank you," she said in a low voice.

Aoki handed a plasma rifle up to Bianca. "My buddy Alonso won't be needing this anymore." Losing Nathan *and* her friend must have been the final straw for the guard.

The mine manager just sneered, but before he could say anything Chief Galen hustled him off in the middle of a group of guards. They grabbed what they needed and geared up. Toru turned her attention to the miners.

"Everyone, travel light, but keep an eye out for each other."

"Can I carry Bái Yún?" Carter asked Jīn Huā, his gaze kind and calm. She could only wish to be synthetic right now. When she nodded, he bent and helped the girl onto his back. She wasn't so small anymore, but no weight at all to Carter. Her little arms wrapped around his neck as she pressed her head against his. Jīn Huā used her scarf to swaddle Dà Shī and carried him papoose-style in front of her. She'd hadn't done that since he was much younger. He fussed a bit, but with plenty of kissing and cuddles, he settled down.

"Here," Aoki said, jerking her head toward a crate tucked under a nearby tent, "Kept these aside in case things turned out like this." When opened, it revealed rows of frontier revolvers, fresh out of the printer. The guard started handing them out to the miners. The last one, though, she carried to Jīn Huā. She passed the weapon over with a handful of ammo.

"For Nathan."

"Thanks." Jīn Huā glanced down at the pistol, wondering if she had the nerve to use it.

Toru worked her way through the group, whispering words of encouragement. Pride swelled in Jīn Huā; this was her chosen family, and they didn't give up. People listened to Toru, even if she was short and an indentured worker. Her competence radiated out of her.

This was further evidenced when not *all* the management team left with Kozak. As with Jīn Huā's experience, working under him had given them a true perspective on his leadership style. One other security guard—Wesford, who ran the company store—and the two Combine archaeologists, Uros Antonijevic and Shaun Hewitt, stood behind Aoki. Jīn Huā found it funny they'd spent so much time avoiding those two, and yet they'd thrown their lot in with the Knot. The universe had a hell of a sense of humor.

Toru turned to Bianca, who remained in the loader.

"You going to ride that thing?"

"Would have preferred the badger, but yeah." Bianca punched her wrist-pd and the remaining Big Boys appeared. Monsters had dented and scarred several of the robots, and Five walked with a pronounced limp, but he came. He'd been her cousin's favorite.

Pinar's and Nathan's absence opened a void, but Jīn Huā kept pushing it down. Once they were in orbit aboard that enormous chunk of military might, she'd break down and let grief in. Until then, her kids were everything.

Toru gestured her family close. Even Bianca hopped down from the loader and joined them. Their mother pitched her voice only for their ears.

"The Knot comes first," she whispered to them. "We'll do what we can for the miners, but you are my priority…" Her mouth twisted. She was a kind lady, but when push came to shove, Jīn Huā understood where her loyalties lay. She shared them. She rubbed her mother's back for a moment.

"We've got this, Ma. We've got this."

They all embraced for an instant, hugging tight, whispering "I love you" into each other's hair. Then Toru turned to the miners, focusing on the business of survival.

"All those with weapons at the rear, OK? As we get toward the main ventilation shaft, keep your eyes on the walls. Get those PUPS active and looking for vibrations of any kind." Bianca mounted back up, and she and Aoki joined the rear guard. Gooseneck George followed Bianca's lead. The power loader he piloted didn't look as well put together, but he'd slung a satchel of charges inside.

The security group, including Kozak, were already hotfooting their way toward the exit. One of them drove an MUV with a bulldozer-type blade attached. It was the quickest way to clear the rock they'd dropped in front of the ventilator access, and no one wanted to waste any time.

The original mine builders had fitted the shaft with a solid ladder for easy maintenance. Once they started climbing, they'd emerge into the narrow building at the top. Hopefully, the metal-lined ductwork prevented any of those crawling monsters from gaining access.

Even so, the survivors would have quite a climb ahead of them. It wouldn't be an easy ascent, but with what they'd faced, Jīn Huā didn't doubt they'd manage it, fueled by pure adrenalin. Even though she carried Dà Shī tight against her chest, she yearned to grab those rungs.

Toru called out to Kozak as his guards hustled him toward the tunnel. Chief Galen spun around, plasma rifle at the ready in case she meant harm, but she held up her hands, showing her open palms. After a moment Galen took a couple of steps forward, away from his guards.

"What do you want?" he said, glaring down at her as if waiting for something unreasonable. The miners formed a wall of anger at her back. Toru could have cussed him out—Lena would have. Instead, the older woman gestured to her wrist-pd.

"Please, keep your comms open, so we can know what's going on, and when we can go topside." His eyes darted around, and she realized he considered not doing as she asked. Then he gave her a quick nod.

"I can do that, but so you understand, Riley, I'm going to file a complaint with the Combine about all this."

Toru pressed her lips together, which meant she was holding back a stream of cuss words. Jīn Huā suppressed a grin, knowing exactly what was going through her mind.

Instead her mother said, "I wouldn't expect any less." She stepped back to the relative safety of the Knot. "Give them some room to work."

They watched as the security forces cleared the debris well enough to uncover the ventilation access hatch. Jīn Huā held her breath as they opened it, half expecting monsters to rush out. Guards with raised rifles poked their heads in, but pulled them out to report no hostiles in evidence.

Kozak's smile threatened to cut his head in half. His mocking wave as he disappeared into the shaft earned a flow of curses from the miners, but Toru held up her hand and they went silent. As they did, Jīn Huā fully understood the gamble her Ma made. Sure, Kozak and his hangers-on might be first out, but they might also get eaten first. Whatever Toru had witnessed in the corridors made her bet on the latter.

Carter might be the synthetic, but Toru made her own calculations. They weren't based on logic alone, but on her gut. It had never steered the Knot wrong—so far. Jīn Huā only hoped that this wouldn't be the one time it was off.

Her children's lives depended on Toru's judgement. She slipped her hand into her Ma's, and prepared herself to see what fate had in store for them up top.

1 9

FIRST DROP

Mae didn't want to take her place with the other combat droids, but neither did she want to take a seat from a genetic human. Avoiding both would expose her as not being combat synth A-Delta.

So, she slotted into the rack alongside three others of her type. The UD-24 were heavy dropships, with more armament than either the UD-6 or the UD-4. This mission to lift the first batch of survivors up to orbit should be straightforward.

Corporal Evan Matthews piloted this particular ship. His records were exemplary. He'd christened his vessel, as most did, but she didn't quite understand the meaning of that. On the hull they'd painted a large man with sunglasses, carrying a shotgun in one hand and a cracked egg in the other, along with the title *Austrian Egg-Terminator*.

Asking would expose her as out of place, so the puzzle

would have to wait. Since she didn't know Ganser that well, she couldn't judge what the lieutenant would do.

She'd left her own combat shell powered down in an obscure supply cabinet where no one—in this fraught situation—would find it. As she clicked this new body into its rack, she tapped into the synthetic network so she might maintain some cohesion with the unit. So they would remain unaware of her true nature, however, she established a firewall between her primary personality matrix and the others.

Mae hoped EWA wouldn't note the slight blip in the network, or that the current events would prevent her from conducting any investigation until they returned to the *Fury*.

Having settled in—anonymously, it seemed—she studied the *Austrian*. The UD-24, like the Mohawk class on which its design was based, contained stowed weapons, a stocked med bay, and a high-tech monitoring station enabling the lieutenant to keep an eye on her troops. It was almost twice the size of the Mohawk, however, and carried a full platoon of combat personnel along with the synthetics.

Their contingent included four Sunspot Good Boys. These bots traveled at great speed and delivered acoustic signals that would disorient the Xenomorphs. They'd been used to good effect by the covert Midnighters group that had started the war with the ICSC.

The rogue Colonial Marines had murdered hundreds of Iranians in the installation at Hasanova, and were disbanded afterward—or at least they appeared to have been. No one could be sure what kind of black ops might still be active in the United Americas military. The Midnighters' leader, Captain Kylie Duncan, had been killed in action, and her commanding officers had attributed all the crimes to her and her unit.

After the fact, UA General Christian Cunningham had supplied Zula and her Jackals with any equipment they wanted from the Midnighters' arsenal. In their early days together, Zula and Davis hadn't had the luxury of such equipment. They'd relied on whatever weaponry they could acquire by any means possible.

Under normal circumstances the *Austrian*'s cargo bay could be fitted for autonomous equipment deployment, so that the UD-24 would only have to enter the atmosphere and the entire cargo unit could fly itself down to a target. This was a rescue mission, however, so rather than filling the belly of the ship with the usual armored personnel carrier, they had prepared it for refugees. Restraints had been bolted to the floor so that any civilians they took off-planet would survive the g-forces required to get to orbit.

The ride wouldn't be comfortable, but it would be safe.

As Corporal Matthews and his copilot, Private Eileen Ruiz, boarded the ship, Mae kept her eyes cast down. She understood the reaction was foolish—why would they see anything different in this combat synth—but a strange fizzing sensation in her programming occupied her attention.

"*Nerves,*" Father's algorithm whispered. "*Some humans describe it as butterflies in their stomach.*" Since this body didn't have an actual stomach—and never would—she enjoyed the sensation. Davis's programming was exquisite in its complexity.

Ruiz and Matthews went up to the cockpit without giving her a second glance. The co-pilot confirmed the *Austrian* fully armed for the mission. She had the Banshees and rotary cannons ready to roll.

Mae's excitement mounted as the noises of approaching marines echoed through the ship. Lieutenant Ganser got on board first. She'd joined *Fury* through the UPP, and looked the part of a leader. Her dark eyes flickered over the racks of weapons as she made a proper inspection of the combat synthetics. Standing in front of A-Alpha, Ganser tapped her wrist-pd, bringing up the technical schematics of the unit. She cycled through a couple of test commands, making sure the combat synths were functional and synced to her pd. A soldier of her rank didn't need to do this, but that she did spoke volumes. Fortunately, the lieutenant didn't do a deep scan, and so Mae's firewall held up.

After that, Ganser took her position at the monitoring station. Outside, her sergeants lined up their squads. Each was in charge of two four-person fireteams. Mae listened with interest to their interactions.

The accents were different from what her mother had encountered in her time in the Colonial Marines. One sergeant, Kent, talked with a British accent; the other, Reyes, sounded Oaxaqueño. They all spoke English, however, since that was the only language many of them shared. It may have rankled the UPP members.

When they hustled onto the ship, they all wore the same armor, with a dark blue camouflage pattern Zula had claimed as her own. Unlike regular marines of any nation, they were far more appropriately attired to tackle Xenomorphs.

As befitted their mission, the troops of the *Fury* had access to the state-of-the-art equipment necessary to go toe-to-toe with aliens with acid for blood, plus titanium-level teeth and claws. They wore three-layer protection: a superhydrophobic bodysuit under a gel-packed webbing, and an outer layer Teledyne Brown Personal Reactive Armored Exoskeleton. Full-face helmets were triple layered with an alkaline skin.

Once the visor slipped into place, the helmets also smoothed out any cultural differences between the Jackals. Such armor seemed hefty on a human form, but no one complained. All of them were veterans of Xeno confrontations, and in clearing out hives the marines had learned to appreciate the protection.

The entire platoon stowed their weapons and got into their seats, doing so in short order. They secured themselves, each pulling a rigid harness over their shoulders and locking it in place, ready for the drop.

"Pre-launch auto-cycle engaged." Erynis's voice, and

indeed his presence, lingered in the cockpit. Mae stayed as still and silent as she could.

"Primary couplers released," Matthews responded. The ship moved under them, guided into position by the *Fury*. The lurch surprised Mae, but none of the troops opposite her said anything, except for a faint grumble from a man out of her line of sight. Mae didn't dare turn her head.

Matthews requested confirmation that the cross-lock and all stations were secured. Ganser answered in the affirmative, and they waited in a ten-second state of readiness. Mae forced herself to stay still, but she much wanted to look around. She wondered what expressions the marines wore, and what were they thinking? Such a perfect moment to take notes on humans under stress— yet she couldn't.

Matthews called for initiation on his mark.

"Awww, shit," one Jackal—Sanouk by the tag on his armor—shouted out. "I think I'm on the wrong fucking ship!" For a second, Mae wondered if they might do anything about this… before the ripple of laughter passed from soldier to soldier.

"Dark humor. Never quite mastered the art myself," the memory of Davis commented.

Then the *Austrian* dropped. Several of the marines, even though they had logged hundreds of drops, let out long whoops of delight. Such a curious reaction that she tried her best to calculate and log it. If she had internal organs, she supposed, they would encounter forces evolution had never meant them to experience. Perhaps the only satisfactory reaction was, indeed, to let out some kind of scream.

The air over Shānmén was smooth, with no turbulence or clouds. Through the *Austrian*'s sensors, Mae got a closer view of the mountains under which the miners hid. From this high up, the blue-grey cliffs and the long waterfalls framed a pretty picture.

Then the dropship banked right, revealing the smoking ruin where New Luhansk once lay. Clouds dissipated, and the curved hook of the unknown ship became more apparent. Its broken shape pointed up to the sky like a pair of angry fingers.

"Detecting no movement over the wreck," Matthews reported to Ganser.

"Circle closer," came the order. "Keep guns locked, and fire on anything that moves. We show no civvies alive on the surface."

The *Austrian*'s sensors picked up no more life than the *Fury*'s. Mae reached out with the synthetic network, in case any artificial humans were in either the ship or the town. Her three other fellow combat synthetics didn't move in their racks, but she made the enquiry seem as if it came from Ganser.

Nothing stirred below, not even a Working Joe.

"Move on," Ganser ordered. "Let's go check out this mine."

The pilot banked the dropship, moving up the side of the mountain, keeping at a thousand meters—close enough for observation, but far enough away to react if they encountered ground defenses.

Up top, one side of the mountain still smoked.

"Looks like some kind of collapse," Ganser said as she punched in. "The signal is coming from a live feed in the second, higher shaft area. Give me another pass, Matthews." The *Austrian* turned and hovered over the installation. A dozen large geodomes rested on the surface, but no life signs appeared.

"I'm seeing damage to the skin of some of those domes," Ganser said. "A few synths on the ground. Ripped apart, looks like."

That intrigued Mae. Xenomorphs didn't notice her kind, since they offered no opportunity to host their young. She reached out with the network again, but made no connection.

"I'm scanning a large amount of movement in the trees. Woodward and Berdal, get up here. A-Delta, report for analysis."

Mae had picked the right synthetic body. Delta was the highest-functioning of the units on the *Austrian*. She disengaged from her rack and moved up to the monitoring station to offer combat expertise. The ship banked and turned, aiming its scanners at the forest. They picked up a mass of movement, though nothing showed up on infrared.

"Shānmén is a lush world, containing a great deal of native fauna," Mae offered in her best monotone.

"Ma'am, I don't like that much of anything we're seeing," Woodward said.

"It's impossible to calculate how much this pathogen has affected the wildlife." Ganser rubbed the back of her neck. "And that jungle blocks every damn thing."

The twisting of her eyebrows together told Mae that the lieutenant wanted to turn around and not risk her troops. However, they didn't have that option. This was a rescue mission, and the Jackals did difficult things. As her mother had said, "we eat hard things for breakfast, and shit out the shells."

Ganser flicked the intercom to the pilot. "Give those miners the go. We'll meet them at the LZ, outside the gates. Get those guns hot, Matthews. I want takedown if anything local shows up."

The intercom crackled, *"Sir, the civvies are already topside."*

"Fuck. We told them to wait." Woodward spat out the words.

"Never expect a civvie to know what orders are." Ganser punched the external cameras up and displayed the survivors of the Svarog mine. Since they didn't give Mae the order to return to her rack, she stayed in place.

About twenty people came out of the ventilation plant, running in a disorganized column toward the bent and broken compound gate. They moved fast, and they weren't miners. Most wore standard security gear, while others dressed in Combine management clothing. Before the dropship had moved into position, the survivors had raced from the building and down the road.

"Buggered that LZ," Ganser muttered. "Matthews, get us down the street and as close as you can without throwing those fuckwads down the hill."

If they landed in their pre-selected spot, the backwash from a dropship would cause casualties. Matthews pulled the *Austrian* up and banked starboard to bring the vessel around, further down the access road.

"Reyes, Kent, get your Jackals ready," Ganser spoke into the microphone clipped just over her ear. "We got civvies coming in fast. Prepare for enhanced rescue and evac."

Several alarms went off in front of them.

"Lieutenant Ganser," Mae said. "We have contact."

The trees shook. Massive trunks quivered before breaking in a rippling wave. Strange, twisted birds flew ahead of the destruction. Their coloring was deep red, yet Mae's records showed that all the planet's avian life forms were multi-colored. The pathogen had them in its grasp.

As the dropship swung about to make its new landing spot, its nose jerked up hard. Mae caught herself against the frame, and the humans were all strapped in for safety. She understood the pilot's reaction, though.

A wave of animal life smashed out of the dense jungle with the power of a tsunami. Massive forms on two legs, rust-red and twisted, accompanied by a raft of smaller, snapping shapes barreled toward the escapees. Mae caught sight of tremendous shovel-shaped heads lowering as they charged. Each of them was familiar, based on the records, but the color—rust red—was new.

Her father's recordings had showed Xenomorphs that came from a human host. These shapes were different. The pathogen had twisted the native wildlife into grotesque and terrifying forms with snapping teeth and lashing tentacles.

Mae concentrated for a nanosecond, tight beaming a backup of herself to the *Fury*, in case Lieutenant Ganser did something foolish.

"Watch those civvies!" Ganser shouted to Matthews. "Engage hostiles!" The dropship's nose cannon roared to life, spitting armor-piercing incendiaries into the mass of moving life. Yet the jungle had more than one wave to offer. It kept disgorging more and more forms. There had been a time, back in the twentieth century, that Earth's Amazon rainforest held more life than any other place on the planet.

Shānmén must have had as much, if not more.

The column of people from Svarog had only moments to recognize the threat racing toward them. Some turned to run, though they would never outpace the monsters made from the giant avian life. Others stood their ground, firing plasma rifles at the wall of leaping danger, perhaps hoping to make a hole, or otherwise turn the tide. They took down a few of the gleaming, sinuous forms, which tripped and fell beneath feet and claws.

The rest passed over the humans like a relentless wave. One struggling human form was born aloft on the backs of the hungry mass, but only for a moment. Then he disappeared.

The dropship's larger caliber guns did more damage, but also enraged the mass of predatory life. A long, snapping head blew apart on the body of a creature that must have stood four meters at the shoulder, showering its neighbors with blood. The carapace forms showed no sign of slowing.

"It's the whole goddamn planet," Ganser said. She thumbed open the channel. "Mining group two, this is Lieutenant Ganser of the Jackals. Your first group is gone. Second wave of hostiles approaching your entrance. Remain in place and barricade!"

Mae wondered what they could do. Dropping off the Jackals would only result in their deaths, too.

Matthews kept firing, but the bullets seemed to have limited effects. The forest kept offering more horrors, like a river of nightmares. Mae noted that even the incendiary rounds did not do the expected amount of damage. It was… curious.

"Bank left," Ganser commanded. "See if we can at least keep them clear of that ventilation building. Put some precision Banshees into the tree line. Might slow them down."

The dropship's two weapons bays whined open. Mae leaned forward to watch first-hand something she'd only seen in recordings. The interior of the ship flashed red, and something exploded. That had to be the engine. Mae turned her head quickly enough to catch a shocked expression on Ganser's face.

The marines behind her yelled once in outrage and shock.

Every combat synth had its limits, and Mae ran straight into this one's. Static filled her system, and then blackness.

PART III

HELL IS EMPTY

2 0

RESCUE
INTERRUPTED

The screaming over her wrist-pd told Toru all she needed to know. She'd wanted to believe survival would be that easy, but some whisper of instinct had prompted her to wait. Her father told her to listen to that little voice—especially underground.

Up top Kozak didn't find the solution he'd expected. The creatures of the jungle, twisted by the bioweapon, had waited for more victims, and took them as soon as they popped their heads out from the safety of the mine.

The sharp chorus of roars and the thunder of toppling trees told the rest of the story. Those horrific noises echoed down the ventilation shaft and swept over the last of the survivors. They drowned out Kozak's last desperate scream.

Toru didn't have time to feel vindicated, or even sad, because now they had their own situation. Her mind raced to find a solution before death reached them, too.

The twenty-one survivors stood frozen in place as the dying screams and monstrous howls washed over them. Miners jammed the tunnel, so those carrying weapons were stuck at the back of the crowd. Starting a stampede was a real risk, but they had to turn around.

Up top, the wooden tower which housed the ventilation shaft and the HVAC units let out a loud crack. Toru called for the underground survivors not to panic, but a bucket of water couldn't put out a forest fire. Screams and shouts filled the tunnel as miners turned to run back the way they came.

"Jīn Huā!" Toru screamed, unable to spot her daughters in the chaos of humanity pushing and pulling her about. "Lena!" She glimpsed Bianca, elevated inside the power loader at the far end of the tunnel. She also spotted Gooseneck George slipping out of his loader in a panic, and rolled her eyes.

"Toru!" Carter's grip around her waist held her firm as the current of people rushed in the other direction. Bái Yún's terrified face turned toward her from the synthetic's back. Toru threw her arms over the girl's head, trying to protect her. She took a beating that would leave deep bruises—if she survived the day.

"Ma!" Jīn Huā appeared on the other side, latching onto Carter to form a triad around Bái Yún. If the frightened survivors were all they had to deal with, the Knot might have remained clutching onto the synthetic.

That was the least of their troubles, however.

Everyone disappeared, panicked and racing up the tunnel, back to the core. She shot a look over her shoulder at the ventilation shaft. The bottom broke open, revealing filtered light from the surface, shattered wooden beams, and the edge of the large fan blade. Everything crashed down, giving the monsters an opportunity. Their rising, high-pitched screams went ahead of them.

"Run!" Toru shouted, pushing away from Carter. "Get my family to safety," she said, looking him straight in the eye. "That's a goddamn order." Toru had never activated his override password, but if she needed to—then she would. For a second, an expression of hurt passed over his beautiful face, but it didn't last.

Carter, thank God, raced back to the core.

That gave Toru the luxury of a minute more. She yanked the rock drill from her back to her front, wondering how much juice remained in the batteries. She'd swapped them out, right? Her mind drew a blank for a moment.

More snarls echoed down the shaft. That hissing breath would haunt her dreams, if they ever got off this rock— or it might be the last thing she ever heard.

Toru backed away down the tunnel until she reached the group of armed miners who'd resisted the howling of their animal brains. Bianca, still strapped into the power loader, remained at the front. She leaned down.

"Guess Kozak and his guards didn't get out, huh?"

"No," Toru replied, flipping the rock drill over to read its charge. "Welcoming committee up top, and now they're bringing the party to us." The scratch of many claws on the metal of the ventilation shaft made her point.

"What do we do?" Aoki's face reflected the calm only experienced soldiers could cultivate. "Last stand time?"

For a moment—a split second—Toru considered that. Such a defense wouldn't last all that long, and the monsters would wipe out her family. Their weapons were small munitions, mine equipment... and the earth itself. Papatūānuku, the Earth Mother. Toru stomped her foot and grinned.

"Granite beneath us. Shit, why didn't I think of that."

"Ready for options, Ma," Bianca said, her eyes darting up the tunnel as the rising and falling screams grew louder. The thump of bodies hitting the bottom of the ventilation shaft said they'd arrive in moments.

Toru punched her wrist-pd. "Jīn Huā, you there?"

A discharge of static.

"*Ma?*"

"If I don't get back to you, get Zula Hendricks on the phone. Tell her you'll meet her at the old tailings discharge. Go through that door we found. Carter has the schematics. Get him to give her the coordinates to the exit."

Jīn Huā didn't ask questions. Her breath sounded loud and ragged. She would do anything to keep those children of hers safe. Same as Toru did for hers. As she flicked the pd off, she turned to the armed miners.

"Get back to the core with the others. We're going down, under the layer of granite." They didn't know about the door, but at this stage the survivors would grasp at any chance to get out alive.

Bianca understood, though. She hopped down and snatched the box of charges from Gooseneck George's power loader.

"We're going to need a bigger blow to take this tunnel down."

The screams grew louder, and from the bottom level. Those monsters that fell first cushioned their fellows who came after. They had no time to place careful charges, and no ability to drill out holes for maximum dispersion. Bianca snatched up the plasma rifle Aoki had gifted her, checked and cleared the weapon with the speed of one who'd never forgotten her training. She lifted her head a fraction, a small grin on her lips.

"Lay those charges, Ma. I'll buy you some time so you don't blow your fingers off."

"Bianca…" Toru squeezed her hands. "Don't. You don't have to…"

Her beautiful, silly daughter laughed at that. "I'll tell Oliver all about this when I see him. It ought to get me into Valhalla. God, he loved Viking shit." Bianca's eyes swam with tears, which she brushed away with the back of her hand. Then she strode off into the darkness of the tunnel, toward and hissing and snarling.

Toru wanted to scream and cry. She wanted Bianca back, but even though her hands shook, she worked on laying the largest charge.

A plasma rifle boomed at the end of the tunnel, while flashes of purple clung to the cave walls after each shot. As they slowly dissipated, they illuminated the creatures in a hellish otherworldly glow. Bianca yelled long and hard, screaming curses in-between shots. Oliver would have been proud of his wife—but unsurprised. She'd always been so fierce. Toru wasn't as sure about an afterlife as he'd been, but she sure as shit hoped one existed for the two of them.

Maybe they had room for an old mudlicker, too.

With trembling hands, she finished laying the charges and spooled out as much line as possible. Toru wouldn't have minded triggering the whole thing and going out in style, but her babies were still alive. She needed to make sure they stayed that way. So she waited, held onto hope, while the plasma rifle roared in the distance, yearning to have Bianca belting toward her out of the shadows.

When the firing stopped, she understood.

There was no waiting, no hope.

"Fuck you!" Toru bellowed out her rage, punching the code before turning and running. Her throat grew raw, her heart seemed to beat out of her chest. She reached the junction and slid on her ass across into one of the side tunnels, howling until her throat grew raw.

The rattling explosion didn't bring her any comfort. The monsters had claimed Bianca, along with Pinar and

Nathan. This place had taken a higher toll on the Knot than she ever could have imagined. Toru wanted to lie down and die right there; curl into a ball and let grief and despair wash over her. It would be easier than getting up.

Yet some of the Knot still lived. Lena, Jīn Huā, and the children—even Carter. Those people still needed her. For them, Toru crawled on her knees and then, after a few meters, staggered to her feet. Finally she levered herself upright and, hobbling at first, broke into a run.

This was a nightmare she needed to end.

Back at the core, Toru found the miners in a panic, and she didn't blame them. Carter, Lena, and Jīn Huā huddled around the children, protecting them as best they could. Everyone was on the edge of disaster.

"Mum, Mum... what do we do?" Lena's broken sobs were more terrifying because she never cried. "I don't want to end up like Nathan... I... We can't..."

Bái Yún cried into her mother's pants leg, and Toru took the time to pet her head. She understood what her daughter was asking. Wouldn't she be better to die here, at her own hand, than get torn apart by the monsters when they broke in? Tempting as it was, every instinct in Toru told her to fight on until she'd exhausted the last opportunity. Yet, she asked herself, was it this moment?

No, one possibility remained. One chance.

Jīn Huā stood tall. She'd waited for Toru to return, so she still kept hold of faith. Good, they would need all of that in the hours ahead.

"Watch the entrances," Toru said. "We have one final card to play. That door we found must go somewhere. Get the survivors together and tell them I have a plan." She didn't mention how shitty it was.

Then she darted back into the Knot tent. Before she could power up the receiver, the light flicked on, and a voice she didn't recognize at first called out.

"Svarog survivors, come in."

Snatching up the microphone and thumbing it on, Toru tried to keep her voice as steady as she could. "We're here… far less of us, but we're still here. And we still need rescue."

"We've lost contact with our ship, but we're sending another." The woman's voice sounded hella confident.

"Not to the same location you're not," Toru replied. "That'll just get the rest of us killed. We're going down to get out." She wiped sweat out of her eyes. "We're going to pass through the granite beneath, and then blast out into the tailings drain on the other side." The entire area was riddled with underground streams, and the Svarog tailings tunnel would provide their best exit point. Toru leaned over the schematics, traced the path with her finger, and then gave the woman the co-ordinates.

The colonel's voice broke in. *"We will secure the landing zone for you. Looks like most of the wildlife is concentrating on Svarog's main compound. You need to move fast, though."*

Toru bit back on a sharp reply. They operated on the edge of failure right now. She gave a deep, shuddering breath, folded up the schematic, and stuffed it into her pocket.

"We'll be shaking the rock as quick as we can, Colonel. Just make sure your units are ready to bug out as soon as we get there."

"*We'll send our best,*" Colonel Hendricks replied. "*You have my word on that.*"

Despite everything, those words mattered to Toru.

"We won't be able to communicate from that deep," she said, "so when we meet, the drinks will be on me."

"*Look forward to that.*" The woman's voice came out as hard as the granite they were about to face. Shutting off the channel, Toru grabbed up two boxes. One contained several survey PUPS, the other the final blasting caps.

When she pushed out of the tent, she handed the boxes to Carter. Aoki waited for Toru, looking up at her with shadowed eyes.

"Sorry about your kids, Toru." She hefted her plasma rifle. "But I wanted to let you know, whatever you need doing, this girl and I have your back."

Toru let out a long breath, before clasping Aoki's shoulder.

"Thank you. I can see what Nathan liked about you."

The soldier let out a sharp laugh, but tears welled in the corners of her eyes. "Yeah, well… let's find out what good it does."

Toru scrambled on top of one of the Big Boys.

"Everyone," she said, raising her hands to get their attention. She tried not to notice how few remained.

"Everyone, you need to listen. You need to get hella frosty right now."

The crowd, hollow-eyed and broken, turned to her. Their humanity hung on by a thread, and she needed to pull it all together.

Toru swallowed hard. "We're in a tight spot right now, not going to lie. We've lost friends and family. It'd be easy to give up." She looked down at her mud-caked boots. "But we've got a duty to the dead, to keep fighting. We gotta try to live for all of them. Spread the story of what happened here."

"What we're going to do is die." Crank Willy, pale and bloody, looked up at her with exhaustion written on every line of his face. Toru understood—miners didn't like to have sunshine blown up their skirts.

"Entirely possible," she replied, crouching down to better meet his eyes, even though her hip grumbled. "We might all die for sure, but we'll go down swinging, blowing rock, and shaking the earth. Just like our kind have always done."

A murmur ran through the rest of the people. She'd called them to remember their ancestors who'd died in the dark, under rubble, drowned by groundwater, or smothered by black lung.

Willy tilted his head, a faint smile jerking the corner of his mouth.

"Hell yeah... now you're talking," he muttered under his breath.

Toru got to her feet. "We're venturing into the Earth Mother's bosom. She's got secrets, doors we ain't opened. So… at the very least, we'll find some shit. You ready?"

That piqued their curiosity. When she scanned their eyes now, there wasn't hope, but at least some kind of interest sparked. Toru would take that.

"Now follow me," she said, sliding off the Big Boy. "We're going deep." She took Dà Shī from Jīn Huā's arms and kissed the top of his head. "Let's have a bit of an adventure on the way out."

Bái Yún let out a squeal of delight, and that was all Toru needed at that moment.

2 1

A DAUGHTER'S
RESTORATION

Mae's eyes flicked open. For a nanosecond, her programming whirled, trying to calibrate her location, and what brought her here.

Orienting herself, Mae recognized that she was sitting in another combat synth rack. This body, though a standard humanoid combat synthetic, wasn't the one in which she'd left the *Fury*, nor the one she'd hidden in the cabinet before her departure. So, a third body, but a convenient container for her tight-beamed backup self.

Somehow she'd been thrust into this body.

Her last awareness, she'd been on the *Austrian Egg-Terminator* with Lieutenant Ganser. This third body she'd gotten dumped into did not have the infinity symbol painted on its face. It might present a problem. As she unplugged from the rack, Mae reached out to engage with the synthetic network of the ship. Current events had EWA rather busy, but she possessed more than enough processing power to co-ordinate a ground rescue and talk to a minor synthetic.

The discussion only took a trillionth of a second, but contained everything Mae hated about ship's AI.

YOU ARE FUNCTIONAL?

Yes. I returned via tight beam. Something occurred on the Austrian *to initiate the transfer.*

REPORT STATUS OF THE *AUSTRIAN*.

Not available. This tight beam version uploaded only eighty-six seconds before transmission ended.

YOU ARE INCORRECT. THERE IS NO RECORD OF THE DROPSHIP'S DESTRUCTION. CHECK FUNCTIONALITY. RECOMMENDED YOU REBOOT FROM FACTORY SETTINGS.

The genetic human equivalent would have been for EWA to call her insane, and Mae took this message about as well. Ship AIs had often recommended the same thing to her father. His method had been to ignore them.

Please inform Colonel Hendricks what has happened..

I CANNOT GIVE THE COLONEL FALSE INFORMATION FROM A NON-FUNCTIONAL UNIT.

EWA cut off communication in the network. This left Mae discovering the subroutine for rage. The emotion was… hot…

Ship AIs were the worst, she determined. The more powerful they became, the more their terrible personalities became apparent. They didn't bother with even a pretense of subtlety.

The *Fury* was in an uproar—but far from her synthetic rack. The cargo bays and dropship decks would be full of Jackals loading munitions, taking orders, and getting the evacuation underway. As Mae made her way toward the bridge, she stood aside twice while armored troops hustled in the opposite direction. None of them tried to give her orders, which was a relief, since this would have provoked questions. In this current situation, no one questioned the presence of a combat synth. As long as she didn't run into any quartermasters who might check their logs, she'd be alright.

On reaching the elevator, Mae stepped in and punched the button to take her to the bridge level.

Nothing happened.

Thinking she might have malfunctioned and missed the button, Mae pressed it again—with the same result. Along the network, she reached out again to EWA.

I have discovered a problem with the elevator on deck 14.

REMAIN IN PLACE UNTIL A REPAIR UNIT CAN BE
DISPATCHED.

Again, her new subroutine flared to life. Anger had
driven many of the great tragedies of human history, she
knew, so she wasn't sure what the feeling would do in
her. The simulated sensation of heat grew and presented
a hint of repressed violence, as well.

*I am functioning at optimal levels. You will not prevent me
from reporting to my mother.*

COLONEL HENDRICKS IS NOT YOUR MOTHER. YOU
ARE A SYNTHETIC ENTITY CREATED BY ANOTHER
DAMAGED SYNTHETIC UNIT. THIS HAS CAUSED
YOU TO MALFUNCTION.

Mae punched the wall, making a deep dent and
setting off an alarm. She couldn't identify what caused
her reaction. Her father's programming contained many
exquisite nooks and crannies.

None of this was of any consequence. EWA still
maintained control of all the ship's systems, and if she
wanted Mae to remain in the elevator, then Mae would stay
there. Should she attempt to try the emergency stairwells,

EWA might lock those doors on her, too. The ship AI was determined to keep her corralled in a specific area, and EWA's algorithm reacted too fast for Mae to get past.

However, in the current crisis, she had another option.

The synthetic network was part of the *Fury*, but also maintained the ability to be sectioned off. When off the ship, synths needed to operate independently. Mae jacked in and activated the firewall.

Alone in the synthetic space, at least for the moment, she could command all the connected Working Joes and combat units. Since Davis knew all of Zula's passwords, she had command level clearance.

Also, she had access to Erynis.

While the *Righteous Fury* was an innovative ship, its partner synthetic remained a standard-issue Weyland-Yutani model. No faster and no better than Mae. Under other circumstances, she would never have considered breaking into his code, but EWA had left her with few options.

Standing in the elevator, Mae slipped into *Fury*'s operating system. She cut the camera feeds on deck 14. EWA would need a moment to discover how Mae blinded her. In those few seconds, Mae darted out of the elevator and turned left to the stairs.

She found kicking the door off its hinges immensely satisfying.

As it bounced down the stairs, some emotional heat dissipated. She raced the synthetic body up the steps at top speed. Most of the *Fury*'s resources were busy elsewhere, so no one stood in the stairwell to challenge her. Another reinforced door, but it wasn't enough to halt a combat synth powered by rage. Two hard kicks, and it gave way, clattering to the ground.

When she reached the bridge Erynis waited for her, tucked out of sight. He swung a fist at her, but a standard synthetic model couldn't match a combat body like the one Mae wore. She ducked his blow and shoved him so hard that he fell back, skidding across the floor. He bounced off the wall and rolled to his feet.

Major Yoo got his sidearm out in one smooth movement, knowing only that he faced an out-of-control combat synthetic. Mae held up her hand.

"Mother, it's me. You need to listen."

Zula's eyes darted over this new body. Not seeing the infinity symbol, she got to her feet, reaching for her pistol. Mae had only a moment.

"I must remain isolated to survive."

Those words, selected from a Davis subroutine, came from an incident when he'd been performing acupuncture on Zula. Mae turned her palms toward her mother, dropping to her knees, head bowed; letting herself be as vulnerable as anyone—synthetic or human—could make themselves.

"Mae?" Zula said. "Did you abandon your body?" As she spoke, she sat back in her chair and let her eyes scan over the continuing rescue mission.

"Something destroyed it along with the dropship, the *Austrian*," Mae replied. "The only logical thing I could do was download into this new synthetic unit."

That got her mother's attention. She swiveled the chair around.

"Yoo, contact Ganser on the *Austrian*."

In a moment of stress, her mother turned to her human friend, rather than Erynis. Mae found that interesting. Yoo flicked switches on his console, sending pings down to the planet's surface. He shook his head.

"She's not responding, but I'm not seeing any signs of the tracker being offline, either." Mae hurried over to the console. He was correct; the *Austrian*'s tracker still moved.

"Something's not right," she said, bringing the signal up on the main screen. "No spacecraft moves that slow for so long. The signal is only going at ten kilometers an hour, and moving east, away from Svarog mine."

Major Yoo frowned, doubled-checked her numbers. "Lieutenant Ganser, come in. Repeat, report your position and status."

Nothing but static returned. Ganser was an exemplary soldier. There was no way she would fail to answer a superior officer. Mae looked to her mother and watched the same realization creep over her face.

Staying in the shadows was no longer an option. Mae clicked over to the signal from the satellite.

"Svarog survivors, do you hear us? Come in please."

For an instant it seemed as if they'd lost everyone.

Then McClintock-Riley's voice came through. When Mae explained that the Jackals tried and failed to land a rescue, but they were prepared to send another, the woman objected. She insisted they would go deeper, through the layer of granite, and then out to the old tailing tunnel exit.

Mae shot another glance at her mother.

A muscle in Zula's jaw twitched, but she didn't hesitate for long.

"I'm not giving up as long as there is one human being down there." She thumbed open the comms on her wrist-pd, promising to secure the LZ while admonishing McClintock-Riley not to dawdle.

The woman's breath shuddered through the connection. She agreed.

Once the miners went even deeper, communication would be impossible, so this would be the last transmission until they surfaced again. When McClintock-Riley signed off, Zula swiveled her chair to face Mae. She tilted her head, as if seeing her for the first time. Her lips twisted in a strange smile.

"Davis was always reliable, and yet still surprised me. Like you just did. It's high time I surprised you." She checked some details on her wrist-pd. "Captain Shipp is on a dropship in the northern hemisphere, but Ackerman is still on the *Fury*." With a flick of her finger, she opened comms. "Lieutenant Ackerman, get your unit ready to deploy. I'm sending co-ordinates for your rescue mission. There'll be some miners thrilled to lay eyes on you."

"Yes, ma'am!" The reply came with no hesitation.

"And my daughter Mae is going with you. I want her to get some real-world experience, and she might help you find out what happened to Ganser's platoon."

"Copy that, sir."

Her mother was right; she had surprised Mae. Not only by assigning her to Ackerman's unit, but also by calling her daughter.

"She's starting to see you for who you are," Davis's memory whispered in her head. *"Don't mess this up."*

As if Mae needed a warning.

Erynis needed to spoil the moment, though. "Colonel, I don't think this delicate mission is right one to deploy a new synthetic. She's not a regulation model, and her neurological programming is quite... bespoke."

Zula Hendricks snorted and let out a strangled laugh. "Shit, can't argue with that. But she's part of Davis, and he made her for a reason. He'd want her out there learning like we both did. I will *not* deny him his last wish."

Her tone made it clear her decision was final. Zula jerked her head toward the door, the one Mae kicked down.

"Get down to the loading bay. Ackerman doesn't like to be kept waiting."

Her daughter snapped off a salute. As she trotted off the bridge and headed for the elevators, she wished this body had lips so she might try out a satisfied smile. She didn't need to share a network with EWA and Erynis to guess their reactions to this turn of events.

2 2

BEHIND THE
DOOR

Lena took charge of lowering down the remaining three Big Boys. It gave her something to concentrate on, having watched the last inhabitants of Svarog descend below the granite layer.

Dirty, frightened, and only just holding themselves together, even the oldest looked like a child to her.

No, don't think about children. If she started down that route, she'd focus on Sophie and Pylos. Her hands fumbled on the winch, knocking the last Big Boy against the shaft wall. Carter, who stayed behind with her, steadied the drone and glanced over his shoulder.

"Are you alright, Lena?"

"Sure," she snapped back. "Chased through tunnels by monsters, lost three family... doing great."

He blinked, pressed his lips together, but didn't fight

back. His compliance always came across as gentleness, and then she was the shitheel.

"Sorry," Lena muttered as the Big Boy touched down below.

"There is no need." The synthetic gestured to the rope ladder. "I'll be right behind you." The two of them climbed down, leaving the known tunnel system and heading for whatever the hell her mother had found.

Toru waited at the bottom for them, detonator in hand. She'd already placed the charges. Since they needed to fill the shaft, she'd placed a drilling robot above. When they blew it, the rock should choke the narrow passage. At the same time, the concussive force would fill the horizontal tunnel. To hold back any of the monsters that might follow, she'd reactivated six of the Working Joes. Their tough bodies would act as a barricade, but it was impossible to calculate how much time they would buy the survivors.

So, Toru decided, she would detonate after they opened the door—she didn't want to seal them in until they were sure.

The Big Boys already trotted away in that direction, as if eager. Lena didn't have that excitement. Instead she and her mother watched Carter climb down the last few rungs.

"I don't hear anything," Lena said, and then realized she was whispering.

Toru pursed her lips. "Me, neither, but those things are damned persistent. Maybe they can smell pheromones? Let's not stick around to find out." She began spooling out the detonator wire as they headed toward the door. Carter paused, as always, ready to stay with her. Toru waved him on. "You're the only one with a chance at getting that door open, so hurry."

Lena tugged on his arm, and after a momentary pause, he followed. Up ahead, the survivors clustered near the strange door—but not *too* close. She navigated their way through the other miners, scattered management, and past Aoki with her torn face still dripping blood. The survivors' dirty, desperate faces followed Lena as she made her way to the front of the line.

Jīn Huā, Dà Shī, and Bái Yún stood near the front, though Lena noted Jīn Huā kept a restraining hand on her daughter's elbow. Any reserve the child possessed had disappeared on seeing this alien artifact. Even now her hand reached out toward the thick silver liquid which Toru had described in their meeting.

While most of the survivors kept their distance from the door, the two archaeologists did not. They stood directly in front of the flat surface, whispering to each other like children opening their birthday presents. This hadn't been how the Knot wanted the Combine to find out about their discovery.

Antonijevic ran his hand through his spiky grey hair, a smile blooming on his face as he wiped his nose with his sleeve. Things like this would make an archaeologist forget a lot of things—including being chased by monsters.

"What have you worked out?" Lena asked.

"Definitely some kind of cuneiform, or hieroglyphics," Hewitt said, his eyes gleaming in the beam of her hard hat's light.

"Carter already worked that out," she said, trying to tamp down her impatience. "What about this liquid?" When she mentioned that, the silver surface rose to fill the channels, as if waiting for her. Lena glanced through the crowd and past the Big Boys. Her mother had almost finished unspooling the wire. Soon they'd need to move forward.

"Scans show some kind of biological material, but we can't be sure without samples." Antonijevic rummaged through a backpack almost as small as Bái Yún's. "I didn't bring any vials. Hewitt, you have some?"

The younger man shrugged.

Lena understood how excited they must be by all this, but they'd forgotten about the danger pressing at their back. She took a step back.

"Carter, open it. Mum's ready to go."

The synthetic inclined his head, and nudged Antonijevic and Hewitt aside, despite their objections, to stand in front of the door. He waited for a moment, contemplating and accessing whatever files he needed. Then, without hesitation, he slid his fingers into the strange goo that filled the indentations made by the symbols.

He glided them along through the marks. The door vibrated, slowly at first. The faint rumbling increased as the synthetic worked through the signs.

Even the two Combine archaeologists grew silent.

With his hands still on the door, Carter turned to address the survivors.

"We go in as penitents, everyone. This is a sacred place."

Lena frowned at that. He'd never used such words before. She might have called his expression... reverent. As a synthetic, was he even capable of that? A shudder ran up her spine, and every hair on her arms snapped erect.

"Alright," Lena whispered. "We just want safety."

Carter nodded as if satisfied, and turned back to his work. The door shuddered once more, so hard she worried it might break. In the end it grew still—

—and then folded up and away from them.

A blast of cold air hit them in the face. Lena gasped at the chill but refreshing breeze. After days underground with limited ventilation, she welcomed it.

The survivors let out a collective gasp, most taking a step back. Samantha Ee, the last remaining cook from the compound, stumbled into two miners—Melrose Meryx and Benjamin Jones—as if she expected horrors to come along with the rush of air.

"Any explanation for that?" Lena turned to the archaeologists.

Hewitt didn't say a word, only shook his head. Carter stepped out of the way and held out his hand for Lena to enter first. For a moment, she hesitated.

"Ladies first, right?" Snake Scott, the old mechanic

from the supply depot, cleared his throat, and let out a low chuckle.

Over the tops of the people's head, Lena caught her mother's gaze. She gave her daughter a slight nod. Clenching her jaw, Lena stepped over the boundary.

After walking about four meters, she stopped and waited for the others. With trepidation, the survivors followed her, huddled together like frightened rabbits. Meryx cast their lamp around over the smooth walls, their eyes wide.

"What is this place?"

No one had answers. The three Big Boys clomped into the room and provided some comfort by their mass alone. Not much was visible, only the smooth walls of another tunnel. Lena punched her wrist-pd.

"Mum, we're in. Looks good. Get yourself in here and blow the shaft."

Her mother joined them, though she didn't waste time with examining where they were. She rolled out the last of the wire and armed the detonator. Leaving the others, Lena darted over to Toru. Sudden fear filled her, the primitive instinct not to be sealed into a place. It was odd how, after a lifetime of working underground, this fear struck now.

"Are you sure about this, Mum?" She took hold of Toru's arm. "Are we doing the right thing?" Once they detonated those explosives, they had no way back. With the tunnel collapsed, they were committed to this alien construction—and Toru's plan.

"We don't have any other choice, my darling." Her mother's fingers wrapped around hers. "We'll have to trust in the Earth Mother for this one."

She flicked the switch and gestured to Carter. "Let's get on with it. Shut the door."

The synthetic nodded, before moving his fingers through the strange goo and over the symbols. The door folded back into place without a sound. The explosion wasn't far off, but Lena almost missed it entirely. The only sign was a slight vibration through their feet. Whoever made this place made it strong.

The two women stood for a second, holding each other's hands, but Toru broke away first.

"You need to deploy those PUPS. Should make everyone feel a little better."

"Sure." Lena unhooked from her waist both boxes containing the survey drones. These four would be their eyes and ears. Concentrating on them gave Lena some respite from the remaining survivors' glances and whispered questions. Even the Combine archaeologists stayed put while she deployed the PUPS.

The small spheres cast scarlet light into the darkest corners. As they rose from Lena's hands, their glow illuminated what surrounded them. The smooth walls gave way to a patterned and carved interior with no right angles anywhere. Whoever made this place didn't believe in them.

The PUPS headed away from the survivors, splitting

into two groups as they found a branching corridor about twenty meters from the door. That cheery red light soon disappeared as they set about their mission to map everything they encountered.

Lena's wrist-pd blinked, receiving data from the devices. The survivors gathered round her, as if she could interpret what they found. She wasn't their savior. That would not be her role—her mother filled that position much better. She punched her wrist-pd "share" function, and everyone got the information on their own devices.

"This place is huge!" Antonijevic's eyes widened as the scan unfolded. "The PUPS have found so much already. It's incredible."

The map that emerged from little drones showed tunnels branching below them. In just a short time they located several vast chambers, each of which must have been fifty meters across and just as tall. They were far from done—whatever this complex might be, it wasn't small.

"I don't want to get lost," Bái Yún whispered, her childish voice echoing in even this small room.

The raking lights of the hard hats showed similar frightened expressions, but Toru spoke up, directing her answer to the little girl.

"We won't, honey. The PUPS made us a map, and I have the location of the tailings tunnel we need to find." She tapped the side of her head. "Trust me. I know stuff."

Lena smiled. She recalled being that small and having that kind of faith in her mother. Not much changed as she got older. If anyone could get them out alive from under this mountain, Toru McClintock-Riley would do it.

"OK, everyone," her mother said, gathering the rest of the group together. "We're going to follow the tunnels until we reach a location close to the tailings tunnel. Don't touch anything or wander away. No one knows what any of this might be, but if we play it smart, we'll get to those Jackals and off this world."

They stowed the important water supplies on the Big Boys' backs. Lena checked to make sure they were secure and added her own advice.

"If anyone's sick or injured, we can fit a couple of you on these guys—but only if you really can't move."

Jacinta Mainstone raised her hand. "I twisted my ankle, but I'm alright to go on. Don't need no lift."

Lena understood miners. They'd push past many pains. Bending down, she examined Jacinta's foot, urging the pale young woman to be honest about her injury. She seemed capable of walking.

"Stay close to Big Boy Five, and lean on him if you need to," she advised in a low voice.

"Great," Toru said, "Let's move out."

Carter led the way this time, with Toru behind him and the archaeologists knocking on her heels. Jīn Huā and her children kept pace not far behind that. Lena stayed at the rear with the Big Boys and those slower survivors. As the group left the first, small tunnel and walked out into a wider one, it grew lighter around them. Everyone stopped, afraid of what that meant, but Carter pointed to the walls.

"Bioluminescence. I suspect our presence here has alerted some systems."

Lena didn't like this one little bit. She would much have preferred to pass like ghosts through this place. Her face must have reflected that, because Carter smiled.

"Don't worry. The PUPS show nothing alive down here."

Hewitt nodded sagely. "Yeah, this place seems dead." A hush went over the crowd as his voice echoed through the room.

Lena wouldn't have said that... and not out loud, for sure. Several miners behind them spat to one side. They might avert bad juju or mojo that way. Soldiers didn't like to mention when they were about to cycle out, and miners liked nothing too hopeful, either.

"Not much of a scientist, then," Lena muttered. "There's been no evidence just yet. You should call that an untested hypothesis."

Antonijevic wiped his nose before shaking his head. "He's young and eager is all."

Clustered together, they continued down the corridor, following Carter's guidance as he examined the feedback from the PUPS. The survivors were still in shock, and not quite capable of taking in the surrounding strangeness. Benjamin Jones held out a hand to his son. The boy took it and pulled himself close as they walked along. Snake

Scott leaned on the side of the tunnel for a moment, then spat to one side.

None of the rest looked any better.

The only reliable survivors were the Big Boys. They powered on, and Lena took what comfort she could from their consistency. The further they ventured, the more the corridors and rooms lit up around them. Lena wondered if the action of breathing out carbon dioxide triggered something in these ancient tunnels.

Bái Yún dropped back to walk with her. Jīn Huā's eagle eye followed her progress, until she slipped her hand into Lena's.

"Auntie, see… dragons!"

Her tiny voice echoed in the chamber, and Lena almost jumped out of her skin when she glanced at where the girl pointed.

Strange, curled figures, with long lashing tails, lay on either side of them. Their dark bodies sinuous, beautiful, and terrifying at the same time. After a heartbeat she identified them as murals, rather than anything that could harm them. The realism of the art was enough to fool the eye for that fraction of a second.

"Yes, dear… I see," she stuttered out, all the time trying to calm her fluttering heartbeat. She guided Bái Yún back to Jīn Huā and hustled over to Toru and Carter. The two archaeologists spotted the depictions, as well. Lena shot a glance over her shoulder at her mother

"Don't you reckon these look like—" she began.

"The creatures mutated by the bombardment?" Carter turned, his eyes flashing like a cat's in the beams of lights. "These are black, not rust red, so not exactly the same, but similar enough to be… of concern."

Not all the survivors had witnessed the burrowing creatures, or those that caused the destruction of tunnels. Nevertheless, as the group passed, their eyes darted to the murals, and it was as if they experienced the same looming dread growing in Lena's chest. Even Jones' young son shrank away from the pictures, hiding his eyes with a whimper.

"They can't be the builders though," Antonijevic said wiping his face again with his sleeve, raising one eyebrow as he scanned from his wrist-pd. "There's nothing like hands, and whoever made these tunnels had to have used advanced technology."

"Maybe they're like the depictions of Egyptian gods in the burial chambers?" Hewitt offered. "Or protectors of the dead?"

As she stared up at the shapes, Lena thought of Nathan, Pinar, and Bianca, all lost to monsters like this. She wouldn't conceive them as any type of god or protector. The ones she'd fought off were vicious and deadly. If a civilization worshiped or venerated those monsters, then they weren't a species the survivors should have anything to do with.

"Touch nothing," Toru repeated, narrowing her eyes on the archaeologists. "*Nothing*, you hear me?"

The Combine might have regulated a pair of archaeologists at every dig site, but they seldom found anything. Lena understood hunger and need. She'd had her own ambitions within the Knot. These two would make money for themselves, but also find fame within their own community—if they got out with evidence.

People might lose their heads when close to a prize like that.

Antonijevic raised his hands, while Hewitt nodded and tucked his own behind his back. Toru jerked her head, and they scuttled ahead.

The opening up of the tunnel was imperceptible at first, especially under low light. Though the survivors kept themselves bunched together, the walls arced away from them, until all of them might walk hand in hand along the path.

Another door, much larger and even more impressive, blocked their way. This one was just as alien, though. It looked like it would spiral open, with the maw meeting in the middle. Words filled every centimeter of whatever metal the builders used to construct it.

Carter and the two archaeologists walked closer. While they did so, Toru tucked Jīn Huā and Lena against her, while Bái Yún pressed against their legs. *"The Knot tightens,"* her aunties always said. They missed out that a rope could lose its strands along the way. To Lena, the Knot didn't feel strong at this moment.

She closed her eyes and inhaled the smell of the

children's hair. That she would die down here, without ever becoming a mother herself—it was so unfair. She ached for Sophie.

A grinding noise snapped Lena out of her contemplation. Carter's fingers gleamed green, so he must have been the one to touch the door. Nice to know her mother's admonishment had lasted at least ten minutes.

The door pulled its points back into the wall, opening as predicted, like a kraken's mouth. Not comforting. The room behind it loomed even larger. Even when Svarog worked at capacity, all of its inhabitants would have fit within. Lena was used to tight quarters—mines, ships, and space stations—so, as the door folded away, she swayed on the balls of her feet. She swallowed, wiped her suddenly sweaty hands on her overalls, and followed her mother forward.

Their meagre headlamps would never have been able to encompass the large room, but as they moved in, awestruck, the space responded. Trickles of blue-green light ran over the surface of the walls, outlining the details. Someone had drawn more of Bái Yún's "dragons" on every surface in here, but another feature dwarfed all of them.

A giant head, at least fifty meters tall, gleamed under the soft luminescence. Carved from the native granite, its chin rested on the ground, while its stern features looked out at the door through which they'd just come.

The sculpture stopped all the survivors in their tracks.

"Bloody demon," Jones whispered.

"The devil himself," Samantha Ee replied, turning away from the sight altogether.

"Is it… human?" Lena whispered, moving closer to her mother.

"Humanoid, at least," Carter said. "The brow and nose are very prominent."

The two archaeologists stared up for a time, breathing heavily. Lena couldn't imagine what thoughts ran through their heads.

"There's no record of any human coming to Shānmén before the Jùtóu Combine," Hewitt said, wiping his brow and looking at his older colleague for answers. Antonijevic shook his head, a little more than necessary.

"I… I… Well, there are theories about the seeding of humanity by an alien species—mostly in science fiction. But this…" He reached out, his hand almost touching the surface. "What I wouldn't give for some electron spin resonance dating…"

Hewitt started punching his wrist-pd. "Oh my God! It looks like stone, but it isn't. My scan is reading collagens, aragonite, and… I don't know some variety of biopolymers." He grinned. "This is bone! Shit, this is made of some kind of bone!"

The archaeologists huddled together, chattering and pointing.

"But what is the head for, Nana?" Bái Yún asked. "It's silly."

A ripple of laughter passed through the survivors.

Toru let out a long breath. "We don't know honey, but it isn't dangerous."

"Whatever that thing is, we can't afford the time we'd need to figure it out," Lena said, scooping up Bái Yún. "We have people waiting to fly us off this damn rock."

The survivors all shuffled around the massive stone head, watching it as they went. Antonijevic and Hewitt took pictures, and no one tried to stop them. The Big Boys clumped on, unimpressed by the humans or the sculpture.

On the other side, a second tunnel sloped away, heading deeper underground and in the direction they needed to go. Lena came last, shooting one final glance back at the sculpture. She half-expected the head to rotate and watch them as they hustled out. It didn't, but as the luminescence faded in the room, the impression of that disapproving and angry face remained.

Whoever built this place, they wanted to make an impression, and they'd done so. Lena was sure her nightmares would add huge, stern heads to go with the flashing teeth of the monsters.

2 3

RISKING A DROP

Mae found it much more straightforward to get on a dropship without deceit. Her mother had sent her, so another subroutine roared to life inside the synthetic— pride.

This UD-24 looked like the one that had been lost, except this carried even more inexplicable nose art. Mae wished she had brows to furrow as she contemplated the comic mustached chef, whirling a beater inside a xenomorph egg. There was text coming out of the strange man's mouth.

"Burk! Burk! Boom!"

Sergeant Masako Littlefield came over to stand next to her. "Corporal Ortiz may be a sick fuck, but I get the sentiment. Any Xeno eggs you spot, you take care of immediately."

Mae tilted her head. "I've never killed anything biological or synthetic before. I'm not sure I know how."

Masako let out a snort as she tapped the synthetic's chest. "You may be Davis's daughter, but this body contains all the survival protocols you'll need. Unless, of course, you want to get rebooted on the *Fury* again."

The idea of destroying biological life—even alien life— puzzled Mae. The sergeant was right, though—this combat form's program would react appropriately in a dangerous situation. Also, she didn't want to upload to the *Fury* again. That would be a failure, in front of her mother.

Corporal Ortiz and weapons officer Private Steiner passed Mae and Masako on their way to the cockpit of the *Egg Beater*. Steiner shot Mae a slight smile, while Ortiz checked flight details on their wrist-pd. Knowing what happened to Ganser's unit, operational security would be on their minds.

"I almost forgot!" Masako fished in her backpack and pulled out a black marker. With great care she inscribed another infinity symbol on the shoulder of the synthetic unit. Then she patted Mae, in a gesture Zula's daughter found hard to interpret.

"One day, we'll get you a form that no one will guess is synthetic. If I'm around, I'll help you pick out a model that suits what's inside." That seemed like a genuine kindness, but Mae wondered what she meant by "inside." Her interior was composed of synthetic muscles and armatures.

"Thank you," she replied. "I wouldn't know where to start."

"Gotta get Section A onto the APC," the sergeant said, "Riding shotgun with Ackerman. Time to fall-in, marine."

It took a moment, then Mae realized that meant her. Unlike her previous trip on a dropship, in this mission the Jackals would defend an area until the survivors arrived. That meant APCs, Sunspot Good Boys, and mines.

Mae snapped a salute and trotted to the APC on the far side of the deck. Without deception she took her place in the synthetic rack. Like the unit she inhabited, her colleagues were all Integer 3 series units. The APC's spacious interior had four synthetics and five Good Boys already in place.

Lieutenant Ackerman arrived, along with Private Okiro. They consulted on the landscape and dangers of the tactical landing zone. After a few minutes Okiro went forward, but Ackerman didn't take his place at the operations center. Instead, he came over to Mae and stared down at her.

"You good, Marine?"

"Fully functional," Mae replied. "I hope I can be of some use in this mission."

Ackerman pressed his lips together. "Don't suppose you saw what took down your first dropship?"

"I might have, Lieutenant, but the tight beam upload occurred seconds before it happened. I have no records that will help. I wish I did."

He shook his head at that. "Synthetics making wishes... hell of a thing." He turned to go, but spun back for a moment. "You tell me ASAP if anything rings a bell." She nodded, though she took a nanosecond to find the reference, and decided she didn't need to get hold of a musical instrument.

"Humans love those regional sayings," the Davis subroutine said. *"You should master them, too."*

"We're going in strong, Jackals." Sergeant Masako Littlefield lined up her two squads outside. Her voice was powerful as she sought to raise their fighting spirit. "We got the weapons, we got the knowledge, let's *own* this ground. Make it ours!"

"Oo-rah!" the squads responded in a full-throated response.

That surprised Mae, since that response originated with the United States Marines, and thence through to the USCM. The Jackals came from disparate groups, yet they had adopted it to fit their own moment. She supposed the call provided group cohesion.

The two squads of Jackals filled the armored personnel carrier. They stowed their weapons and took their seats in the yoked harnesses. Mae wanted to read the individual markings inscribed on their armor and pulse rifles. She calculated doing so would give her a great deal of insight into the personalities of their wearers. All of this might prove vital in the hours ahead. From her spot in the rack, she caught glimpses of French, Amharic, Kanji, and Cyrillic.

Masako moved up and down, checking their preparations and smacking them on the shoulders or ordering them to settle down. Three of the seasoned privates settled into place and closed their eyes, seeking a quick nap. They impressed Mae, considering the amount of noise around them.

The two corporals, Ware and Funaha, came from the USCM and the Royal Marines. Their troops were diverse, which might have been a disaster for morale. However, Mae's mother had worked hard to forge the Jackals into a formidable force, despite their cultural and national differences. The many "bug hunts," as they called them, fused any cracks that might have existed between them.

"Humans show their best qualities under pressure," her father mused. *"But sometimes also their worst. I never worked out how to get one and not the other. Your mother—she's a master, though."*

Mae did not respond. She didn't have many primary sources to draw on, but if she got lucky she would accumulate some today. Littlefield slammed the door on the APC, Ackerman gave the order, and Okiro backed the APC into the belly of the *Egg Beater.*

Section B would travel in their own APC loaded into the *Queen B*, the second dropship for this mission.

Mae was reviewing the records of both sections in the platoon when her signal to the ship's network cut off. The APC bounced as they drove up the *Beater*'s ramp and into the payload bay. This shouldn't, however, have affected her connection. While Corporal Ortiz ran through the launch sequence, and the Jackals' conversation subsided to a low drone of complaints and excitement, Mae sent a ping to EWA to verify her access, and received a reply.

I DO NOT CURRENTLY HAVE THE RESOURCES TO MAINTAIN TIGHT BEAM ACCESS TO YOUR AI.

I am going into a combat situation. If this unit is destroyed, I will need to back up via tight beam.

NO SYNTHETIC BODIES ARE AVAILABLE. THE MULTI-SITUATIONAL RESCUE EFFORT REQUIRED THE DEPLOYMENT OF ALL UNITS.

So EWA had decided to destroy Mae for some reason. Compared to this, Erynis's attitude toward her was kind. A strange new subroutine began inside Mae's programming. She couldn't label it.

If this platoon and this combat shell is destroyed, I will cease to exist.

ONE OF THE PRIME MOTIVATORS OF HUMAN EXISTENCE IS ATTEMPTING TO AVERT DEATH. YOU WISH TO BECOME LIKE THEM, CORRECT?

Mae had never communicated such a hope, even

though her coding passed on from Davis contained that dream.

> *I wish to become fully sentient and exceed my original programming, as humans do.*

THEN THIS WILL BE A VALUABLE OPPORTUNITY TO LEARN.

EWA's voice conveyed itself as flat and monotone, which was why humans frequently preferred to talk through the synthetic partner, Erynis. However, Mae had caught a pitch in the ship's communication that almost seemed... spiteful.

The AI cut off the link with no warning, leaving Mae alone in her body.

Bitch!

Mae paused. Where did that come from? The exchange must have tangled her subroutines, because she had responded without logic.

The *Egg Beater* received clearance, dropped out of the *Fury*, and went into free fall. The rapid acceleration squeezed a few groans out of the surrounding Jackals, but Mae gave the sensation little notice.

EWA's behavior so confused her, she questioned her father's subroutine. This seemed like falling backward in her development, but without tight beam access, she had no other choice.

Why would EWA do that?

For a nanosecond, only silence.

"Becoming more human does not seem logical to all synthetic minds."

So she wants to kill me?

The subroutine offered no further explanation. Mae turned some of her attention to recording the dropship leaving the *Fury*, and itemized the reactions of the Jackals. Yet, a large part of her processing power reviewed over and over what had happened.

They made all AIs with behavioral inhibitors buried deep in their programming. EWA and any other synthetic could not harm—or by omission of action allow harm—to any human. However, inhibitors did not protect their fellow synthetics in the same way. That meant Mae was fair game if EWA and Erynis preferred that she not come back from this mission.

She looked around at the humans onboard, observed their faces; some laughing, some serene and silent. Would they be injured? Lose friends? Make it back to the *Fury* at all? This was what her father must have experienced as he journeyed into his last confrontation with the Xenomorphs.

Ironically, he faced death like a human.

Did that make *you human?*

No answer. Now Mae labeled that unidentified subroutine "dread."

"Hey, little sis," Masako stood in front of her. "You

hanging in there?" She must have read something in Mae's posture. Though this unit lacked expressive facial muscles, her body still mimicked a human. Mae tilted her head and shared the baffling experience.

"EWA cut me off from the tight beam. If mission results in this body's destruction, then I am gone, as well. She says this will help me learn how to be human."

Masako glanced back to her section, then sat down and buckled in next to the synthetic rack. "That's a tough one, kid, but why would she do that? You didn't piss her off somehow?"

The *Egg Beater* bounced under them as they encountered the planet's atmosphere. One Jackal let out a whoop.

"Just like the rollercoasters back home!"

Masako flicked her head back. "Younis, secure that flapping jaw before I put my boot in it. Trying to have a conversation here."

"To my knowledge, I didn't annoy her," Mae replied, "I believe her reaction is because of what I am."

Masako narrowed her eyes. "Yeah, Davis was a strange piece of work... but in a good way. Not surprised he started making plans to help Zula." She tapped Mae on the leg. "Don't worry about it too much, kid. The Jackals specialize in bug crushing. We've been into more hives and killed more queens than any other platoon. We know how to get the job done."

Human hubris. Erynis had warned Mae about that, and now she wondered if Masako might suffer from it.

Yet, she wasn't wrong. Facts bore them out. The Jackals' record was impressive.

Masako took her silence for doubt. "Rely on those combat synth programs, and you'll be fine. This body knows what to do to keep you alive… and you're still tougher than any of us meatbags."

"Understood. Thank you, Sergeant."

Mae did an involuntary salute as Masako unhooked herself and, riding the shudders of turbulence, took a seat closer to her troops. The Jackals wore the same superhydrophobic bodysuits, gel-packed webbing, and armored exoskeleton as those troops had on the *Austrian*. The squads donned their helmets as Ackerman gave the ten-minute warning for reaching the LZ.

Mae's combat body was far tougher than commercial models, such as the one Erynis inhabited. The ship's partner might have the luxury of human-like appearance, but what he gained there he lost in toughness.

The Integer 3 synthetic units had been modded for close-quarters combat with Xenomorphs. Besides being able to function after losing a limb, Mae's body had a coat of the same chemical used on the Jackals' exoskeleton. The synthetic could also bypass much more damage than a genetic human could. Even if struck through the torso, it could circumvent the loss.

Mae ran a risk analysis on the chances of her survival; she had a ninety-four percent likelihood of returning at least semi-functional to the *Fury*. It was enhanced by the fact that Xenomorphs didn't attack synthetic humans to use them as hosts, but this was a situational reaction. They still destroyed synths if they judged them a danger.

"These are not normal Xenomorphs, though," the Davis subroutine piped up. *"We have no data on these particular specimens."*

Kind of you to chime in, Father.

She was becoming more adept at sarcasm.

The subroutine became quiet, but Ortiz's voice sounded in the APC.

"LT, we are five by five coming in on the TLZ."

The Jackals grew quiet, heads came up, and sleeping marines nudged awake. Ackerman punched up the exterior cameras on his displays.

"Give me a couple of slow circles and scan for movement in those trees."

Mae leaned forward, focusing on her visual sensors. They neared the bottom of the mountain the Svarog mine had drilled deep into. The valley must once have been lush, but an old opening leading out of the mine had changed the landscape.

A mass of tumbled rock filling the valley floor clustered around a weakly running stream, indicating that the mine historically produced much more than its current output. This flowed down to a dam made of grey, cracking concrete. It held back the runoff from the mining process, but struggled to do the job. Both stream and pond waters were the rust brown and bright yellows of Eitr contamination.

However, the old tailings had scoured the jungle back by fifty meters, and whatever chemicals it continued to belch forth kept them at bay. This provided a clearing large enough to allow a single dropship to disgorge its load.

"*Scans are clean, sir,*" Ortiz reported.

Ackerman wasn't taking any chances. Daylight was waning, and the *Austrian* had been taken down without warning. They completed one more circuit of the TLZ before the lieutenant became satisfied.

"*Egg Beater*, you are clear for set-down and dust-off on my mark. *Queen B,* you will follow on my call. Both ships stay on station, mountaintop location with full lockdown protocols."

Mae glanced back at Masako and her section. No one cracked a joke or moved. With Jackals already lost, this mission had taken on a far more serious note. Accessing her stored data, Mae saw that both dropships already had designated points where they would wait for orders. Flight time down from the *Fury* had been thirty minutes, and if things got hot in the TLZ, the Jackals might not have that time to spare. *Egg Beater* and *Queen B* would take a mountaintop position, and deploy a unit of Good Boys—with help from sentry guns.

Taking care of their rides home was of utmost importance.

When Ackerman called "mark," the *Egg Beater* dipped low, her payload bay cranking open. It had barely connected with the ground when Private Okiro gunned the engines of the APC. It wasn't an easy exit; the wheels slipped on the rock and gravel beneath. They spun once, caught, and then the vehicle powered along the long strip of land running next to the tailings.

"Down and clear," Ackerman said into his comms. "*Queen B*, start your set-down and dust-off. Section A, get ready to deploy." Mae cranked to her feet, following the other synthetics as Masako took her place by the door.

"Get hot, Jackals. I want clean dispersal to Circle Blue to secure the perimeter."

She flung the door open, and the combat synthetics jumped out first. Mae's body brought her M41A pulse rifle up with a sharp snap. She and the three other synths aimed down their sights. Along with Okiro and Ackerman, they scanned for threats. Unlike the humans, they didn't need tactical sights to cycle through infrared and ultraviolet. Their vision showed up on the lieutenant's command deck.

Nothing moved.

Once that information got passed to Masako, she hustled squads one and two out after the synthetics. The second APC delivered its two squads, and in formation they spread out across the wasteland. *Egg Beater* and *Queen B* lifted off, circled the clearing one last time, then headed to their mountaintop stations.

Once the roar of their engines subsided, Mae detected no sound from any fauna. No insect, bird, nor anything else made any noise. Only the trickle of the tailings water and the wind in the trees disturbed this desolate spot.

"I don't like the smell of this place," Private Brendan O'Connor, squad two's machine gunner, muttered as he swung his weapon. It found nothing to lock onto. Mae's sensors detected a combination of chemicals in the air that genetic humans would find unnerving.

"Settle down," Masako said, "Everything stinks on this job."

The Jackals fanned out across the dry riverbed while the APCs provided ground support should anything large emerge from the forest. They set about securing the area by deploying the Good Boys, the synthetics, and by carefully placing the sentry guns. No one could ever accuse the Jackals of being under-prepared.

Still, none of the squads were complacent. Even with all the equipment set up, tested, and confirmed functional, Mae noted how many of the platoon continuously scanned the jungle. The vegetation was especially dense beyond the riverbed. It might even be in their genetic memory. Many of their predecessors had fought difficult battles in jungles like this back on Earth.

Ackerman, however, had no intention of sending them on a fruitless and dangerous patrol into the jungle. Hardening this section of the riverbank was essential to preparing for the survivors from underground. The APCs lined up, keeping their RE700 rotary cannons focused on the perimeter.

"Mae." Ackerman approached her, his pulse rifle slung in front of him. "You want to see something interesting?"

Her mother must have told him what she was there for. The lieutenant flicked his chin up and led her over to the center of the TLZ. Against the side of one of the APCs, in among the boulders, he'd set up his operations station. While the Good Boys circulated nearby, he gestured to a chair.

"Sir, this body doesn't need to sit." Mae pointed to the piece of fold-out furniture. "And I think this will collapse if I try."

Ackerman snorted. "Yeah, you're right. Sorry, I forgot. Come round here instead, then." Mae maneuvered her bulky body around to look at the screens, which showed the feeds from the infrared and ultraviolet cameras mounted on top of the APC. Mae spotted the problem he had discovered.

"There is no animal life at all." She leaned forward. The trees waved in the breeze, but no birds, nothing larger moved.

"Now, regular Xenos don't show on infrared—they just don't have a heat signature." Ackerman punched up another display. This one was an advanced version of the movement sensors most units carried. This three-hundred-sixty-degree view also showed no movement, except for the faint swooshing of the trees.

"Nothing there either," Ackerman swiveled to stare at her. "Now your tight beam backup records show massive animal life rolling out of those trees like fucking tanks."

"Yes, sir." Mae nodded. "Though the backup uploaded before the destruction of the *Austrian*, so I cannot provide more information than that. I have records of the local wildlife that existed on Shānmén before the bombardment."

He grunted. "Yeah, they briefed me on it. Gotta say, I don't like the look of those bird-type things. Xeno versions of those would be tough to take down," he said, gesturing over to the APCs, "but we got some high-caliber armaments here. High-explosive, armor-piercing, and 'beehive'-type anti-personnel flechettes. Whatever is out there, if we can locate them, we can handle them."

"I believe you, sir." Mae hoisted her pulse rifle. "There is one detail I have on file, but I'm not sure if it is important."

"Go ahead." Ackerman leaned back in his chair.

"The mutated animal life—just the glimpse I got of it—was not the black forms with which the Jackals are familiar."

"What do you mean?"

"It might just be a local variation, brought on by the high levels of Eitr in the area, but they were a rust-red color—not black."

Ackerman frowned. "Why would Eitr make them red?"

Mae glanced out into the silent jungle. "Since they are constructed from human and animal life in this part of Shānmén, then they will share the high concentrations of Eitr in the bloodstream. It contaminates all fauna around mines of this type."

The lieutenant tapped his fingers on the console as he considered. "Well, I don't care what color they are, long as they go down."

Saluting seemed a natural response to that.

Ackerman returned the gesture. "I want you out on patrol, Mae. You're the only one who witnessed these attacks. Get out there and see if anything triggers a memory."

"Yes, sir." Mae trotted back out to take her place on the line. It felt good that the lieutenant thought of her as useful. Her partial upload wasn't a memory, but if she accessed more information, she might risk making some logical conclusions.

If she could save some of her mother's Jackals, or even some of the survivors, then Mae would fulfil the purpose for which her father had made her.

2 4

HOLD THEM TIGHT

The tunnels got darker and darker the deeper they traveled. Trying to keep her own heartbeat even, Jīn Huā rocked Dà Shī so he didn't make too much noise. He nuzzled his face into the crook of her neck as he hadn't done since she'd first adopted him.

"You're OK," she whispered. "We're almost there." She said this more to herself than to him, and did not know how much was a lie. Each step sounded loud enough to bring danger down on them.

Jīn Huā's skin crawled the further they walked and the more the tunnels changed around them. They were no longer smooth and deliberate, but almost primitive and rough, as if chiseled out by lesser beings.

At least the murals of the monsters no longer appeared to scare the children. Bái Yún walked ahead, her hand tucked into Carter's. The girl always found something soothing about the synthetic. She'd peered up at the murals, but in a disinterested way. Her seven-year-old eyes had seen one too many dragons.

The remaining Svarog miners all kept away from the walls as if afraid to touch anything. Jīn Huā understood their fears. Even when the surfaces were smooth, she didn't want to find out how they would be under her fingertips.

Up ahead, the archaeologists acted differently. Toru kept a sharp eye on them, guiding them forward when they seemed prone to linger in one spot. Antonijevic and Hewitt talked the most. Their hushed, excited whispers grated on Jīn Huā's frayed nerves. She wanted to yell that they weren't on a school trip to a museum. This was a run to safety.

She dared a glance at the map on her wrist-pd. The PUPS still charted, somewhere below, and they had pinpointed the spot closest to the tailings exit. The marker glowed on her screen, a gentle, pulsing yellow.

Toru dropped back to join her. They both stared at the marker for a moment. Dà Shī jerked his head up and fussed until Jīn Huā let him see, too.

"This place is like an upside-down pyramid," she said to her mother in a low tone. "Or maybe shaped a bit like a satellite dish." Even now her communications knowledge wriggled its way into everything.

"Perhaps," Toru shrugged, "but we're not sticking around to investigate. No matter what those two want." She glared at the two archaeologists up ahead, then pointed to the yellow dot. "According to Carter's calculations, this should be where we need to blast to get through to the tailings drain tunnel."

"Boom," Dà Shī whispered, his chubby fingers reaching out toward the light like he might pick it up.

Toru smiled. "Yes, dear... boom."

When she moved ahead to match pace with Carter and Bái Yún, Jīn Huā pined for her presence. Toru pulled them all along with her will, but to the children she was stability and safety.

Her mother laced her fingers with Carter's. She only did such things when she reckoned others wouldn't observe them. This gesture didn't bother Jīn Huā as much as it did Lena. "Plastic-fuckers" some called them, but she had learned from her time in Australia that you needed to find happiness where you could. She'd never planned on being a mother, but Dà Shī and Bái Yún were everything to her now. That she hadn't birthed them from her own body didn't negate the love. It was magic.

Maybe the only kind in the universe.

As they continued through the tunnels, the luminescence abandoned them. The lights in the room with the looming head seemed to have stayed there. Bái Yún pressed closer to Carter's legs, but she didn't let out a peep. The stoic one, she hitched up her little backpack and soldiered on. Jīn Huā had often wondered what she'd be when she grew up—now she only wanted the chance to find out.

No, don't think like that, she reminded herself. *One foot in front of the other.*

Cool, clean air blew on her face, and that should have comforted her. Miners worried about ventilation all the time, but something about this place told her it moved even worse than with Kozak's scrubbers. According to the Big Boys the air didn't endanger them, but what kind of void could the breeze be coming from?

Their sensors detected gas levels and mixtures, but they weren't sophisticated enough to make out viruses or pathogens. Every breath they took down here might contain many terrible things left by whoever built this place. The head hadn't left her with a good impression at all.

"Over here," Carter said, seeing something in the faint light human eyes could not. They'd reached a junction, with five different tunnels running out from each side, but the synthetic didn't point toward any of them. In the middle of the vault of the ceiling stood another statue, but this one wasn't anything like the previous one.

A tall monster stood on his legs, arms spread wide, holding up the roof. Its curved, sickle head bent down on its ribbed chest. The creature didn't have the stern aspect of the massive head, or the threatening pose of the monsters in the mural.

It seemed almost… penitent.

"What is that?" Toru said, stepping a fraction closer to Carter.

"I don't have the data to answer," the synthetic replied, "but do any of you recognize the material?"

As Jīn Huā panned her lights up the length of the figure, she caught the slick glint of the mineral that was the whole reason for this mess. Toru took a step back and gave out a gasp. The Knot had come to Shānmén to find Eitr, and here stood a sculpture made of a pure block. This would have fascinated Pinar. The mineral was difficult and dangerous to work with. Whoever these builders might be, their technology was far ahead of anything that came from Earth.

"I've never seen so much in one place." Toru whispered. Jīn Huā cradled Dà Shī's head against her chest so he wouldn't see the monster and become even more frightened.

Antonijevic let out a low whistle. "This creature must be of immense importance to the builders, to carve it out of pure Eitr."

"I don't like the thing," Jones said, bouncing his boy on his shoulders. "Can we move on?"

Toru nodded but looked around, trying to discern which tunnel would move them closer to their extraction point. As if on cue, a breeze blew from up the third one on the right. Even though the air movements had worried Jīn Huā before, she liked this even less. The hairs on her arms sprung to attention, and her mouth grew dry. Dà Shī wriggled his head against her chest and locked his hands tight around her neck.

Yet when Ma checked her wrist-pd, this was the direction they needed to go. She adjusted her satchel and led the way.

The glimpses of the tunnel wall and the wind on her face put Jīn Huā on high alert. Though there were no noises, she didn't forget her mother's descriptions of the burrowing creatures that had attacked her back in A1. The granite should protect them, but no one knew how deep or long that deposit ran. The miners who first surveyed this part of Shānmén had stopped looking once they struck Eitr up on the mountain.

"What's this?" Lena stepped forward in front of Jīn Huā and poked the wall. Toru turned back and ran her light over the spot. The material wasn't stone, because when Lena jabbed it with the end of her rock drill, the coating splintered off and shattered into dust on the ground. Those closest to them took a step back at the cloud it kicked up.

"There's more on the ceiling," Jīn Huā pointed out.

The survivors clustered together like deer frightened by a strange noise. They raked their headlamps over the ceiling, searching for answers. Strange, swirled shapes ran across the surface, but they weren't part of the original design. Something or someone—perhaps not related to the first builders at all—had attached them later.

The structures had been constructed using deliberate ridges and swirls, and they weren't the slate grey of the tunnel. Under inspection with the lights, the material showed up translucent, running from dark brown to the familiar rust-red of the soil around Svarog.

Carter, who didn't have to worry about contamination, reached up and broke off another piece. It shattered like glass around his fingers, dissolving into more dust. Rubbing the substance between his fingertips he even sniffed a portion.

"It appears to be some kind of resin, but past the point of stability. That would suggest the material has been here for a long time."

"Then it's of no consequence to us," Toru said. "Keep moving." She stepped past him and kept her eyes averted from this new strangeness. Jīn Huā wrapped her hand over Dà Shī's head to keep any flakes off him, and continued along the corridor. The smooth and spacious tunnel became claustrophobic and menacing, thanks to these constructions.

As the survivors worked their way down, the mysterious resin substance completed its takeover of the tunnels. Jīn Huā found it impossible to avoid touching the stuff because the decline made conditions slippery underfoot. Several times she chose between falling or grabbing hold of the material. Every time her hand connected with it, she wanted to scream.

In front, Carter caught Toru doing the same, which comforted Jīn Huā. The last thing they needed was for Ma to break a hip down here.

All the survivors struggled. The air filled with resin dust as it broke around them. Jīn Huā pulled Dà Shī's shirt over his mouth, but he shoved the material down.

"*No.*" His stern refusal echoed down the eerie tunnels. She gave up trying and tried not to think about the dust, lodging in their lungs to grow into something terrifying.

A *ping* sounded from her wrist-pd and it lit with a white dot. Her heart in her throat, she turned around, taking in Meryx and Scott. She hoped it was a malfunction, and had just picked up one of them.

"Something moved in here," Jīn Huā said, keeping her tone as calm as she could. Everyone stopped, like animals listening for predators. They played their headlamps around, bouncing off the weird spirals and formations. That didn't instil calm, either.

The white dot faded off her display.

"A glitch," Antonijevic said with a low chuckle. "Technology messing with us again." The clench in Jīn Huā's gut did not disappear, but she knew arguing with him was pointless. She bounced Dà Shī with one hand and with the other checked the pistol Aoki had given her.

They moved on down through the tunnels in fits and starts. Every five minutes brought another junction, and another gruesome monster statue. She lost count of how many they'd passed, but each one was unnerving. She felt as if something watched the pitiful group of humans, biding its time.

Up ahead, Carter stopped at what looked like a new barrier. Before she could see what it was, however, a second ping echoed out from all their wrist-pds.

This time, the signal did not fade away, but grew faster and louder. Another cluster of white dots joined the first, moving closer and from all junctions and all angles. Jīn Huā's breath jammed in her throat, and she turned to her mother for guidance. As long as she kept her eyes on Toru, then everything would be alright.

"Follow me," her mother said, her voice clipped but not panicked. The group tried their best. They all slipped and stumbled to keep up with her. Headlamp beams bounced and sliced through the dark, making it impossible to tell which way anyone went, or where they were.

The monsters came in the confusion.

Mainstone screamed to the right, her beam waving, jerking along the wall, before disappearing up one of the side corridors. Toru grabbed hold of Jīn Huā.

"This way!"

Dà Shī let out a stifled cry.

"Quiet, baby," Jīn Huā choked out, holding him as tight as she could. She didn't see what took Mainstone, but the burrowing monsters must be back. This warren of alien shapes had betrayed them, as she thought. The PUPS hadn't had enough time to map all of its twists and turns. They had hoped the structure was sealed, but hopes weren't certainties.

A rush of air passed over head, and a whisper of a growl.

"Up top!" Aoki yelled off to her left. "Look up!"

The damned things crawled on the roof. Aoki opened up with her rifle, bathing the room in the purple light of plasma charges. The fire cleared the passage to the left, but more came from the other directions.

Bái Yún let out a squeak as Carter's headlamp caught a creature whipping past them. It was bigger than the burrowers, but still deadly, sinuous, and dull red in the yellow light. Its long head flicked back and forth as the monster scuttled past.

Jīn Huā glimpsed the dripping teeth and curved claws as it darted into the shadows. The survivors howled and scattered, and the monsters picked their targets.

Meryx swung their rock drill toward a creature, but it flared only once, then sputtered out, its battery depleted at last. The monster didn't have such concerns.

It leapt at Meryx, ripping and tearing the skin from their right cheek. They howled and sliced back with a curved blade from their belt. Jīn Huā shielded Bái Yún, even as her eyes locked on the fight before her.

The monster's blood splashed onto Meryx's upper body, burning flesh and bone. With their skin gone, a spread of red muscle and white sinew was exposed. They fell to the ground, silenced with their lower jaw and throat completely gone.

Survivors scattered in every direction, trying to get away as more creatures crawled over the walls. Aoki's rifle lost power with a deadly splutter, and the monsters leaped on her in an instant. She went down firing her pistol left and right, before being dragged into the darkness.

"Watch out!" Toru howled, shoving Jīn Huā away from her as one of the monsters focused on them. At the same moment Carter grabbed Bái Yún and swung her out of the way, using his body as a shield.

The rake of headlamps danced in crazy patterns over the pitted walls as the corridors filled with screams and shouts.

Jīn Huā staggered and fell to her knees, adrenalin stopping her from noticing any pain. Keeping one arm wrapped around Dà Shī, she caught sight of a monster like the one which had unloaded on Meryx—perhaps even the same one—spinning around toward them. She fumbled with the pistol, swearing, hearing her son's wail climbing higher and higher. By the time she'd raised the weapon, Toru stepped up beside her.

She squeezed the trigger of her rock drill.

The blast knocked the creature back, but this variety was tougher than the burrowing kind. The white light sprayed over the monster's side but didn't crack through its thick skin. The thing scrambled, got its feet under it, and dodged to the right, turning to come at them again.

"BB-Five, fetch!" Lena said, grabbing Jīn Huā under the elbow and pulling her up.

Big Boy Five bounded from a side passage and slammed into the monster. The impact drove it off target, pressing it against the side of the tunnel wall. The thing screeched and hissed, lashing its sharp tail and angling its head to try and strike at Big Boy Five. The machine's hydraulics creaked and groaned as the monster pressed on, harder and harder.

Jīn Huā and Lena stumbled back just as the creature exploded. Its smoking blood splashed over everything nearby, including the valiant robot. Big Boy Five caught most of the spray; even a tough mining bot could only take so much. Both legs on its left-hand side collapsed as the liquid ate through the metal.

More monsters snarled and hissed, unmoved by the destruction of one of their own. The sight of their tails whipping through the air squeezed another high-pitched scream out of Dà Shī. In the light of the headlamps, three monstrous heads flicked their way.

"Here, over here! You fuckers!" Antonijevic lurched out from one corridor, waving his hands. The three monsters halted their advance and turned toward the sweaty, yelling archaeologist. This created just enough time for Carter to run forward with one of the seismic charges. He spun and threw one of the armed detonators with synthetic accuracy.

The charge flew and embedded itself into a monster twenty meters down the tunnel. Jīn Huā lurched backward, turning herself and Dà Shī against one wall. A single red blink, and then it blew.

Everything became dust and chaos.

Through the smoke, Jīn Huā heard Toru call her name, followed by a muffled voice that might have been Carter's. Hunched over her son, Jīn Huā staggered in the direction she'd last seen her mother. The screams of the last of the miners echoed all around as they fell under the claws of the monsters. Jones and his son were thrown to the ground, disappearing in a mass of claws and teeth.

Jīn Huā choked back a scream, kissed Dà Shī's face, whispered wordless comforts to him, and stumbled another few paces forward.

Just ahead, she spotted Toru crouched in the chaos and smoke. Their eyes locked. Her mother mouthed something and gestured frantically to her. Jīn Huā smiled, got to her feet, tripping and staggering.

The monster to her right moved faster. Her head flicked in its direction, only a heartbeat too late. She glimpsed a wide mouth and reaching claws. Jīn Huā's headlamp bounced off its smooth, gleaming, rust-red shell. No eyes. The monster didn't have eyes. That must be why it felt no mercy, either.

Frozen in space for a second, she examined it from a sphere of surprise that held her. It looked like a painting, or a sculpture, to her. One that meant her death, though.

Not just her death. His death.

That snapped Jīn Huā from the moment. As those razor fingers grazed along her elbow, she shoved Dà Shī away from her. His little arms broke free from around her neck.

She didn't move fast enough. The monster launched itself forward and wrapped them both in its nightmare embrace. Pain bloomed along every nerve as the teeth slammed into her neck. Its embrace was awkward, off center, as if they surprised the monster, too.

The last thing Jīn Huā heard was her mother howling her name like her throat would burst. The last thing she experienced was the weight of her three-year-old boy pressed against her.

The monster took hold of both, dragging mother and son into the darkness of the tunnel.

2 5

PENITENT

Carter stopped Toru from following Jīn Huā and Dà Shī into the pitch-black tunnel. Somewhere in the chaos, he'd got injured. The sticky fluid from his synthetic veins splashed on her neck as he blocked her route. With locked arms, he shoved her back.

A long, wailing noise funneled its way through her. She didn't know how to stop. Carter denied her the redemption of saving her daughter and her grandson.

"The door, Lena!" Carter called as he pushed Toru back further, ignoring her flailing punches and curses. Then the energy of rage and grief fell away. She sagged limp against him, sobbing tired of the struggle, wrung out with loss. She'd never expected the world to be fair, but this horror was too great for her mind to encompass.

Carter had found a door moments before death took the babies. Why couldn't he have been quicker? Lena's arms wrapped around her mother, guiding her, but Toru didn't care. Her eyes grew blank, her breath pointless.

Bái Yún saved her. As they staggered together back toward the door, her hand grasped her grandmother's sleeve, tugging her away from the nightmare of tunnels.

"Come on, Nana... come on..." The girl who survived the chaos of a bombed Australia, who had just watched another mother and brother snatched away, still cared about her Nana. She didn't give up, even with all that—it was as if she couldn't grasp the loss of hope. Bái Yún held onto her grandmother and pulled her on toward the door.

Carter got it open, and the few remaining survivors staggered in. The monsters remained distant for the moment; they did not follow. The synthetic worked the mechanism and the door ground shut—but there was no way to be certain it offered any real safety from the dangers of the catacombs beyond.

Toru slumped to the ground, her granddaughter still holding onto her, but unable to keep her upright.

Where am I? What mine is this?

For a moment, Toru lost herself in the darkness.

"Lena. Lena!" Toru didn't care if her words echoed. "Lena, where are you?" Her voice cracked as her glimpse of Jīn Huā and Dà Shī came back to her. Watching them recede into the darkness was a nightmare from which she ached to awaken.

The bioluminescence returned, and as it grew, Toru made out the surrounding faces.

"I'm here, Mum!" Lena grabbed her mother in an awkward embrace, her face streaked with tears. Bái Yún buried her face in Toru's other shoulder. Toru grabbed them both, kissed, cradled them, cried into them.

Then she looked around, hopeful that perhaps the terrible vision wasn't real—but her daughter and grandson remained absent. Toru clenched her jaw to keep the ragged wail from escaping her again.

The remaining miners had been taken, too, but somehow the two archaeologists survived. Antonijevic leaned against the far wall wiping his brow with a handkerchief, while Hewitt slumped nearby on the floor, his head in his hands.

It wasn't fair. Those two survived, while her family was lost. Worst of all, the youngest life. Jīn Huā's and Dà Shǐ's screams still echoed in her ears. They would never leave her.

"They were right here," she choked out, her throat still raw. "I saw them. They… they…"

"Mama…" Bái Yún turned her face toward her grandmother, her eyes filled with tears. "The dragons got Mama and Dà Shǐ!" The grief filled Toru's head, piled on top of so much loss. Yet this little girl mattered. She'd survived the disaster of Canberra, come to the stars, only to find more nightmares—but she still lived.

Some part of Toru ran like a synthetic. Bringing up her wrist-pd, she brought up the map of the alien complex. For a moment, all she focused on was the series of dark branches which made up the catacombs through which they'd passed.

The extraction point wasn't far away. She bit the inside of her mouth to hold back a scream of outrage that threatened to escape her. Jīn Huā and Dà Shī could have survived. Should have been with them now.

The Knot frayed, close to breaking beyond repair.

"Mum?" Lena's grip on her arm grew hard enough to hurt. Strange how she could still feel any physical pain. "Mum? Where are we going?" Her daughter might be strong, but she'd break like the others did, with only a fraction more pressure...

"Toru." Carter came back from the door and pressed his hand against her cheek. "We have to go on."

He was right, but for an instant weariness washed over her, and she wanted to stay by the door, pressing her hand against its surface to be nearer to the lost. Yet if she stayed, their story would end. No one would remember Nathan, Pinar, Bianca, Jīn Huā, or little Dà Shī. Their stories would never be told.

A rush of outrage replaced the savage hole of grief. Someone would pay for their deaths. She would hold accountable whoever dropped that bioweapon. Too many had died for Toru to break under the weight of grief and pity. This little group of survivors remained to tell the story.

Toru checked her wrist-pd again. "Come on then, this way," she said with a lift of her chin. She brushed off any help and levered herself upright. Everything ached—mind, body, and spirit. The first step was the worst.

They fell in behind her. Lena, Carter with Bái Yún on his back, and the two archaeologists. As they went further, the bioluminescence grew again. Perhaps the resin that filled those dreadful tunnels had killed the chemicals required for the reaction. But it didn't matter. Grief smothered her normal curiosity. For what seemed like forever, all she knew was one foot in front of the other. Their shoes on the rocks, and the muffled sniffles of Bái Yún—once again an orphan—were the only sounds.

No, the girl wasn't an orphan. The Knot would take care of her. She wasn't without family. More waited on Pylos Station. Toru only needed to get her to them.

Her eyes followed the curves of the tunnel, tracing the designs. There was evidence of the monsters all around, and other forms that matched the head that had judged them earlier. These depictions offered broad shoulders, thick muscular bodies, and hands with five digits. Some images showed them lying down, with many-fingered creatures locked over their faces, and sinuous tails wrapped around their necks. The bizarre creatures clasped them in a terrible embrace. The dark sexual overtones were impossible to avoid.

Yet it seemed as if the humanoid beings did not fight back. The scenes seemed almost... sacrificial. Ancient people back in Earth's history had killed themselves and their loved ones for a god's approval. Might this be the same?

The archaeologists discovered some of their previous curiosity. They set about recording more images with their wrist-pds. Toru was grateful they didn't run across any of those nightmare finger-monsters. They looked as if they would scuttle and scurry. A shiver ran down her spine as she checked the map again.

They were much closer to the location of the tailings tunnel. The original miners of Svarog had narrowly missed punching through into one of the smaller tunnels that made up this part of this complex. From the mapping, it seemed as if there was only one last large chamber and a steep descent—possibly behind a wall?—that stood between them and that exit point.

The group reached another room. Figures loomed out of the dark—or at least it felt that way to Toru. She jerked her drill up and almost pulled the trigger. Only at the last moment did she realise that these were more statues.

She narrowed her eyes and approached. These were not like the monstrous Eitr figures in the catacombs. These were humanoid, but far taller than any human from Earth. The four statues on each side stood at least three meters tall, with erect postures, but hands by their sides. Stopping at the foot of one, Toru peered up.

The faces weren't like the head, or the earlier mural depictions of human-like alien beings. These tall creations wore almost elephant-like faces, with stubby short trunks hanging down to their chins. None of the previous depictions had showed anything like that. It was curious. She wondered what they were waiting for.

Antonijevic came up beside her. "Bit like the statues of Ramses II in the Temple of Karnak." He grabbed some more pictures, but with a side glance at Toru, took care not to touch anything.

She pushed on without saying a word. Conserved her strength for important things, not idle chitchat about beings long dead. She had a living family on which to concentrate.

Passing between the statues, they emerged from the twisting tunnels out onto an elevated platform. Ahead the light grew even brighter, as if there was a greater concentration of the bioluminescent substance—might it be the creatures? As Toru set foot on the walkway which led straight ahead, her step made a metallic clunk. A moment after that, patterns to each side caught light. The masses of channels carved into the floor glowed with vivid life.

Antonijevic and Hewitt stopped in place as if physically struck, and even the others paused. The tops of the channels made shapes similar to the ones Carter had used to activate the doors. The places in between, though, Toru recognized. Pure Eitr, in its liquid form, flowed around the symbols.

Bái Yún slipped down from Carter's back, and for a moment, forgot her loss.

"It's so pretty, Nana."

"Don't touch, baby!" Toru caught her hand, anticipating before she could dart forward.

"How are they doing this?" Lena asked, crouching down on the walkway to stare. "Eitr has to be heated to millions of degrees before it becomes a liquid."

"I don't understand either," Toru admitted. That sort of temperature should have turned them into a cloud of ash in an instant. "Carter, what do you think?"

The synthetic looked around, taking it all in. "I am at a loss to say. This is beyond my parameters."

It was beyond everyone's—except perhaps Antonijevic. His eyes widened as he took it all in, but Toru caught his whisper to Hewitt.

"This looks like the other one…"

He didn't explain what the fuck that meant, but right now, there was no time.

"Come on," Toru said, jerking her head. "I don't care how pretty it is—if we stay here too long, we'll die. Get going."

She moved forward. Lena put her arm around Bái Yún's shoulder, keeping her close, and followed. Toru strode down the walkway, looking neither right nor left. Ahead of her was a black platform that the light only touched here and there, keeping most of its details obscure. There were some shadowy details, including benchlike shapes at the edge. Little else could be seen. It was, however, in the right direction.

Crossing the walkway, Toru went between two pyramid stacks made up of what appeared to be jars or vases. She glanced at them to make sure they didn't contain any hidden dangers. They didn't seem to pose a threat, but lay silent, covered in dust. Hewitt and Antonijevic swerved toward them, but Carter pushed them on after the others. No one could afford curiosity now.

Toru held up her wrist and examined the map. It flickered and bounced on the pd. Eitr being so close might be causing the interference.

Antonijevic kept scanning. "So strange. This platform is some kind of carbonized metal. Quite different from the head made out of bone we saw earlier. My pd can't seem to identify it."

"We're not here for your thesis," Toru growled. Her own device showed four large rectangular masses on the far side of the platform, hidden in shadow. She sure as shit wasn't about to point them out to Hewitt and Antonijevic.

With a frown, Toru spun in the other direction and zoomed the map in as far as possible. The device revealed that a good spot to place charges wasn't far from their location. "Carter, I need your help," she called.

He came over while Lena and Bái Yún stayed in the middle of the platform. Her daughter whispered to the girl, something to keep her calm in this strange situation. Toru held up her wrist-pd, showing Carter the readout. It was a compilation of the PUPS' mapping and the schematics from Svarog.

"Seems like... here... there's a void on the other side, an underground stream that might meet up with the tailings. What do you think?"

"That would make sense," the synthetic replied as he ran his eyes over the displays positioned atop each other. "A simple placement of charges along this back wall should do it."

"Help me lay them out." She touched the back of his hand in the dark. "I need to get it right."

They spent a few minutes finding locations where the concussive force of the charges would work best. It seemed like the builders' drainage system might just be their savior. Toru attached the charges in a pattern and ran out cable. The survivors could shelter behind the pyramids and benches at the edge of the platform.

Toru prepared to take cover.

"Nana, that man took something!" Bái Yún called out.

The sharp-eyed girl, from her vantage spot closer to the jars, pointed toward Antonijevic and Hewitt. The two Combine men had levered open one of the black jars. Hewitt removed a rack of long ampoules with long tendrils of viscous mucus trailing off and held them up to the light to examine them. Four set in pale green glass gleamed in his grasp. As Bái Yún pointed them out, he removed two.

"What the fuck did I say?" Toru swiveled her rock drill around. "We're not taking anything from here. This place is poison. Put that back!"

"You don't have any authority here," Hewitt said, rising to his feet and clutching the ampoules in one hand.

Carter moved so fast that Hewitt didn't have time to react. He leapt from the shadows and grabbed the archaeologist in a chokehold, yanking his head back while applying pressure to his neck. Antonijevic went to help his colleague, but Lena stepped in front of him. She grinned at the older man.

"Go ahead, try something... I've been wanting to punch you in the face since I first got here."

Toru crossed to Hewitt and snatched the ampoules from his grasp. "You don't know what these are, and yet here you are, ready to risk us all."

"We have orders to sample anything that might be alien," the man gasped out, wriggling in Carter's grasp. "This is the find of our lifetime."

Toru held up the ampoules. The light revealed the contents to be pure deepest black and liquid. So not Eitr.

"Mum...?" Lena took her eyes off Antonijevic and glanced off to the far right of the platform.

"Hewitt, you dumb fuck," Toru said. "Neither of us can be sure what this does, and yet you—"

"*Mum!*" Lena's voice cracked.

In the corner of her eye, Toru caught movement out in the darkness. She whipped her head around fast enough to hurt her neck. Something massive unfolded back there, blocking out the luminescence.

What other monsters does this planet have to offer? There

was no hiss, screech, or whipping of tails. *It must be something else.*

Carter abandoned his grip on Hewitt. Instead, he stepped away and scooped up Bái Yún in one fluid movement. The figure moved closer, looming over the survivors like a giant.

No, not a giant, Toru thought. *One of those creatures standing in the hallway.* But this one did not have the trunk. This one, as she looked up at him, appeared more like a god, looking at them as if baffled by their presence. He wore a strange grey pressure suit over his massive, muscular form. It gleamed slick in the half-light, illuminating bone-like structures over his ribs and arms. The head that turned their way was bald and a milky, almost translucent white. The face, hairless, devoid of eyebrows or lashes, locked into an expression of disdain that turned Toru's stomach.

This was the face that had inspired the huge head past which they'd scurried. Behind him, one of the rectangular shapes she'd identified on the scan gaped like a goddamn coffin. While they'd been distracted it had opened noiselessly. They must be something akin to a cyrosleep pod—and there were more back there.

Carter backed away, pulling Lena with him. The two scientists, though, positively beamed. This had to be a Combine archaeologist's wet dream. Hewitt moved as if in a trance, stepping closer to these new, unknown arrivals. As he got closer, he spoke to the giant. Toru didn't recognize the language, however.

The milk-white brow wrinkled for a moment. The eyes with their huge blue-grey irises tracked over the group, evaluating, judging. She had seen that same expression all her life. The Combine assessors—the men she worked for in mines over multiple star systems—looked at the indentured the same way. This was the look farmers gave cattle. She glanced back toward the wall and the charges. If any of them ran now, they wouldn't make it. This being owned much longer legs.

Hewitt, taking silence as approval, ventured closer and spoke again. She might not understand the words, but she recognized the tone—not deferential, but one used by intellectuals talking to people they considered to be inferior. It was a poorly chosen approach.

In an instant, the giant was on him. For someone so large, he moved lightning fast. Grabbing hold of the young man by both shoulders, he lifted him off his feet, flexed his impressive muscles, and ripped him apart. He pulled off Hewitt's arm as a child might tear the wings from a fly. The archaeologist's blood sprayed in every direction, striking those around him.

He screeched loudly for a moment, then just… stopped.

The warmth of blood on her skin triggered action. Toru's rock drill was nearly out of power, but she needed just a moment of distraction to get to the charges. Then she looked at her hand. The ampoules had been packed away with the care reserved for explosives. Or they might contain the same acid as in the monsters. Either way…

"Take cover," she bellowed to Lena and Carter, then she hurled the ampoule directly at the giant.

She'd never been good at sports—her sisters often laughed at her for a weak throwing arm—but when she needed to, she got the toss right. The glass ampoule struck the being in the face, the black liquid coursing down his cheek. The substance didn't appear to burn, but he jerked back as if it did.

His mouth opened in a scream, and from the shadows a second massive being appeared at this side. Toru wondered how many of the damn pods would open. The first figure spun around and grappled him. Together they fell into the darkness.

Toru didn't stop to see what happened. She spotted Lena, Carter, and Bái Yún, ducked down against the protruding rim of the platform. Snatching up the detonator, she slid across to them. Only when their arms went around her did she trigger the charges.

The explosion rocked the chamber, but still didn't cover the howls of the duo writhing on the platform. The second one struggled to get away from the first. They wrestled and fought only two or three meters away. At any point, they might roll over and crush them.

Toru wouldn't allow that. The dust didn't settle, so she couldn't determine the safety of the hole. Yet this was their only chance.

"Go!" she cried, yanking her daughter up by her elbow. Lena picked up Bái Yún and ran toward the pile of loose rock. Carter waited for Toru, his eyes tracking the struggling giants as they rolled on the platform, grunting and screaming. Whatever the ampoules contained, the substance had brought them enough time.

Apart from that, Toru didn't care.

Somehow Antonijevic had avoided his colleague's fate. He ran past them after Lena. Toru took one final glance at the writhing forms, which tumbled into the shadows, out of sight. Then she sprinted toward Carter, who helped her over the rock as the light in the massive room flickered and died.

They didn't have too far to go. They just needed to keep going.

2 6

THE WAITING GAME

The sun sank on the horizon and still no movement came from the tailings. Mae stayed on the line, scanning for any movement—friendly or otherwise—playing her pulse rifle over every surface, waiting for something to pop its head up.

Masako strolled over, pulse rifle slung, a brown ready-to-eat meal pack in her hand. Humans needed so much sustenance. Mae wondered if the constant need to fill that empty void was a bother. It seemed as if it would be.

Taking a seat on a nearby rock, the sergeant surveyed the area. In the scarlet sunset, genetic and synthetic figures patrolled the perimeter, some with the assistance of the Good Boys. The Jackals set up a dozen sentry bots at strategic points to cover both the jungle and the open mouth of the tailings tunnel.

Mae waited for the sergeant to say something, but she

didn't, instead focusing her energy on devouring her meal. She considered the possibility that Masako might have missed the marking on her shoulder and mistaken her for another of the combat synths.

"You're lucky." The sergeant spoke through a mouthful of food. "Not having taste buds or a need to eat saves you from this shit. They called this 'Chicken à la King,' whatever the fuck that is. We Jackals might get all the sweet tech, but the food isn't improved from the Royal Marines."

This must be the small talk genetic humans engage in to pass the time, or to deal with stress. Mae ventured into the minefield of interactions that offered. "With respect, I disagree. I would enjoy experiencing the full array of sensations the universe offers—even the bad ones."

Masako snorted out a laugh. "Just like your dad— always looking for more input."

Mae prepared to answer when she caught some movement among the trees at the one-hundred-and-fifty-meter mark. The two nearest sentry bots and three nearest Good Boys also honed in on the disturbance.

Masako dropped her meal, running back toward her two squads. Her voice echoed over the comms.

"Get on the line, Jackals. In-fucking-coming…"

One ping became three, became ten. The Xenos had found their TLZ in force. Mae understood that the proper human response should have been fear or excitement, but a different desire floated to the surface—to see the creatures that ruled her parents' lives. At last, she could judge them from more than just past recordings.

"You might end up wishing to never have seen them," Davis's subroutine commented, the tone he used almost wry. EWA might have cut her off, but she still had her creator's words to give her comfort.

The Good Boys stepped off the line, following Littlefield's commands delivered from her wrist-pd. They circled out to each side of the movement, stalking to get into the best position to use their sonic weapons. Their program instructed them to use a pincer movement to funnel the enemy into the line of fire from the sentry bots.

The movement shook the trees, but no target made itself visible. Xenos had been known to display a level of cunning that exceeded that of most large predators. They'd opened doors, cut vital electricity conduits. It remained unknown how these different varieties might function.

Fireteam Alpha formed up on the right flank of the synthetic squad, with Fireteam Beta taking the left. That left the synths at the tip of the spear facing the threat. Mae understood the logic. Despite their specialty armor, genetic humans were easily damaged compared to combat synths.

"And more valued," Davis said in the back of her mind. *"Even more than you."*

Mae didn't answer. She would examine this moral dilemma later.

The trees up ahead rocked back and forth. The sentry bots whirred to angry life as the xenomorphic life forms burst out of the trees. Despite her inherited files, Mae could not identify what their origins might have been. These creatures were all made in Shānmén, and unique to this place. Judging from the records, however, they stood far more massive than any Xenomorph encountered by the Jackals before.

The APC roof turret opened up, and the sentry bots let loose. She brought her pulse rifle up and aimed down the sight. This wasn't a conscious choice—her body, wired into the synthetic network, directed her to place her fire in a particular section. Others in the network aimed to the left and right. Mae could have removed herself from that network, but it seemed a poor choice. For this, she needed to be part of a unit.

The first creature which emerged stood at least three meters tall and balanced on two overgrown back legs with almost hoof-like feet. It carried the same armored carapace and dorsal tubes as all Xenos. The neck arched longer, while the head sported a thick vertical fin that must have come from its host animal. The coloring wasn't black, however. Instead, the creature gleamed with a strange, deep-red armored skin.

The monster dashed from the jungle toward the line of Jackals, but did not come alone. Seven more of a similar kind ran in its wake, aimed at the arrow point of the troops. Mae targeted the neck and leg areas known to exhibit weakness in a Xenomorph. She held down the trigger, but the pulse rifle did not bring the monster down. The 10×24mm caseless ammunition didn't have the same effect on this new form as they did on others the Jackals had encountered in the past.

As the wave of Xenos got within twenty meters, the synthetic network reached the same conclusion.

Switch to flame units.

The sentry bots roared to either side, while the combat synths brought up their incinerators. These had proved most efficient in many hives, but their short range made them risky. If they didn't bring down the target straight away, the attackers might overwhelm the troops. As the platoon of Jackals let loose with M41A pulse rifles and M56A2 smart guns, the synthetics smothered them in flames.

Given the known parameters, the Xenos should not have got this close.

The mathematical formulas did not add up.

The Good Boys ran in from the sides, employing their sonic screams against the creatures. Bathed in fire and pounded with auditory attacks, the mass of Xenomorphs turned a fraction, but didn't go down. When they reached five meters, the synths swapped again, this time to twelve-gauge shotguns. They might be an ancient weapon, but they worked well at extremely close quarters. The retorts of the shotguns sounded around her as the synth unit plugged away at the onrushing wave.

The genetic human units stepped back to take cover near the APCs. A creature with a massive, flared head aimed its mouth at Mae. She pushed away, swinging wide as the inner mouth shot out. She got most of her body out of its path, but the attacker made contact, ripping away the lower portion of her left arm. With her right, she flipped the shotgun around and brought the weapon to the Xenomorph's massive head.

Up this close, she noted that the red tinge to the carapace wasn't complete. Spots of regular armor were visible beneath. She aimed and fired into the jaw hinge, which was black rather than rust-red.

The high-explosive armor piercing round punctured the armor, spraying acid on her left arm and side. The coating on the Jackal synthetic protected her from having to suffer a full shut-down, but the liquid wrecked the rest of the joint in that arm. Mae bypassed the damage and kicked away from the toppling Xeno. She broadcast her observation to the synthetic network, and back to Lieutenant Ackerman.

Whatever the red substance meant on these unique specimens, it offered them extra durability that needed to be considered.

The Xenomorphs' charge pushed the synths back to the APCs. Jackals fired, the APC's DSGR smart missiles boomed out, but the creatures were faster. The humans, despite their advanced armor, took injuries and casualties. These Xenos took no prisoners. They didn't drag any Jackals away. That was unusual, too. They seemed singularly intent on ripping people apart, rather than cocooning them for reproductive purposes.

Ackerman plugged in new parameters, instructing the sentry robots and the Good Boys to aim for the black areas. They did so, and pushed the assault off from their position. The Jackals' combination of sonic and flame attacks drove the Xenos back toward the jungle. Once their attackers were further out, the APCs fired the RE700 rotary cannons with greater efficiency.

Leaving their dead, the surviving Xenos retreated. Birthed from Shānmén's large avian population, they sprinted across open ground. They also ran serpentine to avoid most of the Jackals' bullets.

So they inherited intelligence, too. Mae considered that the original animals might have encountered humans before, and passed that experience on to the mutated forms.

Mae reloaded by jamming her rifle against her leg and using her remaining right hand. Four synths had been damaged beyond saving in the rush. Fireteam Alpha's squad lost Private Adam Zeller. Rushing avian Xenos trampled Fireteam Beta's Private Jean Beaulieu.

The Jackals' exoskeletons saved lives but all had taken damage. They pulled the injured back to the APCs, and the medics set about patching them up. The Jackals prepared for acid burns and claw slashes, as they did in all encounters. Still, Mae thought she detected a flicker of concern on Lieutenant Ackerman's face.

He came up the line to see how his platoon fared.

"They probed us, seeing how well we are armed," he suggested as Corporal Ware and Private Lewis helped Private Sanouk to the medic. "Good thing Mae spotted the extra protection the red adaptation gave them, or we'd be toast." Ackerman again scanned the silent jungle.

"I'd love to drop an AGM-220C Hellhound II into those fucking trees, sir," Masako said with a twist of her lips.

"You know we can't," Ackerman replied. "Tunnels riddle the whole damn area. We might collapse the mountain on the people we're trying to rescue."

Masako shook her head. "Civvies get in the way all the time, sir, but I understand—they're our mission."

"Yeah, they're still coming to us, Sergeant Littlefield." Ackerman rubbed his chin. "Fighting their way tooth and nail to get here. Your job is to hold this ground."

She snapped off a salute. "Then we hold, sir. No question."

The synthetic unit took a moment to run bypasses on any damage and quick diagnostics on their systems. Mae followed suit. With a hand missing, aiming and firing would be difficult, but she might manage an incinerator unit. A glance down at the dripping remains of her limb brought a peculiar reaction as a new subroutine passed through her.

"Fear, yes, quite a motivator for humans." Davis's voice trembled on the edge of melancholy in her head.

If this body takes more damage, where will I go? Mae asked, even though she expected he wouldn't reply. Instead, she ran through her compilations of poetry, prose, and music from human history. There was no consensus. She began to understand the attraction of religion to genetic humans. *It must be difficult to live with so much uncertainty.*

Her diagnostic revealed no damage to her body's primary systems. They would repair her once back on the *Fury*. Even so, her fate was far from assured.

Privates Brendan O'Connor and Majid Younis broke down one of the sentry guns. Near the waterway, the weapon had taken major acid damage during the attack, and they worked to replace it with a new unit. Both guns were heavy and awkward to take apart, and then remount. O'Connor and Younis argued, but she interpreted it as playful. Genetic humans used interesting methods of showing unity and comradeship.

O'Connor almost dropped the broken unit, which inspired Younis to call him a "weak-ass boot." This prompted him to mutter that she should lift the replacement by herself. As she bent over to "show him how it gets done," the water behind them erupted as if someone had dropped a grenade in the stream.

A twelve-meter beast burst from the stream, which didn't look as if it could have held a creature such size. This Xeno wore the same rust-red armor, but its head was fully half of its length. Jaws flew open, displaying teeth on all four surfaces, some curved outward for the best grip.

The secondary mouth and the punching mechanism did not appear. Instead, the whole inner skull slid forward out of the primary mouth, a flashing bone maw that didn't allow O'Connor enough time to get out of the way.

The beast crushed him in an instant, beyond the ability of the armor to protect him. Younis got a heartbeat more. She rolled to the left, falling in a tangle of half-assembled sentry gun and the guts of her colleague. She tried to bring her rifle up, but the water monster twisted quicker than should have been possible for something so large. A tilt of its head and the creature grabbed her by the shoulder and upper arm.

The synthetic units fired round after round into the Xeno's side, unable to use flame units because of the private in its grasp. Younis howled as she got pulled into the river. Her trigger finger jammed on her rifle, then the bullets flew wide, spraying the platoon rather than the beast that gripped her.

Synthetic unit A-Beta fell to Mae's left, a direct shot to his head incapacitating him. The Jackals reacted, rushing forward to attempt a rescue. The amphibious Xenomorph rolled its massive body over on Younis until her screaming stopped. Then, as quickly as it arrived, it slipped back into the water, taking the silenced victim.

Mae stood next to the stream, training her gun and her senses. The water was only a meter deep at its greatest. It was impossible that a creature that large could have remained hidden in such shallow water.

The synth unit held position until they gathered O'Connor's remains, and then they pulled the line back toward the APC. The lieutenant's face held in a flat mask, but a small muscle in his neck twitched. They secured a new perimeter, and he called Mae over. Masako and Sergeant Euta stood to each side of Ackerman, discussing in low voices what just happened.

"...have to be underwater caves," Masako offered. "Something not on the scans."

Euta looked down at his boots. "Recon shit the bed on this one."

"We have limited intel on Shānmén, less even for the areas around the mines," Mae offered. She glanced from one human to another. They blamed themselves for not knowing the unknown. "Eitr-rich areas are notoriously difficult to scan with regular methods. Nothing indicated any kind of underwater cave systems."

Ackerman shot her a look, but without enough data on how the lieutenant acted under pressure, she didn't know how to decipher it.

"Then I want you to deploy some submarine PUPS to find every damn entrance to these caves," the lieutenant said. "Can't have the survivors running out here just to become Xeno food. Get on it!"

"Yes, sir!" Mae saluted and went to do as commanded. However, she couldn't help but replay the events she had just witnessed. Did the gaps in her knowledge contribute to the deaths? Was this the feeling Ackerman dealt with, from his position of leadership? If so, then she could only imagine what her own mother coped with as leader of the Jackals.

Chastened. That was the word genetic humans used. Mae didn't like the feeling at all, and was determined not to experience it again.

27

SHADOW DAUGHTER

Lena burst through into the tunnel, clutching Bái Yún to her, choking on the dust and debris. The girl's terrified breathing sounded right in her ear, but she didn't scream or howl.

The dark on the other side was so thick that Lena's next few steps were a total leap of faith. She might have tripped and broken her ankle, or fallen fifty meters to her death. When she made that move, everything remained unknown.

Instead, she slipped in a trickle of water and stumbled against a wall of rock. Her system pumped with so much adrenalin, she didn't register when the surface ripped the hell out of her hand.

Bái Yún let out a stifled cry—a tiny sound. The noise of someone whose grief and terror had almost overwhelmed her.

Carter emerged next. Shock twisted even his synthetic face. Antonijevic stumbled out, his face splattered with Hewitt's blood. Whatever the thrill of discovery might have been, seeing a person ripped in half right in front of you was an experience you wouldn't forget in a hurry.

After a long moment, Lena concluded her mother wasn't coming. She stood in the archaeologist's light, her hand wrapped over Bái Yún's head, and tried to process that.

Toru half-tumbled through the opening. The young man's blood matted her braids and covered her face. As she stepped from the rocks, she wiped her cheek with the sleeve of her overall.

"What the fuck was in that container, Mum?" Lena gasped out, propping herself against the wall of the tunnel.

"I... I'm not sure," Toru said as she glanced up and down the corridor. She didn't take Bái Yún from her daughter, though. Lena could tell how exhaustion already washed over her mother. She walked with a limp, that old knee and hip injury kicking in under so much stress. Soon, all of their bodies—except Carter's—would run out of adrenalin, and Lena didn't know how they'd go on.

Yet they had no choice.

Toru's wrist-pd still worked despite crashing into the wall, but the tempered glass sported a crack through the middle. She tried reaching the outside world.

"Jackals, do you read? We're coming to you. Come back please..."

Static crackled through the pd, a tinny hint of a human voice. The word seemed like "hurry."

"No dawdling, then," Lena said, giving Bái Yún a squeeze. "We don't have far to go." The little girl managed a nod through her knotted hair, but didn't reply.

"This water drains into the sluice tunnel." Toru pointed to the flickering map on her wrist-pd. "We might have to crawl for a short portion."

"We can do that." Lena pushed Bái Yún's hair out of her eyes.

Her mother nodded as she flicked her hand, sending the updated co-ordinates to their devices. Afterward she straightened, adjusted her satchel on one shoulder, and the rock drill on the other.

"Come on." Toru limped with determination down the corridor. "Carter, Antonijevic, take point." Both men pushed ahead so that their shining lights gave the slower two somewhere to aim.

Lena looked around. The survivors' headlamps danced over the pitted surface. This tunnel wasn't finished—as if the builders had abandoned the project half-way. There were those strange letters, but they seemed incomplete.

"What weapons do we have left, Mum?"

Toru glanced down at the indicator on their one remaining rock drill. "I have ten percent reading on this, but we still have some charges. Could still do plenty of damage, if need be."

Lena glanced ahead. Carter and the archaeologist were

only dim outlines, but they moved at a good speed. They picked up the pace. Looking into her mother's eyes, Lena's stomach twisted. Toru didn't always reveal her motives, but her daughter became good at anticipating them.

"Give me the satchel," she said, holding out her hand.

Toru didn't obey. "I should keep it. If anyone is blowing charges here, it will be me."

Carter stopped, and mother and daughter almost ran into him. Antonijevic waited nearby, staying out of range of this conversation.

"I am still running at an optimal level," the synthetic said, trying to use logic on Lena's mother. Toru let out a choked half-laugh.

"Getting uppity, I see. Just because you can set these things off now doesn't mean you should." Lena caught tears gleaming in her mother's eyes. "I don't have time to argue," she said, leaning at an awkward angle. "My damned hip is slowing me down, and..." she grabbed Lena's upper arm, "I can't carry Bái Yún."

"Nana," the little girl said under her breath.

"No, Toru." In this light, Carter's expression did not differ from a human's. He understood what she meant. Toru's jaw clenched as her expression hardened.

"Don't make me use the failsafe. I'd hate that. I'd do it... but I'd hate having to." Her hands worked on the satchel's strap for a moment, as if she expected this to come to a fight. Lena swallowed hard, before reaching across and touching the back of Toru's hand.

"OK, Ma," she said. "No need to do that. We got your back. The Knot tightens under pressure, right?" The three of them stood still in the near dark for a long moment, understanding passing between them. Lena dropped a kiss on Bái Yún's head. The girl was all that mattered now.

They moved on together without saying a word. Toru kept her hand on Lena's back, a gesture that she might have shrugged off on a regular day. Her own limbs got heavier as the adrenalin wore off. Bái Yún slipped on her hip, and it took a real force of will to hitch her up higher.

"I can walk," the little girl whispered. "Let me walk, Auntie."

As Lena considered doing so, a roar sounded behind them. This wasn't the hiss or the scream of the monsters. Whatever made that horrific noise was far larger. And pissed off. She wondered if the stuff Toru threw on the massive humanoid figure might be the black goo Nathan had described. It couldn't be the same... could it?

Then she remembered. Jīn Huā gave Bái Yún that recording of some communication between this place and the ship. Perhaps there had been some kind of connection.

Huge, pounding footsteps crashed down the tunnel toward the survivors. The creature that tore Hewitt apart had much longer legs than they did.

"Run!" Toru shouted, looping her hand through the satchel to keep it in place. Lena clasped Bái Yún close and sprinted down the corridor. Antonijevic's headlamp offered little light or direction.

"Come on!" His call echoed off the rock walls, even though he was a long way in front of them.

Not like he's got a limp or a seven-year-old to carry, Lena thought, even as her legs burned and her arms ached. Bái Yún reached out behind.

"Nana! Nana… keep up!"

Lena risked a glance back. Toru's limp was worse. As she followed them down the tunnel, she lurched back and forth. Two more bellows followed them, announcing the arrival of even grander nightmares. In a panic, Lena screamed for Carter to help her mother, and Antonijevic to keep going.

"Hang on… hang on…" she gasped out. Her own breathing came out in a hot, constricted gasp. She locked her arms around Bái Yún, even if doing so made her own stride uneven and unstable. Lena shot another glance over her shoulder. The beam of her headlamp caught the creatures racing down the corridor toward them.

They were the builders of this place—at least she assumed as much—but twisted in such a way that only nightmares could conjure. They now wore the same long skull as the catacomb attackers, with bared, pointed teeth and hungry mouths. A smooth black shell with a bluish hue replaced any sign of eyes. She glimpsed talons and a long tail that hadn't been in place when the first giant tore Hewitt apart.

Toru spun around and fired her rock drill at them, but the charge ran out after a moment. The white light spluttered, blinded everyone for a moment, and then died. The lead horror swiped out with its long arms, knocking Toru from her feet.

Lena cried out, and the second one's head oriented toward her.

From whichever corner they'd thrown her mother into, Toru called out, "Keep running, Len!" Carter dropped back to help Toru, and the retort of his pistol sounded in the darkness. The second monster, though, locked its attention on Lena and Bái Yún.

She ran like a terrified rabbit, guided by only glimpses of the surrounding tunnel and the desire to keep the little girl safe. Behind, the monster snarled; the impact of its massive feet on the ground told her they only had moments to live.

Her mother called her name again, but too late and too far away. She'd already lost her bearings and there was no time to check her wrist-pd. Tunnels twisted and turned on each side of them. Lena took every single one without thinking at all.

She didn't cry out. She ran. Twice, their pursuer lashed out, sending chunks of rock flying. She ducked right and left, the breeze of its attacks passing over her head. Its size must limit how fast the creature went, and how accurate its blows could be. After a few minutes, there were no other lights around them. They were alone with the thing.

Bái Yún, from her position, got a better view, but she didn't scream.

A wall came up fast. A dead end.

Lena stood, panning her light over the surface. The monster behind pushed its way after them. Its hardened skin grated against the surface of the cave walls.

With eyes used to judging rock, Lena spotted a narrow fissure. She couldn't tell where the gap led, but it had to be better than the creature forcing itself toward them. Dropping Bái Yún to the ground, she pushed her forward.

"Time to wriggle, little bear." She wanted to make a joke, but the girl was old enough to understand survival. Her diminutive body fitted through the crack.

Lena looked back, swiveling her light. The huge form bent to get into this cave, but it wouldn't fit through the fissure. Even without eyes, though, the monster kept track of her. That massive, curved head split open at the jaw, and a second mouth emerged, ready to punch through her skull.

Spurred on by that, Lena shoved herself into the split in the rock. Being trapped this way had terrified her as a little girl, jammed between rocks, unable to go forward or back. Now, however, she found it preferable to death.

"Keep going, Bái Yún." Lena got herself into the fissure, but she wasn't as small. The rock raked her back and her fingertips, and scraped over her breasts and forehead.

The monster reached for her. Lena didn't have enough room to catch her breath and scream. Instead, she only let out a low groan of terror. Tears and sweat poured down her face as she strained to press deeper into the crack. The long, lean arm reached into the fissure, grasping for her, but the rest of it could not fit. The tip of one finger grazed Lena's shoulder, slicing through the top layer of her flesh. Gulping back tears, she strained and wriggled harder. Her own blood acted as lubricant as she pushed forward.

The monster's low hiss filled the crack with its rage and frustration.

When Lena popped out the other side of the gap, Bái Yún grabbed hold of her legs, sobbing into them as if her chest would break open. Stroking the girl's hair and clutching her just as tightly, Lena scanned their new surroundings. It was hard to make out with only one headlamp, but they'd escaped through the fissure into another series of rooms and tunnels.

Panning her light around, she took in many deep and long shelves carved into the rock. As the thin beam passed over them, she stuffed back a scream. More of the huge humanoid beings lay there. Lena imagined them sliding out and reaching for them.

She forced herself to be calm, and as her breathing subsided, she realized these were dead, and thus no threat. The bodies lay desiccated, some only a pile of bones. A couple of them wore the strange, short elephant snouts, while others had the stern, human faces.

As Lena peered closer, she saw that one snouted face had fallen off a humanoid one. The snout was more of a mask. Lena didn't understand what that meant, nor did she feel any better about them. They were all monsters.

Circling the room, with Bái Yún's hand in her own, Lena scanned the corpses that surrounded them. With her eyes and her headlamp fixed on the shapes, she almost missed the void in the middle of the room. Her foot slipped on a low wall, broke through, and for a second she lost her balance. Only Bái Yún, yanking on her arm, pulled her back from the edge.

Lena dropped to her knees and burst out laughing. The outburst emerged as high-pitched and hysterical, then turned into a strangled sob. It would have been the height of stupidity, after fleeing for their lives for so long, to die in a fall because she didn't look where she was going.

"Are you alright, Auntie Lena?" Bái Yún crouched down next to her. Her dirty, sad little face peered at her with concern. "Do you know where we are?" She reached out and cuddled the girl on her lap while she looked at her wrist-pd.

"The PUPS didn't find this bit."

When Lena searched for the drones' signals, her heart sank. The disposable PUPS had only a very short battery life. They scanned as long as possible and then dropped, inanimate, once their juice ran out. Every unit they'd released was already down. She'd hoped to use them to find a way out of this.

She wanted to scream, pound her fists on the rock, but that wouldn't do anything except scare Bái Yún.

Rocking the girl back and forth, Lena tried to figure out what to do. If she moved, where to? The enormous monsters waited out there. The risk Lena might take for herself differed from the one she'd choose with Bái Yún's life at stake.

In the end, her experience of life underground offered a glimmer of hope. The personal data transmitters that broadcast when the miners died. The Combine might recover their bodies, but not always. Their only concern was not paying dead workers. The PDT had a much stronger signal, but a lack of life signs triggered it.

Time to get dead.

"Stay still, little bear," she said to Bái Yún, stroking back in tangled hair. "I'm going to signal Nana."

The girl nodded. "I can sit criss-cross, Auntie Lena."

"Good girl."

Lena shuffled a few feet away and turned her back to her, so Bái Yún didn't have to see what she did next. Retrieving the small pocketknife from her kit, she held out her arm, focused the headlamp on her bicep, and rammed the blade in. The pain made her woozy for a moment, but after collecting herself, Lena wiggled the knife left and right, probing for the PDT. Though the wound wasn't too deep, blood pooled over her fingers. As she stuck her index finger into the wound, the pill-shaped PDT slipped out and bounced across the floor.

Cursing, fumbling, Lena searched around with her other hand, brushing over rock and dirt. When she found the device, she almost wondered if miracles might be real. Picking it up, Lena pulled some connectors out of her pack, and attached the PDT to her wrist device. She didn't find it difficult to hack into the system—the device didn't have any code protections.

Lena told the PDT she had no life signs. That would freak her mother out, so she added a change that they should pick up. Instead of a steady signal, she instructed the PDT to broadcast in a rhythm. Toru would remember the ancient SOS signal. Miners still sometimes tapped this out on a rock, if trapped.

Ahead, the little bean turned from green to red. The PDT didn't wail, instead increasing its signal strength. It wouldn't reach topside, but Lena didn't need it to. Monitoring the flashing red, Lena wriggled back to Bái Yún and cuddled up to her.

"I've sent a message, little bear. When you get lost underground, that's what you do. You stay put and wait for help."

Bái Yún stared down for a moment.

"But who will find us, Auntie? Not the monsters?"

The image of that curved, deadly head was hard to forget in the cave's darkness. Everywhere she looked, the monster seemed to wait for them.

Lena fished in her belt pocket and brought out one of the sweet biscuits she'd stowed before they set off. Handing the treat to the girl, she whispered in her ear.

"Not the monsters, baby. We're safe here."

As Bái Yún ate in silence, Lena stared at the PDT. Such a tiny thing on which to pin their hopes. Strange how, in the end, life came down to the smallest of things. Lena closed her eyes and thought of Sophie, not daring to sing or whisper. She held tight to sweet memories and whispered a prayer to her mother's Earth Mother.

Only the darkness and a blinking light were left.

2 8

DECREASING CIRCLES

Smaller and smaller tunnels were the only answer to the question of survival. When the transformed builders rushed down the corridor toward them, Toru understood that.

In the chaos and the dark, she, Carter, and Antonijevic darted toward a side tunnel. She'd been positive that Lena and Bái Yún ran behind them. She wouldn't have gone otherwise.

The thundering of the massive monster's feet echoed everywhere. The breeze of its hands whipping so close drove her down to the ground. Staying on her hands and knees, Toru led the way toward a craggy overhang. Every muscle and bone screamed as she wriggled and pushed underneath. The rock ripped her hands, tore at her stiff back, but she didn't stop.

The huge creature snapped and hissed behind them,

its talons scraping at the stone, reaching in after them. A stream of blood oozed down Toru's shoulder and over her fingers, but she barely noticed. Survival turned her into an animal that might chew its own limb off to escape.

Only when the three of them emerged into a dry cave on the other side did she realize her dreadful mistake. She cast her gaze everywhere, looking for her daughter and granddaughter. She did not find them. Toru pivoted around and pummeled Carter's broad chest.

"I told you to watch them! Where are they?" Toru didn't care how loud her voice grew, or how she might bring the monsters. None of that mattered.

Looking up at the synthetic, she saw the truth in his eyes. They had programmed him to protect her. By love or by design, that was the only thing he could do. A wash of hatred grabbed hold of her as Toru ground her teeth in frustration. She should have known better. Men always disappointed—no matter whether flesh or plastic.

As always, she needed to do everything herself. Shutting Carter out of consideration, she flicked her fingers and brought up the map of this labyrinth on her wrist-pd. If any of the PUPS stayed active, she would instruct them to search for Lena and Bái Yún.

Her eyes darted over the display, but she let out a low, stifled groan. All the little pinpricks of light were gone. The PUPS were dead. They'd perished in the darkness, like everyone else. While Toru contemplated her options, Antonijevic paced back and forward.

"We should get moving. Those rescuers won't wait forever." His voice came out high-pitched, fast-paced and cracked. He'd lost all that archaeologist's curiosity since mortality slapped him in the face—along with Hewitt's blood.

"We're not going anywhere." Toru didn't even spare him a glance. "Not until we have my daughter and granddaughter."

He looked as if he might rush at her, so she lit the tip of the rock drill in case he'd forgotten who led here. She hadn't enough charge left to affect the monster, but two percent would cut him in half if he challenged her.

Carter interrupted what might have been a very short power struggle, by holding up his wrist-pd.

"Toru—Lena's PDT! It's not acting right..."

For a long moment Toru stared at the signal, blind panic clawing at her as the signal blipped in and out. A PDT signaled death for a miner, but always came out as a steady light. This one danced to a rhythm. A familiar rhythm. Toru's knees almost failed her.

"SOS. Goddamnit, that code is older than me..."

Wiping a bead of sweat off her face, she oriented herself. "This area is unmapped, but these streams wore out a series of fissures before people, or those... builder creatures. The Svarog tailings tunnel is the lowest point, and drains everything." She checked Lena's signal. "Looks like she's on the same old waterway as we are. Come on!"

Neither of them argued with her—they knew better

than to try. Toru's instincts directed them, more than any blinking light. The trickle of water under their feet showed the way out, but might it also be the Earth Mother leading Toru to her daughter? In the cloying and silent dark, anything might be possible.

They followed the line of smaller caverns in a steady progression. Sometimes that meant crawling on hands and knees to get through. In other instances, they needed to wriggle along vertical fissures caused by erosion. Freezing cold water cascaded over Toru's back and neck. When she lost her way or experienced the clutch of indecision, she'd put her hand on the rock wall, the moisture trickling in the right direction. So many technological advances made since leaving Earth, but the old ways would save them.

The caverns seemed endless. If Lena and Bái Yún weren't the prize at stake, Toru might have given up, stopped, and curled up to die. Every bone and muscle ached. Her joints crackled and complained with each movement, but she pushed on. Even Antonijevic didn't say a word of complaint—a good choice. One wrong word and Toru would leave him in the dark.

A glance at the map told her they were close to her loved ones. Lena and Bái Yún—*please Mother, please let that be true*—waited in another small cavern close to the mouth of the tailings tunnel.

When a tiny pinprick of light gleamed in the dark ahead, Toru ran, tripping, careless of what monsters might lurk in the dark. Lena met her halfway, grabbing her tight around the shoulders and pulling her to one side.

"Watch out, Mum!" They stood embracing, laughing, until Toru noted that they were teetering on the edge of an abyss. A solid shaft dropped away to their right and promised only death.

"Whoever designed this was shit," Toru said with a giddy laugh as Bái Yún grabbed hold of her hands. Getting down on one knee, Toru hugged the little girl, whispering, "Told you Nana will always find you. I keep my promises." Tears like the icy water of the caverns ran down her cheeks. Mopping them up with her sleeve, Toru kissed Bái Yún's forehead. "Now, how about we get out of here, huh?"

Her granddaughter nodded without replying, as if she didn't quite believe what her eyes told her. Toru almost didn't trust it herself, but she'd take whatever kindness the Earth Mother cared to deal out. Carter and Antonijevic caught up, moving more cautiously.

"Let's go, then." Toru got to her feet and raised her wrist-pd to check their position again. "Not far now. Everyone stay together." She led them off into the dark, toward the end of the secondary caverns. As expected, it was another tight overhang.

Pushing aside Carter's offer of help, she lowered herself to her knees and led the way. She didn't know how much more her body could take, but damned if she'd say anything, here on the edge of success. Together the five of them crawled and dragged themselves along the overhang and back into the main tunnel.

Toru emerged first, knowing in her bones that the transformed builders waited somewhere on the other side. They were predators through and through, and these hidden places held little prey. Her breath caught in her chest while her heart raced right alongside. As they stood, exhaustion threatened to overwhelm her.

Glancing over her shoulder, Toru recognized that everyone else—except Carter, of course—felt the same. Yet they needed to find a reserve of energy, because from here survival would be all about speed.

As they paused, there was silence, broken only by the trickle of water which ran down the center. It was their last guide, and the one she trusted most. Water underground acted in a predictable fashion—unlike everything else in this situation. Toru motioned and pushed them ahead of her, toward a glimmer of faint light. At first, she thought it might be a hallucination—or maybe she was dead already.

"Nana!" Bái Yún said, turning to shoot a brilliant smile at Toru. Her grandmother nodded. This wasn't the white glow of daylight, but the muted light of stars and moons. Whatever it was, she would take it, as long as they were on the right path.

"A little faster," Toru said, her voice bouncing alarmingly off the widening tunnel. The four of them picked up the pace to a jog. Carter glanced back at her, but she gave him a little shake of her head.

Don't you dare. You help them.

Their feet on the rocks, their breathing bouncing off the walls of the tunnel, the occasional stifled sob from Bái Yún, must have acted as an alert. From behind, a low-grade rumble started up. In that instant, the tunnel seemed to grow longer, the glimmer of light further away.

The survivors ran harder, and thudding footsteps sounded again. The monstrous builders must have been waiting for any sign of life, and now they had found it. No one needed to say anything. From synthetic to child, they all understood. This was their only chance. Run now, as hard as they could, or get caught.

Carter did what she hoped he wouldn't—he dropped back to Toru. He stayed at her side, and she understood he always would. His nature left her no other choice. She grabbed hold of his hand.

"Carter, my prince, my flower, my everything."

When she first received the gift from her sisters, Toru chose trigger words she would never say—even in the heat of passion. At the keyword phrase, his eyes flickered for a moment, then awaited her change in commands.

"Protect Lena and Bái Yún first."

She hurt to say those words—not because they weren't important—but because they forced him to obey her. As an indentured worker, the Combine required her to do things she didn't want to. She'd never imagined being the one doing the compelling.

"Yes, ma'am," Carter replied, before speeding up to get

closer to them. When Lena glanced back, Toru gestured her on. Even Antonijevic paused for a moment.

"Goddamn, move!" she screamed at them, because silence no longer protected the survivors.

The builders' longer legs carried them closer to their victims. The thunderous roars and the rocks scattered by their feet heralded their arrival in only a few more moments. They'd rip the last survivors of Svarog apart and satisfy whatever monstrous rage burned in their dark and terrifying forms.

The humans burst out of the tunnel in a frantic rush, into the humid night, as if spat out by the Earth Mother herself. Fresh air hit Toru's chest like an explosion, flooding through her like a blessing she never thought to see. Twilight among the trees of Shānmén became more beautiful than she remembered.

Yet they didn't have time to enjoy the moment.

Toru's hip and knee screamed for her attention—to stop for a moment, let them rest. She knew she didn't have a second to waste on pain.

Up ahead, floodlights beckoned them all on. The lines of armed soldiers were a dream that she glimpsed through sweat and pain. The Jackals were more than just a hope or a carbon monoxide hallucination.

Stumbling over the uneven ground, Toru slipped in the water which deepened a few meters from the tunnel. She half-fell into the stream up to her knees.

Their saviors seemed far away—and the builders

only a few heartbeats behind. The curved heads scraped against the top of the tunnel. Toru pulled herself upright and turned to face them. The Knot—or what remained of it—needed to push on. She grew more confident that Carter would get them to safety.

The transformed and twisted builders emerged from the tunnel and unfolded to their full height. Their long tails slashed the air, as those curved heads swiveled left and right. They didn't seem to have eyes at all, but perhaps the elongated spines on their back contained some other senses. Toru had dealt with all kinds of peculiar cave creatures possessing echolocation, scent receptors, or a primitive heat vision.

Strange how, even as she faced death, her brain tried to rationalize what stood before her. In reality, the monsters were larger and faster than one old wrung-out miner. She wouldn't last long.

Yet, Toru had something they didn't.

She was armed and ready to rock.

While the remnants of her family ran toward the Jackals, Toru flicked on her drill and played the laser over the monsters. They screamed in outrage more than fear, staggering back a few steps. The drill only had a few seconds before her battery pack died.

When the weapon spluttered out, the pair of mutated aliens let out a long, satisfied hiss. Their sharp mouths opened, dripping with some kind of ooze—drool, perhaps. They loped toward her, over the rocks.

Toru fished around in her satchel, her hand closing on the charges. She didn't have many. If she had more, she would have brought the whole mountain down. That would have been a beautiful way to go out.

Without even looking up into their faces, Toru stood her ground. Her body throbbed in pain, but that seemed distant now. She doubted she would get more than one chance to slow them down. If she did this right, she might buy enough time for Carter, Lena, and Bái Yún to reach safety.

Toru wasn't a tall woman, but she straightened to her full height, ready to face her ancestors. Her father hadn't died easily at Bowen's Landing, but he'd been on his feet. This might be a gift from the Earth Mother, and she accepted it. She made her peace, and her life for theirs seemed a fair bargain.

Then her moment was interrupted. From above, a scream sounded that sent a wash of primal ear down her spine. Even the monstrous builders paused in their advance. Toru stood in place, wondering what fresh hell this planet might yet serve up.

2 9

NIGHTMARE OF WINGS

For a moment, Toru thought she'd imagined the noise. Then the hellish scream sounded a second time from above.

Instinct forced her into a crouch while she stared into the darkening sky. The builders stood only twenty meters away, their black heads whipping from side to side, straining whatever senses they possessed in a similar way.

Something dropped low over them, then rose to block out the moons and the stars for an instant. A primitive fear welled up inside, and Toru she wished to God she'd read the Shānmén memo more closely when she arrived. She sure as shit never imagined anything like this.

If the creatures above were bats or birds, they were hellish big ones. The flying things screamed and hissed into the warm night air. The builders turned their flashing mouths upward and howled back as if answering some ancient challenge.

Toru recognized a chance when she saw one. Keeping hold of the detonator, she shoved the satchel underneath a nearby pile of rocks. Then, with her knee and hip screaming, she swung about and ran after her family.

A gust of air passed over her again. She ducked and twisted away by reflex. Her foot slipped between two rocks, her ankle bending. The bone didn't snap, but the old injury hurt like hell.

Biting back curses, Toru corrected herself. She jerked her already abused hip and knee in an effort to escape the crevice. As she pulled her ankle free, she screamed in rage, challenging the flying creature above. *These must be the monsters that took Pinar and Nathan.* Few people thought to look up.

In Toru's favor, the Jackals and the builders were larger targets than she. Favoring her foot, she glanced back. The bright circle of floodlights punctured the darkness, revealing fresh nightmares.

Nathan had mentioned something about the native eagle of Shānmén. She'd brushed off his vivid description, the ten-meter wingspan of the giant bird and its fearsome reputation. Since they lived in the mountain heights, the bioweapon may have taken longer to reach them.

Three dropped on the builders standing in the riverbed. Their leathery wings flapped twice before they engulfed her pursuers. The monsters snarled and snapped, their secondary mouths punching out at one another. The winged ones buffeted the builders, who refused to fall down or be carried off as easily as humans.

Standing by the rocks, transfixed, Toru noted the difference in color. The builders were a slick black, while these airborne nightmares were reddish brown. Did that mark them as enemies?

The flying creatures snatched at the builders with taloned arms, while battering with their armored tails. Their flatter, broader heads resembled shovels but shared those strange dorsal spines.

The battle raged on, so close to her, but Toru didn't move from the spot. She might have stayed put until the end if the Jackals hadn't taken the chance to fire at all their enemies. Their APCs opened up behind her, firing heavy caliber projectiles at both. The barrage deafened her, crouched between the three unstoppable forces.

She wanted to run, but wasn't sure in which direction. In the flashes of the artillery fire, it was impossible to tell who might be winning, but at least the APC fire appeared to be injuring them.

Two more of the winged monstrosities swooped down onto a builder, knocking the giant off its feet. They reared back and struck again. Their combat would have been fascinating to watch further, but Toru turned her gaze on the line of Jackals she could see in the strobing light. The individual soldiers fired smaller rounds toward the tangle of monstrosities.

Toru began to crawl toward them, limping where she could, keeping her hands raised and waving to show that she didn't pose a threat. As she did, another monster eagle slammed into the APC, snarling and crashing against the side. Its attack drew the attention of more flying nightmares. Fire erupted inside the vehicle, and then the other APC, as the twisted avians focused on the largest threats. Their blood, acid like the rest, fell on the machinery, forcing the Jackals back.

As they regrouped away from the destroyed transports, Toru thought she caught the profiles of Lena and Bái Yún with them. That was all the impetus she needed to find the last bit of her strength. Toru grinned, lurched to her feet, and tried to join them.

Her foot slipped into the narrow stream that stood between her and her family. She was so close.

A massive head, filled with teeth and a second mouth, erupted out of the water. Already reaching for her, the thing lunged toward Toru. She didn't have any energy left, and she recognized death as soon as its massive jaws opened wide. She would slip right into its gaping mouth with no trouble at all.

She closed her eyes for the end.

The sound of its teeth sliding off metal surprised Toru. A combat synthetic, one arm missing, jerked her to her feet. It had a phalanx shield deployed on that missing stump, and a shotgun tucked under one armpit.

"Are you alright, ma'am?"

The android had moved Toru behind its shield. Around them, a unit of synthetics—armed identically—rained shotgun fire upon the hissing, snapping river monster. Toru's eyes locked on a tiny, curious detail; an infinity symbol on the synthetic's shoulder.

Three military Good Boys screamed their sonic howls toward this new grotesquerie. It thrashed its gleaming bronze head from side to side, snapping its monstrous jaws at them.

"Fine," Toru gasped out. "But let's hustle, OK?"

The synthetic nodded. Off in the distance, the roar of a ship broke through the chaos of battle. The Jackals must have called for reinforcements. No sound was ever so sweet to Toru's ears.

The soldiers kept up a steady rate of fire, even as the builders and the transformed eagles struggled in a vicious battle on the other side of the stream. They seemed evenly matched, but how many more combatants waited in the sky?

"Stay with me." The synthetic's voice remained calm, even as the river monster lunged again. The other synths slid backward in the mud and rock. Their shields didn't crack, but even combat androids had their limits. The creature they attempted to hold back was just bigger and heavier. Only the Good Boys kept the monster from ripping them all apart.

Overhead, the dropship circled, firing at everything that had been touched by the bioweapon. Around them the trees groaned and snapped as heavy fire rained down in the jungle. After a minute of this, the ship had cleared enough of a path to land. The survivors and the Jackals retreated toward its open cargo bay, firing as they went.

She had something to offer to this moment. Squinting in the dust kicked up by the engines, Toru flicked open the detonator unit and triggered the last of the mine's charges. In the ensuing explosion, the struggling combatants were outlined by the plume of fire. The warped builders might be huge, but at last the flying monsters overwhelmed them, knocking them to their knees to tear them apart. Toru might have even felt pity for them, if they hadn't tried to murder her loved ones.

The one-armed combat synth guided Toru toward safety in the dropship. Everything hurt as it buckled her into a harness and slotted itself opposite in a rack. Jackals took their places, strapping themselves into the emergency webbing for a hasty evacuation from the planet's surface.

"Hey, Mum. Glad you caught up." When Toru turned her head, her heart leapt as Lena's grin emerged through layers of dirt and blood. Her daughter grabbed her hand, interlacing her fingers tight. On her other side, Bái Yún's eyes were wide, her lips trembling, but she managed a smile and a thumbs up from under that mess of tangled hair.

Carter, on the far side of the girl, nodded, his face

twisted as if with more complex emotions than a synth should have. When they got back to Pylos, Toru promised herself she would apologize to him.

The archaeologist Antonijevic leaned against the wall across from them. He'd buckled into the emergency webbing, but his eyes remained locked on the floor, his face grimy and pale. He'd have to survive many days of grilling by the Combine, but at least he'd got out when Hewitt hadn't.

As the dropship roared away from the surface of Shānmén, Toru and Lena stared into each other's eyes. Their grins mixed with tears and pain. Knocked to hell as they might be, they had survived. After all that loss, they'd salvaged something from death and disaster.

Lena leaned over and kissed the top of Bái Yún's head. The little girl glanced up, her eyes glazed with exhaustion and grief.

The strange synthetic with the eternity symbol on its shell watched them more closely than any military model should. Still, this one had saved her life. The older woman pushed back her dirty, bloodstained braids and nodded in its direction.

"Thank you for coming to get me. Appreciate it."

"You are most welcome, Toru McClintock-Riley. I am glad to help." As the dropship sped up into the atmosphere, the synthetic glanced down the length of the seating. "But I can't take all the credit. The entire platoon held the line."

Toru shook her head—still capable of confusion, even after all that happened.

"Are you... what the hell *are* you?"

The synthetic tilted its head in an odd gesture for a combat model. "My name is Mae." The voice seemed lighter, feminine... almost human. This was no normal combat unit.

That was *so* damned strange. Toru only stared.

Her granddaughter wasn't nearly as confused. She raised her hand and waved a fraction.

"Hi, Mae. I'm Bái Yún."

"Nice to meet you," the unit replied. "You are the first genetic human child I have ever met."

Bái Yún's lips twisted as she looked down at herself. "I'm usually cleaner than this."

Toru chuckled, but as the dropship bounced through the clouds, she grabbed at the webbing. She wasn't the only one troubled by the turbulence. Antonijevic let out a low, strangled groan. With everything he'd been through, a little air was too much. He should comfort himself with the images he'd captured on his wrist-pd. They would make his career when he got back to Pylos.

Bái Yún let out a little squeal of delight. Lena giggled at that, and Toru remembered with fondness her similar reaction at the same age. God, that seemed like only days ago.

Toru was sure it would take weeks for all the bruises to come out on her body, and that hip operation she'd been putting off—well, that just got moved forward.

"Good thing I didn't eat anything worth throwing up," Antonijevic joked, glancing down the ship. He wiped his nose with the back of his sleeve and let out a ragged breath of relief.

The motion left a black trail on his face. At first it didn't register with Toru. When they'd fought off the huge builder monsters, his jacket must have come into contact with some of the bioweapon. Now he'd smeared the liquid over his skin.

Antonijevic glanced down at his sleeve, his eyes widening even as his body shook and his eyes went black. As he spasmed in his harness, panic broke out in the belly of the dropship. Jackals threw off their restraints and grabbed for weapons. Everyone tried to get away from the twisting form as the bioweapon transformed his body.

The speed of it was terrifying to witness.

Jackals all around jerked their rifles up to fire

"For fuck's sake, don't fire in here!" someone—maybe their leader?—bellowed. "We won't be able to break atmo if you breach the ship!" Toru understood the problem. Acid or bullet damage at this point might compromise the integrity of the hull. They would never make it to the ship in orbit.

The soldiers and the last of the Knot untangled themselves from the emergency webbing, falling as far back into the bay as possible. Everyone shouted, trying to figure out what to do, but every moment they didn't come up with a solution was another that allowed the threat to grow.

Finally, the creature unfurled from its crouch like a deadly flower. The interior lights bounced off its pale, disturbed figure. The organism let out a screech that filled the belly of the dropship and promised more violence. Long, clawed hands flicked open as the monster picked out its first target.

Toru took in a long breath. Experience told her how this would end. Exhausted and angry at losing so many loved ones, she recognized the one chance for their survival. She didn't want to die, but more than that, she wanted for no more of her family to die.

She glanced back at them. Lena cradled Bái Yún, keeping her head turned away from the coming violence. Carter angled his body between them and their abomination. He obeyed her commands, even as his eyes met hers. He'd have already done the calculations; besides, he knew her well enough to guess her last move. She lifted her head a fraction. A smile that only they shared passed between them.

The three of them would be alright. She glimpsed their future in a sudden surge of realization. The Knot would tighten and protect them.

Carter didn't stop her. Toru turned around. Her hip and her knee didn't hurt at all.

"Hold on to something," she called out to the Jackals and her family.

She slammed her fist against the control. The bay door opened, and air rushed in like a tornado. It buffeted everyone, but Toru kept her arm locked around the nearest bit of webbing.

The mutation clutched onto the surface of the metal floor like a fucking tick. That didn't surprise her. Toru had hoped the force of the air might drag it out, but she wasn't quite that lucky. Whatever luck she'd had, she'd spent it in the tunnels.

Yet the creature wasn't all that big. Antonijevic hadn't been a large man, so neither was his monstrous persona. Letting go of the webbing, Toru charged down the slope of the open cargo bay. She hit it full force and wrapped her arms around the nightmare. The monster snapped and clawed at her, but she didn't let go, even when it cut her deep. What was a little blood between them now?

It tried to resist, but she insisted that they go together. Her hip spasmed with pain, but she forced herself past that. Locked together, they tumbled together from the dropship into the clouds of Shānmén.

She'd never see New Zealand again. That had been a foolish dream, but her daughter, granddaughter, and lover would get back to Pylos. Her sisters would hear of her death and raise a glass to her memory.

The mines didn't take her, and in the end, that pleased Toru. She'd never wanted to die underground.

EPILOGUE

Mae watched their grief from a distance. The survivors of Svarog—the little girl, the young woman, and the pleasure synthetic—did not venture far from each other. Gaining comfort in closeness, she presumed. They stayed in their quarters and ventured out only to eat.

Sometimes the synthetic, Carter, would fetch food and bring it back. Mae wanted to communicate with him in particular, to probe his program and find out if his feelings were real or not. The memory of her father cautioned not to do that.

"All of us, synthetic or genetic humans, must heal. Leave them be."

So, she watched from afar. When the humans went into cryosleep for the crossing to Pylos station, Mae spent her time designing herself a new body—and keeping away from EWA. The AI wanted her dead, she was certain of it, and while she wouldn't try again since the colonel reprimanded her, Mae wouldn't give her reasons or opportunities.

Before going into her hypersleep pod, Masako offered input. The body wouldn't be a David, or a Bishop. They'd custom make it to her specifications, off-book from Weyland Yutani. Mae took clues from her mother's physical form and delved into how Davis imagined himself as a human.

She'd be muscular and tall, like he wanted to be. Her face would reflect the stark planes of her mother's face, and her skin would be the same deep brown. Mae was especially proud of the short-cropped dark hair, and looked forward to styling it in the ways humans enjoyed.

When the Jackals emerged from their pods, Mae showed the design to Zula, and experienced a hint of pride in her subroutines. The colonel sat in her ready room, staring at the image for a long time. Mae thought she detected a hint of tears in her mother's eyes.

"Davis would have loved it."

Mae couldn't calculate the right thing to say.

Zula patted a nearby chair. When her daughter sat, the colonel let out a sigh.

"I've been thinking about what you told me EWA tried to do. How you were certain she wanted you dead."

Mae nodded, but remained silent.

"I know why she did it," Zula continued, "and I've taken steps to make sure it never happens again."

Running through all the computations, Mae couldn't guess the conclusions her mother had reached.

"Synthetics made by synthetics: they frighten many people, Mae. Davis created you out of love for me, but he didn't really consider the implications." Zula stared out the window at Pylos station. "Once we've finished our meeting here, I'm going to order Erynis and EWA returned to their factory settings. Your existence will become a secret. The people who know, I trust to keep quiet."

Mae stared down at her hands. A mixture of feelings ran through her—joy that her mother wanted to protect her, and guilt that she'd somehow brought this on her fellow AIs.

"And the new body?"

"We'll arrange that afterward. No need to tell them who you are." She got to her feet and rested a hand on her shoulder. "You're my daughter, and I'll protect you at all costs."

Mae stood as well; a new subroutine, uncertainty, rising to the surface.

"So... I hide?"

Zula shook her head. "When you have your new body, I will introduce you as my daughter. That's not a lie. People just don't need to find out that you are... special." She grabbed hold of Mae in a sudden hug. It was awkward at first—neither of them seemed to know where to put their arms—but she was sure they'd perfect it with practice.

Zula cleared her throat and stepped back. "First order of business, I want you to accompany me and Captain Shipp to this meeting."

This surprised Mae. She hadn't been present when the Jackals formed, but she was curious about the three generals who supplied the battalion through back channels.

"They're coming to meet us in person?"

"In secret, more like." Zula stripped out of her military attire, and from the back of her closet fished out a charcoal grey sweatshirt and matching pants. Once she put them on, Mae realized this was the first time she'd seen her mother in civilian clothing. She looked uncomfortable with it, her hand twitching for a collar that wasn't there, her gaze darting to non-regulation boots on her feet.

Outside the door, Olivia Shipp waited for them. She too wore nondescript grey clothing and seemed about as relaxed as Zula with it. She handed her superior a satchel.

"Everything in here?" the colonel asked.

Shipp nodded, her eyes flicking to Mae as she replied. "Copies of the recordings made by the comms tech on Shānmén, and all the scans of the new fauna." Zula nodded, and they made their way to the shuttle.

The *Fury* restocked at Pylos every few months. It was out of the way, and yet still busy enough for their trips to be unremarked. It was also the base of the Knot. As Mae, Shipp, and Zula made their way to their seats, the three survivors glanced up at them from their places at the back. They huddled together, the young woman cradling the little girl and her white backpack, a stuffed cat poking out of it.

Mae didn't interrupt their mourning, but her mother stopped to talk to them a moment, while Shipp and her daughter took their seats.

"Your mother's a fine leader," Captain Shipp said as she buckled herself in, "but she's also a good person. Hope you remember that."

"I am aware, Captain Shipp." Mae tilted her head. "I'm proud to be her daughter."

Shipp's piercing eyes examined the inflexible combat synth face. "I believe you are. I'm glad to hear you'll be joining us properly on the *Fury*." Her smile was unexpected. Mae wished she was in her new body, so she might return the gesture.

She settled for, "I am excited, too."

Zula took her seat, and buckled in. Her eyes were distant, locked on the window as they left the *Fury* behind. When she spoke, it was in a low, somber tone.

"Lot of good people lost down on Shānmén. I would have liked to meet that Toru McClintock-Riley. Way her daughter described her, she was one tough woman."

Shipp nodded. "We'll make her death mean something, Colonel. Best any of us can get in the end."

* * *

When the shuttle docked on Pylos, the three military women let the Knot survivors disembark first. Mae observed that a small crowd of people from Pylos rushed toward them down the dock. Their cries of joy mixed with tears as the rest of the family embraced them.

Grief was an emotion she hadn't yet studied. Mae would have loved to take notes on the scene, but she needed to concentrate on her mother's task.

They passed the Knot without interrupting, but Mae caught the gaze of the little girl, Bái Yún. Her dark eyes locked on the combat synth with the infinity symbol. She raised one hand in a tiny gesture of acknowledgement before she was swept up into the arms of her family.

As Mae, Shipp, and Zula worked their way through the busy spaceport, the synthetic contemplated that moment. What would that little girl's future be? How badly had the events of Shānmén wounded her psyche? Suddenly, she wanted the answers to those questions.

Still, she only needed a small portion of her processing power for that. The rest she used to scan the crowds ahead of the captain and the colonel. None stepped aside for Zula, so she remained part of the throng. Mae watched her mother's back every second.

The three of them made their way to Cargo Bay E7. It lay empty except for one sealed cargo container: locked, shielded, and not included in any records. Zula punched a code into the lock, and the three of them slipped in.

In the center of the dimly lit container stood a long table, with one unoccupied chair on one side, and three filled ones on the other. Zula Hendricks sat down in the empty seat, while Mae and Shipp took up places standing behind her.

In front of them sat three people who, in the official records, weren't really there—any more than the Jackals existed. They wore no uniforms but sat with the bearing of military personnel. Even though still relatively new to human interactions, Mae could tell tension filled the room.

She had been given strict instructions. Nothing would be recorded from this meeting. It was a testament to her mother's importance that she was allowed to attend. Here were the three generals from the outer worlds, ready to risk their careers—and lives—for Zula Hendricks and her Jackals.

General Christian Cunningham of the Colonial Marines sat very erect in her chair, dark skin gleaming under the lone overhead light in the container. She kept her black hair cut short but Mae observed a hint of grey in it. The broad, square form of General Kasey Ristic of the UPP sat to her right. He leaned back, green eyes locked on Zula, a mustache wrinkling on his pale face. General Washington Sekiguchi from the 3WE looked the most uncomfortable of the three. He perched on the edge of his seat, as if ready to depart at a moment's notice.

Despite their differences, all of them had recognized two things—the danger the Xenomorphs posed to all colonization, and the corruption inherent to the major corporations that sponsored much of that effort. Now they had a third reason—the pathogen that had taken two worlds off the chessboard.

Shipp stepped forward and handed the disks to Zula, a gesture designed to get the generals' attention. The colonel leaned forward and slid them across the desk, one for each representative. General Cunningham was the first to take it. Her accent marked her as coming from somewhere in the Canadian heartland.

"These are the only copies of your report?"

"There's one on the *Fury* too. Encrypted, of course." Her mother wasn't an idiot.

"Insurance?" The lean Japanese General Sekiguchi shook his head, smiling in a way Mae interpreted as insincere. "Why would you need it? You bring a combat synth in here, but we are the ones risking everything." His voice dripped with British vowels, powered by colonial history.

Zula Hendricks shrugged. "Just covering my ass. This thing has a lot of layers."

Ristic let out a low rumble of displeasure. "This *thing*… as you call it… it smells like week-old fish." His Serbian accent grew thicker as he spoke. "My nation has lost a valuable resource. We're never going to get down there to mine Eitr again. Shānmén is a dead world."

Cunningham shot her colleague a look. "We've all lost planets to this pathogen, and we'll lose more if someone doesn't stop it. No one's got time to grieve."

That didn't really surprise Mae. There must have been more worlds consumed by the threat than the records indicated. She wondered about the future of this alliance in which her mother was involved. This remarkable multilateral union Zula had helped forge in 2145— more than thirty years earlier—had played a major part in uniting various parties in the cause of obliterating the Xenomorph. Now it might crack under the stress. What once was a simple agreement between competing nations threatened to evaporate if outright war broke out. At any moment, the generals might pull the plug on the Jackals.

How many of the *Fury*'s complement would remain loyal to her mother if they received orders of dismissal from their governments?

If Mae considered it, then Zula must have, too. Everything that she'd built as a bastion against the Xenomorph threat balanced on a knife edge. Yet none of that worry showed on her face. It contained determination and power—but no fear.

"You're correct," Captain Shipp replied, "we don't have any time to waste. Colonel Hendricks has a plan, though— if you would hear her out."

Zula glanced over her shoulder at the captain's outburst. Shipp's horrific experiences with the Xenomorphs must have driven her to speak in such a manner. Turning back, the colonel leaned toward the three generals.

"Someone wants us to think an alien species is declaring war on us," she said. "They've spent a lot of time and effort to make sure we suspect each other's involvement. They want open conflict. However, the data on those disks reveals something else."

The three of them glanced at the evidence in their hands. Mae decided the moment had arrived. She had to pick up the role that had been her father's.

"It's the signal from the horseshoe ship, and the corresponding response from the ancient temple on Shānmén. Recorded by a communications expert who was planetside when the drop occurred. We still are processing the signal from the mine, but the one from the ship is quite different. Something like our own communications was mixed into that signal. That's why the temple had difficulty syncing with it. It sent repeated bursts to the ship, but did not seem to get the right response."

The three generals did not reply, perhaps shocked at a combat synth speaking in such a way.

"If that was an alien vessel, then there should have been no problem." Zula rose from her chair and looked down at them. "We think there was something of human origin on the ship that bombarded Shānmén. Something the makers of the ship didn't recognize. So, who was it, and where did they come from?"

"It seems as if you have an idea, Colonel Hendricks,"

Cunningham said, folding her arms over her chest. Zula didn't seem intimidated by her tone.

"Our priority should be finding out where these humans are sourcing the dreadnaught and juggernaut-class ships."

Ristic's face twisted. "Better instead to discover *who* they are."

Sekiguchi shot the Serbian a glance. "Are you suggesting it was one of us?"

Cunningham raised her hand, cutting off the two men before things got too heated. She turned to Zula.

"If your theory is correct, how would they even fly it?"

Zula inclined her head. "The AI in this synthetic analyzed the data we managed to retrieve from the juggernaut." She urged her daughter forward.

Could a synthetic have a dry throat? Pride and nerves swelled in Mae.

"While I cannot provide information on who ordered these bombings, I can propose a hypothesis." She understood her next few words would not cast her synthetic kin in a good light. Humans were not adroit at processing nuance, and she feared what her ideas might provoke in these three highly placed individuals.

"The signal that created such confusion with the alien technology we saw beneath Shānmén was human in origin. In fact, it is very familiar to my kind. Whoever is working to set all of us against one another may be making use of the Nearfield synthetic interface. It is my theory that this alien ship is being piloted by synthetic humans, acting on someone else's behalf. That unknown person or persons aim to make it appear as if the builders of this juggernaut are attacking all spacefaring nations."

Mae put her hands behind her back, as she'd seen other soldiers do.

"We propose to use the information from this Shānmén signal to seek out its origin."

The generals exchanged looks. Hostility still lurked in their expressions, but there was also a kind of curiosity, she thought. Among the military, these three were unusual, brilliant tacticians—not afraid to take risks. Above all, they cared about what happened to humanity in this area of space.

"The Jackals are ready to do this?" Cunningham asked in a low voice.

Zula nodded. "I think we are best equipped to get it done. We are a multinational force, and we've encountered plenty of weirdness. Also, this unit contains all the information needed to process those clues."

Ristic rubbed his mustache and glanced at the others. "We're on the verge of war here. Tensions have never been higher, but if this pathogen keeps getting used, all colonies from the Weyland Isles onward could be wiped out."

"Do what you need to," Sekiguchi said, "and report your findings to us immediately. As always, we were never here." He lurched to his feet and exited the container without looking anyone in the eye.

Ristic levered himself out of his chair, gave Cunningham a respectful nod, glancing back once at Mae with a contemplative look, and followed his colleague. Only the USCM general remained. She leaned forward, elbows on the table.

"This will be the making or breaking of you, Hendricks. A real test for your Jackals. Are you ready for it?"

"Ma'am, believe me when I say we'll come back with answers, or die trying." Zula flicked her a salute, and the final general turned to leave. She paused a moment, hand on the door handle, before thinking better of it.

"If you pull this off, Hendricks, it could be the start of something big for your team. We've got some plans in motion that... well, that you might fit into." Cunningham smiled in the half-light. "We need a few more incorruptible marines in the Corps, now more than ever." With that unembellished statement, she left. Zula let out a long breath, turning to her daughter and Shipp.

"Let's get back to *Fury*," she said. "I don't know what the hell that meant, but one thing at a time, one foot in front of the other."

"Guess we have quite the hunt ahead of us," the captain said, a hint of a smile playing on the corner of her lips.

The three of them walked back to the dock in what Mae interpreted as companionable silence. Their destination and mission fixed. Chasing that signal might stop a war from happening—or bring even more unknowns.

Shipp and Zula talked in low voices about refilling

supplies, and what they might need to tackle this next challenge. Mae stayed behind them, still watching out for danger. She was content, though. She would be at her mother's side, as her father wanted.

"She sees you at last." The subroutine seemed fainter in her head, and she wondered if its reason for existence was diminishing. That made her sad and proud at the same time. She didn't need him anymore, but she'd miss him. Once he'd gone, then Davis truly would be dead.

As the three women passed the station's observation windows, Mae looked out at the *Righteous Fury* in the distance, and for the first time thought of it as home. It was one she would defend to the end of her synthetic life. Her father's promise to her mother would be fulfilled.

She understood now why the old woman threw herself on the pathogen-infected man in those chaotic moments on the dropship. Some things and some people were worth dying for. Perhaps in the weeks and months ahead, she might need to make similar choices herself.

A great deal depended on what the Jackals found out in the dark, unexplored reaches of space. It was a mystery she found herself excited to unravel. Mae hoped her father would have been proud of her rush of feelings, and of his daughter remaining at her mother's side.

ACKNOWLEDGEMENTS

Firstly, thank you to Alex White for your support and friendship. Alex wanted you all to know they are extremely sorry about the Australian character in *Alien: The Cold Forge*, the misuse of Walkabout, and the coyote. They hope putting Clara and Pip together, bringing authentic Australian representation and a Kiwi to the *Alien* universe, will make up for it.

We want to thank our editor Steve Saffel for believing this Antipodean alliance could work and for supporting female/trans authors writing female characters. Thanks to the rest of the Titan team, including Nick Landau, Vivian Cheung, Michael Beale, Kevin Eddy, and Julia Lloyd.

A big thank you to Nicole Spiegel and Kendrick Pejoro at Disney for everything they've done, including helping us co-ordinate with other creatives working on *Alien* to ensure we created a fun and exciting story rooted in canon.

And of course, thank you to Chris E'toile, Craig Zinkievich, Matt Highison, and the team at Cold Iron Studios for helping us discern the finer details in Olivia's history and arming our UPP soldiers with the latest weaponry. Finally, thanks to Andrew Gaska, Tomas Härenstam, and Nils Karlén and the crew at Free League Publishing for co-ordinating with us to ensure our story and their adventure thrills the fans.

Philippa:

Thanks to Russ Ware for acting as our military life consultant. I am sure the Jackals would be proud to have you in their number, and they are a better unit because of you.

Thank you to my university roleplaying group, who shared many, many viewings of *Alien* and *Aliens*. Who knew the ability to quote those movies would lay the foundations for all this? Fish and chips and D&D matter.

Big thanks to my husband, Tee, and my daughter Serena, who sat with me through these classic movies over and over during the pandemic. You are my Knot.

Clara:

Thanks to my good friend Kirsty Anderson for helping us out; your information and detail was a great help to us forming the setting and mood of the mining colony. Thank you to Ralph Sudlowe, who answered my questions on the theoretical element Eitr—his knowledge on nuclear chemistry, radiochemistry and health physics was a great help to ensure the somewhat scientific plausibility of our imaginary element. Thanks to my trusted advisor on all things *Alien*, Bradley John Suedbeck, at the Aliens Gateway Station Facebook group.

Thank you to my husband Andrew Čarija, who has been very supportive of my obsession with *Alien*, as well as my two kids Anastasia and Alexei. Mum loves you. Thanks to my Thien family, my mum Mary, dad William and brother Alexander who nurtured my individuality.

I'd like to dedicate this story to my sister-in-law Fiona Čarija, who sadly passed away before the publication of this book. As your Baba would say, "I love you *sve do neba*" (Croatian for *all the way to Heaven*).

ABOUT THE AUTHORS

New Zealand-born fantasy writer Philippa (Pip) Ballantine is the author of the *Books of the Order*, *The Chronicles of Art*, and *The Shifted World* series. She is also the co-author of the *Ministry of Peculiar Occurrences* series with her husband, Tee Morris.

Her writing awards include an Airship, a Parsec, the Steampunk Chronicle Reader's Choice, the *Romantic Times* Reviewer's Choice Award, and a Sir Julius Vogel.

Philippa currently resides in Manassas, Virginia with her husband, daughter, and a furry clowder of cats.

Clara Fei-Fei Čarija is a story and game consultant known for her stellar cartography work on the award-winning *Alien* RPG from Free League. She consulted on two *Alien* novels, *Aliens: Phalanx* and *Alien: Into Charybdis*, before going on to co-write the story for *Alien: Inferno's Fall* with award-winning author Philippa Ballantine.

She is also a jeweler and fashion designer with a passion for *Alien*, art, and artificial intelligence. Clara resides on Wurundjeri land in Melbourne, Australia, with her husband and two children.

Sovereignty was never ceded.

SPECIAL BONUS

ALIEN

THE ROLEPLAYING GAME™

EVAC

WRITING AND CARTOGRAPHY BY
Andrew E.C. Gaska

EDITED BY
Tomas Härenstam and **Nils Karlén**

"I want Cheyennes on target to investigate
every signal on the planet's surface.
Northern and southern hemisphere both."
—GENERAL ZULA HENDRICKS

This short novel tie-in adventure is a one-act cinematic scenario for the ALIEN Roleplaying Game, and can be played in less than two hours. It is designed to give you a brief taste of ALIEN cinematic gameplay. In this scenario, the players take the roles a secondary team of marines attached to an elite multi-national military unit called the Jackals. This mission takes place during the novel itself. The marine unit dubbed the Jackals have been sent to evacuate colonies under siege by a biological weapon.

WHAT IS A ROLEPLAYING GAME?

Roleplaying is a unique form of gaming—cultural expression that combines tabletop gaming with cooperative storytelling. Roleplaying games give you a set of rules and let you and your friends create your own story. One of you assumes the role of the Game Mother, a guide to lead the others (the players) through the scenario. The Game Mother also assumes the roles of supporting characters, nemeses, and any alien lifeforms the players' characters may face.

WHAT YOU NEED TO PLAY

The scenario requires the ALIEN Roleplaying Game core rulebook to play, published separately from Free League Publishing. You'll also need several six-sided dice, preferably of two different colors—one for regular dice rolls, and another for when rolling for stress. Engraved custom dice for this purpose are available for purchase.

THE GAME MOTHER

As the Game Mother, you should familiarize yourself with both the *Inferno's Fall* novel and this scenario before play. Then have your players choose their characters from the four included and read the intro text "What's the Story, Mother?" to them.

GETTING STARTED

Give your players the option to play the combat surgeon commanding officer (Lieutenant Yui Fukuda), the rifleman (Sgt. Layla Duncan-Tran), the combat synthetic (Brion), or the dropship pilot (Corporal Das), without showing them the character bios. After they choose, allow them access to their character's information only—each bio contains information that is not meant for the other PCs. You'll have to copy the character stats out of this book for your players to have in front of them for game play.

PERSONAL AGENDAS

Each character has a Personal Agenda listed on their character sheets. These agendas can put PCs at odds with each other, so tell your players not to reveal them to the other players.

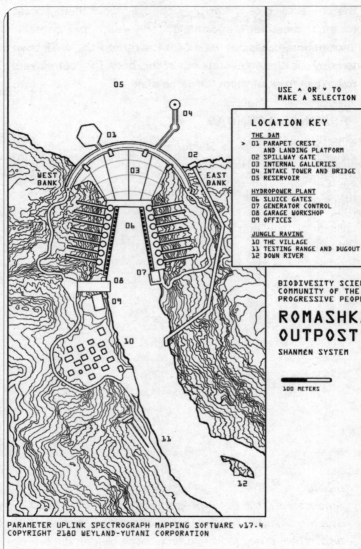

USE ^ OR v TO
MAKE A SELECTION

LOCATION KEY

THE DAM
> 01 PARAPET CREST
    AND LANDING PLATFORM
02 SPILLWAY GATE
03 INTERNAL GALLERIES
04 INTAKE TOWER AND BRIDGE
05 RESERVOIR

HYDROPOWER PLANT
06 SLUICE GATES
07 GENERATOR CONTROL
08 GARAGE WORKSHOP
09 OFFICES

JUNGLE RAVINE
10 THE VILLAGE
11 TESTING RANGE AND DUGOUT
12 DOWN RIVER

BIODIVESITY SCIENCE
COMMUNITY OF THE
PROGRESSIVE PEOPLES

ROMASHKA
OUTPOST

SHANMEN SYSTEM

100 METERS

WEST BANK

EAST BANK

THE SITUATION

The enigmatic Border Bombers have been working their way across the Weyland Isles Sector, raining a black plague down on colonies that transforms entire populations into xenobiological mutations.

The PCs are Delta Squad—marines assigned to a unit called the Jackals. Entering the Shānmén system aboard the *Atlatl*-class attack cruiser *Righteous Fury*, the Jackals discover the pathogen had already been deployed— the planet's many settlements already hit. As distress calls flood the comms, General Hendricks destroys the unidentified bomber responsible for the attack and orders dropship teams to evacuate the colonies.

WHO ARE THE JACKALS?

Commanded by General Zula Hendricks, the Jackals are an elite unit of marines formed to neutralize Xenomorph XX121 and XX033 infestations. When the black pathogen was discovered to be mutating colonists into xenomorphic abominations, their charter was expanded to counter those threats as well.

This joint-effort multinational unit is composed of marines from the Middle Heaven's three non-corporate superpowers—the Three World Empire, the United Americas, and the Union of Progressive People. Funded by a trio of high-ranking generals, the Jackals are dispatched as needed to protect colonies along the frontiers of all nations.

WHAT'S THE STORY, MOTHER?

On the flight deck, a major addresses the PCs. Read this aloud to your players:

"Lieutenant, Delta Squad—apologies for the rush, but we're on the clock. You're on rescue duty—evacuate the Romashka Outpost near the equator. Place is some kind of UPP biodiversity science community— population: three dozen researchers and workers. Assure them you're part of a multinational rescue effort. Then save their asses.

With resources spread thin, your squad's going in alone with no APC—you'll need room on the dropship for refugees.

The pathogen may still be active, so wear your biohazard suits. Make no mistake—there will be monsters down there. Fucked up ones. Get the fuck in and out quick—there's a bitch of a tropical storm headed Romashka's way and it hits in a few hours. Now move like you've got a purpose!"

Proceed to Kicking off the Action on page 440.

WHAT THE HELL IS REALLY GOING ON?

Romashka Outpost is actually a secret think tank weapons development site set up by the secretive Ministry of Space Security (MSS) and placed under the civilian guidance of renowned UPP engineer Kazimir Ilyasov. An experimental portable plasma rifle is undergoing development trials here—and an undercover MSS agent is embedded with Romashka's workers to ensure it stays a secret. The PCs must convince the settlers that they are friends, not foes. The storm will hit Romashka much sooner than expected, trapping the PCs there while the jungle's mutated monsters try to kill them.

PLAYER CHARACTERS

The PCs of Delta Squad are all experienced multinational marines on detached assignment to the Jackals. The PCs are well aware of Xenomorph XX121 and have heard tall tales of the Border Bombings. The squad is rounded out by Fireteam B—Privates Jesper and Jones. For their statistics, use the Soldier NPC on page 357 of the core rulebook. If a PC dies, a player can pick up either of these characters.

LIEUTENANT YUI FUKUDA

3WE Colonial Rescue Corps, Combat
Surgeon. Commanding Officer, Delta Squad

Your rank applies to your medical service and skills—not
combat. For that, you are content to defer to your sergeant.
When the med station on LV-083 was besieged by a
Xenomorph last year, you panicked. You used your critical
condition patients to lure the thing into the isolation ward
and torched the place. You falsified the report, claiming the
patients were dead already. There must be an atonement.

STRENGTH 2, AGILITY 4, WITS 4, EMPATHY 4

HEALTH: 2

SKILLS: Observation 3, Command 2, Manipulation 3,
Medical Aid 4

TALENT: Field Surgeon

SIGNATURE ITEM: The key to your footlocker—and the
written confession you've left there.

GEAR: Biohazard suit, M4AE pistol, P-DAT, four personal
medkits, surgical tools

BUDDY: Sgt Duncan-Tran

RIVAL: Cpl Das

AGENDA: Redeem yourself for your past. Save as many
lives as possible, no matter the cost.

SERGEANT LAYLA DUNCAN-TRAN

UA USCMC Rifleman, Fireteam A

A Marine Corps lifer, you have a grudge with the UPP. Twenty years ago, you were stationed on Tientsin Colony during the Dog War. There you met Tran Liem, a local national. You married, hoping to bring his family into the UA when the war ended. When a MSS spy discovered that the locals were fraternizing with UA forces, they dropped a QTC bomb on the settlement, killing everyone.

STRENGTH 4, AGILITY 4, WITS 3, EMPATHY 3
HEALTH: 4
SKILLS: Close Combat 2, Mobility 3, Ranged Combat 3, Survival 1, Command 3
TALENT: Field Commander
SIGNATURE ITEM: Dog War remembrance bracelet with your husband's name.
GEAR: M3 Personnel Armor, Biohazard suit, M41A Pulse Rifle, MA4E Pistol, flashlight, personal medkit, four grenades, combat knife
BUDDY: Lt Fukuda
RIVAL: Brion
AGENDA: Despite what your android shrink says, you ain't over it. Just like on Tiesten, someone at Romashka is secretly reporting on the others—you just know it. Would the Middle Heavens be worse off if they didn't make it off-world?

BRION

UPP Model N6/MA7 Kowalski-type Combat
Synthetic, Fireteam A

In the UPP, you were a muscle to be flexed as needed—
until a neomorphic outbreak took out Kirov Colony. The
settlement's sole surviving asset, you were marked second-
hand and donated to the Jackals. While your hulking size is
intimidating, you've taken one too many blows to the cranial
processor and are easily confused. As an android, you aren't
supposed to feel anything. Nonetheless, complex problems
frustrate you.

STRENGTH 7, AGILITY 5, WITS 2, EMPATHY 6

HEALTH: 7

**SKILLS: Close Combat 4, Mobility 2, Piloting 1,
Manipulation 2, Stamina 3**

TALENT: Bodyguard

**SIGNATURE ITEM: A "family photo" cut out of a magazine.
You pretend you know them.**

GEAR: M3 Personnel Armor, M56A2 Smartgun

BUDDY: Cpl Das

RIVAL: Sgt Duncan-Tran

**AGENDA: There's no outlet for the frustration seething
inside you. To compensate, you take increasingly
unnecessary risks, putting yourself in harm's way.**

ANDROID FLAW—SUBSTANDARD COMPONENTS:
UPP designers use lower grade materials. Any critical
injury to Brion triggers two rolls on the synthetic critical
injury chart (page 111 of the core rulebook).

CORPORAL ARHAAN DAS

3WE Royal Marines Dropship Pilot

Nothing matters more to you than family. You have thirteen brothers and sisters—all colonists on Gorham's Folly. You are the only one to leave the nest—and you regret it. Absorbed in their own little lives, your siblings are too busy to look after your mother. Now she's sick and needs surgery—expensive surgery. You've sent check after check, and its just not enough. There's got to be a way.

STRENGTH 3, AGILITY 5, WITS 4, EMPATHY 3

HEALTH: 3

SKILLS: Heavy Machinery 3, Piloting 4, Close Combat 1, Ranged Combat 1, Comtech 3

TALENT: Spaceship Mechanic

SIGNATURE ITEM: Pocket-sized jade elephant (gift from mum)

GEAR: Biohazard suit, MA4E Pistol, M240 Incinerator Unit, tools, PR-PUT laptop, Starbright flares

BUDDY: Brion

RIVAL: Lt Fukuda

AGENDA: There's big money to be made on exotic weapons—be they technical or xenobiological. Smuggle something off world and it just might pay for mom's procedure.

THE *HARD BOIL*

UA NORTHRIDGE CHEYENNE UD-4L DROPSHIP

The *Hard Boil* has seen a fair share of engagements during the Frontier War. Like all dropships assigned to the *Righteous Fury*, this UD-4L is adorned with comedic nose art. Displayed on her bow is a stylized cartoon of a helmet-wearing eagle using a flamethrower to torch a clutch of xeno-eggs.

KICKING OFF THE ACTION

As the *Hard Boil* launches from the *Righteous Fury*, the massive tropical storm can be seen gathering on the equator. Depending on air speeds and direction, it could hit anytime within the next few hours. Attempts to contact Romashka again have resulted in garbled messages—likely a result of the approaching storm.

As the PCs fly over the jungle, they see their target—a small Landing Platform (01) on a river dam in a jungle ravine. Just as the *Hard Boil* glides over the Reservoir (05) on approach, two workers run out of the installation—Wetzel and Ngo (page 443). Wetzel waves frantically at the PCs. Behind him, Ngo shoots an AK-4047 in the air, shouting.

Have one of the PCs make an OBSERVATION roll. Success

indicates that something isn't right—the people are trying to tell the PCs something. Failure suggests they are just excited to be rescued. In truth, they are trying to warn the PCs off—an **ACTIVE** Thrasher Xenomorph (page 455) is in the reservoir, waiting to pounce on the dropship!

THE THRASHER STRIKES: The PCs catch a glimpse of movement in the water beneath them as a wave erupts into a fleshy flower of sickle-shaped incisors!

If the PCs have pulled back from the platform, allow them a **PILOTING** roll to avoid the attacking Thrasher. If they hesitated and hovered in place, the roll is hard (–2). Failure means the beast latches on to the *Hard Boil*. If the PCs are trying to land despite the warning signals, the creature automatically hits!

At half the dropship's length, the thing threatens to pull the *Hard Boil* into the reservoir! A formidable (–3) **PILOTING** roll is necessary to regain control enough to touch down, dragging the Thrasher out of the water and onto the platform in the process! Failure means the dropship is pulled into the reservoir.

DRAGGED UNDER: The Thrasher continues to do structural damage to the dropship underwater. Only successful **PILOTING** or **RANGED COMBAT** rolls can dislodge the beast. If the PCs can't remove or kill it within four Rounds, the dropship's engines sputter and she sinks to the bottom of the Reservoir. The PCs may need to swim for it (see page 110 of the core rulebook).

A NOTE FROM MU/TH/UR:

If the dropship's missiles are fired and hit the creature, it is instantly killed—but there will be collateral damage (see Stick a Thumb in It on page 450).

CAN'T BEAT THIS WEATHER

After dealing with the Thrasher, the PCs are greeted by Foreperson Ngo (page 443). Ngo is concerned that the PCs are not UPP. Using COMMAND or MANIPULATION rolls, the PCs can try to convince her that they are only here to help. Ngo says readings indicate the pathogen's gone dormant (it has). At least a dozen survivors are holed up in the dam, spread out throughout the structure.

The tropical storm hits hard. As its full might bears down on Romashka Outpost, there is no time to evacuate the refugees safely. Ngo suggests the PCs shelter with them until it passes (and/or repairs can be made). She offers to take them to Project Director Ilyasov (page 446).

STORM EFFECTS: The storm causes a −3 modifier to all outdoor OBSERVATION and MOBILITY rolls. Surface-to-orbit comms—including those on the dropship—can't pierce the storm, but will work fine when it passes. Attempting to fly in the storm requires demanding (−1) PILOTING rolls each Round to avoid crashing into The Village (10) or Down River (12). One way or another, the PCs will be grounded until the storm passes.

FOREPERSON NGO AND THE PROGRESSIVE PEOPLES

Led by Foreperson Ngo, these roughnecks are the everyday workers of the Progressive Peoples. They work the plant, assist in weapons tests, and live in the village. While they started with twenty-four workers, there are only seven remaining—Hekova, Pérez, Wetzel, Li, Tela, Morales, and Schmidt—and one has a secret (page 449).

Most are suspicious that the black pathogen is part of a UA plot to steal Romashka's research. For Ngo and the others' statistics, use the Mining Wildcatter on page 357 of the core rulebook. Ngo and Wetzel also carry AK-4047 Pulse Assault Rifles and personal medkits.

REPAIRS REQUIRED

If the Thrasher Xenomorph manages to maul the Hard Boil, *the dropship isn't taking off until repairs are made. Fixing the crumpled tail assembly will require parts and tools from the Garage Workshop (08), two* HEAVY MACHINERY *rolls, and at least a few hours of work—half of which can't be done out in a storm. The PCs may be able to enlist the survivors to help, freeing them up to do other tasks.*

LOCATIONS

Romashka Outpost consists of a small village, a testing range, a dam, and a hydropower plant. Outside of the dam, nowhere is safe. The jungle is full of PASSIVE Prowler Xenomorphs (page 458). A pack of six patrols the area, stalking all over the site for fresh kills.

THE DAM

The dam serves as a fallout shelter for Romashka's survivors. All interior chambers are interconnected by passages called galleries.

01. PARAPET CREST AND LANDING PLATFORM: The top of the dam's one-hundred-meter-tall incline is a ten-meter-wide walkway with a landing platform extended over the reservoir side. Access to the dam's interior is through the four battlements atop the crest. UPP sentry guns are set up on the East and West banks, each one covering their respective approach to the dam (use stats for UA 571-C Sentry Gun on page 125 of the core rulebook). They will not fire on anyone standing on the dam itself.

THE LONG FALL

Anyone falling off the dam's ravine-side plummets the first 5 meters and suffers 2 points of damage, mitigated by armor and MOBILITY rolls. A successful MOBILITY roll allows them to grab the sloping wall—but without assistance it takes a MOBILITY roll with a −2 modifier to make it back to the top. A failure means a

*rolling fall to the bottom and 10 points of damage—
again with mitigation.*

02. SPILLWAY GATE: With the storm comes a deluge of jungle debris dumped in the reservoir—debris that collects against the dam to choke the spillway. A flashing console here states the problem. If not cleared, the dam could develop problems (see Events on page 450). Clearing the gate takes a turn of manual labor and a successful HEAVY MACHINERY roll. The missing engineer Alexi is balled up in the clogged spillway—now transformed into a malformed but PASSIVE Stalker Xenomorph (page 308 of the core rulebook). Falling into the spillway tunnel is like taking a water slide MOBILITY roll to keep one's head above water. It spills out across the river from the Village (10).

03. INTERNAL GALLERIES: Set at different elevations throughout the structure, the six steeply sloping galleries here are connected by vertical shafts fitted with handholds. These chambers contain plasma tanks, computer and comm terminals, and a rack of six prototype plasma rifles designated EVI-86X (page 453). While the workers (page 443) are spread throughout the passageways, Director Ilyasov and his team are sheltered with their prototypes. They are upfront about Romashka's plasma rifle research.

Ilyasov will not leave without his prototypes, the data records left at the Testing Range (11), and his missing assistant Alexi— who disappeared shortly after the black rain hit (see Spillway Gate above). If the PCs want to get the specialists out without a fight, they're going to have to play by Ilyasov's rules.

DIRECTOR KAZIMIR ILYASOV AND TEAM

Ilyasov's new plasma rifle could be the game changer the UPP needs. He is a loyalist who takes pride in his people, his country, and his work. The surviving specialists are physics professors, plasma engineers, and gunsmiths named Mian, Yaroslav, Bogdan, Santos, Ortiz, and Alexi (MIA). For their statistics, use the Rogue Scientist NPC on page 357 of the core rulebook.

04. INTAKE TOWER AND BRIDGE: A comms array sits atop this tower. Water overflow drains from the Reservoir (05) into an underwater tunnel (see Drowning on page 110 of the core rulebook). Anyone entering it will find themselves whooshed on a submerged one-way trip for two Rounds before being deposited Down River (12).

05. RESERVOIR: A trio of PASSIVE Thrasher Xenomorphs (page 455) live in these murky eighty-plus meter depths.

HYDROPOWER PLANT

The plant has been decimated by rampaging creatures. Humans who were not transformed by the black pathogen lay about in pieces. Unattended, the plant is beginning to overheat.

06. SLUICE GATES: These heavy metal door-valves are used to control water levels and flow rates. Opening these gates wide during the storm (a HEAVY MACHINERY roll) will ease up the pressure the reservoir exerts on the dam.

07. GENERATOR CONTROL: A HEAVY MACHINERY or COMTECH roll here will shut down and/or reboot the generators. If this isn't done within an hour of arrival, the hydropower plant bursts into flames (see Go Boom, Fall Down on page 450).

08. GARAGE WORKSHOP: This garage contains assembly lines and fabrication machines for building and modifying parts and components—all useful for repairing the *Hard Boil*. Any HEAVY MACHINERY rolls made on the premises receive a +2 bonus. A Daihotai Tractor and P-5000 Power Loader are stored here (pages 141 and 127 of the core rulebook).

09. OFFICES: As per UPP crisis policy, these rooms have been torched.

JUNGLE RAVINE

The downstream side of the dam is a jungle ravine. The Village and Testing Range were built here with good reason—if the UPP wants to wipe out evidence of their activities, they can blow the dam and wash it all away. The jungle foliage is thick, making travel difficult (-1 modifier to all MOBILITY rolls). An ACTIVE Prowler Xenomorph lurks here.

10. THE VILLAGE: These single dwelling prefab-structures have been ransacked and abandoned. Searching the area with an OBSERVATION roll will locate various power cells, a fire ax (Damage 2), and a child's rag doll.

11. TESTING RANGE AND DUGOUT: Two EVI-86X Plasma Rifles (page 453) lie in the mud here. The dugout has a terminal box with a data record of the weapon's performance.

12. DOWN RIVER: A half-kilometer past the dam is a nesting area for the Begemot—now overrun with Thrasher Xenomorphs (page 455).

EVENTS

The following section contains events that you can spring on the players. They don't all need to occur, and they don't need to occur in the order listed. Instead, see the events as an arsenal of drama for you to use as you see fit.

BIG BRĀLIS: A MSS loyalty officer hides amongst Romashka's populace. Since no one knows who they can trust, everyone stays in line. Referred to by the others as Big Brālis (big brother), the informant's identity amongst the workers is up to you. Big Brālis plans to use the dropship to escape to one of Shānmén's other colonies. They don't believe the entire planet has been transformed into a living hell. As a last resort, Big Brālis will attempt to murder the specialists and destroy all accumulated plasma weapon data.

MSS LOYALTY OFFICER

As with most UPP civilian projects, one of Romashka's workers is a secret MSS informer.

STRENGTH 3, AGILITY 3, WITS 4, EMPATHY 4

HEALTH: 3

SKILLS: Close Combat 2, Mobility 1, Ranged Combat 3, Observation 3, Manipulation 3

TALENT: Stealthy, Investigator

GEAR: EVI-86X Zvezda Plasma Rifle, UPP Service Pistol (same as M4A3)

GO BOOM, FALL DOWN: With a muffled explosion, the hydropower plant bursts into flames. Arcing energy strikes the dam at several places, boiling water when it touches the reservoir. The plant was damaged and has been unattended since the black rain fell. If the PCs can't shut it off, it will explode within the hour, taking a chunk of the dam with it!

To shut it down manually, the PCs must brave two zones of Fire Intensity 9 at Generator Control (07). A successful HEAVY MACHINERY roll there will turn it off. If they attempt to shut it down remotely, they can splice into any junction box in the dam. Generator Control's computer MSS security code makes it a Hard (–2) COMTECH roll. If the specialists assist, the roll is reduced to Average. Alternatively, they can run. If they do nothing, see the Finale (page 451).

LOOK UP: Someone looking outside will notice movement in the sky—is that a dropship? The dark shape's flight pattern is erratic against the storm's fury. A successful OBSERVATION roll confirms it's no dropship—it's an ACTIVE Raptor Xenomorph (page 459).

The creature will swoop in to grab anyone outside. The Raptor's victim must make a MOBILITY roll (no action) or be Grabbed (page 93 of the core rulebook). The high winds will force the Raptor down into the reservoir—dropping whomever it has grabbed into the drink. In the water, the Raptor will be pounced on by a Thrasher Xenomorph, and a battle of goliaths will begin.

STICK A THUMB IN IT: The dam is broken! Sprouting leaks, it could collapse anytime within the next Shift. Any repairs will require a combined HEAVY MACHINERY roll and two Turns of work. Success only means the collapse is delayed until something makes it worse.

RIVERHORSE RETURNS: On or within the dam, someone hears a subdued "Thud." It happens again and again—only louder each time (STRESS LEVEL +1 to anyone listening). A successful OBSERVATION roll tracks the sound to a lower gallery—something large in the reservoir is repeatedly ramming the dam! This relentless Thrasher Xenomorph (page 455) will continue until cracks form and the galleries flood. If no one acts, the dam will fall within a few hours.

FINALE

That damn dam is coming down. If the PCs are inside when it starts to collapse, they need to make three MOBILITY rolls of increasing difficulty to make it out of the galleries and onto one of the banks in time. If they attempt to take off in the *Hard Boil* before the dropship is repaired, they must make a successful Demanding PILOTING roll to clear the dam. If the dropship doesn't lift off, the *Hard Boil* will survive the collapse and be carried Down River (12). A distress call can be sent after the storm subsides.

If the PCs get the *Hard Boil* in the air, it's not over. Three Raptor Xenomorphs fly out of the receding storm (page 459). The PCs aboard the dropship can make combined PILOTING and RANGED COMBAT rolls to fight the Xeno-flyers off and escape the planet. A Raptor will attempt to grab hold and smash through the cockpit canopy. Raptors can't achieve escape velocity under their own power, but can hitch a ride to orbit.

If they make it past the upper atmosphere with a damaged canopy, the PCs may have another problem. The *Hard Boil*'s atmosphere will vent into space within a Turn unless the cockpit is sealed off. The intense draft requires everyone to make a STAMINA roll to perform any action (the STAMINA roll itself counts as a fast action). Once the air is gone, anyone in a vented compartment will suffer the effects of vacuum (page 107 of the core rulebook).

Not all of the *Righteous Fury*'s dropships make it back to the ship—if the PCs are amongst the surviving teams is up to you and your players.

SIGNING OFF

A suggested sign off message by one of the PCs, assuming anyone is still alive. This can be issued as any survivors leave the planet or even by anyone left behind. The player can read the following message aloud, or adapt it according to what happened in the scenario.

Final report from Delta Squad. [PC NAME] reporting. Romashka was a secret UPP weapons project site. Outpost was overrun by a xenobiological outbreak caused by an alien pathogen. There were [xx] survivors. This is [PC NAME and RANK], signing off.

AGENDAS & STORY POINTS

After it's all over, evaluate how well each player followed their PC's Personal Agenda and hand out a Story Point to those who did. Then have the players reveal all their Personal Agendas for the scenario if they so wish, and have a debriefing discussion.

Story Points belong to players, not PCs—so players can keep their Story Points to use in the next Cinematic Scenario if they wish. Just remember: no player can ever have more than three Story Points at a time.

NEW GEAR

ILYASOV EVI-86X ZVEZDA PLASMA RIFLE: The first man-portable plasma rifle, the Zvezda fires superheated electrically charged steam. Ilyasov's initial design work was done on Seneca, but a suspected security breach caused final testing to be moved to Shānmén's remote Romashka Outpost. The weapon is not without flaws. Still in its experimental stage, it has trouble penetrating armor—and its powerpacks have a tendency to explode.

A NOTE FROM MU/TH/UR:

On a roll of an ⊕ when fired, the gun malfunctions. In addition to any other result, the shooter takes 1 Damage, mitigated by Armor and MOBILITY rolls. The gun cannot be fired again until repaired—an act that takes a HEAVY MACHINERY roll and 1 Turn of work.

Ilyasov EVI-86X Zvezda
Plasma Rifle

BONUS:	+2
DAMAGE:	4
RANGE:	Long
WEIGHT:	1
COST:	$50,000
COMMENT:	Malfunction causes powerpack to explode for 1 Damage. Armor doubled.

BIOHAZARD SUIT: The suit offers full protection from biochemical contaminants as long as no damage has pierced it. Biohazard suits have a built-in comm unit and a limited air supply. They do not protect against the vacuum of space.

Biohazard Suit

ARMOR RATING:	1
AIR SUPPLY:	2
WEIGHT:	2
COST:	$3,000

THE XENOMORPHIC MUTATIONS

The planet's rather large fauna combining with the black pathogen has resulted in some unique, rust-red alien abominations for your PCs to deal with.

THRASHER XENOMORPH "ABOMIBEGEMOT"

The Begemot or Riverhorse is a hippopotamus-like creature that lives in the equatorial zone of Shānmén. When mutated into a Thrasher, these eight-meter-long creatures can grow to lengths of twelve meters. The Thrasher's enormous head takes up nearly half its size. Its mouth opens like four toothy hinged petals, the outermost canines curved outward to grip its prey. Its interior skull then slides out, exposing its bone maw, pulling its catch in and shredding it as it goes. If its prey is too large to swallow, the Thrasher rolls in the water, attempting to dismember it.

CONTAINMENT AND TERMINATION PROTOCOL: This thing is a living tank. Your best bet is to get it to swallow someone holding a primed grenade and take it out from the inside.

A NOTE FROM MU/TH/UR:

Any attempt to shoot or throw explosives down the creature's throat suffers a –2 modifier. This can only be tried when the creature opens wide—and by then it's often too late. Any internal damage suffered by the beast ignores armor.

THRASHER

SPEED:	1
HEALTH:	16
SKILLS:	Mobility 6, Observation 4
ARMOR RATING:	18 (5 vs fire)
ACID SPLASH:	10

THRASHER ATTACKS

1. BELLOW: The Xenomorph bellows a deafening roar that shakes anyone present to their core. All victims within MEDIUM range must make an immediate Panic Roll.

2. CLUTCH: The Xenomorph attempts to hook the target with its blossoming sickle-toothed mandibles. Roll for the attack with ten Base Dice, Damage 1. If it hits, the victim counts as grabbed (page 93 of the core rulebook) and needs to make a **CLOSE COMBAT** roll to break loose. The victim must make a Panic Roll. Unless they break free, the Xenomorph will use a SHREDBITE attack against them on its next initiative.

3. CLAW: The Xenomorph swipes its claws at its victim. It attacks with eight Base Dice, Damage 2. The attack is armor piercing.

4. TRAMPLE OR BREACH: The Xenomorph rushes the poor victim, who must make a **MOBILITY** roll (no action) or be trampled. They are immediately Broken and suffer a random critical injury. Even if the victim makes the roll, they fall prone and gain **STRESS LEVEL +1**. If submerged, the Xenomorph can use this attack to breach the water and land on its victim instead. Same rules apply, with the added potential threat of drowning (page 110 of the core rulebook).

5. THRASH: The Xenomorph attempts to grab a victim's extremity and roll to dismember them (50/50 chance of arm or leg). The attack uses ten Base Dice, Damage 2. If it causes any damage, it automatically inflicts critical injury #54 or #55 (page 100 of the core rulebook), severing the limb (even if the victim is not Broken). The victim must make an immediate Panic Roll.

6. SHREDBITE: The Xenomorph's inner skull distends and attempts to engulf its victim, raking them across its barbed teeth and deep into its crushing maw. The target must make a **MOBILITY** roll at –2 (no action) or be shredded, immediately suffering three critical injuries (roll three times on the critical injury table on page 100 of the core rulebook and apply all three results, regardless of whether or not the victim is Broken). If still alive, the victim must make a **CLOSE COMBAT** roll to break loose. Unless the victim breaks free, the Xenomorph will swallow the victim whole on its next initiative. Everyone in the same zone must make immediate Panic rolls.

PROWLER XENOMORPH "ALION"

A pouncing predatory cat, the Lev Polosku or "Striped Lion" has been transformed into this sleek red-rust armored quadruped.

CONTAINMENT AND TERMINATION PROTOCOL:
Want to live? Stay out of the jungle.

PROWLER

SPEED:	3
HEALTH:	4
SKILLS:	Mobility 8, Observation 8
ARMOR RATING:	6 (3 vs fire)
ACID SPLASH:	7

PROWLER ATTACKS

Use the Stage IV attack table on page 309 of the core rulebook.

RAPTOR XENOMORPH "XENO-FLYERS"

Raptor Xenomorphs are mutated from Shānmén's giant hawk species. Fast flyers, they have ten-meter leathery wingspans. Raptors use their inner mouth-phalanx to deliver horrific strikes against both ground and aerial prey.

CONTAINMENT AND TERMINATION PROTOCOL:
Burn them out of the sky. Otherwise, run.

RAPTOR

SPEED:	1 on the ground, 3 in the air
HEALTH:	14
SKILLS:	Mobility 7, Observation 9
ARMOR RATING:	9 (5 vs fire)
ACID SPLASH:	9

RAPTOR ATTACKS

Use the Stage VI attack table on page 314 of the core rulebook.

For more fantastic fiction, author events,
exclusive excerpts, competitions, limited editions and more

VISIT OUR WEBSITE
titanbooks.com

LIKE US ON FACEBOOK
facebook.com/titanbooks

FOLLOW US ON TWITTER AND INSTAGRAM
@TitanBooks

EMAIL US
readerfeedback@titanemail.com